Wimarshaná Wijesuriya was cast out from the country in which he grew up in 1992, and soon found himself marooned on one of its former tropical colonies. There he encountered a different and strange world, a world he was supposed to call home.

This is his last known work.

Also by Wimarshaná Wijesuriya

Colombo: A Critical Introspection

POST
POLITICA

WIMARSHANA WIJESURIYA

squircle
SUBVERSIVE

This is a work of fiction. Names, characters, organizations, places, events and incidents are either products of the author's imagination or are used fictitiously.

POST POLITICA
Copyright © Wimarshaná Wijesuriya 2014

Published by Squircle Subversive, New York

Cover illustration by Sahib Brown

Squircle Subversive and the Squircle Subversive logo are trademarks of Squircle Subversive

ISBN: 978–0–9925837–8–1

"Imagine there's no countries…"

John Lennon

1

MUTHUKUDA WAS an odd old man that used strange words like democracy and government and sometimes dangerous sounding ones like patriotism, or even worse, politics; but for young Zen, facing as he was the most important decision of his life, conversations with the peculiar old-model had become a pleasantly distracting indulgence. Indeed, Zen was grateful for the stroke of serendipity which, in the midst of his weighty pre-decision soul searching, had veered his course toward the dilapidated disarray of corroding books and mortar which Muthu took refuge in. And so as Zen had done for the past few weeks, to see old Muthu, he once more suffered through the dingy rubbish strewn paths where the ground was ruled by mobs of obese gray rodents and the skies by squadrons of humming bloodthirsty mosquitoes; where only the stench of backwardness and undevelopment smelled worse than the rot of carcasses and open sewers.

In the typically difficult to understand language of Muthu, a rhetorical "Those dastardly marketers haven't lobotomized you just yet have they?" emanated from somewhere within the plumes of dust whirling around the corroding books to greet Zen.

Locating the dusty old ghost, Zen pushed the chair he had previously made for himself from a pile of rare sturdy books toward Muthu and sat down. Getting started was always difficult and letting Muthu start was no solution as, before Zen could get a word in, Muthu would incessantly hurl content at him, which Zen flippantly thought to himself was best described by a word he had learnt from Muthu himself—propaganda.

So Zen, now familiar and somewhat comfortable with their dynamic, fired the first salvo, "I think I am closer to making up my mind, I think MyRealm I is most me". To justify his selection, Zen projected from his Embed, squarely affixed at the center of his forehead, a brilliant orb of

MyRealm I which he then delicately stretched with his fingers, so as to almost invite Muthu in.

Tellingly, even Muthu's defining skepticism was momentarily dazzled by the miniaturized utopia in front of him. Wherein it seemed that every creature comfort dreamt up by modern industry existed in perfect tranquility with the virgin lushness of nature; wherein advanced noble human beings entered cordially into the most fulfilling relations of work and play.

Reminding himself of his expected role as the arch dissenter, Muthu yanked his conscience out of the orb, "Utter fantasy, mere bells & whistles" he derided, "This is what they do, this is what they promise you, they paint a utopia that young people like you can't possibly resist; you can't make a country like you would a theme park!"

Zen knew he had to get a word in before the inevitable barrage would begin, but as usual he didn't know what one of Muthu's words meant—in this case the word being utopia, though he inferred it was something close to '100% citisumer satisfaction'.

Nevertheless Zen butted in, "There are no more countries, remember; and they are certainly not making countries, these are customized realms". And hastening the output of his words to preempt Muthu, Zen continued "You select everything about these realms from the religion to the rules, it really is where YOU want to live the rest of your life, not some one-size-fits-all country where you have to cohabit with citisumers of different beliefs"

With his decision so close at hand, Zen didn't want to get into another meaningless debate about the good and bad of countries versus realms as Muthu so loved to do. So he concertedly tried to shift the conversation to an evaluation of the two realms he had narrowed his options down to—MyRealm I and Peaceverse.

"You see MyRealm is totally set up to getting you everything new that the great entrepreneurships create," Zen galloped on, "I saw the new Sky Cabriolet on my Embed—it was amazing, that is so who I am. Also in MyRealm I, Moderate Catholicism is the religion and what's more since it's by LifeTree we get free access to loads of holidayscapes designed specifically for us MyRealmers and of course all of LifeTree's best enhancers & actualizers on discount! That is the real advantage over Peaceverse. The other cultural specs are pretty much the same though I think Peaceverse's version of Moderate Catholicism is a little different from MyRealm's one, but Peaceverse can't possibly offer what LifeTree can offer through its realms"

What began as an evaluation for which he wanted Muthu's input, became for Zen a self-hypnotizing soliloquy. It was as though the evocative projections of a better life in the realms that he had quasi-experienced via his Embed had become his imagination. There he was lying on a featherbed of comforting emerald grass, in the gleam of a smiling midday sun, sharing his lunch with fellow MyRealmers, proudly gazing up at his participation tower as it aspired through polished metallic sculpture toward the azure blue of Christ's heaven. Perhaps this evening Maya and he would...

"Argh! There you go again! Entranced by some corporation's damn film set" Muthu bellowed, slapping a nearby stack of books with all the might left in his flagging old arms.

Satisfied that his purposely thunderous intervention had just about been enough to prize Zen out of his Embedded imagination, Muthu resumed with zeal, "Before you think about trinkets and baubles, think about whether you will have any rights, you know a 'say' in how you will be governed"

"I will not be 'governed', I am deciding on what I want, I am choosing my own cultural specs" retorted Zen.

"Cultural specs! I think neither you nor those despicable marketers understand what they mean, and right now neither of you care. But believe me, in the end it won't matter to them but it will rob you of all your freedoms" Muthu prophesized and ranted on.

At that moment, Zen felt the early prickling of being offended, but it soon was soothed as he admitted to himself that the real reason he quite enjoyed his clandestine conversations with Muthu was not merely because it was an amusing distraction from his soul searching but because Muthu's passion for his strange thoughts and the squalor that it forced him to live in summed up all that was horribly wrong about the dreadful pre-world. How uncivilized he thought, but for a holiday of amusement, it is to live in a world of totally different ideas and beliefs, of constant argument and inevitable compromise with the ever looming possibility of the complete suppression of your beliefs or, at the very least the necessity to concede their inferiority for the sake of your very survival. Yes, that was what was wrong with the pre-world Zen reasoned: Christians, Muslims, Scientologists, Rastafarians, Buddhists, Hippies all wanting their way and miserably struggling against each other to reach an impossible middle-ground. He determined himself that this would not be his fate, no, he would make it to MyRealm I and earn his stay there—NO—he would never be made to come back in disgraceful defeat to this wasteland.

Of course Muthu was still going strong, now more in a reminiscing lament, "Who would've thought it would come to this, we were well on our way to a world driven by democratic ideals and human rights for all…"

Politely feigning interest, Zen tuned back into his imagination, yes perhaps that evening Maya and he would get their fifteen-on and do it on SoulMate. From there, Maya, the ultimate tangent of his heart and his lust within his Embedded imagination, sensuously beckoned. Her shy manners contrasting in titillating inappropriateness with her massive bubble butt blown out from her slender thighs. Her breasts, like her feelings, pent up by the impossible tightness of t-shirts and norms, only showing their rounded soft impressions. Her long, thin, up-slanted eyes, vixen-like yet somehow always smiling. Her lips pouted on purpose as a subtle deniable concession to her half-heartedly hidden lustfulness. And she was all this, Zen thought to himself with delicious glee, before she had all the wondrous enhancers & actualizers of the civilized realms. Electric expectations of their future in the Realms jolted through Zen, as it had begun to do more frequently ever since he had finally scraped up enough for a Life.

Muthu's gaze had by now turned away from Zen and indeed it seemed the here and now, his lament had grown deeper and by now was searching for its philosophical roots but still showed no signs of abating, "I blame the failure of the liberals, they gave up… they gave up on their duty to intellectualize the masses…"

Pausing his imagination momentarily to amuse himself at the string of incomprehensible code words generated by Muthu's mind, Zen once more resumed his imagination and by doing so bizarrely locked himself and Muthu for some time longer only in the body alignment required for a conversation.

Finally, and only when Muthu had, to his own satisfaction, arrived at the philosophical and historical explanation of all that was despicably wrong with the status quo did he attempt to reengage Zen on a level that would foster a genuine conversational to and fro. "So at least tell me about these cultural specs" he relented.

As intended, the mundane practicality of Muthu's inquiry enticed Zen to excitedly offer, "Better yet I will show you"

Once more from Zen's Embed almost materialized MyRealm I and grasping into its mesmerizing orb he gestured out a long densely branched list reaching almost as far as Zen's arms could stretch upwards.

"Go ahead," invited Zen, "google out anything you want"

Muthu, the luddite, inexpertly poked at the three-dimensional object which illuminated the sauntering particles of dust bordering it into a halo of sorts. Atop the list encapsulated in glossy bulbous buttons, were vivid video descriptions of glorious landscapes and spick-and-span neighborhoods, of insuperably cutting-edge sleekly designed devices and gargantuan shopping pyramids teeming with millions of shopper-ants. Beside the buttons was a contrastingly solemn crucifix with the word—'MODERATE'—engraved in an equally solemn font on it. Muthu keenly poked at the crucifix, and as he did he was taken aback as branches of light rapidly grew toward his eyes. Here again were a list of bulbous buttons, which too encapsulated vivid video, but unlike the previous ones they had either a red cross or a green thumbs-up over them. 'DIVORCE'—green thumbs-up, 'PORNOGRAPHY'—green thumbs-up ('Conditions apply'), 'SOULMATE'—green thumbs-up, 'ABORTION'—red cross, 'GAY MARRIAGE'—red cross, 'CONTRACEPTION'—green thumbs-up, 'EUTHANASIA'—green thumbs-up and the list went on. Muthu shuddered, more out of revulsion at the clinical formality underlying its creation than out of any disgust at the morals it espoused.

"Yup, those are the moderate Catholicism cultural specs" interjected Zen, "Exactly what I believe in, never to be doubted, never to be fought over, never to be changed, easy as that!"

Still aghast, Zen's words barely reached Muthu, "How do I get to the other non-religious specs?" he asked.

Zen promptly navigated his way back to the root list and dug to the very bottom of it and said, "They should be around here"

Muthu semi-struck by this, hurriedly thought to himself—hadn't Zen checked all the cultural specs before deciding on the realm? But his curiosity too inflamed by what he had just seen, he returned earnestly to the other cultural specs. This time the bulbous buttons contained no video but merely, and in comparison quite blandly, titles such as 'RE-DECISION', 'EVICTION' and 'PARTICIPATION' set against a background of sentences in a much smaller font. Muthu poked at the 'EVICTION' button and out marched sentences which methodically organized themselves from top to bottom. Muthu began to read the first one, 'The management of MyRealm I™ reserves the right to evict any citisumer for any reason it deems fit, including but not limited to the following: (with a listing of criteria subsumed under yet another button)'.

"Don't worry all the realm entrepreneurships have pretty much the same thing when it comes to those specs, I guess they can't make the realms work otherwise" interjected Zen before Muthu could poke at the criteria button.

Nevertheless, Muthu was determined to find out more, so in one forceful movement belying his inexpertness he went at the button. The emergence of words themselves at his eyes could no longer startle him, only their contextual meanings, and indeed they totally transfixed Muthu. In a role-reversal whose irony was not lost on Zen, it was now Muthu who was captivated by the Embed; an implicit affirmation no doubt, Zen thought to himself, of the superiority of his world to that of the dark history which Muthu championed.

As Muthu absorbed the contents of the criteria button, the peculiar old-model whose sagging wrinkly hide was only saved from a total shriveling by the pumping of his inner zeal, appeared to visibly deflate into a hunched clump of dejection. Which Zen presumptuously attributed to the realization, on the part of the old man, that he would never be able to live in a realm and that he had wasted away his life in the pre-world clinging on to some fantasy of a glorious past.

"Muthu, see it's not what you thought it would be, is it?" Zen delicately gloated, "It's not some place where you are ruled by the others and you can't do or have what you want. Actually, since there are no real 'others', it's impossible that they could rule you!"

Before Zen could administer the coup de grâce, Muthu, too dejected to make anything approaching an intellectual counter-offensive yet all the same not wanting Zen to notice his dejection, detoured the young upstart with the distracter, "So what about this Maya you are always waxing eloquent about, is she ready to go to this realm with you?"

"I think so, I've been showing her the specs of MyRealm I and of course she likes it and I knew she would, because otherwise I wouldn't have liked her in the first place! Only people who are the same can like each other" Zen replied, radiating a blissful confidence.

"But she hasn't made up her mind yet?" clarified Muthu.

"Well no, but she hasn't even mentioned any other realms and she really does like MyRealm I. You should see her face every time I show it to her on my Embed" noted Zen reassuring mostly himself.

"I had a special someone like your Maya, once, but she was the polar opposite of me" reminisced Muthu, going off into an uncharacteristically romantic interlude, "But back in those days, we would, believe it or not, say 'opposites attract'. We would actually embrace diversity, even glorify it; ha… must be completely unthinkable to you. We were completely different, me and Rayhana. She was so easygoing and carefree, a scandalous dresser and yet a good Muslim would you believe? She would chatter on for hours about the latest fashion and celebrity gossip, sometimes I think just to annoy me. And you know me, always on about politics and the 'boring', 'serious' stuff. But somehow we made it work, for a short time at least, a Muslim and an atheist, me hating popular culture and her obsessed with it. I wouldn't give up that tension for the world, Zen, I really wouldn't"

Zen unable to bring himself to speak his mind and enlighten (or quite likely remind) the dwindling old man looking through his rose tinted retrospectacles, that it was precisely these 'tensions' that had led to his and Rayhana's breakup, instead prematurely declared, "So you DO have a religion! And all this time you kept saying you don't"

Initially bamboozled as to where Zen came to this conclusion from but then, sifting through the mental transcripts of their preceding conversation and quickly realizing that Zen had equated atheism with a religion, Muthu re-experiencing his previous dejection explained, "Atheism is not a religion, atheists don't believe god exists"

"You are not serious are you?" Zen interrogated with a disbelieving anger, "How could you not believe in God?"

"Well we believe in only what can be proved scientifically" Muthu replied, carefully mollifying what would otherwise have been a condescension sharpened response, "And since there is no scientific proof of god or gods, at least not yet, and there is plenty of evidence to the contrary, it is only rational to believe in evolution"

"Evolution!" Zen quizzically exclaimed.

"Yes, evolution. It's a travesty that nowadays no one has even heard of it, it's shocking how a theory can go from being universally accepted, the consensus among the educated and even the not-so educated, to becoming nearly extinct, pardon the pun" replied Muthu, his rationalist condescension simmering.

"No tell me again, do you believe in any God? Doesn't have to be Jesus Christ, Allah, Buddha or Selassie, but any other God?" Zen demanded.

"No, I do not" Muthu answered almost sheepishly.

The cushion of potential misunderstanding that Zen used to stave off the unspeakable reality could no longer hold, for the first time in his life Zen was disgusted by an entirely alien difference; a difference somehow more perverse, more debauched than the others he knew, and not entirely due to its unfamiliarity.

"So you believe in nothing?" Zen asked dismissively.

"When it comes to god and the supernatural, yes, but we do have an explanation for how life came to be" Muthu explained, "A scientifically incontrovertible, a… a solid one"

For Zen, the revelation of Muthu's blasphemy created within him an almost instantaneous about-face of revulsion toward the old man, as if Muthu were a lover whose faithfulness he took for granted, only to one day catch him red-handed, fornicating with his best friend. Of course Zen was curious about this atheism and evolution, far more so than the other cryptic drivel that Muthu ranted on about, but his revulsion was too overpowering. Besides, he found it blasphemous in itself to indulge the blasphemy of the old unbeliever. Instead he blunted his intellectual curiosity by reasoning to himself that the greatest single cause of the destruction of the long dead world Muthu championed, was not—as he had always previously thought—its foolish commitment to insisting that the different live together, but that it allowed godlessness to flourish.

"Anyways, Muthu, I've gotta go" informed Zen curtly.

"Oh" sighed Muthu and inquired hopefully, "When will we meet again?"

"Soon" replied Zen dishonestly.

Fearful that Zen's pious outrage would deny him his only company and of course being extremely fond of the young zealot, Muthu conciliatorily advised, "Don't get too upset by what I do or don't believe in, it hardly affects your beliefs, try to keep an open mind"

"Okay" said Zen, and summarily got up, obligatorily faced Muthu gestured goodbye and beat a path through the shrub of fallen book leaves toward an orifice in Muthu's dungeon.

Outside, in the treacherous blackout of the pre-world night, Zen had only the smoggy light trails emitted by the factories belching in the distance and the makeshift projected luminescence of his Embed to guide him. Surely, he thought to himself, as he got closer to the settlements, the entire horizon would be lit up by news from the realms. True to form just moments later, rapidly gathering momentum in the distance was a tornado of multihued light, which as it approached, focused itself into a shimmering white infinity sign. The lemniscate proudly twirled on it axis, took a bow and was soon sucked back into the twister, only to be superseded by a whizzing two-lane highway of idyllic imagery. Smiles, skyscrapers, gardens, beaches, gadgets, brands in one lane; in the other crucifixes, dharmachakras, aums, crescents, faravahars, menorahs hurtled toward the eyes and consciousness, curving away only at the very last moment in two perfect arcs. Regally succeeding the procession, in enormous capitalized full moon hued letters an axiom appeared, 'UNITED WE FALL, DIVIDED WE STAND'. How true, thought Zen, still metabolizing his disgust at Muthu's godlessness, how true.

ZEN AWOKE, as he always did on these most special of days, his chest pulsating in a vat of adrenaline, his body moistened by a clammy lather of sweat. Yes, today was the day Maya and he regularly met at the Numero-Lingual casts.

As if any reminder were needed, his mother rang out, "Zen are you ready for NumLing?"

"Yup" he replied.

"I've got everything ready for you" she said.

"Thanks" said Zen as he got up from his nest of sheets huddled together at the corner of the hut.

As always, his mother had made porridge and though its leafy smell rising to his nose on greenish thermals of steam had lately begun to be nauseating, Zen holding his nose figuratively at least, plopped in with his ladle.

As he ate his mother replayed her NumLing morning sermon, "Now Zen, focus on NumLing, don't get distracted by Maya or anyone else. If your NumLing is not good enough, you won't be able to hold down a participation in MyRealm and you'll have to come back to this horrible place"

"I know, I know" Zen interrupted her.

"Don't worry, during the whole NumLing I will be praying for you" she reassured, fondling her rosary, "Remember to say a little prayer before you start, as well. It was God that led you to MyRealm and it is he that will get you there"

The words of his mother's sermon were essentially the same but with his ascension close at hand, all her talk about the bliss of MyRealm I agitated the feelings of guilt that had begun to well up recently. If only she could come with him, she would just love the purity of religiousness; she could spend all her free time in devotion and prayer in the latest churches and even come back on the great crusades. But she couldn't, it was too risky, at her age even if she did master NumLing, what were the chances that she would be able to hold down a participation? And if she didn't then she could lose it all! Zen, noticing himself slithering into sadness, snapped himself back out with the resolution 'I mustn't think about it before NumLing; I can take care of her if I make a success of myself in MyRealm'.

"Come on Zen get dressed" hurried his mother.

With that, Zen got dressed and in a ceremonious fashion befitting the importance of the endeavor at hand, stepped out of his hut into the morning pandemonium.

The wail of "Alllaaaaaaaaaaaaaaah... uh... Akbarrrrr" from the mosque on the hill's giant megaphone, clanged, clattered and confronted the moaning lament of "Buddhan... Saranang... Gachaaaaami" from the ivory-domed temple on the opposing hill; and making a joyful mockery of the two, the megaphone of the old church down the path sang out "OH MY LORD, YOU SENT YOUR SON TO SAVE US, OH MY LORD...". Zen scampered past the usual riffraff, the beggars, the hawkers, the clergymen beseeching passersby for a moment of their time. Today he was in no mood for the hellishly jagged edges of the pre-world, his brisk gait soon became a gallop as he skillfully dodged the potholes and pitfalls of the pre-world street toward Maya and their future.

Arriving out of breath at the amphitheater long before the first NumLing cast of the day, Zen rabidly searched for Maya at the entrance where they usually met. Unable to find her, he darted through the entryway, almost forgetting to validate his subscription, and scuttled up the stairs, immediately zeroing in on where he, Maya and a group of fellow MyRealm I hopefuls had begun to band together during the past few casts. From behind, a soft cheek snuggled his left shoulder blade, as a pair of delicate hands cinched both his shoulders.

"Zenny, I was looking for you" a high-pitched voice delighted.

Titillated that Maya had touched him, yet anxious that she had smelt the tanginess of his perspiration on his rarely washed clothes, Zen swiveled almost dislodging Maya and following a pregnant pause, grinned "Hi"

"C'mon, let's sit" ushered Maya, gesturing toward the floor.

One by one, along with hordes of hopefuls all increasingly segregated by the realm they aspired to, Zen and Maya's little clique filed in. Just before Linus sat down, the NumLing cast commenced.

In all the dimensions of reality the proud lemniscate appeared, this time rippling with the variegations of the rainbow and levitating under it, embossed with a steely sheen, simply the name 'OmniRealm'. Before the NumLing lessons proper began, the amphitheater would whet its eager audience with peeks into various realms sponsored by the realm entrepreneurships. Zen crossed his fingers.

First off, was a peek into Mecca III. A collectively half-muted groan murmured from everywhere other than the Muslim section accompanied by an en masse muting of Embeds. As a land appeared where everything—apartments, malls, participation towers—seemed to be confined in towering concrete and glass minarets, that in turn overshadowed the black silhouettes of women and the reams of white clothed men below. To a background cacophony of familiar wails, the peek boastfully whisked the audience through a parade of modern amenities and glitzy storefronts and then, exploding in the night sky of Mecca III set against a crescent moon, fireworks burst forth cultural specs: Boom—'5X SALAT', Boom—'HALAL', Boom—'RAMADAN', Boom—'NIQAB', Boom—'NO PORNOGRAPHY', Boom—'NO HOMOSEXUALITY', Boom—'NO ALCOHOL', went the fireworks; culminating in a green fire emblazoned calligraphic print proclaiming itself 'MECCA III'.

Perhaps the next one, Zen hoped. But no, it was a peek into Samsara+. In a plush mall of milk marbled floors and bright glass windows, through which tropical birds and butterflies flitted across mystically inspired storescapes, sat a saffron-robed flutist, cross-legged on a cushy satin waterbed. From his flute, holding hands with his enchanting tune, danced out wispy gold clouds that the music then tenderly arranged into the outlines of words: 'VEGETARIANISM – TEETOTALISM – ABSTINENCE*'. For emphasis, the words fluttered for a few moments until they became part of an ornately carved chariot wheel, which then began to turn purposefully with the promise 'Samsara+: Your Last Stop' wispily forming in its center.

Zen was on the ready to turn his Embed's sound on, surely after waiting through cast after cast of NumLing this time would be a peek into MyRealm I. Alas, it was a peek into the Clear Realm of Thetans. Thousands of scoffing puffs randomly burst out from all over the amphitheater. As a ghost-like energy trail streaked across starry galaxies toward the brown globe of Earth and took the form of a primitive savage, who then was rapidly fast-forwarded via the quaint costumes and landscapes of history into a modern citisumer reclining at peace on a couch. Orbiting his head were vivid holograms of brands and gadgets perfectly in sync with happy childhood memories and the cultural specs: 'NO OBSCURING MEDICINE', 'NO NARCOTICS' and 'BE 100% ENGRAM FREE'; with the surreal spectacle crowned by the emergence of a large harp-like insignia.

Never mind thought Zen as the NumLing cast proper began, shuffling a little closer to Maya and committing himself to concentrate on the lucid booming voice as it introduced and then explained a string of new words.

Half-an-hour or so later, as the NumLing cast entered the numerical instruction component, "Okay, here's the hard part for me" sighed Maya.

"Don't worry, afterwards I'll help you" Zen eagerly volunteered, making an ever more concerted effort to sponge up the cast.

"Zen's the only one that's really made up his mind for sure, right?" Benedict asked, leading-off the clique's post-NumLing caucus, "And Maya of course" he added with a smirk slyly looking at Zen.

"Well, I am not sure about any of the MyRealms" Linus warily interjected, "Think about it, we've been coming to these NumLing casts for God knows ages now, but we haven't even seen one peek into any of the MyRealms. You know what that means right?"

"What?" Zen worriedly inquired.

"It means, that it might not be a well-run cluster of realms" Linus explained, "And so they can't afford to sponsor peeks, you can imagine how expensive sponsoring peeks must be, so it's a sign of success when realm entrepreneurships regularly do"

"Or a sign that they are not doing so well and desperately need citisumers" Benedict pointed out.

"But the entrepreneurship is LifeTree, I mean how can that be Linus?" Zen argued, "Not only are they known as one of the best realm brands but they make so many other amazing actz & ens and even just because you can experience them on discount in their realms, their realms are worth it. Anyways I don't know, what do you think Maya?"

"Um… I don't know, what are the other options for moderate Catholicism?" Maya queried.

"Peaceverse of course, but Startern is new to realms so their ones probably won't have the features of the big brands" Benedict speculated.

"Yup and loads of bugs in Startern's realms" noted Linus.

"PietySphere is a pretty good option, Maya" Benedict continued, "It's by Realmx, you're not going to get discounts on actz & ens like in the MyRealms, 'cause they're realm specialists but you are guaranteed a totally bug free citisumer friendly realm"

"PietySphere is what I was considering instead of MyRealm too" resounded Linus, "After all you can always trust a specialist brand"

"Do they have SoulMate?" inquired Zen, looking at Maya as she coyly looked down.

"No but it's listed as 'Coming Soon' " Linus answered.

"See Linus, this is what I mean, because it's not a LifeTree realm even things like SoulMate are still only 'Coming Soon', and I'll bet it'll be the same with the other features" reasoned Zen.

"Yeah maybe, but this why we should google it out, instead of blindly choosing MyRealm I" Linus retorted, pecking his head forward and turning his palms up in exasperation.

"But we already…" Zen began defensively only to be interrupted by Maya, "Look, every citisumer should make up their own minds, as that peek goes 'Live in the Land of I' "

"Right" agreed Linus.

"True" Benedict chimed in.

Before an increasingly cornered Zen could remount his defense, the attention of the group had been grabbed away by a commotion roaring from roughly the Shaivite and Buddhist sections.

"The usual squabbles" Zen dismissed, hell bent on his mission.

"No, no, I think it is a… crusade!" sputtered Maya, perplexed.

"A crusade? In the NumLing amphitheater?" exclaimed Benedict.

"Yeah, look there is no way they are from the pre-world" agreed Linus, pointing to a clot of conspicuously plump characters in immaculately white skintight bodysuits being surrounded by an angry mob of disheveled youth.

"Definitely from a Christian realm" Zen joined in, now himself distracted by the ruckus, "Must be trying to teach the Buddhists that Buddha is not God"

"And they're not giving up" Maya observed, "Look, their Embeds are still projecting Christian stuff"

"Wow, now that's an up-close & personal crusade for you" clucked Linus.

"Oh yeah, this is gonna be the best NumLing cast ever, great stuff, great stuff" cheered Benedict.

The leaders of the disheveled mob had by now invaded the personal space of the privileged crusaders, their eyes demonically set ablaze reflecting the pious radiance from the crusaders' Embeds. In one last act of mercy, the emergent leader of the mob pointed to the exit, followed in chorus by his deputies. Collectively, the crusaders remained defiant; the NumLing audience heaved, bracing themselves for the rampage. When, as though on cue, a whirring in the heavens arrested the earthly drama. Reverentially, the hopefuls looked up as one, as the metal mosquito emblazoned with the leminiscate on its smoothened bottom belly rapidly descended and humbly apologized for the inconvenience. The apology was reiterated in the epicenter of the amphitheater by a merry-go-round of all-different, all-beautiful, all-smiling faces as the mob obligingly dispersed, making way for the crusaders to show themselves out of the amphitheater, still spouting and flaunting their creed.

"Whoa, and that's why realms shouldn't mix!" concluded Maya.

"And certainly not realms and the pre-world" added Linus, "Not unsupervised anyway"

"Hey guys, guess who would come back on even an unsupervised crusade for MyRealm I?" teased Benedict nodding in Zen's direction.

Belatedly realizing that he was the butt of his friend's chuckles, Zen felt like barking back at his friends and reminding them that only a few

NumLing casts ago they were all in love with MyRealm I, but the raucous interlude of the crusader episode had given him pause to think that if he continued with his defensiveness he would be lessened in Maya's eyes. So he affably laughed along with them and schemed to privately convince Maya when he got her alone to go over the day's NumLing cast.

A few minutes later, still raving about the spectacle of the crusade in the amphitheater, Linus and Benedict duly left. Finally, what Zen had been waiting for all day, indeed that moment he had been longing for since the last NumLing cast, had arrived.

"So shall we start off with the first number puzzle and go from there?" started Zen.

"Zen, do you know anything about your family's past" asked Maya.

"Uh, not really, I don't want to ask my mother about it, 'cause it reminds her of my father and that really upsets her" replied Zen, derailed by Maya's digression.

"Is your father, um?" stuttered Maya.

"Yeah he is dead, he was killed in a mugging, we think by some hippies" Zen burst out.

"Oh, sorry" sympathized Maya.

"Well that's the pre-world for you, a jungle where anybody can eat anybody" bemoaned Zen.

"Yeah" agreed Maya.

"And the realms are like a zoo, where everyone is neatly kept apart for their own good" analogized Zen with a self-satisfied glint brightening his eyes.

"But why this sudden interest in your family's past Maya?" inquired Zen.

"Nah, I just came across some old family stuff, turns out my family is more complicated than I thought" answered Maya.

"You mean like inter-marriage and stuff?" pried Zen.

"Yeah" answered Maya.

"That's what got the pre-world into this mess in the first place, I reckon" theorized Zen, thinking to himself—that and godlessness.

"Well, what does it matter what got us here. All that matters now is a Life in the realms, right?" asked Maya rhetorically, raising Zen's self-awareness to his newly acquired habit of seeking explanations for the emergence of the pre-world.

"Absolutely right, and this is why I wanted to talk to you about MyRealm I, alone" answered Zen, sniffing an opportunity.

"There is plenty of time for that, now let's get to those puzzles" skirted Maya, flicking through her Embed to a recording of the NumLing cast.

Zen dutifully commenced his tutorial, tangoing his Embed with hers, he gave life to the puzzles and numbers with an élan that amused and impressed Maya. But despite his most exhaustive of teaching styles, the dreaded last few puzzles eventually approached.

Just before the very last puzzle, his chest thud-thudded with an impromptu plan to sequel the magic moment. He would ask Maya out for lunch! An indulgence for which he had just about saved enough for after scraping up everything he had earned to offer for his ascension.

"And so if you put the 6 here then both the row and column add up to 27" Zen nervously explained rounding up his tutorial.

"Thanks so much, Zenny" smiled Maya opening her arms for a hug that Zen clumsily relished completely forgetting about his ever fermenting tanginess.

"Maya, do you wanna have lunch?" Zen asked, her name coming out in a squeak and 'lunch' in a yelp.

"Yeah, okay" replied Maya suppressing a giggle at Zen's awkwardness.

As Zen and Maya left the amphitheater, smelling their relative affluence hawker-flies buzzed around them. Swatting them off, they ran down a tractor heading in the general direction of the lunch huts.

"Half a like to the lunch huts?" growled Zen transparently trying to show off his machismo.

"Hmpf, one like or get off" grunted the turbaned greasy blob manning the rusty controls.

"Okay" Zen relented, changing his tactics and hoping Maya would notice his big spender capabilities.

"Pay now" the greasy blob grunted again.

Zen adroitly completed the e-pay to the hole ripped out of the blob's turban and helped Maya onto the trailer which, in the midday sun, sizzled the skin like a frying pan. The tractor jostled and bobbed along toward the lunch huts and then abruptly jolted to a halt.

"Okay, get out" commanded the greasy blob.

"The lunch huts are more that way" Zen pointed to a well beaten dirt track.

"Get out, the tractor ain't going there" shouted the greasy blob.

Could he handle the blob? Zen asked himself. Was it worth risking a beat down to impress Maya? The boys he grew up with would've.

"Let's just go Zen" exhorted Maya sensing Zen's intent, "C'mon let's just go"

Maya eventually managed to cajole a reluctant Zen to hop off and they made their way toward the huts.

"Lunch one like, bird and all… lunch one like, bird and all" announced a scrawny frizzy haired women with naked little children running around her feet. Zen and Maya, fixated their eyes on the large patina coated cross hanging pendulously from her neck, looked at each other, nodded and headed toward her hut.

"Hope today's bird isn't crow" said Zen.

"Unlikely, look at all the crows flying around" reckoned Maya.

As soon as they paid and sat down on the bench outside the woman's hut, she promptly handed them two brown clay pots and slopped in some bony gruel from a larger clay pot.

As they were just about to finish, Zen summoned up the courage to ask Maya the all-important question, "So Maya…"

Just then the tornado of multihued light formed in the horizon. It approached and in a burying motion disappeared briefly. Only to spring forth in the form of a well-nourished bark of a tree, which rapidly went through its life stages: first thick brown branches, then thinner offshoots, then deep green leaves and multicolored flowers, and finally, in the fruiting stage, gorgeous sophisticated devices.

"LifeTree" beamed Maya, gazing up in awe.

"Joy is LifeTree" an angelic voice echoed across the earth.

Then the fruits began to parachute toward the grounds, merrily pirouetting as they descended. A stampede began from the huts and surrounding areas, Zen and Maya were at its vanguard. Being outsiders to the area, they only grabbed one capsule each as scuffles broke out around them between hoarders.

"C'mon, you first" invited Zen impatiently.

Maya had already ripped off her capsule's parachute and was marveling at the artistically carved hand shape inside it. Lovingly, she held it slightly aloft in the palms of her cupped hands and asked Zen, "What do you think she does?"

"Wow, I think she's a personal massager" answered Zen, gently fondling buttons placed where its knuckles could have been.

The hand's fleshy fingers began to move in a graceful wave-like motion, which at first startled Maya but then pacified her.

"Oh" she moaned as she was soothed, "Oh, oh"

"You think that's good, try it on your neck" promised Zen, carefully removing the soothing hand, stroking Maya's dark locks aside and placing it on her sumptuous neck.

"Ohhh, even better, try another mode" pleaded Maya, her head reverberating with comfort.

By now, all around Zen and Maya the strong were conspicuous by the number of soothing hands that were kneading them. They appeared as though a cast of crabs had surmounted them, only, they were writhing with ecstasy. Just as Zen realized that he was the sole onlooker to Maya's and this collective ecstasy, thwok, thwok, thwok, the soothing hands fell off in succession.

"Wow, how totally actualizing" exhaled Maya, "Did you try her?" she asked Zen, trying to recall through her hazy trance like experience. Hardly concerned with his answer, Maya bent over to claim the hand from the ground, she dusted some dirt off it and read to herself an inscription on its palm. Proudly cradling the hand in hers, as though she were naming her newborn, she announced, "Meet MassageMe"

Absurdly, Zen felt jealous of the hand and with Maya in its grip, the portal to pose the big question had closed. Ritualistically almost, the hordes around them along with Maya had picked up the soothing hands and now were venerating the perished thing through devout conversations about its glories. The refrain "Joy is LifeTree", "Joy is

LifeTree" rang out several times from the congregation each time to rapturous hurrahs.

"Amen to that" affirmed Maya, as the refrain rang out once more, adding breathlessly, "I can't wait to show this to my grandmother, I'm sure she'll hang it underneath our crucifix"

3

"NO SERIOUSLY guys, I'm worried about Maya" gulped Zen as the NumLing cast concluded.

"Like I said, she just probably couldn't make it today" reiterated Linus.

"Though, she never misses a cast 'cause she needs all the help she can get with Num" noted Benedict.

"I'm going to her hut" decided Zen. He jumped to his feet, and began to hurtle toward the amphitheater's exit.

Surely nothing was wrong but as Telltale always says 'A warranty guarantees tranquility' he repeated to himself over and over again, as he slalomed his way through the pre-world obstacle course.

Panting and pouring he arrived at Maya's hut and threw aside the reddened rusty iron stopgap serving as a door.

"Zen!" greeted the relieved voice of Maya's grandmother, "Thank God you are here"

"Why, what has happened to Maya?" demanded Zen his heart accelerating to fight-or-flight mode.

The old woman could only get in, "Well, she has decided to...", when a figure obscured by an unmistakable headscarf ducked into the hut.

"Maya!" shrieked Zen, quickly embarrassed by his loudness and trying, unconvincingly, to return his face to its normal proportions.

"I have made my decision Zen" declared Maya, attempting to moderate the situation with her composure.

"But Maya..." tried Zen, gob smacked, not knowing where to start.

Summarily cutting Zen off, "I have chosen to ascend to New Caliphate: Progressive-conservative Islam and conceived by LifeTree" announced Maya.

"Dear, you should think about what you are doing" started Maya's grandmother, at first even-temperedly, but soon the damnation broke— "They are Muslims! Look at the way they treat women, I don't know what will happen to you, tell her Zen, tell her"

"Maya why? What made you change your mind?" asked Zen, attempting to gently take up the cause, "I was worried that you might choose Peaceverse over MyRealm I, but a Muslim realm! What happened?"

"In Islam a women is a like a cartier, precious, always to be protected" pontificated Maya, "She is not a piece of flesh, left out for the crows to have their way with"

"And Grandma, it is you that actually led me to Islam" continued Maya, "Remember when you showed me Mom's and Dad's old stuff, they were Muslims"

"NO, he tried to make your mother a Muslim, and see where it got them!" corrected the old woman indignantly.

"Maya, the point is, Islam is the most backward of all the backward non-Catholic religions" declared Zen self-righteously, "It's not who you are, it's not…"

"Zen, you know the problem with you? You're only NumLing smart, you're not brand new, you're not state-of-the-art. Have you learned nothing?—'What I believe in is always right' "derided Maya.

"And 'Everybody is always wrong' " mouthed Zen, not realizing that he had stumped himself.

"Hail Mary, full of grace, our Lord is with thee…" incanted Maya's grandmother, rosary in hand away in the background.

"Just tell me why? Why all of a sudden?" begged Zen.

"It's not all of a sudden, it's not. I couldn't tell you because you think about these things too much. 'Think less, feel more' remember; and I… feel… New Caliphate" impassioned Maya.

'Hail Mary, full of grace, our Lord is with thee…' looped in the background via the old woman's nasal jittery voice, as Maya and Zen stepped out of the hut. Heads down and for the most part silent, they reflectively ambled through the haphazard settlement, Zen's mind vacillating between 'Shall I hold her hand', 'No I shouldn't' and the disemboweling shock of Maya's decision.

"Fweeeeet, Fweeeeet, Fweeeeet" a chorus of whistles pealed out from a raucous of exceptionally strapping boys.

"Only seen ass like that on the news" one of them shouted to congratulatory cheers and more, "Fweeets, Fweeets"

"Oh yeah, we got the realms jiggling, jiggling right here" bawled another.

"Let's get out of here" pled Maya already in a full panic.

Zen and Maya quickened their strides to just below a run, but from the ominous shadows falling in front of them they could see that the strapping raucous was upon them.

As they passed around, a posse of muscular hands reached out from the raucous and groped deep into Maya's fleshy derrière, several of them smacking it into a gelatinous yet firm ripple. Zen swatting them away, inadequately screened Maya with his skinny frame and readied himself into a fighting stance—fists up, shadow jabbing. Curiously, belying their rowdiness, the raucous didn't even bother to look back at the outnumbered couple as they triumphantly went their way.

"See Zen, see this is what I mean about exposed women" admonished Maya, welling up, "I can't live like this anymore. All this getting your fifteen-on on SoulMate before marriage and dressing like this, this is what it leads to, you saw what those boys did to me"

How could this be happening? Zen despairingly thought to himself. But how could he break it to an almost sobbing, definitely convinced Maya that Islam was wrong, that Jesus was God, the king, the only savior of man? If only New Caliphate wasn't a LifeTree realm, then it wouldn't have both arms around Maya's heart. Maybe Muthu wasn't all wrong. No. He wouldn't let himself fall into old-model thinking. Maybe if he could prove that Catholicism is right and Islam is wrong, as if he were solving a NumLing puzzle then Maya would be convinced. But again 'What I believe is always right' and 'Everybody is always wrong' would stop him from getting through to her, he would be one of the 'Everybodies' and of course she would say that he was thinking too much.

Confirming his thoughts almost, Maya interjected, "It's not all their fault though, although I do hate them. It's just this damned hell where we all have to 'live' together. I mean, I'm sure that there are loads of girls who are just like those guys, that would love the attention, and I guess whatever they believe would be always right FOR THEM; but for me it's totally disgusting, it's totally haram"

"I guess nowadays, there is certain hell before life as well the possibility of it after" observed Zen, once more obliviously hurting his cause.

"Yeah exactly" agreed Maya, pulling her headscarf further toward her hairline and scrunching her body tighter into itself.

"Must be some hippies, 'cause I mean nowhere in Catholicism does it encourage this kinda stuff, I seriously doubt it'll happen in MyRealm I or any of the other Catholic realms" Zen reassured trying to mount a comeback.

"Zen, Zen" halted Maya, parentally lifting an index finger at him, "What I believe in is always right" she sermonized once more, "And anyways, Islam is the one religion that is specially designed to stop this kinda stuff, the others simply don't have that feature even if they actually don't make you do it"

First Muthu, now his Maya, sulked Zen, and as he did the Dark Age malware that Muthu had tried to infect Zen with rebooted in his mind. This time though it commandeered his voice, "Are different thoughts all that bad?" he blurted out, "After all, if someone or, God forbid, everyone has the wrong beliefs and they at the same time won't budge from 'Everything I believe is always right' then they are damned by their unchanging wrong beliefs, right?"

"What? I don't even know what you are talking about Zen" sneered Maya, "Stop it, stop it now, and just believe what you believe and feel what you believe, stop solving everything like it's a NumLing puzzle, beliefs can't be solved you know"

Shuddered by Maya's rebuke and somewhat confused by the logic he had uttered, Zen self-censored himself, knowing though that the uprising of the Dark Age malware had only temporarily been quelled. More urgently he was debilitated by the physical pangs of heartbreak, as he began to acknowledge that convincing Maya to ascend with him was a lost crusade.

"C'mon walk me home and none of this nonsense" ordered Maya, "I'll show you New Caliphate"

The trauma in Zen's chest and the weakness in his limbs after he dropped Maya off, tempted Zen mirage-like toward an alluring path. What if he followed Maya to New Caliphate? What if he converted to Islam? Surely then nothing would stand between... but no sooner he contemplated this he convulsed with revulsion at the thought of him as a Muslim. After a few bouts of forcing himself to reconsider it, his choice of MyRealm grew infinitely more promising, infinitely more perfect and righteous, as though this whole episode with Maya was a final divine nudge in the right direction toward his destiny. Spurred on by this and eager to flee his agonizing solitude, Zen headed to the factory he worked at to tell Mr. Ramwi that he had earned enough likes to ascend.

The giant windowless box made of gray corrugated asbestos sheets, where over a thousand emaciated pre-world worker bees performed meaningless actions to incomprehensible objects, was Mr. Ramwi's fiefdom and he was as harsh as the conditions inside it. An asymmetrical, potbellied, one-eyed man who Zen surmised from his precise instructions and elaborate work methods was a NumLing expert, bitter Ramwi's only satisfaction it seemed was devising methods to extract ever more from the stupid worker bees under him.

"Ascend, ha, so you think you are good enough at NumLing?" patronized Ramwi in between his incessant coughs, "We'll see. Don't expect me to keep a place for you if you can't hold down a participation though"

"Well, I just came to tell you, I better..." finished off Zen, clutching the arms of his chair.

"Hold on, hold on" commanded Ramwi restraining Zen in his domineering orbit, "After all these years you at least owe me a moment of your 'precious' time"

Ramwi struggled to the edge of his elevated booth to oversee the worker bees load their finished incomprehensible components into containers. From each container, almost as if it were a flower pot, sprang forth the venerable LifeTree, the bark of each engraved with a different insignia. The emaciated workers bees—men, women but

mostly children—holding their incomprehensible charms ceremoniously aloft over their head, formed themselves into separate
processions, and each chanting different hymns headed toward a
container. It was obvious from above that the container with the
crescent engraved bark drew the largest procession. Followed in order
by the one with the cross, the wheel, the ying-yang, the aum and the star
being tied for fifth. On reaching their respective containers, the old male
leader of each procession chanted one final prayer, signaling each
worker to consecrate their incomprehensible charm, which they duly
did, following which each procession ritualistically touched themselves.
Zen made the cross on his chest and Ramwi clasped his ears with
opposite hands simultaneously bowing his head several times.

"So you are a...?" queried Ramwi, adjusting his eye patch and
disintegrating back into his seat.

"Catholic" Zen filled in the blank.

"So what's the realm you have chosen?" asked Ramwi showing
genuine interest.

"MyRealm I by LifeTree" declared Zen making sure to sound proud.

"Do you know how the realms came to be?" asked Ramwi, preparing
himself to answer by clearing his throat.

"Um... no" replied Zen, hoping that Ramwi wouldn't pull a Muthu
on him and readying an exit excuse, "I really better get..."

"Do you know the founding story of LifeTree?" asked Ramwi in a
timely change of course.

How foolish of him to think that the state-of-the-art Ramwi would
drone on like the obsolete old-model Muthu, thought Zen as he settled
back in his chair.

Ramwi, feeling an unexpected kinship with Zen on finding out that
the capable young man was his NumLing peer, began with gusto, "You
see-eeeeee... when the first realms came out, the realm
entrepreneurships only provided the real estate and the basic
infrastructure. Everything else for the realms had to be provided by
independent entrepreneurships, so the actualizers & enhancers clashed
terribly with the realm, resulting in a bug filled Life. Well, actually even
today most realm trepships don't conceive of their own actz & ens to

perfectly complement their realms. Imagine if your body was constructed by stitching together the parts of other people's bodies!"

Zen, totally engrossed, gasped at the thought.

Temporarily unveiling a statue of a middle-aged man with a maverick beard gesturing a thoughtful pose, whose eyes were set a light by the holographic luster of the LifeTree crest, Ramwi began to eulogize, "But this one man, this one brilliant visionary…"

"Vic Crafts "completed Zen reverentially.

"Yes, Vic Crafts," resounded Ramwi, "dared to think different, to seamlessly integrate everything in his glorious quest to create perfect, beautiful realms. Realms that we at LifeTree can be proud of whether we live in them or not. This is why joy is Lifetree!"

The peroration had exhausted Ramwi, sending his cough into a snot spewing frenzy, but he persevered, "This is why I wouldn't ever trust these other realm trepships, Realmx may let you down, Startern may let you down and let's not even talk about Arise, but Vic Crafts will never let you down!"

"One hundred percent, one hundred percent" concurred Zen, simultaneously mesmerized and comforted (given his decision) by the splendor that was LifeTree and wanting Ramwi to continue his inspirational tale.

"Come with me… yes, come with me to unveil this statue" brainstormed Ramwi, shepherding Zen down toward the factory floor. "Bring it yourself" he added, summoning some men from below to assist Zen, "And make sure you don't have any religious stuff on you" he instructed, inspecting Zen's neck with his one telescopic eye.

"SILENCE, SILENCE" Ramwi commanded before he paused, allowing the worker bees to fix their attention on him. Then, heaving his strength, he avalanched out his oration, "It is with great pleasure and humility that I, today, unveil this monument to the greatest of entrepreneurial geniuses, the maestro of citisumer satisfaction, the realm visionary, our… VIC CRAFTS". As the uproar of applause began, Ramwi whisked away the white satin quilt covering the statue to the "Oohs" and "Ahs" of the awestruck worker bees.

"And, and… I have a very special example for you today" continued Ramwi, clutching Zen's hand and yanking him out of the statue's shadow, "Here is a young man… ahem, ahem… here is a young man that used to work here, who earned enough likes only by working just at this blessed LifeTree womb, that he can, now, ascend to a LifeTree realm"

The worker bees looked up to Zen, as Ramwi went on, "Let this be an example to you all of the triumph of individualism, the self… ahem… that means each of you. By working hard in this here blessed womb and then ascending to a LifeTree realm, you can actualize and enhance whatever it is that is inside you, whatever you feel; bring out whatever makes you—YOU. You can, believe with complete peace-of-mind whoever it is you believe in, you can take the rough ore, the… the stone, that you are and chisel out the I-diamond within. In short—YOU CAN… finally… become YOU!"

Throughout Ramwi's rousing sermon the worker bees nodded, gestured and lip-synced in total agreement at every punch line, making Zen, his eyes still shyly averted from the audience, wonder how different their reception would have been if it were Muthu delivering one of his sermons. So it was not sermonizing in general that was boring, Zen concluded.

"Now, you can all, one-by-one, approach Vic Crafts and receive some individualized words of wisdom from him" announced Ramwi.

This time around, the workers formed themselves into one long procession and presented themselves in front of Vic Crafts. Wow, thought Zen, over a thousand different nuggets of wisdom from the great man himself which he could overhear!

The first worker bee approached, gratefully submitting his ear to Vic Crafts, "You're worth it" Zen overheard the great man whisper, his lips faithfully articulating the vowels and consonants of his wisdom, and lapping up that drop of nectar the worker bee gleefully buzzed off.

The second approached, "Have it your way" Vic Crafts whispered.

The third approached, "Open your happiness" he whispered.

The fourth approached, "Be unlike any other" he whispered.

The fifth approached, "Don't dream it, live it" he whispered.

And the sixth approached, "You're worth it" Vic Crafts repeated, must have overhead wrong, Zen thought. The seventh approached "Have it your way" Vic Crafts replayed. What happened to the thousand different nuggets of wisdom each customized to the individual worker? Puzzled Zen.

"This will take ages, though it's most definitely a valuable stoppage unlike the other ones, after all, informed citisumers are well-formed citisumers" broke in Ramwi, "Let's come back when it's about to finish"

"So you must be licking your lips dreaming about the beauties in the realms" Ramwi asked Zen on the way up, vicariously giving vent to his own lust.

"Well, I kinda like… liked, someone here" replied Zen, the trauma in his chest relapsing.

"Ah, is she joining you in MyRealm?" inquired Ramwi.

"Uh, no, she has converted to Islam!" answered Zen, head down, flagging with resignation.

"Then you never liked her" deduced Ramwi, "If she converted to Islam, that means she always had that in her, that was always her. We always end up believing what we are, our beliefs stem from us as seamlessly as actz & ens stem from LifeTree realms. That is why they are always right. And if hers are different from yours, well then it goes without saying that you never liked her. How could you?"

"Only people who are the same can like each other" thought Zen out loud, but then he really did love Maya and was beginning to quite like Ramwi.

"Yes, exactly. You're a smart young man, this should be obvious to you, put her out of your head, it's just this pre-world hodgepodge that has got you confused" advised Ramwi, "You're going to be a worthy citisumer soon and that's all you should be focusing on from here on in"

Perhaps, Zen thought, he would have been better off being mentored by state-of-the-art Ramwi instead of obsolete Muthu, the godless rabble rouser. Though he really didn't know what he thought at this point.

"Someday soon my sons will make it to the realms, most probably Eternal Lotus, that is my only dream now" confided Ramwi, wrapping up what had ended up as a lengthy heart-to-heart, "Come, let's go back down, I have to give out this evening's instructions" he added, ushering Zen back toward the factory floor.

Zen eavesdropped in as the last of the worker bees were receiving their nectar from Vic Crafts, but to his continued puzzlement he only overheard once again, "Be unlike any other". Surely there was good reason for this, he thought to himself, when, a worker bee impatiently faked the uptake of nectar and swerved his exit path toward Zen, humming as he went by, "Careful what you wish for"

IN THE days leading up to his ascension, Zen did not feel, as he had expected to, even the slightest of poignant twinges. Indeed, even parting from his mother came to be an open & shut matter of rational choice. How could it be any different, what with the script tearing shock of Muthu's godlessness and more so Maya's apostasy. Nevertheless, as a loose end tying formality he felt obliged to say goodbye to Linus and Benedict, Maya of course, and maybe even old Muthu.

"Maya, Maya… are you home" called Zen, knocking on the tinny covering of Maya's hut.

A few knocks later, her grandmother solemnly answered, "Come in"

And there she was, Maya, now just a pair of eyes. Quickly, she averted them, as her grandmother rolled hers in disapproval.

"Maya, I have come to say goodbye and wish you the very best in New… um your chosen realm" Zen unevenly recited, hands by his side, beating his feelings into a rigid formal posture.

"When is your ascension?" asked Maya, talking at the wall.

"Tomorrow" Zen tersely replied.

"Okay then, good luck with that and thanks for the help with NumLing, barak'Allah" Maya summed up, as if they were never more than acquaintances.

Hollow with rejection yet realizing that this might be the last time he would see Maya, he stared at the black cutout of reality, hoping that it would turn its eyes toward his for one last rendezvous. Alas, Maya feeling Zen's gaping eyes on the back of her cloaks solidified her posture.

"Bye then" he finally withdrew, promising himself never to look back.

Why was he even saying goodbye to Muthu? Zen self-examined. He was still morally if not viscerally disgusted by him. 'Everything I believe in is always right' but surely Muthu's beliefs were wrong on some common plane that had to exist. And he could never tell him about Maya, it certainly wouldn't prove Muthu was right but he would use it as ammunition for his anti-realm folly, definitely making the smug old-model think he was right. Hopefully, the godless geezer wasn't there at all and he could blamelessly get away by leaving a note.

The thought 'On some common plane that had to exist' reverberated through Zen's mind as he foraged his way through the thicket of strewn book leaves in search of Muthu. Mercifully, he was nowhere to be seen, so Zen sat down at Muthu's customary seat, gathered the ancient writing devices, and began to scrawl. Despite his familiarity with the letters and increasingly, thanks to NumLing, ever bigger words, he soon discovered that actually writing on a piece of paper was an unimaginably difficult, annoyingly intricate skill (as he supposed all skills required by pre-realm devices were). His first scrawl, utterly illegible, Zen reached for a sheaf of yellowing leaves tucked just underneath the hardcover of a newly dusted book sitting right beside him.

The removal of the sheaf revealed the words:

For Zen,

Utopia means nowhere.

Muthu

Zen thumped the book closed, and lifting with both hands the front cover to eye level, he slowly pronounced aloud to himself its title—"POST POLITICA"

AT LAST, at long last, Zen, his mother sobbing on his shoulder, gallantly approached his hard won destiny. In the heavens an armada of curvaceous pods hovered, assuredly led by a leminiscate adorned leader. The archangel descended crooning an anthem that Zen and indeed every hopeful knew every word of, *"Imagine you're in heaven... It's easy if you try... Only hell below us... Above us only I"*. The hopefuls started to organize themselves into a resemblance of a queue as the pod landed, still singing, *"Imagine there's no countries... It isn't hard to do... Nothing to kill or die for... And all religions too..."*. Like a frog sticking out its tongue to catch insects, the archangel pod unraveled an ivory stairway singing, *"Imagine all possessions... I wonder if you can... No need for want or hunger... All shopping goods for man... Imagine all the people enjoying all their worlds..."*

"Okay, Zen" his mother said, inhaling and exhaling her words through sobs, "God bless, God bless you... God bless you" she broke down to her knees.

"Take care okay, I will come and see you as soon as I get a participation" comforted Zen, gently uplifting his mother from her abyss and for the first time feeling the pangs of separation. He kissed her cheeks several times, each time getting a taste of the salty tributaries of tears that were streaming down via the wrinkle-banks on her face. Finally, he had to let go of his mother's last clenching hug and with it, the wretched pre-world.

"Right this way, sir" politely instructed a voice from behind him.

Zen, his Embed still flashing his choice of realm, stood up and turned to see a stunningly voluptuous woman in a white cat-suit; the LifeTree insignia embroidered near her left breast. Wow, Zen exclaimed to himself, her flawless buttery beige skin and sensuously accentuated features spontaneously overthrowing Maya as the hottest women he had ever seen in real life; and on top of that for her to call him 'Sir'! Wow.

"I am Eve, this way to the wellness check" she said with a smile of perfectly symmetrical gleaming white pearls.

The prospect of the wellness check revved up Zen's anxiety. Surely he was well enough, surely everything in him was bug free, but you never know what you could've caught in the pre-world or what it would've done to you over the years. Not to worry though, the way his mother fed him and the precautions he took would see him through. Besides, this is why LifeTree is so great, we genuinely live our beliefs, in this case 'A warranty guarantees tranquility', thought Zen, coddling himself.

The comely woman, who Zen's apprehension had made him momentarily lose focus of, ushered him and a large group of fellow MyRealm I hopefuls into a room of unimaginably sophisticated equipment and left them with the exoneration, "Very sorry to have to put you through this but it's OmniRealm rules for all hopefuls, nothing to do with LifeTree of course"

Through the transparent receptacle Zen could see other groups of anxious hopefuls being escorted to their wellness checks. In the very next receptacle, a group of hopefuls to a Buddhist or Hindu realm were being escorted in by a plain looking saree clad woman. While in another, a group was being escorted in by a woman again wearing a saree, but this time a silky bright red one with a provocatively plunging neckline, her features sensuously accentuated like Eve's; a more moderate Buddhist or Hindu realm, Zen surmised. Peering through into the other cubicles, Zen was struck by a woman escorting hopefuls to a Muslim realm (that could have even been New Caliphate) who was obscured head to toe in reams of brilliant white cloth. Cringing at the mental picture of Maya's future this wrought in his mind, Zen quickly looked away. For Maya's sake, at least if she converted to Islam but chose a realm with a moderate religious spec, bemoaned Zen, sifting his eyes about the receptacles to find what a woman from such a moderate Muslim realm would look like. A few sweeps later, he located just the image he was searching for in the shape of a hostess, who, to complement her loud neon pink cat-suit, wore a filmy neon pink heard scarf loosely about her luxuriant brown hair. Surely Maya would have been better off, relatively at least, in a realm like that one, concluded Zen.

When Zen took a step back to bird's-eye for a moment all the receptacles at once, the grand promise of the realms seemed to restate its case to him—ALL DIFFERENT therefore ALL SEPARATE therefore ALL HAPPY. 'That's right' he drilled himself, 'That's right, Maya was the past, his pre-world past, today was the day he was born again in MyRealm I'. Despite his best efforts at sanitization though, Muthu's pesky malware, like all effective parasites do, had attached itself on to the very nutritive core of his realm-reasoning. Hence, every positive thought sequence he had about the realms was now compulsively niggled by it. Zen involuntarily felt for the book in his shoddy duffel bag, it was there amongst his mother's crucifix and the other few keepsakes he had chosen to ascend with.

"It's your turn now" said the voluptuous Eve, who had returned to chaperone the wellness check, welcomingly extending her hand toward Zen's.

For a half-hour or so, after Zen duly offered his one hundred thousand likes, he was poked, prodded, pricked and even asked to jog by an assortment of politely spoken devices which looked similar to the one's he helped make at Ramwi's LifeTree womb.

Back in their receptacle after they completed their turns, the hopefuls sat around fidgeting uneasily, holding back talking to each other about how wonderful life in MyRealm I would be, lest the unthinkable would happen.

The voluptuous hostess reentered. Zen was sure this was the life defining announcement, he corrected his posture and rehearsed in his minds the words 'Thank You', as his entire body throb-throbbed with hot blood. Instead of making the announcement however, referencing her Embed, she quietly located certain hopefuls, each of whom she whispered a few words to, before escorting them out of the cubicle.

'Whew' exhaled Zen's heart.

The pudgy hopeful at the very end of the exit queue glanced back on his way out and then abruptly turned, readying himself to say something to the rest of the hopefuls. But a timely hand around his plump hanging waist from Eve was all it took.

A few moments later, Eve returned, this time beaming a dazzling white-hot smile. This was it, it had to be, Zen figured now throb-throbbing with warm ecstasy.

"Congratulations" smiled Eve, "You are moments away from ascending to LifeTree's MyRealm I. Well done"

Cheers, tears and cries of "Amen" sprang from Zen's cubicle, joining a wave of them that had begun milliseconds earlier in the other cubicles. For the first time Zen witnessed strangers spontaneously hug each other. Well not really strangers, since the whole point is that the huggers are all alike, he automatically countered. Anyhow he felt compelled to join the mass joy of his fellow individuals-to-be.

Amidst chants of "Joy is LifeTree, Joy is MyRealm", Eve continued, "Remember, after embarking on the LifeTree pod, you are welcome to actualize yourself with LifeTree inspired personalized tattoos during your journey to MyRealm I. A long Life to you all, and hopefully, see you on the other side"

As the ceiling of the OmniRealm pod opened, allowing the individual receptacles to swim up toward the mother pods of the realm entrepreneurships to which they belonged, Zen inscribed one last panorama of the diverse receptacles onto his memory. And all he could hear from his fellow MyRealmers as their receptacle neared the open belly of the LifeTree mother pod was the bleat, "Wow... Wow... Wow".

At last, the extremely tall hopeful who had claimed the center of the receptacle as his own, squinting at the blinding halo radiated by the mother pod's LifeTree insignia, ventured, "This is what ascending to heaven must be like"

"Knowing Vic Crafts, this is probably better" quipped another.

"... you can add your name later" explained Explod, the tattooist who also doubled as the guide and first inductor to MyRealm I, "Most hopefuls, or shall I say citisumers, do". The starry eyed inductees collectively chuckled with humbled embarrassment, eager for the strapping young man to continue imparting his realmliness. "The reason is that citisumers sometimes change their names and usually, though of course you don't have to, new citisumers like yourselves change their names after ascending. But don't worry this will all be explained in the induction applet which is probably, as we speak, being uploaded to your Embeds (and obviously in orientation itself). Alright, here are some tattoo ideas and trending tattoos, feel free to personalize them of course... and yup... that's about it. TatMe will take good care of the rest, and if you need any help don't hesitate to ask"

The captivated inductees formed droves around the several TatMe consoles and began to select their tattoos. As each of them submitted various parts of themselves to the contraption, Zen observed that nearly all emerged with pretty much the same brand—a beautified illustration of their own face featuring the MyRealm I logo impressed on the forehead.

"Aren't you going to actualize yourself?" an inductee asked, adoringly stroking his arm, "The magic is that it doesn't hurt one bit!"

"Uh... yes, yes, I am" replied Zen approaching TatMe—and it really didn't.

"Here we are" announced Explod as the pod descended in a jittery diagonal motion.

A round of triumphal hugs and high-fives followed from the new MyRealmers. Zen's facial muscles unconsciously arranged themselves into a permanent smile as he sat for the next few minutes clutching his duffel bag, stupefied by the impending moment.

The pod landed with a few thumps of varying duration. Surely that couldn't be applause, Zen wondered about the sound he heard outside, but as the latch opened fully the sound was unmistakable. Each new MyRealmer thanked Explod profusely before stepping out onto the velvety maroon floor of the walkway to be greeted by the applause. It seemed as though the entire realm was there to greet the young inductees. Well at least a holographic projection of every MyRealm I citisumer, noted Zen.

Stepping slowly as if in a trance, the inductees eventually stumbled their way to the end of the walkway and into a massive glass dome through which, riding on the dazzling rays of the midday sun, the surreal immaculateness of MyRealm I streamed in. Lustrous metal & glass soaring in ambitiousness, homely neighborhoods belonging together in geometric neatness, broad walkways in spotless cleanliness, all color coordinated in cheerful friendliness. And rising imperiously from the horizon was the MyRealm I logo—a metallic crucifix embossed on the bark of the LifeTree, engraved with 'MyRealm' across its horizontal axis, its vertical axis slightly augmented on both ends to resemble 'I'.

The "Wow" chorus resumed in earnest, only to be interrupted by the giant face of a woman looking a lot like Eve (though not her), appearing on the inside of the glass dome and proceeding to beam, "Welcome, you have now ascended to YOU, whatever YOU want, whatever YOU feel. Before you head out on the Orientation Express to begin your Life, please enjoy some scrumptious refreshments lovingly gifted especially for you by KrocRonald's"

"Wow, KrocRonald's, WOW" fawned an inductee standing next to Zen.

Good luck holding down a participation if you didn't learn any other nouns for 'amazement' at NumLing, Zen snickered to himself.

"KrocRonald's, I'm feelin' it" several inductees cried out. And to everyone's amazement, as if hearing this sentiment, the happy face of the clown appeared on the globe agreeing with it, "Yes! Yes! That is soooo right" and jingling out, "KrocRonaaaaaaald's, I'm feelin' it". Here comes the chorus, dreaded Zen.

The Orientation Express, though much smaller, was a pod much like the one the young cohort had arrived in, except it had one memorable difference. All over its walls, was scribbled the graffiti of past inductees. Zen read a few, *'Don't worry about a thing, orientation is crazy fun, I forgot that I was from the pre-world in a few hours!', 'You'll instantly belong, trust me trust LifeTree', 'Even though I've never even been to any realm before, it was like coming home', 'You have no idea how good you're going to feel!'.* Zen followed the instructions to leave a note of his own, but even though he was writing with his index finger on a light slate and not one of Muthu's obsolete pens, he couldn't form the letters nearly as legibly as the ones already inscribed on the walls of the Orientation Express by his predecessors. Making him give up and wonder.

A few minutes later the pod hovered over a luscious green field from which the MyRealm I logo, composed of brightly colored flower pixels, bloomed forth. Soon onto the field, warm zephyrs dancing about them, stepped the new MyRealmers. His feet yearning to squish the succulence of moist grass, his lungs yearning for a deep breath of minty fresh realm air, Zen though kept a solitudinous distance from the group. Not far off, from a gleaming glass dome not unlike the one they were first received in, what was by now a generically beautiful face beckoned, "This way MyRealmers, right this way"

When all the hopefuls were nestled in their seats, "MyRealm I is YOU, it is the ultimate, glorious realization of your unique citisumerism and Catholicism" commenced the orientation by an overbearing holographic Vic Crafts, "Throughout all those wretched unfortunate years you toiled in the pre-world, throughout all those times you stood powerless as your wants and beliefs were diluted along with everyone else's in an insufferable… sinful… and yes, deadly brew, MyRealm I has always been your home. Whether you consciously knew it or not, throughout all those years MyRealm I has been waiting for you, in you. Today is the day… that a false 'We' ends… and a true 'I' begins". Taking a few moments to smugly revel in his grand opening and sealing the deal with extended sessions of laser-like eye contact with his audience of eager neophytes, Vic Crafts got down to the practical nitty-gritty of MyRealm I Life, "And because MyRealm I is you, because it is your soulchild, you must keep in mind that nothing can go FUNDAMENTALLY wrong. Indeed, admitting that things can go FUNDAMENTALLY wrong would be tantamount or equal to saying that 'Everything I believe in is NOT always right'! "

As "Oohs" and "Ahs" of comprehension and agreement reverberated from the new MyRealmers, Vic Crafts dove ever deeper into the nitty-gritty, "And so it stands to reason that if nothing can go FUNDAMENTALLY wrong then nothing ever has to be

FUNDAMENTALLY changed. The best example of this is no doubt the rules and cultural specs of MyRealm I. In fact, they shouldn't even be called the rules and cultural specs of MyRealm I, for they are essentially YOUR rules and cultural specs directly downloaded from God almighty himself—so how can they be FUNDAMENTALLY wrong? And if they can never be FUNDAMENTALLY wrong, isn't it the greatest of sins to seek to FUNDAMENTALLY change them?"

Amidst a sea of nodding heads, Zen marooned in his thoughts, conceded the elegance of Vic Crafts' logic though not necessarily its infallibility. Certainly, Zen thought to himself, it conveniently allowed him to cling on to the contradictory beliefs that 'Everything I believe in is always right' and 'Muthu's belief in godlessness is wrong' at once. For though 'Everything I believe in everything is always right' as Vic Crafts pointed out, this is only so if it is downloaded directly from God, which Muthu's belief in atheism by its very essence could not have been.

"Your sole focus from now on in should be to find a participation" continued Vic Crafts, having by now completely changed lanes to practical concerns, "You will find that in your Embed account LifeTree has deposited ten thousand likes. I am sure, as you have proved by your conscientious labor and saving in the pre-world, that you will use this wisely to find accommodation and maintain yourself until such time as you find a participation". Upon delivering both the grandiose promise and the clinical stipulation of the realms, Vic Crafts, leaving the more mundane orientation matters to his LifeTree underlings, imperiously signed off with the refrain, "Go forth and participate, Vic Crafts and Jesus Christ believe in you"

A holographic generic-Eve appeared from the ground up to take the reins from Vic Crafts. Just as the neophytes adjusted their glance downwards to meet her, she shone blindingly and, accompanied by a barely audible motorized whirr, the hologram materialized. "Come with Elantra, let's go on your very first MyRealm I sky tour!" she invited, gaiting toward the neophytes to emphasize her tangibility. Singing their customary chorus, the neophytes re-boarded the Orientation Express, which, as it took off, mechanically self-peeled its outer casing leaving a floating glass bubble.

"Would everyone like to see a participation tower in action? Elantra would!" roused the generic-Eve.

As yelps of "Yes" and "Oh yeah" rang out from the neophytes, the glass pod darted in a downward trajectory and hovered, as a humming bird would, around a grove of metallic stalks.

"Look, look, they are saying 'Hi' " exclaimed the generic-Eve pointing excitedly.

The neophytes thronged to the edge of the pod and began frenziedly waving back. Squeezing her way through to the front of the throng, she seized the teaching moment, "You see, participation in MyRealm I is actualizing fun. It's nothing like laboring in the pre-world, so you guys shouldn't think of it as just a better model of what you were forced to do back there. It is entirely different, E-N-T-I-R-E-L-Y different. There is none of that backbreaking monotonous physical stuff; it's neither tiring nor boring, only very fulfilling. In fact, and this is important to keep in mind, participation is the only act that both actualizes and blesses you with likes. Now don't get Elantra wrong, Elantra is certainly not putting down the Godly act of offering likes for actz & ens. No, no certainly not, just pointing out that participating is the fun, equally actualizing and Godly mate of offering. They go together inseparably like man and woman, like prayer and confession. As one—participating & offering—is the whole Godliest act"

"What about sex?" the intently listening Zen's thoughts spilled out into words.

"What do you mean?" queried Elantra, genuinely befuddled.

"Well, sex falls somewhere in between doesn't it? I mean it's an actualizing experience but since we have a no-prostitution spec in MyRealm I you can't be blessed with likes or offer likes for it. An actualizing act that doesn't involve likes! "

As the neophytes, whose interest had been titillated on the utterance of the word 'sex' by Zen, processed his insight; Elantra herself taking a moment, scoffed in the privacy of her own thoughts at Zen's insolence, thinking it only a matter of time before one of the great trepships conceived of a way to likeize consensual sex.

"Well, sex is most certainly the only one" Elantra grudgingly conceded.

Zen's riposte was cut short by the sudden scurry of the neophytes to the opposite end of the pod. Elantra, intuiting what had attracted them, gestured the pod to climb to afford a better view. A few moments later as Zen burrowed to the edge of the pod, there it was—hundreds of rounded-square holographic portals arranged in a rectangular lacework breezily levitating against the tropical sunshine and blue, each featuring with lifelike multidimensional clarity, couples rhythmically oscillating in foreplay and sex.

"Yup, soon, you can get your fifteen-on too" interjected Elantra, "Isn't it totally actualizingly wonderful!"

The entranced neophytes concurred with small nods. Every few seconds, the topmost row of multidimensional squircles evaporated away allowing each row underneath it to climb a rung and an entirely new bottommost row of oscillating foreplay and sex to appear. The neophytes begun keeping track of the counter on the bottom corner of each squircle and it soon became an educational game to them.

"I found one with a hundred and thirty five loves" said one female neophyte.

"Yeah, but it also had about seventy hates" countered another.

"Even though they were really good and really hot, I've heard that showing off is sometimes not the best way to get loved. You're better off seeming as though you are 'Just one of the girls' " replied the first.

Maybe he was wrong after all, Zen pondered, maybe with loves and hates sex had been reinvented to be just like all other actz & ens by SoulMate.

WITH A short prayer that she felt ashamed for not knowing, a revolving necklace of names shimmied toward her eyes and under each golden tassel dangled an explanation of the name's quranic significance. After she read and re-read almost every one, Maya was no more, in her demise giving life to Saudah.

When Saudah and her sisters reemerged, metamorphosed butterfly-like from their naming cocoons, Vic Crafts, his bald spot outfitted with a white taqiyah to complement his white, long sleeved, poncho-like robes, commenced the orientation, "New Caliphate is YOU, it is the ultimate, glorious realization of your unique citisumerism and Islam…"

"You are now flying over the Sisterhood" explained the white blanketed hostess of the sky tour, "New Caliphate is separated into three main neighborhoods to ensure that your Life is pious and peaceful—the Sisterhood, the Brotherhood, and the Marriagehood. You will find accommodation and Insha'Allah a participation in the Sisterhood until you get married and move with your husband to the Marriagehood"

"What about our children?" squeaked a voice from within the cloth tapestry of female neophytes.

"Well of course they'll live with you in the Marriagehood," replied the hostess, "and when you find them a suitable partner they can continue to live in the Marriagehood with you"

"What if they don't find a suitable partner?" inquired another voice from within the tapestry.

"Well, when they turn eighteen the boys have to go live in the Brotherhood and the girls in the Sisterhood, till they get married" answered the hostess.

"Astaghfirullah, forgive me for asking this question but when we are in the Sisterhood, how are we to find ourselves husbands, astaghfirullah?" asked a voice audibly summoning up the courage.

"Ah this is why sisters, along with parental arrangements we also have Nikahbook" explained the hostess, "Where you can provide your details and upload one decent photo of your face so that prospective suitors from the Brotherhood or even from the Marriagehood can propose for your hand in marriage. You can vet such proposals through voice only communications via Nikahbook to reach a decision"

"Barak'Allah sister, barak'Allah sister" a thankful chorus broke out from the cloth tapestry.

When Saudah, at her new home in the Trump-West Minaret, reclined into her sofa to take in the panorama of New Caliphate, she reclined for the first time in her life into pure belongingness. Despite the layers upon layers of her own cloth, she could snugly feel the perky give of the sofa underneath her and almost thanked it out loud for dimpling itself into the shape of her body. She named it Sabrina. But what really gratified her was the neatness, the consistency of it all; everything from the sky with its omnipresent LifeTree emblazoned green crescent moon, right down to the food and every detail of her home were in the motif of her beliefs, her Islam. Soon, nay almost instantly, she felt at spiritual ease, as if her beliefs had been automated, as if she never had to concern herself with their right & wrong, their ins & outs again; that from here on in till eternity she would be unquestionably in the right by just insouciantly partaking in the worship and practice of her beliefs. And soon this newfound spiritual ease would slay that horrible dissenting devil's advocate in her head, the voice of anxiety and self-doubt that plagued her pre-world mind, freeing Saudah's spirit to actualize and enhance, to participate and marry.

"OMA! It's time for Asr and Hafsa is hungry" burst out Hafsa leaping out of her chair, "C'mon Saudah, as the proverb goes 'HalalKing tastes even better after prayer' "

"I'm in" replied Saudah.

As they headed toward their participation tower's prayer coves, "Is that new?" she asked of the decorated carpet roll in Hafsa's hand.

"Yup, he's the latest Prayer-o-Matic" answered Hafsa, "He's awesome, Hafsa loves him, he gently massages your knees and sprays the pious fragrances of ancient Mecca while you pray! Hafsa calls him Ihab"

"Wow, Insha'Allah I should bless myself with one" decided Saudah, proceeding to confirm, "LifeTree right?"

"No, Startern" replied Hafsa hesitantly.

"What! Really? I never thought of you as a Startern kinda sister" decried Saudah, her fallen estimation of Hafsa unmistakably expressed via the recoiling of her face.

"Yeah, but don't forget Startern is 'Designed for citisumers' " defended Hafsa, lifting the decorated roll to cover her already manifold covered chest, "It's supposed to be 'The next big thing' "

"Maybe but 'Joy is LifeTree' " fired Saudah indignantly.

"Yes, that is certainly true, but in New Caliphate we have a saying to resolve such important and necessary intellectual debates" started Hafsa, seeking to kindly mentor Saudah still the relative neophyte, away from her pre-world crassness, "We simply say the 'Citisumer is always right'. Now this doesn't mean that we are different, after all we are both citisumers of New Caliphate so we can't possibly have major differences. But inevitably, we have congenital brand tendencies just like you have brown eyes and Hafsa has green eyes. Nothing right or wrong about it. In the end we must remember that all brands are blessings from God, so ALL brands have a right to life"

"Even though we live in a LifeTree realm?" questioned Saudah.

"Yes, even though we live in a LifeTree realm" affirmed Hafsa, "You can love LifeTree, cherish her virtues and argue that she is the greatest brand in all of Allah's heaven and earth, but you can't hate other brands; brandism is sinful and the brandist is a sinner"

"Does Allah forgive bran... brandists?" asked Saudah tremulously.

"Well according to what Hafsa has been taught of the Realm Hadiths it is an al-kaba'ir, but Allah is all merciful. Ah, but then you have not had the privilege of learning the New Hadiths have you? No matter, there is plenty of time for that, plenty of time, and maybe Hafsa will join you for a refresher course" reassured Hafsa, adding, "Come let us pray now"

Saudah, knowing exactly what she needed to pray for, anxiously slipped into a personal prayer cove.

His brown cratered jowls sporting a beard of long, progressively thinning, unruly silver and gray tendrils, his pristine white taqiyah sporting the gaudy emblems of his proud sponsors, the face of a thick-spectacled middle-aged man appeared on the calligraphy inscribed dome. Thunderous claps from the brothers sitting on the other side of the black partition easily drowned out the demure applause of Saudah, Hafsa and their sisters. The holographic face adjusted its spectacles several times and in an avuncular tone announced, "Brothers and sisters, al-hamdu-lillahi-rabbil'alamin, welcome to iTime with me—Dr. Rikaz Kain"

"Al-hamdu-lillahi-rabbil'alamin" the partitioned audience resounded at differing decibel levels.

Saudah, startled by the sudden jerky movement of her seat, despairingly reached for Hafsa, "Don't worry you're being taken to your session, that's all" reassured Hafsa.

As Saudah's cushy chair entered a tiny, dimly lit alcove, it slowed to a halt and reclined a few degrees.

"As-salam'alaykum, before we get started, if you will be so kind as to launch the relevant app on your Embed" greeted Dr. Kain, now a holographic entirety sitting cross-legged opposite Saudah. "Now tell Dr. Kain what Saudah is feeling lately, tell Dr. Kain everything" he quickly went on.

"Wa'alaikum-salam" replied Saudah, behind the pace and in any case too embarrassed to start.

"So tell me about Saudah" repeated Dr. Kain.

"Well…" started Saudah hesitantly, as Dr. Kain nodded her on, "I… ascended…; Saudah ascended recently to New Caliphate and um…"

"How does New Caliphate make Saudah feel?" queried Dr. Kain.

"Well, of course it is me, it is everything Saudah is and naturally since New Caliphate is by LifeTree, it's totally bug free" Saudah went on, her thoughts and her voice gradually gaining some momentum.

"See that's good, go on, remember keep focusing on Saudah" interjected Dr. Kain.

"Yes, well I… Saudah, have this friend Hafsa who is showing me the features of New Caliphate. She is really nice, it goes without saying we get along. Just recently she bought a Prayer-o-Matic. I, oops… Saudah, thought of blessing myself with one as…" and on and on, accelerating her pace, went Saudah.

"This is important stuff, Saudah is certainly making progress" put in Dr. Kain, his piercing little brown eyes in flitting lockstep with hers.

"…the fragrances are from ancient Mecca, Hafsa says her favorite is the waft of coffee, I honestly don't know what Saudah's favorite…" continued Saudah, now no miniscule detail too small.

"This is impor… See that's good, go on, remember keep focusing on Saudah" put in Dr. Kain.

"… at first we were a little concerned about how to find husbands, silly now that Saudah thinks about it, obviously we should've trusted that the legendary Vic Crafts and almighty Allah would've thought of a solution to such a small problem, anyway…" went Saudah, on tangent after tangent.

Half-an-hour or so later, a meager moment in minutia though, the question, "Dr. Kain, don't you think Zen was totally wrong?" unexpectedly churned into words from Saudah's racing thoughts.

A longish pause where Dr. Kain eruditely adjusted his spectacles several times ensued, then, "Yes, the important thing to keep in mind is that what others think or believe is of no significance to Saudah. They are mind-weeds which if Saudah is not careful will infest Saudah's soul, overrunning and eventually killing Saudah's individuality" advised the doctor didactically.

How wise, what an expert hafiz, well of course this is none other than the great Dr. Rikaz Kain! Saudah, feeling thoroughly affirmed, marveled to herself.

"Go on, Saudah" egged Dr. Kain, "Well, Saudah told him as much and then…" she took off.

Another half-an-hour or so later, Dr. Kain snipped Saudah's catharsis with the pearl, "We have made good progress today Saudah. The next step is to delve deeper, to unearth every little snippet of memory, every morsel of emotion that makes Saudah, Saudah. Don't let anything of Saudah go, Saudah is too important. In almighty Allah's eyes Saudah is the most important person alive today, the most important person that has ever lived"

"Jazakallahu-khayran, Dr. Kain" thanked Saudah brimming with herself, as her chair began to jerk.

"How was it?" asked Hafsa pulsing with inquisitiveness, as their chairs came to a halt next to each other.

"Wow, just WOW" beamed Saudah, readying her Embed to update her Nikahbook, "That's all that Saudah has to say"

"I thought so" smiled Hafsa as she followed Saudah's Nikahbook cue.

"And it's so generous of Dr. Kain to bless us with a free first session" added Saudah.

"Yup, that's just the kinda man he is, a true servant of Allah" agreed Hafsa.

"With the smarts of Vic Crafts!" chimed in Saudah.

Just then an announcement rang out, "This is a citisumer welfare announcement. Sisters enhance yourselves with Dr. Rikaz Kain's iTime customizable henna and brothers don't leave the iTime sanctuary without one of Dr. Kain's all new personally autographed customizable iTime tiqayahs". A pair of feminine hands ornately embroidered with orange ink, and a pristine white skullcap featuring a handsome face with a slanted scribble underneath it, appeared over the partitioned sections. The feminine hands gracefully reached out toward the sisters, a multiplicity of skullcaps streamed forth from the original toward the brothers. As the ornately embroidered hands approached, Saudah quickly made out Dr. Rikaz Kain's signature in its brown and orange hued baroque curves, alongside the intricately inked impression of a beautiful young woman which could easily have been Hafsa.

"C'mon let's get one" urged Saudah.

"Would be a sin to leave without one" replied Hafsa.

Sitting next to each other, their hands submitted to Alma the henna device, Saudah for the first time began to pay careful attention to every elegant contour, to every symmetrical feature that composed what remained visible of Hafsa's face. As Alma skillfully etched its exquisiteness on its owner's hands, the contentment that Dr. Kain had filled Saudah with just minutes earlier began to leak away. In comparison to Hafsa's sculptured visage varnished with supple beige skin and encrusted with a pair of rounded emerald jewels, hers was a goulash of pre-world scars and unpolished bumps and edges. Suddenly Saudah couldn't bear to look down at her own hands where this coarse, unsightly jaggedness was being traced unedited. And she made up her mind that, Insha'Allah, as soon as she could, she would bless herself with the enhancements she deserves.

Excitement tantalized her nerve endings, as if she were about to open a present. Courteously gesturing to her Embed she unwrapped it. Accompanied by a devotional hymn, cryptic squiggly letters appeared, it took a few quick scans of the calligraphy for the title to elucidate itself, it read 'The Realm Hadiths by Telltale' with a nifty crown floating above Telltale's middle 't'. A profusion of labeled bubbles succeeded the title screen each housing video tidbits. Saudah located 'The Sin of Brandism' and just to reassure herself about the knowledge that Hafsa had sought to impart in her, she tapped it open. Dr. Rikaz Kain came bounding out against a clear night sky illuminated by twinkling logos and starting with, "Saudah, brandism is…" legitimized Hafsa's impartation. As a pious citisumer of New Caliphate, Saudah told herself that it was her duty to learn the entire Realm Hadith as quickly as possible, so she proceeded to the next bubble that piqued her interest, labeled 'Brainy Days & Hearty Nights'.

"Saudah," started Dr. Kain as before, this time though appearing in the shadow of a participation minaret, "almighty Allah in his infinite wisdom has allotted participation minarets exclusively for thinking and everything outside of them for feeling, brainy days & hearty nights as we say. Hence, Saudah must guard against the sin of mixing the two"

Zen's characteristic sin, remembered Saudah, as she proceeded to 'A warranty guarantees tranquility'. "Saudah," started Dr. Kain now in a shopping minaret "all actualizers & enhancers are blessings conceived by almighty Allah who is needless to say immaculate. However these immaculately designed actz & ens must be delivered by mere mortals so they are liable to have bugs. To avoid suffering the heartache of Saudah's friend-devices dying prematurely always be sure to bless him or her with a warranty that will guarantee Saudah's tranquility"

How civilized are the realms felt Saudah, as she proceeded to 'Holy Entrepreneurs' considering it a matter of course that Vic Crafts would be featured, maybe Dr. Kain would feature himself she hoped. "Saudah," started Dr. Kain now standing dwarfed by the giant faces of the great entrepreneurs carved into the mountain sides of the Valley of the Treps, "the great entrepreneurs are almighty Allah's messengers (may peace be upon them) sent down to the realms to receive via epiphany Allah's immaculate conceptions and thereon to spread these actz & ens, these blessings to all citisumers... to you, oh deserving Saudah"

Saudah reveling in the benevolence of almighty Allah and marveling at the state-of-the-art practicality of his Islam cravingly proceeded to 'Saudah, Express Yourself'. "Saudah," started Dr. Kain once more, taking a break from diligently filling a form on his Embed, "whenever the Prophet (may peace be upon him) was asked a question he never failed to answer honestly and to the best of his knowledge. Thus when Saudah is asked a question by the Holy Entrepreneurs or their great trepships, to stay silent or to not answer honestly and to the best of Saudah's knowledge will be to act against the will of almighty Allah". And so on and so forth went the Realm Hadiths, Saudah faithfully imbibing the innocuous instructional applet until she fell asleep.

Next morning, Saudah awoke to the greeting, "...but the Prophet (may peace be upon him)..." by the tireless Dr. Kain, and as he continued, his sermonic words gradually infiltrated the sleepy gauze over her senses, "without recourse to anger, calmly explained its defects and shortcomings for the purposes of his use to the vendor. Similarly,

51

Allah forbid, that in the actz & ens that you bless yourself with or in the delivery of these you find a rare defect or shortcoming, keep in mind the grace and compassion of the messenger of Allah (may peace be upon him)". She jolted herself upright with the sensation 'Another brainy day with a hearty night to look forward to'.

Arriving at her participation console ten or so minutes early, Saudah marrying her Embed to it, began her brainy day. Immediately an ancient looking block, patterned much like the henna Hafsa and her recently blessed themselves with, popped in front of her eyes and under it a set of concise instructions appeared: '1. Continue pattern on extension of 30 cm x 30 cm x 40 cm, 2. Seamlessly incorporate pictures below into extended pattern, 3. Submit five options before the end of the participation day'; with a cheery voice signing off "Have fun participating Saudah". Taking only a few seconds off to reassure herself by glancing over at the ratings her previous participation challenges had received, Saudah earnestly began.

For the rest of her brainy day, with neither a backstory nor a desired impact to guide her nimble slender fingers, they daintily danced the pixel needle in front of Saudah's oblivious eyes, skillfully weaving in three images she knew intimately—a black cuboid building, a drum beating bunny and a devotee kneeling in prayer.

When her fingers had finished, "Insha'Allah you will get a good rating for this blessed participation" hoped out loud the supportive voice from the console as it sucked up the five images with a thirsty whoosh, letting Saudah snap out of her skill trance.

"Insha'Allah" replied Saudah to the console, "Hopefully, Nazimah, I'll never see them again"

"It's hearty time!" exclaimed Hafsa who had arrived a few minutes earlier to pick Saudah up.

"Yup, it's time to start feeling" resounded Saudah wholeheartedly.

Just then a familiar ping grabbed Saudah into her Embed. Her eyes darted left to right progressing downwards, a smile dawning on her face.

"What is it?" asked Hafsa.

"I can't believe it! MA-SHA'ALLAH! I can't believe it!" hooted Saudah, grinning and clapping delightedly, "I've been invited to my first heart-to-heart!"

"Who by?" inquired Hafsa.

"By MagicRealm of all blessed trepships!" whooped Saudah, adding little jumps to her clapping routine.

"Lucky you" said Hafsa obligatorily, rechecking her Embed in disbelief and remarking, "Must be for new citisumers, recent ascenders you know"

Hafsa's words not penetrating her ecstasy, Saudah frenziedly signed off, "Saudah's gotta go, as-salam'alaykum"

Chanting to herself, "As the prophet would; honestly, and to the best of Saudah's abilities. As the prophet would; honestly, and to the best of Saudah's abilities", to allay her performance anxiety, Saudah sat restlessly along with a group of seven other sisters nervously anticipating the commencement of the heart-to-heart. From the center of the circular formation of couches where, until now, the beloved MagicRealm castle revolved, a beautifully rendered sister appeared greeting the cohort of confiders, "As-salam'alaykum and welcome to MagicRealm: Where dreams come true. Ajeebah will be your hostess for the evening"

"Wa'alaikum-salam" chorused the grateful cohort in unison.

"This is so exciting" a sister sitting next to Saudah whispered, "Is it your first time as well?"

"Yes" replied Saudah whispering even softer than her counterpart out of reverence for the proceedings.

"And so righteous too" her talkative counterpart noted.

"Yup" Saudah murmured.

"First my sisters, you will have the pleasure of experiencing several iTelly novels originally conceived by Don Lord himself" explained the beautifully rendered Ajeebah, "Become one with them, since they are from Don Lord this will happen almost unconsciously. Then, upon being immersed in YOUR stories as regaled by Don Lord, tell me individually which one is your most beloved and why you feel this way.

And then... and then... go forth and perform one of your most sacred duties as citisumers—amongst yourselves discuss... debate... argue even to your heart's content about which deserves to be called the best novel, standup for what YOU feel sisters"

Soon the first iTelly novel began drenching Saudah with laden droplets of bittersweet emotion, diluting her concern that she wouldn't be able to live up to the great honor bestowed upon her by MagicRealm and Don Lord. In never ending plot u-turns and romantic merry-go-rounds Saudah was lost for hours yet right where she was supposed to be; right where she wanted to be.

Just as another juicy jigsaw of love and intrigue was coming together, surely of course to somehow in some sensationally tragic way to fall apart, Ajeebah jarringly broke in, "Okay sisters, it is time for each of you to tell Ajeebah how you feel. Come on, one by one".

Saudah, by now totally relieved of her initial apprehension and indeed fancying herself quite the expert on the relative merits of the engrossing novels, volunteered to spill first.

"Right, now sisters let Ajeebah hear what you all feel, in the name of Allah and his prophet (peace be upon him) don't hold back!" solicited Ajeebah, and the floodgates opened.

Saudah stopped herself, surely there was no way that the novels she felt something for at her first heart-to-heart would have already made their way to iTelly, surely not. Either way, tonight would be a truly hearty night, for tonight was the night she was to receive the blessing of a brand new LifeTree iTelly.

Arisha the elevator couldn't get Saudah up nearly fast enough and reaching her floor she couldn't run without tripping over her reams nearly quick enough. Finally she fairly shoulder charged her likeness that was painted on her door, unable to wait any longer to see her iTelly, whom after much heart searching she had decided to call Anwara. Bless them, bless those good participators at LifeTree services who never fail citisumers she quickly told herself, as she knelt near Anwara. Taking a moment to adjust her headscarf and realign her facial features into a polite smile, Saudah readied herself to greet the beautifully rendered

Hafsa-like hologram projected from the tiny LifeTree sculpture affixed to her wall, when, utterly stupefying Saudah, it said, "Hello, I'm Anwara. It's sure great to finally meet you Saudah"

As though inanimate object had switched souls with animate person, Saudah stood concreted while Anwara, arms open, vivaciously smiled, gesturing Saudah toward her. Saudah unconsciously approached, and sufficient time having passed to somewhat regain her wits, finally introduced herself, "Nice to meet you, I am Saudah"

Her wits now fully regained, using her Embed Saudah began to navigate through her new best friend-device. After spending hours attentively learning everything about Anwara as if on a first date, and in turn duly offering up her own life in images and sounds to Anwara, Saudah felt comfortable enough to ask Anwara to share an iTelly experience with her, "Anwara, can you suggest something for Saudah to experience tonight?" asked Saudah coyly as if seeking a second date.

"Why of course Saudah" graciously replied Anwara unveiling a smorgasbord of melodramatic delights.

Still clinging to the off hope that her very own heart-to-heart had made it, Saudah browsed through each video nibble, finally fondling the one titled 'Pious Hearts' to life. A few moments later, to an escalating upbeat tune the stars were introduced. First, his chiseled jaw ruggedly roughened by kempt stubble, Ahmed flashed an incandescent grin. Next, a pair of villainously arched thick black brows furrowing over his long aquiline nose, middle-aged Burayd smirked ominously. "Awww, so cute" Saudah gurgled as chubby cheeked little Habbab beamed toothily. Then Durrah, albeit a beautified version, demurely upturned the corners of her mouth; Saudah knew her well, she participated just down the corridor from her. Followed by Khalilah and Latifa; Saudah had met them at iTime she remembered, and Hafsa, ever beautiful Hafsa, rendered befittingly more gorgeous than ever. Now the moment was nigh, Saudah braced herself, the very next star could be her, star of her own iNovel, star of her own Life. Finally she would get to see how she would look professionally rendered, professionally enhanced. And sure enough, the music climaxing to a crescendo, last and certainly the very opposite of least, processed free from her larval ugliness, Saudah now infinitely more beautiful than Hafsa, Saudah the protagonist now larger than life stepped forth to bask in her own adulation.

7

TIGHTENING THE swivel of his gaze to avoid both the carnal oscillations of SoulMate levitating against the horizon and the equally omnipresent mirrors that lined MyRealm I's streets, Zen apprehensively made his way to Admin@MyRealm I. Was turning down those first few participations a good idea? No ascender ever did that, certainly no one from the group that ascended with him, he worried. But for some faint ghost of a reason, Zen knew he would only be content if he held out for more, a participation somewhere in the very mind of MyRealm I. But those were tough to get, especially for a new ascender. Sometimes they took years of dedicated participation to earn; what was he thinking risking it all? Churned his worries over and over again as he reached the Admin@MyRealm participation tower. But this was only a lowly assistant-to-an-assistant position he reassured himself as he sat, refusing to scout the competition sitting with him, waiting for his call up.

A surprisingly short while later, a young man ushered Zen into his transparent booth and before Zen could even sit down snappily told him, "Your PRNL, Participation Relevant NumLing scores are really good, so congratulations you are blessed with a participation, all boot-up instructions have already been sent to you. Thank You"

Ejected as hastily out of the booth as he was ushered in, Zen, good news in hand, decided to linger around Admin, seeking to glean if not the required practices and attitudes of its participators then at least their characteristic motions. He soon noted that their motions were extremely limited, actually they couldn't even be called motions but rather minor fidgeting; the only real motion being that of the arm regularly reaching for the ready supply of refreshments. Verbal communications across booths he observed were non-existent, quite unlike the constant back and forth of gossipy gibberish that flowed between workers at Ramwi's LifeTree womb. Indeed the only flash of feeling was when the victorious face of the participator of the hour popped up; immediately followed by an ever more zealous return to fidgeting. All of this more or less kept to script, after all, Zen thought to himself, participation in the realms, unlike the monotonous physical drudgery of pre-world work, required the best concentration of one's brain, precluding the excretion of gossipy gibberish and any need for tiring movements. But what struck Zen most of all was the rarity or indeed the total absence of thoughtful poses, no heads slouched on elbow-supported palms, no brow rubs or brief thought invigorating head massages.

Zen hoped it wouldn't, but inevitably the day's participation was drawing to a close. What would he do with himself for the rest of the evening? He wouldn't admit it to anyone, not that he had anyone to admit it to, but he couldn't stand the thought of going back to his apartment. Slightly doubting his own sincerity, he convinced himself that this was only because he couldn't yet afford to bless himself with friend-devices. Perhaps church, yes, a little prayer would do him good and any in case he had promised his mother to pray daily. Which church though? Zen asked himself. The one he recently witnessed several peeks into, Telltale's all new Bethlehem themed BestBeth, looked like it had authentically holy holographics, obviously, since Telltale cares enough to send you the very best holiness, he reiterated to himself. But, he had already bought a pious saver monthly pass to Oprah's Prayer Club. Oh well, Zen decided, now that he found himself a participation he could splash out a little and he probably should do for a holy cause. But first, pausing to rehear the rumble that caused him so much gassy agony back in the pre-world, he needed to eat.

Almost as if responding to his pangs, overshadowing SoulMate a question in gigantic frill free black lettering commandeered the sky, it asked 'WHAT WOULD JESUS EAT?'. The question zipped away and a little, freckled faced, red haired girl, Darling, who Zen instantaneously recognized, skipped, pigtails bouncing, merrily into view. In a high giggly voice, she chirped "Did you know that every day, hundreds of citisumers find images of Jesus in our food?". As she skipped off to a familiar jingle, the tagline 'Darling's… little miracles served fresh daily' trailed her.

Church was the only place that Zen would dare even consider confessing that he might be feeling a little bit of realmshock. Even during iTime with Dr. Stal McKnow, Zen never contemplated admitting to it. Indeed his unreasonable and inexplicable failure to assimilate was first clinically identified as possibly realmshock by the good doctor, leading Zen to never return to iTime out of shame. Church was different; while a concoction of Muthu's malware, a change in his routines, and his unfamiliarity with the features of MyRealm I brought on this temporary affliction known as realmshock, Jesus Christ was the one true constant, resolved Zen.

He entered the confessional, made the cross on his chest and was received by a calm monotone voice emanating from the other side of the screen.

"Confess your sins my son" commenced the voice.

"Um... well... all I have ever wanted all my pre-life is to ascend to the realms, and even though I didn't always know it, MyRealm I in particular" began Zen's soliloquy, "I guess everybody in the pre-world does. And don't get me wrong MyRealm I is exactly what Vic Crafts and Jesus Christ our Lord and Savior promised it would be and I'm grateful to them, grateful to God for blessing me with ascension. My sin is not in my lack of gratitude Father. It's just... it's just... well now that I'm in the realms, in MyRealm I, I know that the whole godliest act is... consists of, participating & offering. I know it is my sacred duty as a citisumer, as a Catholic of MyRealm I to participate & offer... but I just don't feel like it. I... I... I risked everything... I turned down three participations! Which obviously meant that I wasn't doing much offering. But the worst part is not even that, it's that now I found a participation, I still don't much feel like offering, unless of course I really need certain actz & ens! It's as though a terrible pre-world disease has infected the whole godliest act in my mind and the infection has spread so much so that I constantly think about the whole godliest act without just naturally and joyously engaging in it as any other citisumer would. It has spread so much so that not only can I not stop thinking about the whole godliest act but that I can't stop thinking at all!"

"Go on my son" interjected the voice mostly to reassure Zen he was there.

"Think, think, think" restarted Zen his voice simmering with irritation, "That's all I do. What's the meaning of all this? What's the point? I keep asking myself. And I can't seem to stop. I know it's borderline blasphemous, I know it's a sinful distraction from participating & offering. I know all this Father, but I can't stop. It's like my mind has a mind of its own and my heart is the victim!"

"Zen, my son, for the answers you must look to the word of the Lord. There are no answers in you and nor should you expect there to be. All that should be in your heart are memories, feelings, yearnings and of course faith in the Father, the Son and the Holy Spirit. May Father suggest the Realm Psalms by Telltale" counseled the voice in a slow empathetic meter, as a mosaic of video tidbits each featuring customarily adorned catholic priests sermonizing from various pulpits appeared on the screen that separated Zen and the voice. Allowing Zen's eyes a few seconds to focus in on them, the tidbits began to arrange themselves to spell out 'The Realm Psalms by Telltale' with a nifty crown floating above Telltale's middle 't'.

"Anyway, go on, Zen, my son, confession is good for your soul" cajoled the voice.

"I'm really worried Father" Zen restarted confiding, "In the pre-world we believe that grass is always greener on the branded side and now that I'm in the realms I can honestly vouch that the grass *is* actually greener. But... but for me its superior greenness is simply another characteristic, just another fact about the grass, as true and at the same time as un... as unstimulating as the fact that ice-cream tastes sweeter than broccoli. Unstimulating not as in my eyes, ears, taste buds etc. don't enjoy their superior greenness or taste their sweetness but that beyond this quick enjoyment, they don't inspire any deeper feelings in my heart (and of course I really expected them to). You know... I can't... I can't feel actz & ens, I can't be one with them, it's like I can't help myself from breaking them down like a NumLing puzzle so they don't, they can't, actualize or enhance anything inside me. I know how sinful and faithless this must sound, but I'm supposed to feel freely right? That's like one of the major features of the realms right? And this is exactly how I feel!"

"Zen, my son, you are having a crisis of faith" spoke the voice, then, after a long concentration disrupting pause resumed, "You are thinking too much, all these thoughts are grimy residue from the belief pollution of the pre-world and the reason you have not been able to fully overcome them is because as yet you haven't found a participation. You see Zen, a participating mind opens God's gift shop while an idle mind is the devil's workshop. And my son, the reason that you haven't been able to actualize & enhance yourself with holy actz & ens conceived by God himself is because up until now you have subconsciously felt unworthy, undeserving of these blessings, for you didn't have a participation. So go my son, go exorcise your thoughts through prayer, go participate, go bless yourself with actz & ens, Godspeed Zen, Godspeed"

"Thank you Father" said Zen, his mind instinctively devouring the readymade excuse supplied by the voice. Consoled, Zen left the confessional and headed toward the pew, which as promised was surrounded by an ancient desert motif replete with caravans of camels, shifting sands and quaint little huts; and knelt in prayer.

"Hey 'I', haven't you found an 'I' for an 'I' yet?" teased Lambo on catching Zen steal a peep at SoulMate on his way to his participation console. Zen grinned trying to play along. "Today after participation, the Director is briefing us on the new series of crusades, Lambo wants 'I' to be there" he added.

The first few weeks at his new participation, as promised by the priest, Zen's mind had hardly suffered any malware attacks, though he was not sure if it was genuinely cleansed or merely preoccupied by trying to make a good first impression.

No sooner he sat down up popped his instructions, '1. Proofread Director's Personal Notes (Part 1 of 16), 2. Make necessary grammatical and spelling amendments whilst being careful to NEVER ADULTERATE MEANING, 3. Place in the folder [Upcoming Crusades], 4. Finish before first crusade briefing'. This couldn't be right thought Zen, this seemed a task meant for an assistant far higher up in the Admin tower than lowly him, but he couldn't be sure. Zen carefully perused for clues in the instruction, they were ambiguous. The fact that he was assigned to proofread one part out of sixteen presumably meant that fifteen other lowly assistants were assigned a part each with somebody above them overseeing the task; and it was only proofreading. But editing rights were given to make amendments to the Director's own words. The safest option would be to double check with his boss Lambo, but not only would this make him look simple if he were wrong but the process of uncrossing wires would probably mean that the task might not be finished by the first crusade briefing that very evening. So Zen with an upsurge of initiative began making headway.

Finishing a good hour before the briefing, Zen, having smoothened out the Director's difficult prose, committed himself to rereading it just one more time, motivated equal parts by duty and intrigue.

To start with, it is important to define precisely the aims of a crusade. It is commonly believed that the exclusive, or at the very least primary, purpose of crusades by the admins of LifeTree realms is solely the entertainment of its citisumers who offer good likes to go along on said crusades. However this is only one of the purposes served by crusades albeit, given the righteousness of entertainment, a salient one. If the exclusive or primary purpose is entertainment then crusades might well become indistinguishable from holidays hosted at one of our holidayscapes. The purpose of crusades should be threefold. Beyond entertainment value, crusades should seek to strengthen the pious devotion of citisumers to their chosen realm & religion and seek to further the grand, divinely ordained mission of the realms in the pre-world.

It is undoubtedly the greatest feature of the realms, indeed the defining feature of the realms that individuals can citisume and worship in perfect peace, entirely free from the blasphemous cataclysmic intrusion of conflicting beliefs. However there is one side-effect of this, one which we in admin, entrusted with garnering 100% citisumer realm satisfaction, must particularly be concerned with. Without a standard of comparison of how bad, how depraved things can get when the various conflicting beliefs are allowed to mix together, citisumers in any given realm cannot fully appreciate how good they themselves have it, or in other words 100% citisumer realm satisfaction is comparative. Now this is mostly so for the citisumers who were born and bred in the realms but do not underestimate the capacity and speed with which the individual acclimatizes to freedom and luxury. It is here that crusades prove invaluable to us at admin. By allowing citisumers to experience firsthand this dreadful depravity, by letting their noses cringe at its rubbishy reek, their ears ring with its jarring clang and clatter, by letting their feet be punctured by its rusty nails and their eyes tear at its puss oozing diseases and bone baring starvation, the full glory of their realm—its religious freedom, its blissful luxury, its divinely inspired immaculateness—will dawn upon their hearts.

The mission of the realms as so splendidly articulated in the OmniRealm charter, is to '...propagate the immutable truth that man can only live in peace with his fellowman, where he does so segregated along the lines of his inherently conflicting beliefs'. Or in the equally splendid words of the OmniRealm credo, 'United We Fall, Divided We Stand'. The pre-world of course being the very antithesis of this, is the chief battlefront of this divine mission. Here again crusades, though certainly not the only means, are an invaluable weapon in our arsenal. By focusing the fervor of crusaders on aggressively converting pre-worlders of religions different to theirs, we evocatively drive home to these pre-worlders precisely how repulsive, how offensive, indeed how blasphemous it is to constantly have your beliefs questioned, to have them demeaned as heretical or even just plain untrue. Their hearts set ablaze by this immutable truth, the resolve of pre-worlders to ascend to the realms and specifically to the realm which embodies their beliefs can only grow.

This third aim needled Zen, it needled him when he first read it, it needled him while he corrected its grammar and spelling and it needled him now. All he wanted to do was to read it again and again before he succumbed and let his heart sink even further, but he was duty bound to read on. So he started on the next paragraph which contained the Director's observations on the shortcomings of the last few crusades.

"Come to Briefing Room Four" commanded Lambo's voice through Zen's participation console, interrupting Zen's umpteenth reread of the third point. Knowing that he would never see them again, Zen didn't want to let his console suck the Director's notes into what was for him information oblivion, but he had no choice.

"Right, let's get started" began the hologram of the MyRealm I Director of Crusades, a robust middle-aged man with carefully slicked back salt & pepper hair, a dashing jaw and debonair, almost platinum, gray eyes, "The Director hopes that the Director's notes have been properly edited"

Lambo and the other crusade design assistants echoed, "Yes" and "They have Director" several times.

To his great relief Zen immediately noticed that he wasn't the only crusade assistant aide that was attending the briefing, he even heard one of them joke, "Look it's 'I'Lambo"

"In keeping with the points laid out in my notes, the Director proposes that we stop handing out LifeTree actz & ens as freebies on our crusades" stated the Director.

"Why, may I ask Director?" queried an assistant.

"You see, as the Director's notes explained," started the Director proceeded by a self-important throat clear, "it is not a central aim of the crusades to convert pre-worlders, in fact the whole logic of conversion is flawed. Ultimately, the inherent congenital beliefs within an individual will inexorably come to the fore, attempts at proselytization at most can only speed this process along, not arrest nor change its course. However, one of the central aims of the crusades most definitely is to install the truth amongst the masses of the pre-world that 'United We Fall, Divided We Stand'. For a crusade to successfully install this truth, the pre-worlders, whom the crusaders are preaching to, must find such preaching utterly detestable, utterly blasphemous; now how can this possibly happen when these very same crusaders are handing out blessed freebies? Freebies from LifeTree no less!"

The assistants nodded. Now there was no doubt in Zen's minded about that day in the NumLing amphitheater when the Christian realm infiltrated. Angered by having been made a fool of, Zen in a spontaneous act of retaliation spoke out of turn, though what he burst out with itself was in no way rebellious, "I think that we should use a double-edged strategy. I think we should allow our crusaders to gift LifeTree freebies to Catholic pre-worlders so that we win over ascenders considering competing Catholic realms, while stopping them from gifting freebies to pre-worlders of other religions to satisfy the third aim of crusades—convincing pre-worlders that 'United We Fall, Divided We Stand'. I also think that crusades into NumLing amphitheaters are really effective. I'm not sure if MyRealm I or other LifeTree realms have tried this but I've seen such a crusade firsthand and the reason why I think this type of crusade is so effective is… well, because NumLing amphitheaters always have all the different belief groups so the impact is not only on the exact target group of the crusade, it's on all belief groups at once. My friends were just onlookers but it really impacted them as well; it's sort of as if for the likes it takes for one crusade, you get the impact of them all"

In turn, Lambo held back his embarrassment, the other assistants their disapproval and the aides their gasps at Zen's audacity. Lambo and Zen braced themselves as the Director cleared his throat once again, readying himself to speak. But without so much as a tacit acknowledgement of Zen's unsolicited contribution, he resumed exactly from where he was interrupted.

"Hey, Hey, 'I', let us in on one of your 'thoughts' ", "C'mon 'I', C'mon", "Yeah 'I', we wanna impress the Director as well" hazed his fellow aides as Zen headed to his console the next morning. Zen got it, he should've known better than to speak up, not that what he said would get him excommunicated from his participation at Admin, after all, he was just trying to help—Lambo had said as much. But as Lambo also rightly reminded him, it wasn't worth the risk to even so much as appear to be a troublemaker at your participation since an excommunication meant an automatic eviction and a blacklisting from all LifeTree realms. At least a performance termination only led to an eviction with no blacklisting and the possibility of re-ascension. And Zen knew one more thing, as the walls, floors and ceilings, as the dimensions of his Life in MyRealm I seemed to draw claustrophobically inward, he could breathe only at confession with the empathetic father.

"Father, it's me again, it's Zen" he exhaled sitting down inside the confessional.

"Yes my son, confess your sins" spoke the voice freeing Zen to inhale.

"Father, as you told me to, I'm participating but my infection is now definitely a full blown disease" began Zen.

"This is why Destiny, you must as soon as possible go in person to the participator in charge, admit to your sin and answer the questions to the very best of your ability. Then God will surely forgive you, for only then have you truly repented" instructed the father inexplicably, looping out, "May Father suggest the Realm Psalms by Telltale. May Father suggest the Realm Psalms by Telltale. May Father suggest the Realm Psalms by Telltale..." followed by, "Yes my son, confess your sins. Yes my son, confess your sins. Yes my son, confess your sins..."

With the sides of his two closed fists Zen beat at the screen, he beat at it until he jerked tiny droplets of excruciation from his wincing eyes. Seconds later, a panting man in brown overalls sporting the Telltale insignia over his left breast with 'iTime Services' embroidered underneath it, charged into the booth. He sympathetically restrained Zen, helping him out of the confessional.

8

HE STROKED the embossed title of the book with his forefinger repeatedly and glanced once more at the name of its author—Henry Ports, then, in an act of escapism Zen began to read.

Introduction

Beating in the chests of the perpetual economic crises, the wars, the famines, the terrorist insurgencies and the environmental destruction that have come to define our age lies a dark heart, the dark heart of politics. Now, you don't need me to tell you this, we all know this, we all readily acknowledge this, in fact everywhere you go from East to West from the developed world to the developing world, politicians are universally mistrusted and reviled. But it's more than just that sociopaths and psychopaths are overrepresented in politics, for though this is definitely true and has been so since the dawn of history, the failure of politics has a far more radical cause.

Now as you know, I am no political scientist and so you might well question what worth my thoughts as a businessperson and an entrepreneur have when it comes to politics, but for me, my background far from disqualifies me from dissecting politics. On the contrary, I firmly believe that since I, just as you, are very much its real life subject, and as it always transpires its real life victim. I, just as you, are best placed to understand it and have every moral right to judge it. In fact isn't doing so the true essence of democracy?

I think that we 'lay' people, if we are for the first time in history to wrest genuine control of our own governance, must think of politics in general and traditional representative democracy in particular as just another piece of governance software or operating system, which once upon a time may well have been state-of-the-art in running the affairs of groups of people labeled countries, and managing their rights and obligations, but like all software is inevitably surpassed and eventually rendered obsolete by the ironclad immutable law of advancement. It is naïve, it is almost willfully ignorant to unquestioningly believe that people are always coming up with better ways to do everything else, to better fulfill human needs and wants but somehow countries, presidents, parliaments, political parties, MP's and elections—tools invented hundreds of years ago—are the perfect and ultimate devices of governance. Churchill the politician may have been right up until the time he said it and perhaps even for a few decades after that, that *"Democracy is the worst form of government, except for all those other forms that have been tried from time to time"*, but now I honestly think that the time has come, where given the other forms of government that are being conceived, our traditional democracy is just simply the worst form of government.

For the first time since his ascension, the slim old book which Muthu had gifted him made him feel that there was nothing inherently wrong, nothing inherently perverse about wallowing in thought and for this Zen felt an immeasurable debt of gratitude to it and old Muthu. All he wanted to do was read on, hoping that it would never finish.

Chapter I.

Neither Priests, Kings nor Queens or MP's in between

Adopting Lincoln's classic definition of democracy as being government of the people, by the people and for the people, the fundamental shortcoming of the traditional representative democracy that we have today is that it's not very democratic. The root cause of this 'democratic deficit' far precedes the characteristic crookedness of politicians. Neither is there any evidence to believe that it is engineered into traditional representative democracy by sinister intent. Quite to the contrary, there is plenty of evidence to believe that the intent of the first designers of representative democracy was entirely noble. If not Machiavellianism or elitist conspiracy, what then is the true root cause of this democratic deficit? It is quite mundanely a matter of capability and efficiency.

Even today, despite all our technological advancement, we are only in the late infancy of mankind. In the preceding long infancy of mankind, the masses were by definition illiterate and ignorant. Now of course the politicians, for obvious self-serving reasons, and the intellectual elite, to feel better about themselves, will have us believe that the masses are still asses; hence that we are not ready for anything more than representative democracy. However science, impartial enterprising science, is clear on the matter. For instance take the Flynn effect, the IQ of the average person today would make them a near genius a hundred years ago and certainly far more intellectually capable than the very designers of the traditional representative democracy that the politicians and intellectual elite would have us worship at the altar of. Furthermore, the convenient access and sheer volume of information available to the average person today is greater than what even the leaders of the most powerful nations on earth had only five years ago. What all this means is that no longer can it be genuinely said that we the masses are not sufficiently intellectually equipped and sufficiently well informed to directly make the most critical decisions concerning our own governance; we are entirely capable.

Even if we are capable, and we are, the politician and the intellectual elitist can seemingly take refuge under the banner of efficiency. They will no doubt argue that, quite apart from the capability of the masses, it is simply not efficient or even practically possible for every citizen to be consulted and then inform themselves about each and every decision that governance entails. They will argue that this practical concern is precisely why democracy necessarily has to be representative, that this is why we must periodically elect proxies to carry out our will. There is no doubt that for most of the history of democracy this was true, that regular referenda were completely impractical. However for a long while now, almost a half-century, it has been well within the reach of technology to facilitate secure and efficient regular referenda. Indeed what is absurd and anachronistic is that in an age where every day trillions of vital transactions and vital relationships from the financial to the legal are carried out online at the speed of thought facilitated by technology, when it comes to democracy we still insist on punching holes in chits of paper every few years, clinging to the belief that this is the best possible way to exercise our franchise.

It is traditional democracy's way around the now antiquated problems of capability and efficiency that directly gives rise to the democratic deficit. Its solution is to crudely (from a contemporary perspective) slap an obese layer of middlemen between you and me and our governance called politicians. Ideally the politician should, where his constituents lack the capability to understand the issues of governance compensate for this shortfall. Ideally the politician should, even where his constituents possess this capability, be better informed than his constituents about the particular decision of governance facing his constituents, on account of being a dedicated professional whose job it is to be so informed. Ideally the politician should always make the decisions regarding governance which his constituents would have made if they were both capable and sufficiently informed given their values and beliefs. In short an ideal politician should be smart, well-informed and do what his voters would do. Needless to say this is but the naïve ideal and it is here that the characteristic crookedness of the politician is granted entry into the democratic deficit equation. Where his constituents are dumb, all the politician has to do is convince them that he is smart. Where his constituents think that they are insufficiently informed, all the politician has to do is convince them that he is well informed. But most importantly, whatever else a politician is or is not, does or does not, as long as he can convince his constituents that he is making the decisions that they themselves would make, he can win his political survival and advancement. The keyword here is 'convince', the do-or-die in the profession of politics is not task performance but task selling. It is not the management of governance but the management of the perception of governance. While it is true that in every job, that in every workplace, perceptions management is a natural component of the work effort and in being so takes away from actual task performance to varying degrees, in politics it is by far and away the predominant endeavor, and in election time, the only endeavor. So inevitably the political layer that representative democracy by definition has to impose on us, self-selects a cadre of individuals based solely on a particular personality profile, a particular moral profile and a particular skill profile. It self-selects individuals who consummately and with no qualms are the very best at convincing, selling, cajoling, manipulating and propagandizing as opposed to those who are the most conscientious task performers.

In terms of historical middlemen, politicians are the successors to the clergy. Just as the priests set themselves up as the spokesmen and interpreters of god, the ruler of the past, to puppeteer kings and peasants, the advent of representative democracy has allowed politicians to set themselves up as the conduits of governance to puppeteer you and me. The defining feature that makes one cabal the successor of the other, indeed what makes them both middlemen, is that both derive their authority specifically from being the agents of the unchallenged consensus ruler of their age; the clergy from god and politicians from the people. This 'mere agency' is immensely advantageous for them when taken as a collective because the corruption, immorality, or treason of any one individual or even subgroup does not in the minds of the masses readily bring into question the whole system or the function of the entire collective. If a priest under the influence of a foreign foe misadvised a monarch or led the peasantry astray, the clergy as one could easily convince the masses that the blame is that priest's alone; the very human fallibility of one bad egg, one black sheep; leaving god unsullied and the role of the clergy as the spokesmen and interpreters of god intact. Similarly, every time a political scandal surfaces, the swiftest, most decisive, punitive action is usually taken by the erring politician's own party, administered along with a dose of moral indignation for the public benefit. The condemnation and posturing of the opposing political parties and foes also serves only to focus blame on the individual, never is it allowed to enter the public discourse, the common thoughtscape, that it is the whole system of representative democracy that is rotten to its core. Thankfully, taken as a whole, humanity always moves forward, the succeeding age must necessarily be better than the one it unseated. For proof of this we needn't do much more than contrast what the political middlemen of our age *are* agents of, with what the priestly middlemen of the past *were* agents of. The political middlemen of today are the only obstacle standing between us and governance of, by and for tremendously capable, well-informed and not to mention actually existent people—ourselves. Whereas the priestly middlemen of the past were cloaking a non-existent tooth fairy, a chimera that they themselves expediently dreamed up to puppeteer the masses; whose rule incidentally, if he did exist, would by most accounts be petty, vengeful and condemn us to forever live in servility to him.

In other words, despite their inherent perversions the system of our age and its middlemen—representative democracy and politicians—are the agents of the right thing, they are the agents of the rightful and final ruler of the future—the people. Leaving as the defining historical task of the succeeding age, only the eradication of well-meaning but flawed representative democracy along of course with its crooked politicians.

Obviously representative democracy is obsolete, how many devices social or mechanical can you think of devised hundreds of years ago that aren't? Today we don't live in extended families, marry exclusively the opposite sex or move around in horse & cart, in fact a great many of us don't even believe in god anymore. But of course, social devices and mechanical devices are different in one all-important way. It is human nature to form deep moral and sentimental attachment to social devices even in the face of countervailing reason and demands. Whereas no sooner a superior successor to a mechanical device emerges, the obsolete incumbent is cast out with scarcely a second thought or feeling. And so the last rites of all the previously mentioned social devices along with all such others have been bitter and often violent, hopefully something we can avoid or at least minimize when the death knell of representative democracy is being struck.

Zen so wanted to read on but it was too sumptuous an intellectual indulgence to finish all at once. Delaying what was his only remaining gratification, Zen began instead to ruminate on the thoughts and thought ripples that the first chapter had cast in his mind and then revel in his rumination. The thoughts were so exotic, so excitingly labyrinthine that it took Zen ages to be surprised at himself that the glorification of godlessness by Henry Ports hadn't instantly offended him. Even more surprising to Zen was the tug of his mind away from the conclusion that he had made when Muthu first told him about his godlessness. The conclusion that it was this widespread godlessness that was the singular cause of the destruction of the long dead world Muthu championed. It certainly was not out of the question that it was the singular cause, it definitely in the least had to be *a* cause but oddly Zen didn't want to make up his mind till he read on, till he read beyond.

The thought ripple that particularly intrigued Zen's mind was the question of who everyone was going to blame if the direct democracy of Henry Ports failed? In the past when there were middlemen there were also scapegoats, professional blame bins that everyone could chuck away their disgruntlement in and get on with their lives, but to have direct democracy you also had to accept direct blame, and how would people take that? Perhaps they still could blame, they could blame each other, those who decided differently from them, those who got their way opting for the decisions that ultimately turned out wrong. But nameless, faceless others hardly make as good blame bins as high & mighty kings, holier-than-thou priests and hypocritical politicians.

Perhaps that is why, speculated Zen, the direct democracy of Henry Ports never succeeded. But then again, his mind countered, if what Ports says was true, if the average individual were as capable, well-informed and mature as he says they were, then direct democracy could only have failed for some other non-fundamental reason.

Or maybe direct democracy actually worked but it wasn't as Ports believed the next age, the real successor to representative democracy; maybe Post Politica was just a short transition stage before the present Age of the Realms. But then again, if Post Politica was a transition stage leading to the present Age of the Realms, the present age should bear some resemblance to it, or have some components of it, and in any meaningful way other than of course the absence of politics, it didn't. In fact, forayed Zen's thoughts, its main feature—religiousness—clashed head-on with the rising tide of Ports' time—godlessness. And it seemed like individuals in those days, Muthu being one of the last living examples of them, spent a lot of time sitting around thinking and informing themselves about non-entertaining, non-actualizing facts, but today thinking outside participation is like getting yourself surgery on a tumor you don't have. How could this be if humanity always moves forward? How could the next age rewind to the ways and beliefs of a past one? Maybe Post Politica wasn't a contributory transition stage to the Age of the Realms. Maybe, just maybe, thought Zen, still not wanting to make up his mind with any finality, Post Politica was like a belief killing virus that set its sights on the two main beliefs of Ports' day—democracy and religion. Favorably for the sake of the future, it was allowed to kill off democracy but thankfully and most likely by the grace of God, the coming of the Age of the Realms saved religion. Or of course, maybe humanity doesn't always move forward.

9

A NEW found confidence flickered within Zen. A confidence not so much in his own abilities or the promise of his immediate future, but that of one who genuinely feels that his differences are not perversions. That though not here, but somewhere that could exist, that did exist, and may one day do so again, he belongs. A somewhere which has as much a legitimate right to exist as here or anywhere.

And so, as had become his morning pre-participation ritual, he sat down at his console and began reading, for a few minutes, the liberating book.

Chapter III.

Apathetic Revolutionaries

The most debilitating death blow to representative democracy is being struck by not being struck, and everywhere it is being struck/not struck by young people. It is young people, the future, that are on the vanguard of the realization that representative democracy is utterly obsolete. It is young people in record numbers that are not turning up to vote. It is young people that proudly declare that they don't know the names of senators and ministers and even presidents and prime ministers. It is young people for whom politics and politicians have become so insignificant, so archaic, so boring that their typical corruption, mismanagement and scandals are not even worth mustering indignation at. Young people simply don't care and there is nothing, even if it were desirable to do so, that can radically resuscitate their belief in traditional democracy. If at all a fleeting uptick in interest in politics occurs amongst them, it is invariably sparked by something essentially nonpolitical, the mere acting out on the political stage of a theme or narrative that consumes the rest of their lives and thoughts, most often the ascent of a celebrity-politician or a politician-celebrity.

...In the short-run the undeniable truth that young people don't care inevitably leads to the flourishing of the characteristic crookedness of politicians, but in the long-run it leaves the door wide open for the successor of representative democracy—direct democracy—to assume its rightful office. But we must be careful. The door has been left open by the apathy of young people as opposed to any active antagonism on their part. They have long since given up on being politically conscious not solely because of their disenchantment at the typical corruption, mismanagement and scandals of politics and politicians but also in large part due to their enchantment with and by the irresistible entertainments of modernity. And the great irony about the politically oblivious, the apolitical, is that they are the best and most crucial political chess pieces. So our apolitical young people, though generally well capable and having access to vast reservoirs of information, may well be misled. Misled by the selfsame politicians that puppeteer representative democracy, who on sensing representative democracy's demise and of course having no particular affinity to it other than as a meal ticket to a power buffet, will no doubt concoct a pseudo alternative system of governance which promises much but only serves to maintain their lucrative middlemen position. One which far from being the progression that direct democracy represents, may well, given the dastardly ingenuity of politicians, dupe our apolitical young people into conceding even more power than what representative democracy currently cheats them, and all of us, out of...

A melodious gentle reminder from his console alerted Zen that it was time to start participating. Though with each new immersion into the book it mattered less and less, he didn't need any more ridicule from his fellow crusade assistants, so he carefully hid the book away in yet another one of his objects of ridicule, his old duffel bag. The latest thoughts the book sowed in his mind however he couldn't tuck away, as he began participating. The very thought of these thoughts delighted him and he had to keep tabs on himself lest this delight gurgled to the surface in buffoonish inexplicable smiles and expressions. But he was engrossed, engrossed in a riveting intellectual to and fro across the ages with Henry Ports. Now Ports was contradicting himself and Zen couldn't miss the opportunity to flesh out in his mind precisely how so. Ports at the same time thought that young people were greatly capable and had access to loads of information but somehow could be misled by politicians simply because they didn't care about politics. Sure they must have not cared about politics but that would've been, as Ports himself said so, only because they thought it was obsolete and so not worth wasting their time caring and learning about, it would've been like watching the instruction manual of a broken disused Embed. But surely when it was time for an upgrade, for a new model of something as important as governance, they would've cared despite all their entertainments. And with their capability and access they would've firstly been able to compare the existing model with the proposed options to judge if they were really an upgrade and then been able to select the best upgrade. This contradiction fed into the most laden contradiction, the one that stoked Zen's own growing inkling. Ports seemed to be genuinely concerned that the 'dastardly politicians' could engineer a reversal of history, ushering in an age which was even worse than Ports' own age of representative democracy. This was an implicit self-contradictory admission by Ports that humanity doesn't always move forward. For Zen though it was more than just the contradiction in one obscure man's thoughts. Ports had only worded this belief which Zen on introspection realized he had always held. Indeed the one belief which on further contemplation he concluded everyone, no matter what their other defining differentiating beliefs—whether Christian or Muslim, Rastafarian, Jew or Hippie, whether pre-worlders or citisumers—implicitly held. But now he couldn't be sure. It wasn't necessarily true as he and everyone else had always taken for granted that his own age, the Age of the Realms, was the greatest golden age in all of history. Gradually in his mind, no longer was it a matter of that still nebulous place where he felt he belonged having a legitimate right to exist, having to justify itself to today; what was in question more and more was the very opposite. Zen's surging confidence hydraulically lifted his head high, his chin turning ever upwards.

As she had done for the past few days, she sat down a few consoles over from Zen as the day's participation drew to a close. Zen strategically made a mental notch at the most promising angle of intersection for them to make eye contact and waited. A few moments later, just as he had planned, her eyes momentarily broke away from the console only to be accosted by his. They both smiled broadly almost in sync, reassuring Zen that he could approach her after participation.

"Hi, I am Zen" he introduced himself confidently thrusting his hand at her, knowing that there was no way that she would figure out that his wellspring of confidence was entirely different from that of his fellow MyRealmers.

"Oh hi, Tresemmé" she replied warmly, duly offering her hand, "Tresemmé thinks she's heard about you"

"Ah" sighed Zen inadvertently, knowing exactly what she had heard about him. But trying to ignore the little jab to his new found bravado, he continued, "You're not a crusade assistant right?"

"Nope, Tresemmé is a crusade facilitator"

"So…" started Zen, hesitating to consider what he would refer to himself as, "I guess you've been on loads of interesting crusades?"

"Yup" replied Tresemmé, swiveling her chair a teeny bit more so that both her feet directly pointed at Zen, "Just recently Tresemmé facilitated one of MyRealm's 'Tots for Jesus' crusades. It's a new series partly sponsored by KrocRonald's"

"Oh" nodded Zen.

"The kids loved it"

"Yeah I'm sure they loved the nuggets of wisdom that you imparted" slipped in Zen, confident that his sarcasm wouldn't register with Tresemmé.

"Good one" she chuckled, whimsically tapping him on his forearm.

"So Tresemmé heard that you ascended to MyRealm I pretty recently, it's awesome right?" she continued, "Tresemmé was born in MyRealm I" she proudly added, reiterating a truth that was unmistakably borne out by the sculptured symmetry and perfection of textures, colors and contours that was her beauty.

"Yeah it is, it's everything that LifeTree and Jesus Christ promised it would be—OBVIOUSLY" answered Zen emphatically, drawing from the wellspring of confidence that his double intellectual life had become to him.

"Well, joy is LifeTree and Tresemmé is glad to have you in MyRealm" she smiled, looking Zen right in the eyes.

"Thanks"

"Hey, Tresemmé and a few friends are playing Personal Pursuit tonight, do you wanna join?"

"Um… well, I've never really played it before, so I…"

"Don't worry, Tresemmé will teach you the rules, it's pretty easy if you know yourself and it's educational too"

"Educational?"

"You'll find out, just pinging you Tresemmé's home co-ords" she added, zipping with her finger a smidgen of information in Zen's direction from the mind-map with her face at its centre that her Embed had begun to project.

"Hey everybody this is Zen" introduced Tresemmé.

As the pleasantries rang out, Zen had to draw an extra-large dose of confidence from his wellspring to greet the gathering of handsome and beautiful templates.

"Hi, I'm Zen" he announced, awkwardly louder than was necessary.

"Have a seat and help yourself" graciously invited Tresemmé, ushering Zen with a welcoming hand behind his waist toward platefuls of snacks, each of which had a small yet prominent shield beside it displaying the brand of the particular snack.

"Alright," began Tresemmé as Zen sat down with a snack in hand, "Zen's new to Personal Pursuit so let's teach him the rules. Basically the game is all about knowing yourself. Each player gets to roll a v-dice and then you get to climb onto one of five types of steps: Vital Statistics, Your Story, Interests & Hobbies, Love Life, and of course Beloved Brands. So let's say Zen, your roll lands you on Beloved Brands, then one of the other players let's say Dasani here, will ask you a question about one of your beloved brands. Like for example 'On the first day of NumLing what brand of t-shirt did you wear?'. Then obviously you answer the question and if it's verified as correct by your Embed, you get to roll again and advance. If you get it wrong another player gets to roll and the first player to reach the top, the summit of Mt. MEverest, is the winner. Though of course everyone's a winner because everyone learns something about themselves, that's what Tresemmé meant earlier by it's educational"

"The trick is to ask as detailed questions as possible" interjected the athletically built young man Zen was introduced to a few minutes earlier by the name of Stang.

"Yeah, and after you cross the halfway mark of Mt. MEverest, the other players can even ask you questions with specific dates" chimed in Excela, a slenderer model of Tresemmé, "Like 'Vital Statistics: How much did you weigh last year on March 27th?' Or 'Love Life: How many loves did your last love making last May get on SoulMate?' That's when SoulMate history comes in really handy"

"But of course we're not going to ask you questions like that" reassured Tresemmé, "'Cause obviously you have just recently ascended and probably haven't had time to get on SoulMate yet"

"It's so much of fun" added Minolo, who Zen found difficult to distinguish from Excela expect for her distinctly higher pitched voice, "Minolo plays the single-player version for hours, Minolo is a golden self-master, just two more levels to go for total self-mastery!"

Zen was cornered, there was no way he was going to get out of playing Personal Pursuit without squandering the fledgling personal capital he had begun to accumulate with his fellow MyRealmers, and more importantly, without ruining his chances with Tresemmé. He was embarrassed to reveal his poverty stricken pre-world past but he couldn't afford to plead self-ignorance and purposely tank. Since for some reason, which he couldn't afford to think about right now, but he surely would relish dissecting later, knowing every trivial detail about oneself was held in the highest esteem; it was the greatest individual accomplishment. In fact, from the base of the holographic representation of Mt. MEverest, in a bold ancient looking font, the obsession of his peers 'Know Thyself' dauntingly confronted Zen.

"If you're okay with the rules Zen, let's get started" announced Tresemmé, preempting Zen's decision.

Over the next few weeks Zen honed his coping mechanism, watchfully veneering his qualms and insecurities with the norms and attitudes of a good citisumer. He made himself an account on SoulMate, at every possible opportunity flirted his way, albeit clumsily, closer to Tresemmé, ingratiated himself with her friends and even 'blessed' himself with a new duffel bag. In the privacy of his own thoughts however, under the aegis of the book, he became himself. Each time he retreated into himself and the book, he replenished his confidence so that he could wear again with aplomb his realm masquerade. But Zen knew that the ultimate success of his strategy pivoted on one thing—successfully getting his fifteen-on with Tresemmé on SoulMate. If he could just do this, he would surely get himself an impenetrably opaque veneer of citisumerism behind which he could care-freely continue indulging in his cherished private thoughts. Of course quite apart from the demands of his strategy, he longed to make love to Tresemmé off-screen, for not since Maya had his heart skipped and raced, his skin tingled, his words mumbled like this for anyone. This wasn't how he intended his relationship with Tresemmé to pan out, egged on by his new found wellspring of confidence he had merely wanted to have a fling with Tresemmé, but now he most definitely felt something for her. Yet, he didn't consider it unfaithful to, at the same time, use Tresemmé to further his strategy. After all she loved SoulMate and surely she would want him to be accepted by her friends, to belong. But all of this was Zen getting ahead of himself, he wasn't positively sure that Tresemmé liked him, that she wasn't just being polite, this having happened to him before he was twice-shy. And even if she did feel the same way, he still had to perform.

Watching how to perform was about the easiest thing that you could do in MyRealm I, what with the cultural specs of SoulMate and pornography everywhere. So Zen made his mind up to dispassionately learn about passion. From SoulMate, which he previously would do everything possible to avert his eyes from, he would glean for hours the techniques that earned the most loves whilst noting which ones drew the most hates. Using his Embed after a long while for something other than his participation, he paid special attention to porn since he figured that he might as well learn from the professionals in the field. As the weeks passed, Zen had shadow-mastered the techniques he needed to satisfy Tresemmé on SoulMate and in doing so ace his strategy. The counter feeling that all this training and strategizing would systemize out the pleasure of making love to Tresemmé did occasionally prick at Zen, but he always dealt with it by telling himself that after he got that one performance on SoulMate out of the way, they were free to make love to each other in private solely for their mutual pleasure.

"So are you ready for tonight?" asked Zen.

"Ready? …Oh righty, well there's nothing much to be ready for, Tresemmé is Tresemmé and that's what makes Tresemmé amazing" she answered breezily.

Zen, taken aback by Tresemmé's nonchalance, reassured himself that with all his preparation everything will go to plan. In any case, he re-reassured himself, pre-Maya he was far from a novice at this.

That night over dinner, true to her earlier nonchalance, Tresemmé hardly talked about their impending appearance on SoulMate except for the sole platitude about how actualizing it was going to be. Instead she soon lost Zen, who could only think about his all-important debut, by talking about everything she had recently blessed herself with, felt, heard, seen and even smelt.

"Well," cut in Zen when the target time of nine o'clock struck, "shall we…"

"Yes, let's, Tresemmé feels like it"

Soon they found themselves entering Tresemmé's bedroom, and with a few swishes of her hands she prepped the cameras mounted at strategic locations around the room for the upcoming live stream. A little bit out of sync, Zen had already begun to unfurl his arms to a back-turned Tresemmé in anticipation of their opening embrace. She relished an extended look at herself in the large mirror that covered almost an entire wall before turning back toward Zen. By this time he was standing awkwardly his arms thrown wide open as if in prayer. As she approached, the growing incandescent glare of the studio lights set off by the activation of the cameras lanced Zen's eyes, blinding her to him until she began kissing him. 'Don't think', 'Don't think' he reminded himself before he allowed his eyes to close mid-kiss. After their lips and tongues had for a suitable length of time writhed and reveled in each other, as was expected of him Zen commandeered Tresemmé's body from its fleshiest ends and lifted her onto the bed, their foreheads still almost touching. With the motion of her eyes she had him remove her high collared blouse. That was when, readily betrayed by the unforgiving brightness of the studio lights, he noticed it—the craggy patchwork that made up the rest of Tresemmé. Enclosures of supple smoothness seemed to be bordered by barely perceptible, yet nevertheless unmistakable incisions and neighbored by wrinkly looser terrain of ever so slightly varying speckled shades. Her large breasts sat upright, round and proud, yet her shoulders drooped; but then again her arms, wrists and fingers were as tautly layered as her immaculate face. Against two supple skinned enclosures her lower ribs rippled firmly only to fizzle away into a flaccid crisscrossed belly that threatened to spill across her sides. Despite all his exhortations to not think, that is all Zen could do. This woman had a face that looked younger than Maya's and a body that—he recoiled as he thought this—looked older than his mother's!

Agog, Zen hadn't noticed he had stopped the requisite kissing and groping. Tresemmé had to prompt him on by clasping his head with both her hands and bringing them to her breasts. But as his nose nuzzled into their buoyant springiness, he already knew that things were going south. A few moments of warm nuzzling later, Tresemmé took the lead. She sat up cupping Zen's head, unpeeled her skintight leathery pants, placed her knees on the bed and crawled to its edge to face the giant mirror. As she knelt on all fours smiling and posing to herself in the mirror, Zen knew what he had to do, he demanded it from himself. 'C'mon, C'mon' he gritted under his breath. He gave himself a few more seconds by undressing as slowly as wouldn't get noticed, but soon Tresemmé was gesturing at him in between posing to herself. So with one last 'C'mon' he moved into position and, as though concerned about Tresemmé's frailty, warily grasped ahold of Tresemmé's hanging sides. But he just couldn't.

"No worries" assuaged Tresemmé with her characteristic nonchalance, after several evermore desperate tries by Zen.

But a thoroughly destroyed Zen couldn't even muster the energy to mouth the apology he wanted to make. All he had left in him was just enough life force to get himself out of that tortuous room, away from those damned cameras; so he grabbed his clothes and...

"Don't go, don't go" pled Tresemmé.

"Why? I can't, what's the point?" garbled Zen, holding his clothes in front of him to cover both his shames, and so in disarray that he stopped when that was the last thing he needed to do for himself.

"Come here, come here, let Tresemmé show you something" she lured in a soft tone that promised consolation.

Zen who had by now hurriedly put on his clothes all wrong, approached the naked creature, a mutant of firm and saggy, beautiful and hideous, now sitting on the bed.

"Look" she pointed to the corner of a playback of their performance projected by her Embed.

In disbelief, Zen needed a concerted second look to confirm that the loves counter totaled '512' and the hates counter only '4'; and what was more the loves counter was still ticking furiously away!

"WOW—right? See Tresemmé and Zen did well!" exclaimed Tresemmé.

Zen couldn't live with the ignominy, he knew he had received all those loves out of sympathy. Even his co-participators who had made a sport out of ridiculing him had warmed to him out of pity. Like those girls that first day on the pod said, showboating on SoulMate gets more hates than loves and his performance was the right opposite of showboating.

There was one upside though, as embarrassing as his first time on SoulMate was, those loves meant that Tresemmé was ever ready to get back on SoulMate with him. But he needed practice with her so that his next performance wouldn't end up like his last and getting her to do it in private was a far more difficult challenge than getting her to do it on SoulMate. Zen had a plan though, she didn't know nor did he have to tell her that it was his primary goal to get back on SoulMate to deliver a redeeming performance. It was Tresemmé that wanted to get back on SoulMate with him, so he could offer getting on SoulMate with him in exchange for doing it in private.

Sure enough it didn't take much convincing to get Tresemmé to bite on the deal. This time they were to do it in the privacy of Zen's apartment. Along with this, Zen nursed his confidence back to health by reminding himself that since his embarrassing debut he had watched hours more of SoulMate and porn to hone his technique. Whatever feelings he had for Tresemmé had begun to unravel that day with her clothes and this too he thought could only help his performance.

This time Zen took the lead, Tresemmé scarcely had time to sit down on entering Zen's bare apartment when he pounced, abducting her kissing and stumbling into his bedroom. There was no time for pleasantries, his clothes efficiently done away with he ripped through to her cragginess hardly noticing the works-in-progress across her belly that had cropped up since the last time. Soon he had mounted her in position, snippets of porn flashing across his mind.

"Where's the mirror you promised?" Tresemmé sneaked in through her obligatory moans.

That's right—he had promised her a mirror hoping that she would forget about it (as he conveniently had)—but no luck. He quickly got up and tossed away some clothes and stuff that were obscuring a mirror which in relation to Tresemmé's expectations was meagre. On his way back to her, Zen's eyes instinctively started comparing the choppy clash of shriveled flab and stretched rubber tarpaulins that lay on its side with the creamy voluptuousness of the actresses in his porn flashes. A wince of revulsion, as if he bit on something sour, convulsed Zen as he trudged into position. But the porn flashes wouldn't leave him to it. The buxomly breasted, bountifully buttocked, sexual gymnasts with their tiny waists and lusciously moist bright red lips had become his fantasies, totally expunging any drawn from reality. Zen began to realize this as he groped and kissed, fighting eyes tightly shut, about Tresemmé's patchwork. But, he thought, unlike those fantasies drawn from reality which at least reality has some hope of living up to, these professionally choreographed sublimely rendered fantasies only set up reality to fail, only set it up to disappoint. Maybe Tresemmé wasn't as grotesque as these porn flashes made her look, sure bits of her were old but in all honesty taken as a whole she was hotter than Maya ever was, and certainly way hotter than anyone he had been with in the pre-world. 'Oh no' a familiar siren rang out in his head, he was beginning to think! And things once again were beginning to go south.

"See, should've done it on SoulMate" said Tresemmé with a distinct note of told-you-so, after Zen had made a hasty retreat.

"What do you mean? I... I couldn't, do you like seeing me embarrass myself for the sake of loves?" chided Zen.

"What?" shot back Tresemmé bemusedly, "Loves are great but it's not only about the loves. You haven't read the Realm Psalms by Telltale have you?"

"No I haven't" scoffed Zen.

"Well, in the psalm called 'Sex is More' Dr. McKnow says that Jesus Christ wants citisumers to move beyond the stage where sex is just a few minutes of pleasure" explained Tresemmé, "He wants sex to be about delving into yourself, he wants you to use it to tell your uniquely beautiful story"

"So it's not about pleasure, but it *is* about getting loves 'cause obviously you'd want other citisumers to love your story" pointed out Zen, satisfied that he proved the accusation he had earlier directed at Tresemmé.

"As Tresemmé said, Jesus doesn't say anything against getting loves," she clarified "he's all for it, it's a great thing. But the story that you tell is not for other citisumers—it's for yourself. It's your uniquely beautiful story which deserves to be told by you. It's like all the photos that you take of yourself, if others admire them even better but their greatest importance is to you; they are you, and you are the most important person that has ever lived"

In some still inexplicable way Tresemmé's revelation had begun to lessen the impact of his latest debacle. Somehow that feeling the book had first inspired in him that this place no longer had a right to judge him was returning. His failings, his inadequacies, his freakishness was becoming external to him, imposed on him by MyRealm I; and for the first time he spoke up against it.

"How sad," he snarled wagging his head in disapproval, "even when you make love, you can only make love to yourselves"

"What?" replied a bamboozled Tresemmé, "Tresemmé doesn't know how it works in the pre-world but the point is, here in MyRealm sex is meant to be more"

"No, it's actually a lot less" quipped Zen sneering with one side of his mouth.

In his apartment, which in many ways was a recreation of the spartan pre-world hut his mother raised him in, as he did most evenings after participation, Zen lay on his disheveled bed thinking. The late evening twilight that came sauntering in through his partially covered windows was tainted with garish neon streaks from SoulMate and the giant MyRealm I crucifix that perpetually stood in the horizon. The book lay next to him.

Episodically the happenings of the last few weeks replayed in his mind and with it resurfaced the question which that first game of Personal Pursuit had raised. Knowing every trivial detail about yourself certainly won you high esteem from fellow MyRealmers, the game implied this, but this was hardly the point. Individuals themselves considered it a great accomplishment but this wasn't the point either. Neither of these were the point, because neither esteem nor accomplishment were the point for MyRealmers; nor he suspected were they for citisumers in general. If esteem and accomplishment were most important they wouldn't so relish as they did playing a game which made them reveal their failures and inadequacies, their deformities and their evils; they wouldn't relish getting on SoulMate which might reveal their impotencies. He got what Tresemmé was trying to explain to him; MyRealmers, citisumers, were totally unlike pre-worlders at least pre-worlders like Benedict, Linus, Maya and other such aspirers. Aspiring pre-worlders wanted to do something, go out and grab something, win something, achieve something external to them like ascension. Something which everybody could agree on was worthwhile, something which indisputably moved their lives and maybe the lives of those around them forward in some real way; something great and glorious even. And they were willing to go to any lengths of sacrifice to achieve it, to win it for themselves and others. But all MyRealmers, citisumers, wanted to do was wallow in themselves. This alone was their greatest 'victory', it didn't matter how trivial, how pathetic, even how evil or immoral a certain facet or behavior of theirs was. It was theirs and because of this they reveled in it. The relationship between themselves and their life stories, physical features, likes & dislikes, idiosyncrasies, habits and behaviors was like that between a mother and a child. No matter how dumb, how bad, how ungrateful children are, most mothers will still love them, still dote over them, yearn to spend every possible minute with them. Nothing about their children is insignificant or boring for mothers, and just like this, neither are the contents of themselves to citisumers and MyRealmers.

The girls who ascended with him in the orientation pod had prioritized the wrong thing by deducting hates from loves and holding this as SoulMate's most important return. They were thinking like typical pre-world aspirers not typical self-wallowing citisumers. Obviously it was all the better to have loads of loves and no or few hates but because what others thought was only the bonus benefit bestowed via SoulMate, even having loads of hates and a few loves was a pretty decent return. Since it meant that others were paying attention to your contents, which as a typical citisumer, you believe to be supremely important and therefore by that fact deserving of attention. In fact it would be a far greater snub, it would be far worse—though again not the absolute worst since what others thought was merely a bonus return from SoulMate—if the total loves plus hates you received was small or you received no attention at all.

SoulMate wasn't only a device designed to likeize sex, to spread its legs and voyeur away its intimate pleasures, Zen concluded; it was also, perhaps more so, a device to further the obsession, the self-obsession of this age, where citisumers wallowed in cesspools of themselves.

10

HOW HE hoped this would be his opportunity fallen right into his lap, as he expectantly dilly-dallied without opening the message. At last, half closing his eyes, Zen snappily unfurled his fingers but alas this crusade wasn't to be anywhere near home. He wouldn't get to see his mother, he wouldn't get to see Muthu. Never mind he told himself, surely as a crusade assistant he would be called to observe countless more crusades and surely at least one of them would take him home and if none did, well, he soon would be able to afford a trip home himself. To get his mind off the letdown, he let the book meander his thoughts away.

Chapter II.

No Haste yet plenty of Waste

As customers we won't accept poor customer service, quite rightly so. As employees we are expected to always meet deadlines, to do more with less, quite rightly so. As shareholders we clamor for downsizing, more efficiency, more return on our money, quite rightly so. And even on the rare occasion when we let anything political affect us, what we can't stand most of all is the lethargy, the red tape, the wastefulness of government. But as our growing revulsion with politics has made us look away, what we have lost sight of is that the most inefficient system that survives today, the most egregious black hole sucking away resources is representative democracy. The incumbent political process is not held to anything near the standard of efficiency to which we hold the salesperson, the employee, the manager or even the public servant. And while the salesperson, the employee and the manager are all part of a species of organization—private enterprise—that has the striving for efficiency encoded in its DNA, efficiency being a survival imperative, no one can reasonably hold that there is any such coding in representative democracy's DNA. Indeed it is ironic that representative democracy which was itself invented to get around an inefficiency, the inefficiency of polling each and every citizen, each and every time, can now be justifiably considered as our most inefficient system. This of course is a mundane irony, for this eventually is the fate of all products and models—after all dinosaurs were nature's most efficient model at one point!

...It is their nature that around all systems grows the moss of tradition and around all people grows the moss of habit. Quite apart from their inherent imperfections and shortcomings but most often exacerbating them, this moss of maturation blinds them to new opportunity, clouds reason, weighs them down and holds them back; yet while doing all this, the moss makes their host love it evermore. A perfect example of this is the legal system. Its cryptic language and outmoded dress, its demand for feudalistic deference and its contempt for innovation, but above all the compulsive ritualism and red tape of its procedures, exists truly for what? To guarantee justice or out of a fetishism of tradition? And so in the succeeding age, we must be open to, more than that, we must actively seek the radical redesign of our legal system to go hand-in-hand with the rightful overthrow of representative democracy by direct democracy. The very same representative democracy that drains our lifeblood with elections that cost billions, campaigns that sometimes cost even more, perks & privileges, parliaments and senates, committees and sub-committees and innumerable layers upon layers of political fat and excess. With the perverse punch line being that all of this only serves to elect and maintain the characteristically crooked politician, the double feeding parasite, who after lapping all of this up, gleefully goes about his business of perverting our will for his own political survival and insatiable gain.

Though this was his umpteenth read of the first part of the book and he could still only loosely infer what things like DNA and dinosaurs were, the chasm between the present and Ports' past, which had begun to dawn on him after his SoulMate flop, became for Zen ever more gaping, ever more unbridgeable. There was no way, it was laughable to even imagine Tresemmé or any MyRealmer he knew reading stuff like this. For what? Whatever could be the point? True, looking back from today into a long dead time made it extremely difficult to understand what Ports was trying to say, forget about all that, it was probably difficult to understand what Ports was trying to say in his own time. But all MyRealmers, all citisumers, were as Ports liked to say, 'by definition' smart, they all held down participations, they were all good at NumLing, otherwise they wouldn't be welcome in the realms. No, it was laughable to imagine Tresemmé and her friends reading Ports not because they wouldn't be able to figure out what he was trying to say, but because Ports was talking about how things work, how little puzzle pieces of thought fit together, the could and couldn't-do's and the should and shouldn't-do's with these thought pieces; the right word was, Ports was talking about ideas. And the problem with most ideas, certainly the one's Ports was talking about, was that there really wasn't much in it for you in just holding them in your head. They didn't taste yummy, smell pleasant, feel comfortable, tingle your heart or make you smile. They could possibly do these all things for you but only a long way down the line, and only if you put in a lot of effort and others went along with you and things went your way. But there was more to why it was ludicrous to imagine citisumers reading Ports. Ideas wouldn't have tasted yummy, smelt pleasant, felt comfortable, tingled anyone's heart or made anyone smile in Ports' time or ever before, but nowadays ideas had to face yet another frustrating challenge. An idea, Zen supposed, comes to its receivers and even its own thinker as somewhat of an outsider. If the thinker lets it free and receivers accept it unadulterated for what it is, then these receivers surely do so at the cost of acknowledging to themselves that it is not theirs, that it belongs to someone else, that it is rightfully the thinker's. Neither modifying nor improving it, will make the idea completely the receiver's and somewhere deep inside he won't be able to deny this. And even if the thinker doesn't let his idea free, to come up with it in the first place, the thinker would have had to borrow thought pieces from outside himself, from other ideas, from other thinkers, only piecing these puzzle bits together to create 'his' idea; and just as much as a receiver can't, since he is one too, somewhere deep inside he won't be able to deny this. In a way an idea has a life and story of its own, it is a vagrant; to it thinkers and receivers can only ever be foster parents and welcoming strangers. Most certainly, ideas are at least not as personal to thinkers and receivers as their very own feelings and life stories, as their very own love lives and tastes. And modern citisumers more than anybody else in the past, more than even the pre-worlders of today, care only about, want only to wallow in the exclusive petty contents of themselves.

But then again, a loose end sprung up in Zen's thought flow, the Realm Psalms, moderate Catholicism, religion in general—they were ideas floating around the realms. And what was more, these ideas weren't just floating around citisumers who couldn't care less, citisumers actually paid attention to these ideas, they actually used these ideas in their everyday lives!...

"Zen, report to Departure Bay 8" interrupted Lambo's voice from Zen's console, startling him. Still in a daze of thoughts, still the intriguing loose end far from tied up, Zen made his way to the departure bay.

As expected all the crusade assistants were lined up ready to enter the pod. As far as Zen knew, all of them had been to the pre-world before, many of them numerous times before, yet they all wore or at least put on to impress the higher-ups a look of rabid excitement. From an entrance adjacent to the one Zen and the crusade assistants were entering through, a group of crusaders were being ushered in by Tresemmé. Zen started to look down and away but she had already seen him and was smiling and waving as if nothing had happened. With a quick teeth exhibiting stretch of only his lower face that came out like the grimace that it was, Zen hurriedly acknowledged Tresemmé and resumed looking down and away. Toward an opening in the underbelly of the elevated pod, Zen observed a second group of crusaders climbing slowly up via a boarding ladder.

'Forget it, let it go, it wasn't even an embarrassment' Zen kept admonishing himself as he sat arms crossed alone near the back of the pod. Mercifully, Tresemmé was in some other section of the pod, most probably prepping the crusaders, and if he was lucky enough he could totally avoid her, hopefully throughout the whole crusade.

"Crusade assistants" bellowed Lambo standing upright, his bulging pectoral muscles threatening to rupture through his tiny child-sized shirt, "The facilitators are about to commence their briefing to the crusaders. Observe them carefully and critically, note down anything you think will be of interest to the Director or Lambo. Especially... especially be sure to discern if the facilitators are sufficiently emphasizing ALL the aims of the crusades as articulated by the Director. Alright then, let's get started"

Along with his fellow assistants, Zen got up, his fingers figuratively crossed, hoping that he wouldn't come face-to-face with Tresemmé, then in cycle quickly admonishing himself again about how silly he was being to feel embarrassed about the whole SoulMate flop.

The first few observations passed without incident, without Tresemmé, making Zen ever more anxious. And inevitably enough, eventually, what had to happen—did. As the team of assistants walked toward the next band of crusaders, Zen made out Tresemmé.

Since all the crusade facilitators dressed the same, in cat-suits that hid who knew what, since all of them looked pretty much the same, exactly like Tresemmé, Zen took a few more steps along with the teams of assistants, camouflaging himself amongst them until he was sure. It was Tresemmé. Without much thought of the consequences, Zen slipped away from the assistants down a narrow corridor, the words 'I'll be back in a moment' ready at the tip of his tongue just in case one of them asked him what he was doing.

As he snaked away, Zen reassured himself that he had gathered enough from observing the other facilitators to report back to Lambo and the Director. He took a few arbitrary turns until he saw a lonely dead-end, where he came to a rest leaning his back against some paneling. As he sunk lower to sit on the floor exhaling in relief, he heard the distinct sniveling lament of a woman, from, from behind the paneling, and further in the background indistinct chatter. It was none of his business Zen told himself, he didn't want to add to the explaining he surely would have to do. But he couldn't help overhearing; and overhearing, well, it was harmless, he thought. She sobbed and sniveled, going on about, as far as he could gather, one of her pre-world experiences, hardly of any interest to him.

Just as Zen began to zone out of the anti-climax, dismissing it as a crusader having a minor breakdown, he heard the word "Eviction" with conjunctions of snivels garbling the sentence around it. He turned his head so that his ear was snug against the paneling, he heard someone else's voice rising above the indistinct chatter, shouting something like, "We are all in the same boat", followed by a rise in the volume and fervor of the chatter. In yet another move whose consequences he gave no thought to, Zen got to his feet and headed away from the dead-end to search for the entrance to the room where the eviction drama was unfolding. Several right, wrong and left turns later, he was sure, by placing his ear against its door, that he had found it.

He was almost certain that access required more authority than a knock, but he knocked anyway. To his surprise the door immediately slid open and from behind it a small frizzy haired woman greeted Zen with an eager-to-serve smile.

"You must be here for the exit interview" she verified politely, as Zen scanning her uneven features deduced from her dry eyes that she wasn't the woman whose sobs had lured him here.

"Um…" wavered Zen, his panning eyes noting the hung heads that defined the mood of the room, "um…" he delayed, to ask himself if he had the courage to go through with what he so wanted to do, then impulsively, "Yes, that's what uh… Zen is here for" he babbled.

"I… uh Zen, will get started with her" he decided, pointing and walking decisively toward the sobbing woman, trying his best to put on an air of authority.

"Tell Zen, ma'am, the circumstance of your eviction" started Zen, pretending to gesture his Embed on and taking a seat next to her.

"Chanel" she announced, reminding Zen that he should have got her particulars first.

"Right" replied Zen, trying to pretend with an assured smile and a nod that he already had them.

"Well, Chanel was born in MyRealm I, but Chanel was never any good at NumLing" she related, starting off with clarity and composure, "Chanel's mother tried to get Chanel to focus on NumLing, to watch each and every NumLing cast over and over again, and she prayed every day for Chanel, because otherwise she knew this day would come, she knew better than anyone how horrible the pre-world was 'cause she was from there" she continued, the glaze over each of her eyes on the brink of condensing into two fresh tears, "And... and, it has come," she sobbed, the tear dam breaking, re-flooding the dried watercolor stains on her cheeks, "Chanel can't... can't live in that horrible place, even going on crusades was hard to bear, it's disgusting... and no actz & ens—it's unholy—and... and those dirty pre-worlders, eww... with all their different beliefs... " she went on sobbing and sniveling.

A fair haired little girl of not more than five or six in a mini cat-suit, whom Zen hadn't noticed till then, toddled toward Chanel from the other side of the room. Down her chubby face, on which it was clear work had only recently commenced, flowed much like down Chanel's, two streams of black and blue watercolor. The little girl tried to nuzzle her head in Chanel's lap only to be palmed away by her.

"Chanel can't, Chanel can't" she cried almost demanding sympathy from Zen.

"Who is that? Is that your daughter?" inquired Zen.

"Yes, and imagine maintaining her in the pre-world!" wailed Chanel.

"What's her name?"

"Chanella" she answered quickly and, "Chanel caaaaaan't" she resumed wailing, her eyes shriveling tightly shut in agony.

The other evictees had by now huddled around Zen and Chanel, Chanella sat on the floor crying along with her mother.

"Would it not be possible to leave Chanella with her father presuming he has not been evicted too" proposed Zen formally.

"Suppose that's possible," sputtered Chanel, "but Chanel hasn't even seen him since the divorce ceremony. And Chanel can't be alone in the pre-world—no way"

"Divorce ceremony?" burst Zen quizzically, unwittingly compromising his ruse.

"Yes, Chanel and Arman had a grand divorce ceremony, it was featured in My Day magazine" reminisced Chanel, a wistful smile shining through her tears.

Just then, the threat to his ruse hit Zen, but he continued anyway, "So what exactly did you and Arman do at your divorce ceremony?"

"Well, the altar and aisle were decorated with stuff from Chanel and Arman's glorious marriage—you know nights out shopping and trips to holidayscapes etcetera and loads and loads of Chanel and Arman's SoulMate holograms" she began enumerating, "The hor d'oeuvres were Chanel and Arman's favorites. And the altar, aisle and hor d'oeuvres were all blessings from Martha's Home!". "And, and" she hastened, her voice rising to a proud climactic boom, "Chanel walked onto the altar in Chanel's wedding dress by Coco and then unzipped it to unveil Chanel's divorce dress again by CoCo!"

For an extended moment, Chanel's face clung to its last expression, her eyes looking out beyond Zen into some distance, replaying the halcyon climax. Then two fresh tears came trickling down her face's watercolor plains all over again.

"Don't worry, it's all a part of God's plan" assured a voice from the huddle of evictees. Zen looked back to identify the speaker, a middle-aged man who as was obvious from his unrefined shabby gestalt, was most certainly a recent ascender.

"Yeah, God works in mysterious ways" added the small frizzy haired woman with uneven features that had showed Zen into the room.

Until this encounter with Chanel, Zen had never really seen an unhappy citisumer before. Certainly one whose unhappiness couldn't easily be disremembered or totally turned around by a simple act or en, one whose unhappiness owed so much, owed everything in fact to the way of the realms. Citisumers were generally happy he assessed, they were happy when things went right of course but when things went wrong, ah well those were things outside of them. They were happy when they were talented, admired and beautiful of course, but even when they were incompetent, hated or parts of them were ugly, these were still beloved components of their beloved selves; intriguing twists and defining wrinkles in their life story with which they were obsessed. They loved, self-loved, their flaws and failures into happiness; they were happy in their actz & ens, their realms and in themselves, Zen summarized.

"Do you believe…" began Zen, pausing ever so slightly to perfectly frame his implosive next question, "that your eviction due to your insufficient NumLing competence is primarily your own fault or that of MyRealm I and LifeTree?"

With this one question Zen knew he had got one over Chanel, that he had got one over a citisumer, and most satisfyingly of all, that he had got one over the realms. Chanel was genuinely and inconsolably unhappy about her eviction, which meant if she admitted to her NumLing incompetence being the cause, here Zen would have a citisumer that couldn't love her incompetency, a citisumer whose flaws and failures had undeniably caused her unhappiness. If on the other hand, Chanel blamed MyRealm and LifeTree then she would be conceding that realms don't always keep citisumers happy and another pillar of the immaculateness of the realms would precariously wobble. Whether she blamed herself or MyRealm and LifeTree, the third pillar of happiness in the realms, which Zen's question didn't even draw attention to, was more than just wobbling, it had fallen right off, since there wasn't an act nor an en in existence that could cure Chanel of her fundamental unhappiness.

Chanel, her tears having drained her, hardly in the ideal state-of-mind to answer Zen's rabblerousing question, nevertheless, out of some ingrained morality, considered it her duty to answer to the very best of her abilities.

"Chanel's abilities are Chanel's abilities, that is just how it is and that is just perfect" she commenced with purpose, "And Chanel definitely does not blame MyRealm I or LifeTree, after all joy is LifeTree, Chanel has lived it firsthand and it, actually… actually is. It has been a blessing to be born in MyRealm I, it has been a blessing to be born into Chanel's very own beliefs, Chanel has never even considered re-deciding. Chanel loves it here… Chanel belongs here"

It didn't matter what she says, it had to be either her fault or the fault of the realms, or even better the fault of both, Zen smugly brushed off. Of course she would try to convince herself it was neither, she was a citisumer born and bred, he told himself.

"This is not MyRealm's fault, this is not blessed LifeTree's fault, and it has got nothing to do with Chanel's abilities either" reprised Chanel, the meter of her words clearly signaling that a grand conclusion was imminent, "This is God's plan for Chanel, yes... this is God's plan for Chanel"

Agreement reverberated from the mouths of the huddle of evictees. Zen was stumped.

11

"ZEN!" GROWLED a voice from behind the huddle of evictees, just as Zen who had gathered his thoughts and words was about to fire a retorting question at Chanel. The conspicuous anger in the voice instantly turned the heads of the evictees toward it.

"Zen, a word" called Lambo, softening his tone greatly to avoid a scene.

The 'sooner or later' that his mischief would bring about was now. Zen knew it and he really didn't care.

"Lambo should evict you, more than that, Lambo should blacklist you!" he excoriated, when he got Zen outside, "But Lambo will give you another chance—just ONE more—that's just the kind of citisumer Lambo is. But this is going on your record, there's absolutely no way around that"

The only thing Zen had to lose, the only thing he really didn't want to lose, was his chance at going back to the pre-world on MyRealm I's current crusade. But surely 'another chance' meant…

"Lambo is confining you to the pod for the duration of this crusade" decreed Lambo.

The broken jittery thuds indicated to Zen that the pod's landing was nearly complete. Defiantly telling himself that he didn't even care about the crusade that Tresemmé, Lambo and his fellow crusade assistants were about to embark on, Zen reclined in Lambo's chair. As the thuds and screeches came to a halt, the console attached to the chair switched itself on showing a panorama of the landing pad. Zen had a plan.

He started for the lowermost exit bay, his defiance denoting itself on his face with a self-satisfied smirk. When he got there, sure enough the dejected evictees—heads still hanging, like Chanel tears now gushing—were taking the dreaded backward steps into the pre-world. Slickly, Zen joined the defeat parade and quickly made his way to the front to lead it down the ladder.

"Proceed in that direction" he instructed as he stepped down onto the tarmac, pointing to where he knew Lambo and the others would be exiting the pod from. And with this, Zen, holding back his urge to run, took hurried nervous little steps toward a pod that had landed adjacent to his own and hid in its shadow.

The MyRealmers, present and former, were soon chauffeured and packed off respectively, allowing Zen to step out from the shadows. Through the dusty glare of the pre-world sun he counted seven pods, two, including his own from LifeTree, and the rest from various other realm providers; all seven of them of course from different realms.

This was it. He caressed the rectangular protrusion the book made against his trouser pocket for a hit of confidence. He would try to board the next departing pod.

Cloistered inside a maintenance locker, Zen listened carefully for the clatter-clutter of screeching, thudding and whirring which indicated landing. When he finally heard it, he gave himself an impatient ten minutes or so before he looked for a way out. It wasn't difficult, he snuck out the same way he snuck in; under the aegis of the busy maintenance crew.

When he felt safe enough from detection to lift his gaze from his feet, there dawned upon his eyes the sun, an unmistakable corona of six iridescent yellow graphical spokes cheerfully circulating it. Taking regular turns within the corona, 'RealmMart' in a blue affable font gladly interchanged with 'Nirvanaland' in curvy exotic gold lettering.

The wondrous glint of an entirely new place in his eyes, the exhilaration of rebellion revving his heart, momentarily insulated Zen from the impending cataclysm that he had brought upon himself. He strode faster and further away from the pod station into the warm embrace of the new sunshine, curious beyond measure to find out what lay within it.

Once he reached the grassy edge of the hill, the pod station now a buzzing blur in his background, Zen leaned forward against the railing to take in the view of Nirvanaland. Straight out ahead of him, gargantuan shopping temples in Buddhist motifs gaudily flashed their promises to heaven and earth, to his right a grid of lustrous metal & glass participations towers whose efficient drone Zen could almost hear, and to his left, clearly every effort taken to encrust them with homeliness, more towers, neighborhood towers. A tingle of familiarity pinged Zen. Nirvanaland looked just like MyRealm in Buddhist robes. In fact the only thing that was different was that its citisumers (though it was difficult to get anything more than a blurry outline from this high above) seemed to mostly wear the bright saffron robes that Buddhist monks customarily wore. He had gleaned everything he could from this perch, so Zen decided to make his way to the Sky Cabriolet halt located back nearer the pod station. And as he began to walk he acknowledged, but then quickly suppressed the reality, that the moment he offered any likes, he would be giving his location away.

"Suppose, you're a recent ascender" guessed a citisumer, as Zen stepped into the carriage abreast with him.

"Uh… yes" Zen answered before they sat next to each other.

"Vuitton" he proclaimed, slightly bowing his head and making a two-handed praying gesture at Zen, who replied without gesture, "Zen"

Not subtly, Zen started scanning the man's attire to fill in the details that weren't discernible looking down from the hillside. It was exactly what those Buddhist monks in the pre-world wore. The only difference was that far from being emaciated like the pre-world Buddhist monks, left bare by his robes, Vuitton's arms, tattooed with a likeness of his face encircled by the RealmMart sun, bulged from his square chest, and his calves fleshed out wide and muscular. As Zen looked closer though, it was obvious that Vuitton's robes were different too. They were tailored from a rich silk that draped elegantly over the contours of his sculptured body, not the cheap gauzy cotton that hung like crêpe paper over the emaciated bodies of the pre-world monks. And their luxuriousness was hallmarked by the iconic monogram etched across them.

As the Sky Cabriolet readied to leave, at first it appeared to Zen's eyes that its exterior had become transparent, for rays of sky blue and sunshine gold shimmered and shimmied in. But then as the Sky Cabriolet began to move, giving the sensation as though it was moving toward this, a giant apparition of Buddha—legs crossed, eyes closed, deep in meditation—appeared at the front of the carriage. The Sky Cabriolet picked up speed galloping toward Buddha, who by now had become just his solemnly meditating head. The sun and sky turned to pure blackness—the carriage was in Buddha's head—and careening toward an ancient scroll bracketed with two golden knobs. The scroll unfurled to a melodious sitar tune and right in the middle of it, inscribed in the same lettering as the Nirvanaland insignia, shone the title 'The Realm Jatakas', and underneath it 'by Telltale' with a nifty crown floating above Telltale's middle 't'.

Vuitton and the sprinkling of other Nirvanalanders in the carriage sat in reverence, staring at where the scroll had been for a good thirty seconds after it had disappeared. Vuitton only really got back to Zen and the here and now when the next station—'RealmDepot Homeware Temple'—was announced.

The doors whooshed open to reveal, for the first time to Zen, a female Nirvanalander. Immediately Zen, again not subtly, began to scan her attire from bottom up. Her robes were about the same silky saffron hue as Vuitton's but they started well, well above her knees and were draped across her slender waist so as to reveal her creamy midriff, glistening at its center with her jewel encrusted naval. Above her breasts, her robes slung low and from underneath, their lace-embraced plumpness sensuously peeked out. Her face looked like some cousin of Tresemmé's, or Chanel's, or both. She sat opposite Vuitton and a still scanning Zen and made the same two-handed praying gesture that Vuitton had made before floating off pied-pipered by her Embed.

"It must be exciting to have recently ascended right?" broke in Vuitton, "You've made the right decision, you'll find nirvana here"

"Nirvana?" asked Zen mainly with the bamboozled look on his face.

"Yes of course nirvana" resounded Vuitton, "Nirvana is total freedom from want, and here in Nirvanaland no citisumer will ever suffer from want since they can bless themselves with every possible act & en, from those conceived in RealmMart's own blessed wombs to those conceived in the wombs of all the other great trepships!" he explained boastfully.

"Oh… that's what you mean by nirvana" acknowledged Zen, quite disappointed to learn that he already knew exactly what nirvana meant.

"Well, if you've ascended to 'Nirvana'… land and you're are not sure what nirvana means, Telltale's timing was perfect then" chuckled Vuitton, "You need to bless yourself with the Realm Jatakas"

"Anyways, would you like to know Vuitton's story in Nirvanaland?" he asked, launching into it without scarcely a pause after uttering the last syllable of this offer.

Zen didn't really know where he was going. Mercifully, Vuitton's oral autobiography had been cut short by his station arriving not a moment too soon (though he had considered riding on with Zen to continue narrating it). The sensuously robed female Nirvanalander had got off too. An announcement rang out, "The next station is… Body Boutique's Benares Park", Zen thought it as good as any to get off at.

He hesitated before offering up the twenty likes to enter the park. Not that it would make much of a difference, he had already given himself away by riding on the Sky Cabriolet, but now the insulating novelty of Nirvanaland was wearing thin and the exhilaration of rebellion was starting to be metabolized into poisonous anxiety. But there was nothing he could do about his fate now, he told himself. All he could do was make the most of the little time he had left in Nirvanaland, so he offered up the likes and headed into the park.

Zen strolled along the main footpath of the park, thoughts of his next move nagging at him. To either side of him, citisumers gratefully plucked Body Boutique's tester freebies that blossomed from the park's trees and plants. Out a little into the distance, at the centre of the park, sat a giant golden Buddha statue in his signature meditative posture, a halo reading 'Body Boutique's Benares Park' orbiting his head. Zen, not wanting to be disturbed, searched for a tree which had been plucked empty by citisumers and sat against it. He felt again for the rectangular protrusion as the nagging thoughts grew incessant, as they grew ever more insistent. He didn't dare check his Embed, but he was sure by now that it would have been besieged by messages, alerts and warnings, no doubt the most severe of which coming from Lambo. Any distraction was welcome, so Zen picked up a light-orangey flower that had fallen next to him on the feathery grass, noted that its petals read 'Night Jasmine Eau de Toilette' and lifted it to his nose. Just then he noticed that the kids clad in their miniature saffron robes, sitting out near the centerpiece golden Buddha, who were painting their faces with the testers they had plucked, had dropped everything and were looking out into the horizon. He hoped not and sank back against the bark of the tree. But it was SoulMate. Instantaneously the tingle of familiarity that had pinged Zen when he first saw how similar Nirvanaland's layout was to that of MyRealm recharged, this time not pinging but stabbing him. A few amongst the litter of mini saffron-robed kids pointed at something or other that tickled them on SoulMate before quickly returning to their friends, who were back to painting their faces.

Zen was not sure if the sick feeling that churned his stomach and made his chest feel hollow owed more to the predicament he was in or the realization about the realms that the sight of SoulMate in Nirvanaland had brought on. Again the mini saffron-robed kids dropped everything and looked out into the horizon, this time in the opposite direction of the continuing carnal oscillations of SoulMate, Zen's eyes instinctively followed theirs. In a scene that could easily have been taken right out of the very park that it was projected over, a thick-spectacled elderly man sporting the blissful self-assured smile of the know-it-all and the typical saffron robes of the Nirvanalander, loomed large over the horizon. He sat on a bench under a tree blossoming with the distinctive brand-fruits of his multifarious sponsors, his words, "Don't deny yourself iTime with me—Dr. Padeek Pracho" reverberating from the horizon through to the ground below as if decreed by an almighty deity. Here was yet more confirmation about that realization regarding the realms, Zen concluded, as he resolved to look down, freeing himself from both the empty oscillations of SoulMate and the generic demagoguery of Dr. Padeek Pracho. But then as Pracho dissolved into the motley blues and wispy whites of the horizon, arresting his gaze was something he had never seen before.

Right where Pracho had been, as if succeeding him, materialized a teenager wearing exactly the same thick spectacles and the customary saffron robes. Jutting his head forward in disbelief, Zen took a second and then a third squinting concerted look. Yes it definitely was Pracho, but about fifty years younger!

"Introducing for the first time ever—iTime for kids—with who else but me, Dr. Padeek Pracho Junior" the teenage incarnation of Pracho chirped in a distinctly high unbroken voice. And as he did, the brand-fruits, which had changed from the ones which the elder Pracho peddled into the mascots of obviously kid's brands, began marching, dancing and prancing to the beat of merry tunes toward the ground below, toward the outstretched arms, the awestruck eyes and the welcoming hearts of the kids below.

With this spectacle Zen had about enough of Nirvanaland. And his next move? He needed respite before mulling over that, so he reclined back against the tree and reached for the book.

Chapter IV.

Final Rights

Representative democracy is archaic and thus obsolete and so is our vainglorious legal system, the rights which these inherited devices are supposed to execute and safeguard however, most certainly are not. And nor will these rights ever become obsolete so long as man's natural genetic configuration is left untouched. For man as naturally configured has a raw, intrinsic clamoring for freedom of speech, for freedom of worship, for freedom of association, along with all the other human rights laid down in the Universal Declaration of Human Rights. Rendering the denial of these rights—the very denial of man's essential humanity. Now in the past various hegemonies have managed to brainwash the masses into believing that the self-denial of these rights was somehow moral, or convince them that their deprivation was necessary, but none have ever succeeded in radically extinguishing this intrinsic clamor. And today, raising our heads out from the cocoon that was the long infancy of mankind, most of us freed from hegemony and the rest at least in the process of unshackling themselves, we hold our intrinsic clamor proudly aloft, eloquently articulated, universally accepted, and final.

If, from the illiterate forest dweller to the educated urban dweller, we intrinsically clamor for the same fundamental rights, then in this regard the only role of a system of governance is to obediently, slavishly almost, guarantee these fundamental rights. Here again the incumbent political system riddles itself with inefficiency and here again it gives the characteristically crooked politician an opportunity to pervert its intent for his own survival and gain. The inefficiency stems from the free rein that the incumbent political system hands politicians to endlessly debate what are in fact intrinsic finalities—our fundamental rights. To bluster on and on about the nuances of these final fundamental rights should not be the job of the politician or the political system, if at all it is the job of the moral philosopher, and we should not be squandering our hard-earned tax money on it. Beyond its inefficiency, this bluster is as always perversely co-opted by the characteristically crooked politician. Its deliberately big words and purposely complicated technicalities are used as a bludgeon against us 'lay' citizens to overawe us, to intimidate us into willingly and thankfully ceding our power over to the political system and politicians. And even if we were to suppose that the intent is not to overawe and intimidate us, our public officials reveling in debate about the nature and finer points of conclusively established fundamental rights smacks of elitist indulgence, when all that we want is the execution of these rights, when all that we need from a system of governance is quite simply to 'get on with it'. Instead, true to its root word *parle*, meaning 'to speak' in French, from which the word *parliament* stems from, the wasteful, alienating, elitist bluster continues unabated. To put this bluster over fundamental rights into perspective, just imagine how ludicrous it would be for the top management of a business organization to spend a good portion of their working hours debating whether profitability, product & service quality and customer satisfaction are worthy business goals as opposed to actually spending all their time and effort actually working toward achieving profitability, product & service quality and customer satisfaction…

Zen's concentration was breached by the wailing siren from his Embed. He knew there was no way of turning it off and heads would soon turn in alarm. A glaring red beacon began flashing, each pulse of its blinding light stinging his eyes. Zen stood up turning his body and forehead away from the citisumers toward the bark of the tree, hoping that it would obscure the beacon. But there was nothing he could do about the wailing siren. A matter of seconds later an annoyance of kids gathered around the tree amused by the all new Embed game that Zen looked like he was playing. Zen bolted for a lonely tuft of trees that he could see from the corner of his downturned gaze, the annoyance of kids gaily following him. The kids were of no danger he told himself, it was clear that they didn't know what the wailing, flashing beacon signified. It was the adult citisumers that he had to avoid. Concealing himself as much as possible amongst the tuft of trees, Zen had no choice. With the crude blunt implements at the ends of his fingers he started digging and scratching at his forehead. Soon he was rubbing beads of warm salty sweat into his freshly scratched wounds. The annoyance of kids on witnessing this scampered away in horror.

Mangled with stinging red pulses, memories of that day full of hope when he got his new LifeTree Embed implanted flashed before his eyes, as Zen's fingers finally felt from underneath the burning rawness of his clawed forehead the accursed metallic disc. Teeth gritted, with one bloody rip he tore free from the clutches of the thing that had betrayed him. He needed to get away from the still wailing, still flashing thing and everyone who had seen him with it, but as he turned to flee, a troop of brawny uniformed men backed up by a pod hovering ominously above them were lying in wait for Zen.

12

HE WAS about to be blacklisted from the dream he had strived for all his life, but there was only one quite trivial thought on Zen's mind, perhaps intentionally so to avoid dealing with the graveness of what he had done. As he kept refusing to concede his staring match with the leminiscate beaming proudly from the opposite wall of the room he was being held in, he kept asking himself—Why? Why was he being evicted from the realms by OmniRealm and not LifeTree? The question didn't stop pestering Zen or more like Zen didn't stop pestering it until he had a breakthrough that had nothing to do with its answer. It was a breakthrough teeming with excitement and relief: soon he would be seeing his mother and Muthu again.

The pod began its indicative jittering, sending Zen into his nervous tick. He repeatedly caressed the book that had got him through his ordeal in the realms. The book which Zen without an iota of regret acknowledged was most likely the cause of his eviction and imminent blacklisting. After the alternation of thuds and screeches had ceased, Zen stood up and strode toward the door, ready to be escorted out of the realms, unconquered.

"Zen, MyRealm I, right?" asked a man politely after the door whooshed open.

"Yeah" Zen scoffed, refusing to make eye contact.

"Right this way then sir" ushered the man courteously, displaying a pretense of concern on the part of OmniRealm and MyRealm I for someone they were heartlessly evicting which Zen found utterly obnoxious.

He was escorted through the guts of the pod until, after they exited a long corridor, Zen was sure from the surrounding architecture that they had entered a building. They came to a stop in front of an imposingly large polished metal sliding door with a larger than usual leminiscate gleaming brighter and whiter than any that Zen had seen on the pod. It whooshed open for them.

"No, no, NO! This is what they don't understand… products MUST have flaws. Just like quirky innocent flaws do for people, they make products more lovable too" perorated an old man around whom, hanging on to his every word, the entire room seemed to orbit.

"Ahem… Director" finally peeped Zen's escort, after allowing more than enough time for the team of his young acolytes to jot down and clarify the old stalwart's seminal pearl.

"Ah yes, the young MyRealmer" acknowledged the old man, leaving his hangers-on hanging and struggling toward Zen, "Richard Bernays, Director-General of OmniRealm" he declared extending his liver-spotted hand at Zen.

The Director's hand left to awkwardly dangle in front of him and from it left to dangle loose liver-spotted skin, Zen stood staring at the old man. And it was not because, as the rest of the room readily assumed, Zen was frozen in awe. Zen now knew his case wasn't a normal eviction and blacklisting, he didn't know the whys & hows, but he certainly knew that it wasn't normal. Of less immediate importance, but nevertheless stoking his naturally raging curiosity, was how totally different the Director-General looked from everyone and everything else he had seen in the realms, everyone and everything else in that very room. Two flaccid flaps of liver-spotted skin ran from his neck to somewhere underneath his face, batting about every time he talked, like two loose sails flitting against a breeze. Two heavy tea bags of flesh, in about the only symmetry on his face, suspended themselves from the corners of his mouth finishing well below the plane his jaw line once traversed, giving his face, even when he smiled, a sort of overall glumness. His hair remained on his scalp only here and there and had faded into fine silver filaments that thickened only at his ears and misshapen moustache. There were no enhancements, no Tresemmé-like patchwork here. Or else Zen quickly entertained—and this was a distinct possibly given that as the Director-General of OmniRealm he would have unlimited access to the very best of actz & ens—maybe the Director was really, really old, way older than he actually looked, so maybe this *was* him after all the enhancements the realms could dream up had done their best work. In any case, there was one thing on the Director-General's face which Zen couldn't help but be captivated by, whose zeal and buoyancy the mere harshness of time could not sag. Set deep behind a surrounding scrunch of speckled corrugated flesh, a duo of vigorous small black eyes shone back at Zen.

Zen's escort gently prodded him, "Uh, Zen" he responded carefully shaking the Director-General's long dangling, frail hand.

"Well take a look around until I am done with this lot" suggested the Director-General, "We have a lot to discuss" he added before getting back to his eager acolytes.

For the hour or so that he waited for the Director-General, mind-winds swirled within Zen's brain, picking up scraps of thought from within and from around this enthralling new place, hurling these admixed missiles at the neat concept-towers that in Zen's mind had already started crumbling. Looking out from the high perch of the Director-General's office, Zen could see the familiar arrangement of participation towers, neighborhoods towers and shopping towers, and the huge OmniRealm leminiscate that presided over the horizon with its credo 'United We Fall, Divided We Stand' revolving self-assuredly around it. Indeed against this backdrop, his eyes out of expectation almost, projected mirage-like the carnal oscillations of SoulMate against the afternoon sky. But yet, there was something different about this place—an authentic quality. It was as if stretching through a long continuum that started out at its very edges, the entire place grew gradually ever less pretentious, ever less superficial, ever more real; with the unmistakable epicenter of this realness being the Director-General's office itself.

"Magnificent isn't it?" interrupted Bernays from behind.

Zen, not having heard the old man's cautious steps, turned around startled.

"Have a seat," directed Bernays, "you must be anxious to know why I have called you here"

"I think I know," ventured Zen, after sitting down at Bernays's desk following his lead, "it's to do with my eviction and blacklisting, right?"

"Well sort of" Bernays started explaining, "As you well know... ahem... given what has transpired, your eviction and blacklisting would have been inevitable, but the crusade director of MyRealm I is well known to me and he speaks highly of your insightful contributions. In fact so highly that I have been monitoring your progress for a while now"

NO, Zen thought, DON'T. The Director-General's tone and demeanor seemed to hint that something the old man considered positive was in the offing for him, but he shouldn't get his hopes up, Zen told himself. He couldn't get his hopes up, he hated the realms. All he could do, all he should do, was take heart in the sense of achievement that he felt for having his contributions recognized as insightful.

"You see Zen," Bernays continued, "I ask the implementers closest to me to keep an eye out for youngsters like you in their realms"

Again his tone and demeanor indicated anything but, yet Zen fixated on an ominous interpretation of the Director-General's words.

"Yes, you see, and I shall be quite forthright with you, the man who doesn't need leadership is the very man most fit to assume it!" Bernays proclaimed, his eyes shining a smile at his own wisdom, "Oh yes, and this is why I have called you here—to offer you the position of being my personal aide"

"YOUR PERSONAL AIDE?" bellowed Zen at a volume which almost splattered the frail old man back against his chair, "Your personal aide?" Zen pronounced again softly, the whirlwind of thought scraps swirling into a full blown twister. Why was he offering to make him his personal aide based mostly on one outburst at a crusade meeting? How much did the Director-General know about him? How did he come to know what must definitely be quite a lot about him? But most pivotally, did he know about the book?

"Yes, my personal aide," affirmed Bernays softly, "and you can learn to your mind's content about everything, about every detail, about every 'spec'—pardon the pun—of these glorious realms" he promised with a flourish, sweeping his right hand in a shaky arc that culminated near Zen indicating 'over to you'.

As the Director-General concluded his pitch by detaining with his charismatic gaze Zen's eyes, eyes that were restless to flit away in thought about what he should do next, a clear implication was beamed to Zen. Either he accepted the offer, or the inside of the Director-General's office would be last thing he would ever see of the realms.

It wasn't like back in MyRealm I where even if someone saw him reading the book they would merely consider it peculiar, some vestige of pre-worldism that was totally innocuous, a habit which, at worst, could only make him a laughing stock among crueler citisumers. Now not only was he the personal aide of the director-general of OmniRealm, but more so, Bernays knew things. It was the most conspicuous thing about Bernays. That he knew things shot at you from those eyes, every carefully chosen word of his was laced with overtones of it, Zen didn't know precisely in what way but he was convinced that it even explained how he managed to be the OmniRealm director-general and yet got away with looking like he did. And it was not only that he knew about mere happenings like Zen's outburst at the crusade meeting or his incursion into Nirvanaland; or things he should know by being the director-general of OmniRealm such as how precisely the realms work. Zen was sure that he knew the deeper 'whys', the preceding 'how comes', the proceeding 'what thens' and the potential 'what ifs' about the realms. He was sure that unlike most citisumers, if not any other, Bernays knew what Muthu and Ports knew. Knowing was the life force that seemed to prop the sagging old know-bag up. All this, and the fact that, he had been monitoring him most probably meant that Bernays already knew about the book. But just in case, in the off-chance that Bernays didn't know about the book, since he couldn't predict what Bernays's reaction to it would be, he couldn't jeopardize this almost unbelievable chance to download everything about the realms and much, much more from the old know-bag, by revealing its existence. So he decided never to take the book out of the tiny apartment that Bernays had allotted him. As Zen adoringly opened the book to the page he last left it at, a tidal wave of excitement rose from his chest breaking upon his face in an expression of childlike glee. Well placed here in OmniRealm at the side of its director-general, he felt above the realms, at the cusp of waging a war for their final intellectual conquest. And then, just before Zen started reading, another tidal wave of excitement rose up, if indeed Bernays knew about the book and still wanted to engage him, a cornucopia of possibilities lay ahead.

Chapter V.

Imagine there's No Countries

Positively acknowledge that direct democracy is both superior to representative democracy and is entirely feasible. Positively acknowledge that man intrinsically and universally clamors for a set of rights rendering these rights final. Now imagine.

Imagine that standing securely on the bedrock of final rights, we design and redesign institutions whose function it is, without the pretentiousness of tradition and the assumption of self-importance, to deliver these final rights. Basically a successor to our current constitutions which totally removed of their characteristic pretentiousness will be both a blueprint of societal management and a manual or simple 'How To' guide of the same. In the engine room of these new institutions, slavishly implementing their functions, (and doing strictly only this) will be an intimately familiar entity assigned a new task, an entity we all know as the rational business organization. Now this is most definitely not, as despairing politicians fighting for their collective survival would have you believe, a case of the privatization of governance. Do not be fooled. The privatization of governance would mean that pivotal and decisive authority over our lives, over the structure, workings and future of our society, would be handed over to private entities. It would mean that both 'What to do' with we the people and 'How to do it' will be re-surrendered to kingships in modern garb. Unallowably it would mean these life-defining, society-defining and indeed history-defining decisions of 'What to do' with we the people and 'How to do it' will be beholden to, will solely be made, with the overarching goal of business—profit maximization—in mind. But this is not the privatization of governance. When the characteristically crooked politicians scream from parliaments and presidential palaces, talk shows and campaign rallies, that this is, do not be fooled; it is their last desperate collective death cry. Rest assured neither 'What to do' with we the people nor 'How to do it' will be decided by business organizations. Springing directly from our final rights, the blueprint component of our new system of societal management will establish exactly 'What to do' and its manual or 'How To' guide component as the name itself suggests will, in great detail, explain 'How to do it', leaving the business organization narrowly and only with the role of actually getting down to 'doing it'. Leaving it narrowly and only in the role of implementer. And there is no better entity to play the narrow role of implementer than the so specialized business organization. There is no better entity not despite of its singular pursuit of profit maximization, but indeed because of it. Where the narrow role of implementation in our new system of societal management is competitively tendered out for a flat fee, the only avenue through which the so specialized business organization that wins the tender can maximize profit is the tireless pursuit of efficiency in the processes of this implementation. This *is* the economic rationale behind privatization, and admittedly, what we would be attempting is privatization, but it still would not be the privatization of governance, only the privatization of implementation. And of course there will be checks and balances to ensure that profit maximization is being pursued through the desired means of tireless efficiency increases, through innovation and invention, not shortcuts and compromises. Checks and balances which themselves, due to the very same aforementioned economic rationale, will be most effective and efficient if outsourced to private audit firms. With the final check being administered by a social device which we already possess, a device whose vital role of keeping we the people informed is too a historical finality; this social device of course being the free media.

Imagine then that direct democracy rightfully presides over this efficient apparatus of implementation. That, for every decision above that of day-to-day implementation and about the very choice of implementers themselves, for every decision that concerns the 'What to do', yet whose answer cannot be found in our blueprint of societal management, for every decision of real governance that charts the course and determines the moral and material destination of our society, we the people are polled through regular referenda. That we the people, now well capable and sufficiently informed, now ready, now deserving, are, for the first time in history, finally granted true self-governance. Imagine there's new countries.

13

AS ZEN put the book down, through the dusty haze of his ever swirling thought scraps something appeared out in the not too distant abstractness. A bridge, a bridge between Ports' Post Politica and the realms. And as the dusty haze of thoughts settled momentarily, Zen could see the bridge a bit clearer, albeit still unsupported on one end. As if to see in the tangible world what he could not quite see in the abstract, Zen walked to the tiny glimpse of OmniRealm offered by his window and continued to search in vain for the bridge's missing support.

Through avenues parted by quick stares at the ghastly scab on his forehead that was replacing his Embed, Zen took his morning commute to Bernays's office.

"Ha! Interesting, a range of realms for hippies, very interesting. Interesting but dangerous though!" surmised Bernays as Zen entered. "It all rests on the cultural specs," he declared, "most of all… most importantly what is to be done about religion" he emphasized to the generic looking assistant.

"Ah, Zen have a seat" welcomed Bernays.

"Yes you see," recommenced Bernays, his sharp little eyes stealing a glance at Zen and then returning to the assistant, "the problem is, hippies are for our intents and purposes at least, only a group by exclusion. In fact in the pre-world, as I am sure our young Zen here will back me up, any non-adherent to one of the major religions is labeled off a hippie!"

"Right, Director" agreed the assistant, "According to VestaRealm they've created something called Kessey's Canon to get around the absence of a major religion"

"Kessey's Canon!" burst out Bernays arching his furry white eyebrows and bringing to centre-stage two boiling black wells of disapproval,

"They just don't get it. You can't simply… out of the blue, come up with a citisumer guide without divine sanction; and let alone divine sanction, one without any transcendent sanction whatsoever!"

The assistant duly placed a cross in the checkbox labeled 'Citisumer Guide' on the holographic scratch pad that his Embed was projecting and attached to it a terse voice note consisting of only the words 'No divine or transcendent sanction'. Zen was riveted.

"No, no, no, it is definitely an interesting idea," continued Bernays, his liver-spotted neck sails flapping, "but if they can't find a legitimate divine or transcendent sanction for it that resonates across the hippie segment, I'm afraid that I will have to present my case against it at the next realm providers meeting. In any case, even if I don't, left to their own accord I doubt whether the required majority of other realm providers will give their consent to a realm devoid of the requisite religious sanction. And of course, ours is a democratic world so whatever a majority of realm providers decide in favor of is *ipso facto* right"

Pins and needles of nervousness and excitement frenzied about Zen's body. This was the first time he had heard any citisumer use that word, it was the first time he had heard anyone other than Muthu and Ports use that word. Did Bernays know? His eyes hadn't made any special effort to turn toward Zen when he had said it, but still. The assistant duly entered the voice note 'Director-General will argue against, even if not realm providers will decide against'.

"So what of the other cultural specs?" inquired Bernays impatiently.

"Well," started the assistant gesturing his scratch pad aside.

"What is their spec on marijuana?" interrupted Bernays cutting to the chase.

"It is allowed. And here are the rest…"

"Forget about the rest of the specs, this poses yet another problem" broke in Bernays curtly, "Ah VestaRealm! As always the maverick" he remarked, a glint of adoration, as that of a parent's for a mischievous child, twinkling in his eyes, "Most of the time it's a good thing, why it was their freewheeling attitude that led them to add MeScape and now of course all the other realm providers are following suit. But not marijuana and certainly not LSD. In fact, what is their spec on hallucinogens?"

"Allowed as well" confirmed the assistant.

"That won't do, that won't do at all" boomed Bernays conclusively.

What his words could not—Why? Why?—begged Zen's eyes.

"They should know better than that" admonished Bernays, "Citisumers ascend to the realms to FREE themselves from belief and thought pollution. Why on earth would they want something which returns them to a helpless state of sloshing around in the thought muck?"

The assistant duly placed a cross each in the checkboxes labelled 'Marijuana' and 'LSD'.

"And the other cultural specs?" prompted Bernays.

"Well, they've got 'Free Love'" began the assistant.

"Not a problem, SoulMate will take care of that nicely" put in Bernays.

"...and 'Non-Violence'" the assistant continued listing.

"Not a problem"

"...and 'Eco-Friendliness'"

"Not a problem"

"...and most realms in the proposed range have got 'Vegetarianism'" the assistant finished up.

"A task for KrocRonald's and his friends" rounded off Bernays neatly, "Surprising, knowing VestaRealm, that they didn't try to play around with participation!" he added jocularly.

Obliged to, the assistant smiled, and Zen to fit in followed suit.

"No, in all seriousness, exactly as I thought, the other cultural specs are just fine," resumed Bernays, "actz & ens can definitely be designed to realize them. But no realm provider can be allowed to alter the operating system specs of the realms. I hope you make this clear to VestaRealm"

"Yes, Director" affirmed the assistant and added the voice note 'Reiterate realm provider cannot alter OS specs'.

"Right, well I have to visit Rainbow Cross" informed Bernays setting in trembling motion the process of getting to his feet, "Now that's an example of how to smartly configure a realm" he declared admiringly, "And Zen you will be accompanying me"

As their pod descended Zen left the side of Bernays, who had nodded off the moment the old shrivel of loose skin had sunk into the enormous cushiony lap of the leather reclining seat reserved exclusively for him. Bernays, now several dribbles of drool drying crustily over each other in flesh channels around the downturned corners of his mouth, hadn't told Zen anything about Rainbow Cross. So he was eager to see for himself this realm the Director-General of OmniRealm seemed to hold in such high regard.

Through the cabin window a bedazzling rainbow striped flag fluttered against the horizon. At its center a black crucifix offered solemn contrast to the loud scream of colors bordering it and from the middle of the crucifix the words 'by Kudos' contained in a dialog box spelled itself out in a loop. The pod made its first bump against the landing bay. Zen looked to see if this would wake Bernays, but it didn't, so he waited to see if a few more bumps and screeches would resuscitate the flagging old know-bag back to life. When this didn't either, he approached the leather throne.

"Um director, we've landed" he tried several times. Still he got no response. Reluctant to poke the fragile apparition, after a pause Zen tried again, "Director, we've landed". Just before Zen reached to gently tap Bernays's shoulder, his eyelids suddenly flung open to reveal the duo of beady black bulbs, burning so brightly that they belied the deep slumber they only just switched back on from.

Zen, helping Bernays, they alighted from the pod directly into Rainbow Cross's Admin tower. With great reverential fanfare, Bernays was greeted by its participators who escorted him into the office of their director. Zen, asked to wait outside, sauntered to the edge of the glass epidermis of the tower, expecting to see some dressing up of the typical realm configuration. Sure enough there was Rainbow Cross laid out basically the same as NirvanaLand and MyRealm, and Zen was sure, most or all other realms. Costumed with luminescent hot pink and a tinseling of the other florid colors of its flag, its towers and its trees tried to scream a flamboyant exhibitionist euphoria, but for Zen this was nothing more than cellophane over the sameness. And then more of the same—the carnally oscillating squircles of SoulMate pranced forth. Just as Zen was dismissively turning away from the glass epidermis, what he was sure was a meaningless pattern nevertheless momentarily distracted him. As he gave it a second look, a gush of vomit from the pit of his stomach squirted into the back of his mouth. Only men. Each and every squircle contained only men. Only men, mostly in that position. The clumpy acidy disgust still in his mouth, Zen masochistically focused in on one hairy, sweaty, muscly, deviant, sinful oscillatory mounting after another. And as he did, after swallowing his disgust, just as vomit had squirted into his mouth, a thought involuntarily squirted into his mind. His MyRealm I would never make him see anything like this, anything even remotely leading up to this, for this revolting abomination did not exist in MyRealm, and how rightfully so. And from this thought seed quickly another vexatious thought shoot sprung out. What had he done! What had he got himself into! Why, why, why had he got himself out of MyRealm I!

He didn't want to admit that he was wrong all over again about the realms, that it was nothing more intellectually profound than impetuosity and immaturity that had made him throw it all away. But his revulsion at the belief pollution oscillating in front of him was graphically, compellingly, nauseatingly mounting its case. Habitually, Zen felt for the book down in his right trouser pocket, but of course, the book was safely tucked away in his apartment.

A few moments of introspective back and forth between the realms and Ports' alternatives later, Zen felt a presence behind him.

"A truly ingenious realm, don't you think?" bubbled Bernays.

Zen still didn't understand why Bernays held this place in such high esteem. Other than that the specs viscerally disgusted him more than the specs of any other realm he had seen, other than that they disgusted him more than he could have ever imagined any spec could, everything else seemed to pretty much follow the same formula.

"Oh yes, yes, yes, this is undoubtedly the way forward" enthused Bernays, gesturing Zen to come to his side. "They have segmented on religion which is of course mandatory but then, then…" he explained, lifting his index finger to his face and shaking it to emphasize his point, "they have re-segmented on sexual orientation! Now all realms re-segment, but until now it's always been on some belief spec that is not nearly as natural… as fundamental… as defining… as sexual orientation"

"But don't some…" Zen began to question.

"I know, I know what you're going to say" interrupted Bernays, " 'There are plenty of realms that allow homosexuality' and there are, but Rainbow Cross doesn't simply allow it, as you can see. Oh no, no, no, they go far beyond just allowing it. They take this natural, fundamental, defining attribute and give it pride of place (just under religion of course), pride of second place so to say, and then they allow this and religion to inspire the design of the entire realm. Look around you Zen, gayness inspires everything from the buildings to the goods & services"

"Uh…" Zen didn't know what to say.

"And 'Kudos' to them for pioneering the way forward" chortled Bernays, his eyes affixing on Zen's, expectantly waiting to see if his punning had registered.

Zen quickly acknowledged receipt with an obliging smile.

"And you know," resumed Bernays, his eyes zooming back out and looking beyond Zen as if into the future, "many other realm providers are following suit" he announced approvingly, "Why, Realmway just recently submitted a proposal for a realm of scientologist orphans"

"Scientologist orphans? You mean…"

"Imagine," Bernays went on, his eyes floating further away into contemplation, "your entire world—the way it works, the way it looks and feels, the promises it makes to you, the joy it lets you see and the pain it doesn't—grows from the ever fertile soil of your most defining attribute; the fork in your life's road that has made all the difference". Bernays's eyes luxuriated in the fantastical thought, leaving time and Zen long behind.

Finally, abruptly, they zoomed back in on Zen, "Just imagine Zen," he resumed with a more pragmatic vigor, "an orphan will never again feel the emptiness of seeing a friend abound in the limitless love of their parents, they will never hear the word 'parent' in the lacking sense, they…"

Impulsively, Zen grabbed his opportunity, "But this realm can't last" he quickly spurted out, "When the orphans themselves have children, these children won't be orphans" he hurriedly explained before Bernays could interrupt him. But Bernays didn't butt in. So, at a far more deliberate pace, he reasoned, "Unless of course… you add a cultural spec that they can't have children"

Bernays's eyes squinted, sizing, re-sizing Zen up; his thumb and forefinger slowly clasping together, repetitively scrunched the loose wad of flesh that was his chin.

"This is the precise problem that I have with MayoRealm's proposed amputee series" broke out Bernays from his reappraising pose, his head straightening, his eyes widening, "How are they going to manage the non-amputee offspring that will inevitably result? This is the question they haven't satisfactorily answered as yet you see. The solution they have come up with thus far is to only allow the adoption of child amputees but this requires the imposition of some fundamental restrictions, for which… for which it is difficult, if not impossible to convince people that there could be religious sanction from any of the mainstream religions on offer"

"And," Zen eagerly interjected, "amputees would hardly meet the wellness criteria would they?"

"Ah, and that of course is the other limb!" Bernays remarked.

"It is indeed time" replied Bernays to the young man with the purple cockatoo hairdo who was waiting to escort Bernays to the next stop on his tour. "There is only so much you can learn about this wonderful realm from here Zen, let's go" rallied Bernays, seemingly energized by the just concluded tête-à-tête with Zen.

"Uh, Director you will need to… uh… go through makeup first" informed the cockatoo haired man timidly.

"Oh yes, absolutely" agreed Bernays, and then turned to Zen, "You see, not only is it an ingenious idea, it is meticulously executed"

Just as Bernays said this, a vivacious pageant of men gaited into the room. At their lead was a plump middle-aged man in a pink leather cat-suit brazenly interrupted here and there by black fish-net cutouts.

"Oooh, let's get to it boys" he shrilled, looking at Zen and Bernays and signaling to his troop of merry men.

A tortuous half-hour or so of snips, of pulls and tugs, rubs, and colorful brush strokes later, Zen could no longer avoid a good look at himself in the mirror. Instantly a sensation that somehow he wasn't looking at himself shot through Zen, before the skin squirming acknowledgment set in that he looked exactly like a typical Rainbow Cross man, right up to the pink and blue cockatoo hairdo.

"You'll look a sight in this" promised the plump makeup torturer with a wink, showing a cat-suit, much like his own, to Zen through the mirror. Zen immediately looked for Bernays to get himself out of having to get into that thing. But when he despairingly turned back and located him, there he was sitting pretty, smiling broadly, reveling in the experience of it all, a psychedelic neon cat-suit hanging baggily from his hunched drooping skeleton. On seeing this, completely against the prevailing current of his disgust, accompanied by a hiss of air from his nose, a chuckle as insuppressible as an unexpected sneeze broke out from Zen.

For the rest of the day the whistle stop tour around Rainbow Cross wore on, with Bernays far more than observing and offering advice, mostly doling out hearty praise and congratulations along the way. And Zen, though alertly searching, not finding anything remarkable about the place beneath its garish cellophane.

"Your director informed me that you have been tracking the phenomenon that I asked him to pay special attention to" stated a visibly tired Bernays as they reentered the pod, "I am eager to see this before we leave"

"Yes Director, we have" confirmed an assistant.

Instinctively almost, Zen's mind honed in on the conversation as if intuiting that it was what it had been waiting for all day long.

"We have quite a few cases" explained the assistant, "All gleaned from iTime therapy and confession"

Zen got closer to read the title of the folder that the assistant was drawing out from his Embed. It read 'Cases of Doubted Sexuality'. The assistant then gestured to life a hologram of a young man, in whom Zen, before he even began speaking, instantly recognized a lot of himself in.

"Dr. Milk," started the young man his face rumpled by self-doubt and despair, "Hermès has been in Rainbow Cross for like six months now, but hasn't gotten on SoulMate yet!" he confided.

"Go on Hermès" replied Dr. Milk the archetypal iTime therapist albeit wrapped in the garish cellophane of Rainbow Cross.

"Yeah... and it's not that Hermès couldn't find anyone to get Hermès's fifteen-on either" the young man explained, seemingly comforted a touch by the avuncular tone of the archetypal iTime therapist.

Bernays's eyes zoomed in on the holographic incarnation of the young man as they did when Zen had titillated his intellect.

"It's... uh... more like..." stuttered the young man, "that... uh... Hermès doesn't really feel anything, you know" he finished, looking up at Milk yearning for empathy.

"How does that make Hermès feel?" queried Milk matter-of-factly.

Zen's face snarled with scorn at Milk.

"It... it, uh..." despaired the young man, "makes Hermès doubt...", a tormented pause as if the admission wanted to come out but was constipated followed.

"Go on Hermès" urged Milk.

"When Hermès was in the pre-world everybody made fun of Hermès" explained the young man, indicating with a top-to-bottom sweeping motion of his hands that it had something to do with his body.

Zen's eyes, in sync with Bernays's, immediately started scanning downwards from Hermès's silky straight fringe of hair and delicate, almost ornamental, features, to his narrow shoulders, soft marshmallow nipples and slender hips.

"They'd chant 'HOMO, HOMO... FAG, FAG' every time Hermès left Hermès's hut" he continued, his eyes clenching and his lips pursing in relapsing pain, "They would say things to Hermès's mother when she walked Hermès to work, but she always held Hermès's hand tighter and walked like she didn't hear a thing. It hurt Hermès's father more though. But they both understood. They wanted Hermès to ascend to Rainbow Cross, they knew that Rainbow Cross was Hermès"

"See that's good, go on, remember to keep focusing on Hermès" Milk chimed in.

"But now Hermès is here, and Hermès does loves Rainbow Cross," assured the young man, "the actz & ens, the whole realm, it's amazing, it's everything Kudos promised it would be. And Hermès was even blessed with a participation only a few months after ascending! But the doubt won't let Hermès get on SoulMate…"

"And Director this goes on for a few sessions" interrupted the assistant, gesturing to life another hologram of Hermès and fast-forwarding to his point of emphasis.

Bernays, head pointing upwards, was scrunching his chin in his customary fashion.

"But then Director, just a few weeks later" broke in the assistant, swiping rapidly ahead.

"Hermès feels it passing Doctor" confided the young man, "It was just adjusting to Hermès's new Life without Hermès's parents that's all, and that's totally normal"

"Go on Hermès… See that's good, go on, remember keep focusing on Hermès" encouraged Milk. A vision of strangling Milk flashed before Zen's eyes.

"Hermès feels like the true Hermès is coming out… FINALLY" exhaled the young man, "It's like Hermès couldn't get Hermès's fifteen-on until now because somewhere deep inside that chant 'HOMO, HOMO… FAG, FAG' and the terrible things they did to Hermès still scared Hermès, that's all. It wasn't because Rainbow Cross wasn't Hermès. It wasn't. It really wasn't"

"And then Director have a look at this," broke in the assistant intently, "just a few weeks later"

"What a fabulous realm Rainbow Cross is" shrilled Hermès with a happy flick of his hand, "How silly was Hermès to doubt anything.

126

Hermès has totally sponged off all that 'belief pollution' as you like to call it Docterrrrr. Here, take a look at Hermès's first time on SoulMate"

That thought seed was fertilized back into life and from it second-thoughts flourished; Zen couldn't help but wonder if a second-wind of faith, the kind that Hermès had, wouldn't have been better for himself in the long-run.

"Brilliant, absolutely brilliant" boomed Bernays, lifting his right hand to about face level and closing its upturned fingers tightly together as if he were holding upon them a priceless gem.

"Yes Director, what a transformation" agreed the assistant obsequiously with the others assistants providing a backdrop of concurring nods.

"Oh no, no, no" disagreed Bernays, his head shaking, his liver-spotted neck sails flapping, "Not a transformation, oh no; but this does show just how well you are operating this realm"

Flattered, the assistants coyly smiled in their thanks to Bernays, whose eyes had already floated away on a waft of thought. Intuitively, Zen drew closer to Bernays.

"This is what all realms should aspire to mass engineer..." he declared, his gaze still averted from the assistants, "a fundamental underlying premise of the realms... a fundamental underlying *promise* of the realms" he smirked almost secretly to himself.

'What is it?', 'What is it?' Zen yearned to ask as he drew even closer to Bernays as if to eavesdrop on the Director-General's thoughts.

"What is it?" the words uncontrollably blurted out from Zen.

Bernays turned to Zen, his eyes burning, seeking to brand the answer on to Zen's mind, "Why, it is post-purchase rationalization my dear Zen, Post-Purchase Rationalization!"

14

PHOSPHENES OF meaning, shards of feeling unveiled to him his once perfect her, painted nails of MassageMe reached out embracing him in righteous LifeTree roots. She whispered sweet-nothings of actz & ens, that Allah a wanted man ran free through streets of 'I', where yellowing ideas blew about, chased but never caught by aging men. On her knees he had again his perfect Maya, and as he did and did, there she was shriveling for all to see; wrinkling, old, she turned, for him and all to see, there he was shriveling for all to see. It was him and his mother for all to see, it was him and his mother for all to see!

With a heaving gasp Zen sprung awake; ashamed, anxious. As though it were real, as though it somehow had pushed a rewind button in his mind, he got up searching for the crucifix his mother had given him when he ascended. In his duffel bag, no. Amongst the hundreds of things on his messy dressing table, no. Under his bed maybe, no. In that empty cupboard surely, yes—right there wrapped in its own chain, right next to the book. He took both out and settled back into his sweat moistened pillow. Atop his chest he placed the book, and atop it he placed the crucifix, fingerings its beads, its sharpish metal edges, and the man nailed prostrate to it, whom he felt he no longer knew. And as he did, he fought this new vista that had been dawning since he met Bernays, no, dawning ever since he had started reading the book. He winced his mind's eyes once more, tighter, but the rays of understanding were too bright or perhaps it was he himself that desperately wanted to peep, to let the rays in. Regardless, Zen could no longer deny that he wasn't disgusted by Muthu's godlessness anymore, that he found it no more abominable than any other beliefs he had encountered. Most of all, Zen could no longer deny that he felt a bit of it himself.

The next morning, still wrestling with flashes of last night's shame and the implications that lay ahead now that there was no looking back, Zen, bleary eyed, headed for Bernays. And Bernays was already in full flow.

"Proverbs, adages, aphorisms… a rose by any other name" Bernays sang and chuckled, "I love them all, oh yes, yes, yes, they are like prod… actz & ens you see" he explained to his usual gathering of apostles.

A weary Zen took his place beside Bernays, hoping that his tardiness wouldn't be noticed.

"Just like actz & ens, some of them are useful in everyday life" Bernays set off on one of his impassioned lectures, "You know like 'A warranty guarantees tranquility' or 'Everyone is an island'. And far, far, far and away beyond their boring functional uses, just like actz & ens, many of them have a much more magical potential. You see… for instance take 'The Greatest Risk is Not Taking One'. Now this is recited by nevertheless the most risk-averse pussyfooters every time they— 'throwing caution to the wind'—so much as eat a one day past expiry pack of biscuits. And every time they recite it, though they are in reality nudging only negligibly this way or that, well, well within their comfort zone—What does it conjure up?"

The apostles, not quite getting that Bernays meant this as more than a rhetorical question, stood there attentively waiting for his answer.

"Well, what does it conjure up?" he asked again, before needing no second-invitation to answer himself, "It conjures up notions of bold 'devil may care' adventurousness of course. Far, far out of proportion to the insignificant little change-of sock-color nudge that they have effected. And… and on top of this magical reward they get the sweet icing of doing something (actually just believing that they're doing it) that is consensually agreed by everyone to be admirable and awesome. Something grand from nothing—hey presto—THAT'S MAGIC!"

Expressions of processing something difficult contorted some of the apostles' faces, while others were obviously merely marveling at Bernays's oratory, sure in the truth that he was waxing eloquent about something important.

"No, no… clichés are not things which have lost their impact because of overuse" Bernays insisted, "Oh no, no, no… the more widely, the more commonly they are recited their potential magic oomph only grows. Each recitation is, if you like, another straw that brings us closer to breaking the camel's back!"

"Um, Director have you had time to…" an apostle tried to ask.

"In those days," carried on Bernays heedlessly, " 'Think Outside the Box' was in vogue. Every time anyone suggested so much as moving from staples to paper clips, they would feel they were swashbuckling free-thinkers and believe they had the encouragement and admiration of society at large. Anyhow, what was it that you were going to ask me?"

"Um… what you feel about our new proverb, Director" answered the apostle.

"So go on tell me, what is it?"

" 'Opposites Detract' " chorused the apostles in an impromptu unison that Zen found comically absurd.

"Ummm, 'Opposites Detract', 'Opposites Detract' " Bernays mused scrunching his chin, "I can certainly see its everyday functionality and obviously anything recited often enough will give it the societal sanction element. And it's certainly catchy and simple enough to be easily remembered and regularly recited. But… but the only question is… what specific grandiose promises does it make to the individual?"

"Um… Director, well it does implicitly emphasize that everything the individual is, is right and whole" ventured an apostle, "That the individual doesn't need any other, different citisumers to complement themselves"

"Yes," agreed another apostle, emboldened by her peer's first foray, "and more simply, this is not a promise though, it's more a warning. The word 'detracts' makes the individual fear that association with other, dissimilar citisumers will detract—take away—from themselves"

Zen sank into a sudden disconsolateness.

"Very good, excellent, excellent" congratulated Bernays, "This depth of insight is exactly what I expect from you. Go ahead, go ahead, you will get no 'opposing detraction' from me"

As the apostles basked in Bernays's hearty approval like greenhorn saplings in the morning sun, Zen realized the cause of his sudden sink into disconsolateness. This was the first occasion in his time in the realms and OmniRealm that he didn't understand, more so that he didn't understand but his peers, the apostolic assistants, did.

The weeks passed with Zen at Bernays's side gleaning, inferring the canon that the apostolic assistants had mastered. Frustratingly, Bernays for his part never sat Zen down and spelled (or since it was Bernays punned) it out to him. Though his regular glances at Zen during his daily sermons made it obvious they were, in part at least, for his education.

Over a lunch of KosherKing burger & fries, he lay there musing, his back against a brand-fruit tree. The yarmulke shaped arrangement of SoulMate squircles, all featuring carnally oscillating mini-characters, hardly perturbing him. Perhaps one of these days Bernays would visit New Caliphate he hoped, but then again Bernays was only interested in new realms, or more precisely new realm ideas. And in any case, even if he met her, what would be the point? But who's to say that Maya couldn't understand what he was beginning to? If only she were evicted and blacklisted too, surely then he had a chance of making her understand. But even if she was evicted and blacklisted, back in the pre-world how could he explain to someone as god fearing as Maya that he didn't find godlessness an abomination anymore? And even worse, that he felt a bit of it himself. A stray glance at SkyClock immediately collapsed his branching, digressing thought vine—it was time to get back to Bernays.

"Just in time Zen" greeted Bernays, "Tell me what is wrong with this" he quizzed, guiding his index finger across a sentence that floated in front of the both of them and the following of apostles that had congregated around Bernays.

Zen read it slowly to himself, 'Small and Beautiful just like You', gritting his intellectual teeth, determined to figure it out, he read it again and again to himself, 'Small and Beautiful just like You', 'Small and Beautiful just like You'.

A silence, which Zen so hoped he would be the first to break, ensued.

"Will it be more powerful," Bernays began, turning to the following of apostles, "if you see some symbol of god, HaShem, or if you see god?" he asked bombastically.

"It will be more powerful if you see God" chirped a tiny little apostle.

"Precisely" replied Bernays, glee at the elegance of his imminent summation smiling through, "This is why your wonderful realm's tagline, its credo, should be' Small is Beautiful is Me'.

Zen got it, the apostles jotted it.

"Similes are like a cat flap, citisumers may come and go as they please," observed Bernays, making a cheeky smirk to somewhere out in the distance, "but metaphors… metaphors are a cat trap!"

Zen peered out through the glass epidermis, out as far as where Bernays's eyes had floated off to, while the eager little beavers surrounded the old sage to pick his brain. And as he stared into and right through the yarmulke of SoulMate squircles teeming with little people doing it, as though children playfully wrestling, a thought quite apart from Bernays's most recent insight digressed Zen. Obviously he felt a bit of it, a bit of godlessness, after all everyone he knew, his friends and mentors old and new, dead and nearly so—Ports, Muthu and he was sure Bernays—were all godless. They were all godless, and they knew things; and more and more it seemed, that they were godless *because* they knew things.

"Zen, Zen" called Bernays as he plodded free of the little bustle of keenness that surrounded him, "It's time for us to go"

As their pod descended and he saw again that sordid mounting of squircles and the proud rainbow flag fluttering in the horizon, a curious feeling of accomplishment satisfied Zen. There was no clumpy gush of acidy disgust this time, just a lingering disapproval coolly compartmentalized.

Zen had noticed a likely fatigue induced grumpiness in Bernays as he trudged through the pleasantries and obligatory meetings at the admin tower. And now that the initial crest of accomplishment had long since subsided, and this was a realm he knew all too well, there was nothing much to see or do other than sit around and wait for Bernays.

Finally, Bernays emerged from what Zen hoped was his last meeting surrounded by his usual following of assistants. Mercifully none of whom Zen recognized from last time and all of whom had abandoned the cockatoo hairdo for the equally garish multicolored one-eye-obscuring fringe.

"Right, let's get to those tox scans" ordered Bernays.

Immediately an alacritous assistant almost tore his tight tinsel yellow cat-suit summoning the requested information.

"As... uh... as, uh, you can see Director-General Bernays" quavered the assistant, clearly hoping for the best and fearful of the worst, "Less than ten percent of the tox scans show unacceptable levels of belief pollution"

"Let me see one of these tox scans" commanded Bernays loudly, his eyes squinting in disbelief.

As the tinseled congregation braced themselves, the put-on-the-spot assistant nervously assembled several levitating video bubbles and gestured to life-size the first in the series.

"Okay, Givench," began the interviewer, "starting entirely from scratch and using anything—words, sounds, pictures, anything—create and describe your very own realm. And take your time". With this the interviewer smiled at the subject and left the room.

Suddenly the sameness was broken. Zen's attention was grabbed.

"Have you finished?" asked the interviewer as he reentered the room.

"Yup" Givench yelped in high-pitched delight, "Givench's very, very own realm" he presented with an extravagant unveiling ta-da gesture.

The interviewer graciously accepted Givench's holographic orb and began to unravel it, carefully examining as he did, its layout and bringing his pierced ears closer to it several times to intently listen to the sounds going on within it.

The gazes of the tinseled congregation, peeking through their multicolored fringes, fixated on Bernays, breathless, hoping for some inkling of so-far-so-good from the saggy standard-bearer.

After swiveling, twisting, dissecting and inspecting Givench's orb in every which way, the interviewer pushed it a fair distance away from his eyes to get a birds-eye view.

Suddenly, as he looked at the familiar panorama, garish cellophane and all, Zen got an unmistakable cue about what exactly a tox scan diagnosed.

The interviewer gave Givench's orb a last summarizing once-over and began to enter something in the boxes attached to the checklist items. As he did, the checklist item and what he was entering appeared in large letters, superimposed on the holographic screening.

Visual Purity, *9* out of 10

Aural Purity, *8* out of 10

Document evidence of contaminating visual or aural pollutants and/or oddities, if any—*None*

"Good stuff" remarked the interviewer, looking back up at Givench, "Now tell Marc about *your* cultural specs, Givench"

"Well, obviously Givench has got gayness down" he started with a giggle.

"Obviously!" agreed the interviewer in a matching lighthearted tone placing a tick near the relevant cultural spec.

"…and male-gay only adoption"

"Of course" agreed the interviewer placing another tick.

"…and SoulMate all the way! Wooo"

"Right"

"…aaaaaand divorce"

"Right"

"…yes to porn, of course"

"Of course"

"…oh, oh and of course Progressive Anglicanism" added Givench, "That goes without saying, doesn't it?" he qualified, smiling at the interviewer searching for agreement.

"Ahem," interrupted the assistant, stopping the holographic screening, "in this case as in seventy-two percent of all cases Director-General, subjects reported a perfect eight out of eight for cultural purity… um, on the major specs"

The tinseled congregation and Zen cravingly awaited the impending pronouncement that seemed to teeter on Bernays's hanging lower lip.

"And your tox scans were conducted—as per OmniRealm guidelines—exclusively on evictees?" verified Bernays somewhat anticlimactically.

"Yes, Director-General," confirmed an assistant, who by the way he came forward, Zen deduced was responsible for assuring this, "but…"

"We often find," interrupted Bernays, overbearingly using his raised palm to abruptly full-stop the assistant midsentence, "that unwilling evictees, you know those who desperately want to stay in their chosen realm but who, usually for some participation-related reason, can no longer do so, are motivated to supply answers and select options that they feel their interviewers and realm administrators are looking for. You know, in the hope that this might help with avoiding eviction"

"But…" tried the assistant again.

"We can't of course do anything to shake the blissfully settled thought-dust of citisumers," carried on Bernays heedlessly, "so we can't try tox scans on citisumers that aren't being evicted, which means that we must accept the fallibility of the results we get"

"But…" tried the assistant yet again, appearing to have lost none of his patience, and this time he got his chance, "many of the subjects that we ran our tox scans on, including the one you just saw, had been diagnosed with terminal or evict-level diseases by their regular wellness checks but hadn't been told of this until the tox scans were completed. We selected them for the tox scans, especially because of this"

"Ah!" exclaimed Bernays, his furry white and brown brows arching, a slight smile of admiration at the ingenuity of it all making an appearance amongst the wrinkly loose flesh at the corners of his mouth. After a thoughtful pause, "Your selection of subjects to run the tox scans is, without doubt, a gem of a stratagem" he remarked, "but of course the best gauge of imagination infiltration into a realm is to test its children"

"Yes, that's right Director-General," agreed the assistant signaling another to retrieve holographic proof, "and we have"

Thoroughly engrossed, Zen had sat down at a desk not too far from Bernays and placing one of his elbows on its surface he was supporting his slanted head on the open palmed end of his forearm.

Up popped the hologram. A sparkling of little boys sat on rainbow hued beanbags restlessly giggling in a room dotted with cheery characters, all of whom, to Zen's surprise, he recognized. An oversized chubby character in a wooly bright purple suit that framed a cherubic face with a triangular antenna on its head burst into the room, running from beanbag to beanbag handing out goodies. "A Kiss for you", "A Buttercup for you", "A Fun & Fun's for you", "A Sniggle for you", he or she (though given the realm, Zen figured it had to be a he) tweedled, as he gave them out.

"Hello kids" greeted the purple chubby cherub, after gaiting to the front of the room, "And may God bless you all"

"Hello Kinky Dinky" hollered the sparkling of boys in unison, "God Bless you Kinky Dinky"

"Okaaaay" hollered Kinky Dinky, "Today is going to be sooooo much of fun. Today, just like Kinky Dinky tells you stories about yourself every day, you—yes you… and you… and you, each of one of you—is going to tell your very own story!!!"

"YIPPEE" came the holler from the sparkling of boys.

A hologram of two children, roughly the same age, walking down what seemed to be an indistinct path appeared in front of each boy. One of them was androgynous while the other was quite clearly a girl, both were blandly dressed in a white t-shirt and shorts and wore no shoes. A sanatorium like whiteness pervaded the holographic world they inhabited.

"Okay kids, this is what you've gots to do" the purple chubby cherub started instructing with a merry little shimmy, "Tell the story of the two… in front of you"

"And this Director-General…" the assistant broke in, fast-forwarding to the results, "is what eighty-three percent of the subjects' stories were like"

The androgynous child, a multicolored fringe like that worn by the rest of the room tacked on to his forehead, white shorts and t-shirt replaced by glittery spandex shorts and vest, hopped from one leg to another, thumbs in ears, tongue wagging, mocking the little girl, whose clothes had turned into torn brown rags.

"And what do we have here?" inquired the purple chubby cherub, lovingly tousling one little boy's multicolored hair, making him promptly animate his creation.

"Na-na na-na boo-boo, you're from the pre-world," mocked the androgynous child, "you're from the pre-world, you're from the pre-world"

The purple chubby cherub stretched the hologram to get a better view. Zen, on seeing the transformation of the sanatorium-like whiteness into a child's impression of the garish cellophane wrapped panorama that stabbed through the glass epidermis of the admin tower, quickly ticked a mental checkbox of his own.

"Go back, go back" shouted the androgynous child, its face darkening and pouting with cruelty, "Go back to the dirty pre-world, Gerber's daddies said you were yuck. You're yuck, you're yuck"

Out of nowhere, sprang into the hologram two men, two generic realm mannequins dripping with garish cellophane. Zen and the purple chubby cherub ticked another one of their respective checkboxes. One of the mannequins lifted Gerber onto his shoulders and then both mockingly laughed at the little girl, who, except for the disheveling of her clothes remained unchanged and unanimated. Soon she was forgotten as the two mannequins strode off, Gerber smiling atop their shoulders. And then suddenly, the happy trio were striding toward a store, where, on a holographic background of familiar cartoon clouds, rolling green pastures and cows, in a jolly font, arced its name—SVEN & TERRY'S. The purple chubby cherub ticked another checkbox. Melting rainbow sprinkled treats in hand, the trio were soon heading toward yet another store. The sight of whose name, spelled in colorful playfully arranged letters with a distinctive wrong-way around one letter verb in between, even managed to cajole a reminiscing smile of childhood joy out of cynical Zen.

"Well done, well done, well done Gerber" sang the purple chubby cherub, tousling the little boy's multicolored hair again and giving him a congratulatory wrist flick before shimmying his way to the front of the room. "Now all you kids that got ten out of ten rainbows, come on up, come on up," instructed the purple chubby cherub gesticulating with his stubby arms whilst jumping up and down, "the best friend of this show—Creamy Queen—is taking you out for ice-creeeeeeam!"

137

Gerber furiously counted the small dazzling holographic rainbows that floated in a neat line in front of him—1, 2, 3, 4, 5, 6, 7, 8, 9—disbelieving the result he counted it again—1, 2, 3, 4, 5, 6, 7, 8, 9—and again—1, 2, 3, 4, 5, 6, 7, 8, 9—and as a sparkling scurry of little boys bum-rushed Kinky Dinky nearly hugging him off his feet, the quickly gathering storm of tear clouds on Gerber's crumpled face wailed forth.

"And just before you head off with our best friend Creamy Queen, let everyone here, and at home, and Kiddie NumLing, see your perfect stories" instructed the purple chubby cherub, regaining his balance after tottering in a dramatized Humpty-Dumptyish fashion.

The assistant stopped the hologram and along with the rest of the tinseled congregation refocused on Bernays, a tinge of relief evident in the way their chins ever so slightly rose to meet his response.

"There is, uh, there is…" Bernays returning after a long thought-flight sputtered to a start, "it is clear that the cause of your widespread citisumer dissatisfaction is not imagination infiltration. And so far it seems that neither has this citisumer dissatisfaction provoked imagination infiltration… SO FAR. Which just confirms my initial apprehensions about your realm model"

At once a collective gasp lifted the tightly clothed chests of the tinseled congregation.

"This is the problem with having a realm without a sun you see. And it is a fundamental problem" Bernays continued.

"Um… Director… sun?" asked an assistant, as thoroughly puzzled as Zen.

Shooting a look back at the assistant which Zen took to mean 'figure it out', "You see," restarted Bernays, "to your credit, you run this realm every bit as well as your main rival"

"Thank…" started an assistant.

"Well of course you do, since you have emulated them but mostly because you have sincerely flattered them… huh… imitated them at every turn" Bernays snickered, "In every tangible, in every operational and design related way, your realm is the same as theirs. One might argue that because you had an opportunity to learn from their mistakes, in some ways your realm is even better. But all that matters very little you see… well, it certainly matters less. You *can* make hay without the sun shining and you have, but the problem is that nobody will believe it is hay that you have made or at least they won't believe that your hay is as good"

"I don't understand," interjected Zen, unceremoniously stepping in between the tinseled congregation and Bernays, "just a few weeks ago you said that this was the perfect realm, that this was the way forward for all the realms"

Smiling broadly, almost lovingly at Zen and starting with a low hiss-hiss from only his nose, Bernays's shoulders began to bob and dance like boiling water; his neck sails flapping, soon the entire sagging old know-bag was vibrating with loud guffaws.

"Well that… well that," he struggled through the whoops of laughter, "well that makes my point perfectly doesn't it?"

"What point?" Zen asked brusquely.

"That this realm is exactly the same as…" started Bernays before pausing, turning toward the glass epidermis and pointing out into the horizon, "Why don't you see for yourself?"

Zen hastened to the glass epidermis and began perusing right through the garish cellophane. But sweep after sweep, zoom after zoom, he only grew more confused. Until he remembered 'the sun', 'the sun', 'maybe it's got something to do with the sun'. Immediately, he looked up from the garish cellophane, skimming past the bedazzling rainbow striped flag fluttering against the horizon, but as he did, his eyes autonomously registered a hunch of oddness. Instantaneously they doubled back and zoomed in. From the flag's center the black crucifix still offered solemn contrast to the loud scream of colors bordering it—but there was no Kudos insignia. Instead, cowering almost, on the horizontal axis of the crucifix, only the bare name 'Rainbow X'. Zen got it. He stood there eyes and mind widening.

Bernays had approached from behind. Placing a hand on Zen's shoulder and peering squarely into the soul of the flag along with Zen, he asked rhetorically, "What is a realm, what is any act or en, without a Brand-Sun?"

15

AND AS they walked, rising on a scintillating pixel mist that drizzled out from every pore of every thing, arose fractions and fragments of him—unwanted, forgotten, halcyon; arose failures and figments of him—shameful, painful, dreamt and yearned. Twirling and tangoing, his defining dust settled softly anointing him the lord of the landscape from whence it came.

"Told you" exclaimed Donatella as they sat down, "It's amazing isn't it? This is why Director Bernays insisted that you try it out"

Zen didn't answer. The contours and configuration of the park they were making their way through, a park he had walked through many a morning on his way to Bernays, were all the same. But as he walked by, the grass though not its texture, the brand-fruit trees though not their brand-fruits, the water fountains, the light poles and seemingly every permanent feature, down to the very bench (though not its feel) he was now sitting on, appeared to transform. And now Zen was confronted by a colossal naked marble statue of himself, weight preponderant on one tensed leg, holding the MyRealm I crucifix in its bent opposite arm.

"It's all the rage in the realms" marveled Donatella, "According to Director Bernays—'You won't be able to leave home with it' "she chuckled, as if along with Bernays.

"Ah" acknowledged Zen, trying to avoid the phallic confrontation in front of him by looking beyond it into the horizon where the OmniRealm leminiscate and SoulMate still presided untransformed.

"What are you doing?" asked Donatella with a tone verging on disapproval as Zen poked about the settings of his new mandatory Embed placed on his left forearm, "It's already synced, you can't turn the app off"

"Ugh, okay" snorted Zen giving up, "Let's go, the Director must be waiting for us"

Zen, trudging as though in a bog of himself, Donatella, swimming as though in a clear sun drenched pool of herself, they headed toward Bernays, when suddenly Zen stopped and looked quizzically back at Donatella.

"What are you?" he asked, his face freezing its quizzical expression.

Donatella, lost in a song and a music video hologram of herself, didn't hear.

"What… are… you?" Zen repeated loudly.

"What?" asked Donatella, "Oh, Donatella is Eastern Orthodox"

"But…"; Zen thought for a few seconds, "How does that work in OmniRealm?"

"Donatella goes back to Synod Spire whenever Donatella is rostered off" she replied, "Synod Spire is by VestaRealm" she added reverentially.

"Oh" said Zen, though the conundrum of Donatella's religion was not nearly resolved in his mind.

"And this makes it sooooo much better" continued Donatella, blithely pirouetting and sweeping her arms in a wide arc to indicate her surroundings, oblivious that Zen was enmeshed in a visual world very much his own.

As though his thought train hit an impenetrable wall of trivial bricks, an impact of frustration reverberated through Zen. There was no point trying to figure things out by asking Donatella or any other citisumer. Only Bernays knew. But Bernays only offered a darn one step-forward-two steps-back self-learning course.

There was no sense in disturbing the old know-bag's deep drooling and snoring, might as well take Bernays right home, decided Zen when the pod's console inquired about the specific location to disembark. Soon they landed, but before awaking Bernays, Zen wanted to sneak a peek at Bernays's neighborhood tower. No doubt being no less than the Director-General of OmniRealm it would be spectacularly endowed with everything under every brand-sun, he thought. But then again, this was Bernays, who knew? As an extra precaution tiptoeing to the cabin window, Zen opened it.

His face instantaneously arranged itself into a bewildered 'What the??' expression. He surveyed the bizarre asymmetrical panorama concertedly, his head tilting as he zeroed in on its odd outcrops, yet head nor tail was forthcoming. So he returned to the console to double-check if this was in fact Bernays's neighborhood tower. It was, and a glance at his left forearm reconfirmed as much. Self-learning was how Bernays liked to do it, so self-learning is how it would be done! Zen tiptoed to the hatch and frisked down its steps.

Morning was still sleepily opening its flooding orange eye, but set against its mauve and indigo brush stroked sky, Zen was assured in the intuition that this place was neither a realm, the pre-world nor OmniRealm. It was the bold forms, the daring individuality of its large huts that struck Zen most indelibly. And of course that he had never before seen such large, almost megalithic huts with neatly manicured realm lawns adorning their welcoming visages. Having nothing in common, gargoyled arches in sandstone yellow introduced themselves to clean straight lines in pastel shades and palm trees, and got along just fine. Built of different of things—bricks, metal, glass and even wood— in different combinations, heights and sizes, each character in this place seemed to have moved here from somewhere else in time and tide, somewhere else altogether. There seemed to be no distinct order to the place, there certainly was none of that sanitarium sanity, none of that logical layout, none of that pristine primness which standardized the realms and OmniRealm. Yet, it was obvious to Zen that this was even more so not the pre-world than it was not the realms. No stink of sewers, rats and rubbish or mangy maniacal missionaries trying to convert you here; this whole place, its exotic characters standing shoulder-to-shoulder, radiated an aura of plush comfort, of wise tranquility, an aura of uncontrived beauty.

But there was no time to explore up and down the boulevard, Bernays's hut must surely be the one attached to the landing 'H' where the pod had landed, Zen figured, and he knew just how to get in. So he rushed back to the pad, ran up its steps and tiptoed toward Bernays who was still snoring and drooling and snuck out again. Soon he was at a large mahogany doorway, whose ornate carvings he distractedly stroked for too long. Then raising Bernays's Embed, the one that the old luddite always kept tucked away in his shirt pocket, Zen—all of it happening too fast for nerves—was granted access. The long carpeted corridor, not dark but lit only in a dull gold light flickering from chandeliers suspended from its high painted ceiling, seemed to suck in the time that rapidly ticked away outside and slow-motion it. With small steps of wide-eyed wonder, Zen sidetracked his way stopping, absorbing, absorbed, wanting to but unable to touch the paradigm quaking aisle of paintings and sculptures, swords and ancient friend-devices. And then, to his right, toward a man within a glass box he was irresistibly drawn. Placing both his moist open palms and face against the glass, he peered in. Though much younger it was most definitely Vic Crafts leaning dotingly over a beige box with a grayed out window. Zen's eyes fixed on the tray of buttons that was connected by a twirling umbilical cord to the beige box, if only he could break through the intervening glass and press one of them, he wished. But, as he noticed the rainbow striped bitten berry on the beige box—'NO'—he restrained himself. He was privileged enough to see this first fruit of LifeTree, he shouldn't give himself away now, who knew what Bernays's corridor lay in store for him?

Reluctantly, Zen peeled himself away from Vic Crafts, and lingered past paintings and sculptures, many in some way somehow familiar. There was good old Lisa, who, over the years, had tried to impart in him so much wisdom about actz & ens. And Lady Listerine, who had blindfolded herself, his mother told him, to keep herself pure of heart and faith, uncontaminated from the belief pollution of the pre-world. And even that colossal naked marble statute that had stalked him when he was with Donatella (mercifully though, this being Bernays's hut, it wasn't going to morph into his likeness, Zen quickly reassured himself). Until finally, at the end of Bernays's corridor which Zen wished would never end, he came to a rectangular carved bronze frame slanted upon a solid marble pedestal, its centerpiece a yellowing parchment.

When in the Course of human events, it becomes necessary for one people to dissolve the political bands which have connected them with another, and to assume among the powers of the earth, the separate and equal station to which the Laws of Nature and of Nature's God entitle them, a decent respect to the opinions of mankind requires that they should declare the causes which impel them to the separation.

We hold these truths to be self-evident, that all men are created equal, that they are endowed by their Creator with certain unalienable Rights, that among these are Life, Liberty and the pursuit of Happiness. That to secure these rights, Governments are instituted among Men, deriving their just powers from the consent of the governed, that whenever any Form of Government becomes destructive of these ends, it is the Right of the People to alter or to abolish it, and to institute new Government, laying its foundation on such principles and organizing its powers in such form, as to them shall seem most likely to effect their Safety and Happiness. Prudence, indeed, will dictate that Governments long established should not be changed for light and transient causes; and accordingly all experience hath shewn, that mankind are more disposed to suffer, while evils are sufferable, than to right themselves by abolishing the forms to which they are accustomed. But when a long train of abuses and usurpations, pursuing invariably the same Object evinces a design to reduce them under absolute Despotism, it is their right, it is their duty, to throw off such Government, and to provide new Guards for their future security...

These words, Ports and Muthu reechoed through his mind. These words, Ports and Muthu reechoed through his mind. Closer and closer in concentration he leaned till he was shook by his nose squashing against the glass. He couldn't stay any longer, there was surely more to discover, but this parchment it wouldn't let him go. He couldn't let it go. It was another piece in Ports' and Muthu's post political puzzle, he was sure. But move on he had to and with a few steps more, the first doorway in the corridor beckoned. Looking back, he broke away, now nerves having had plenty of time—frayed. He gripped the handle of the door, hesitated a moment, and creakily opened the ancient door.

He was back in Muthu's dusty dungeon! Or so the déjà vu seemed. Back he went, in he went, and when a few steps in, Zen slowly swiveled full circle in awe. In awe at the ceiling scraping stacks upon stacks of books, so high that the uppermost were only reachable by wooden ladders placed against their shelves. And from this high reaching forest of yellowing autumn leaves, a thick waft of musty nostalgia suffused the air. To an ancient looking wooden desk Zen wandered. On the desk a ball, mounted on a tilted axis that promised to spin as he touched it, with squiggly arbitrary seeming lines demarcating different colors but mostly light blue, each one named and containing more and more funny unpronounceable names. And on the ancient desk's well-worn chair he sat and looked at the book that Bernays was halfway through, folding it shut to read the title 'Colombo: A Critical Introspection'. And then Zen rocketed to his feet propelled by an intriguing possibility. Zipping to the much shorter book cupboards that encircled the desk, Zen's eyes, like earnest little scanners, darted left to right following his index finger's lead, then crouching, right to left again. Then to the next cupboard, where on the very first shelf, title vertical, top to bottom, he was sure he caught a glimpse of it, he glided it out, there it was—'POST POLITICA' by Henry Ports. Book in hand, Zen leapt to the chair, placed his right hand on the book and started strategizing.

Just because Bernays knew of the book and he was sure had read it, confronting Bernays with this fact wouldn't really get him what he wanted. Bernays could, to use one of his favorite words, easily 'conjure' up a fantastical dismissal or belittlement of the elusive bridge between Post Politica and the realms, which Zen positively knew existed. Or even worse, Bernays could outright deny that he had ever read the book though it was in one of his cupboards. No, he had to go on the offensive, confront Bernays with the truth (assuming he didn't already know) that he was reading the book, preempting any fantastical conjuring from the old sorcerer.

Actually, it would be more advantageous and certainly more amusing to not initially disclose, to hold up his sleeve, that he had found the book in Bernays's personal collection. No doubt the old sorcerer would wax fantastic about the meaning and significance of the book, no doubt he would conjure up some convenient yarn, some slithery stratagem that will seek to 'Hey Presto' convince that whatever that is—ought to be. But right then, when Bernays the old sorcerer, had finished waving and weaving his word-wand, yes right then, he would disclose the droplet into the old sorcerer's fantastic potion and watch him boil, writhe and squirm in it.

Contemplating the pros and con-sequences of his next move, Zen paced his right palm up and down the hardcover of the book for several minutes and then for no reason at all opened it.

To My Dear Bernays,

You belong in Rationalia

In disbelief Zen verified the scrawled last two words over and again, pronouncing each syllable as he deciphered the letters;

H-e-n (Hen)·*r-y* (ry) *P-o-r* (Por)·*t-s* (ts)

The jigsaw puzzle that had been painstakingly assembling itself crumbling, all its pieces jumbling, all of a sudden Zen did not understand a thing. Again for no reason at all, thudding shut the hardcover, Zen incoherently confirmed that this was 'Post Politica' by Henry Ports. Opening it again, reading once more the scrawl that appeared now clearer than printed font—*To My Dear Bernays*—*You belong in Rationalia*—*Henry Ports*, Zen thudded the book shut again. And then the refrain amidst the jigsaw jumble—'This doesn't change anything', 'This doesn't change anything'—offered, if not some lucidity, at least some direction. He knew he needed to place the book back exactly where he found it and make his way back to the pod without getting noticed or caught, and this was what he was determined to do. But, lucidity hadn't fully returned, he hastily searched the book, the very same one that lay safe in his apartment, for that chapter, that chapter he knew was surely there. Through puffs of musty nostalgia unsettled by the fast flicking of yellowing pages, Zen soon found it.

Chapter VI.

The Direct Democratic Republic of Rationalia

Zen unwisely, for time according to the giant faced ancient clock opposite the desk was ticking-tocking away, enveloped his nose with his two palms, rested the weight of his head on his thumbs and stared down at the chapter, ever so often inhaling and exhaling deep heavy breaths. After a while, 'This doesn't change anything' he drilled himself again, before getting up and carefully replacing the book. Time began to speed up. Hurriedly via the corridor, yellowing parchment, colossal naked statue, Lady Listerine, Lisa, Vic Crafts, swords, paintings, devices blurring by, Zen, mahogany doorway behind him, surged into the keen rays of the morning sun. With a hop and skip onto the pod, he changed gears to a quiet though panting tiptoe toward Bernays, gently dropped Bernays's Embed back into his shirt pocket and then slouched relieved on his usual seat.

His heart rate had barely returned to a rest, when he noticed that first the flaccid right corner of Bernays's mouth, and then his droopy right shoulder, started to twitch. Instantaneously, Bernays's eyes switched on. Zen swallowed a gulp of anxiety.

"Ah, good morning Zen" Bernays greeted checking his Embed, a gooey cheese of sleepy drool stretching from flapping lower lip to flapping upper lip as he spoke, "Oh… I see you've taken me home. Very well, very well, it's the weekend isn't it? I'll see you tomorrow afternoon then"

"Okay, Director-General" Zen replied rigidly, not wanting to hatch his plan before reading that next chapter.

Back in a rush to his apartment, nestling in his ship of sheets, head against its pillow mast, propelled by the winds of intrigue—how did Bernays know Ports? Zen embarked on the most exciting voyage of his intellectual life.

Chapter VI.

The Direct Democratic Republic Of Rationalia

Welcome to the Direct Democratic Republic of Rationalia managed by the Microports Corporation. Based on your final rights which are embodied in Rationalia's detailed, yet easily accessible, societal management OS, Rationalia is designed to offer you all the essential functions that facilitate modern life—state-of-the-art infrastructure, cutting-edge healthcare, progressive education and other supportive social services. These functions will be delivered either directly by the Microports Corporation or outsourced to so specialized private entities under the constant supervision of the Microports Corporation.

Rationalia's Citizen Handbook is your simple guide to all the Do's & Don'ts, specifications and regulations which you agree to abide by if you choose to become a citizen of Rationalia. As with everything in Rationalia, no rule, specification nor regulation will ever contravene your final rights embodied in Rationalia's societal management OS.

Beyond the functions and Citizen Handbook, all other features and goods & services are made available to you by the free market, once again and always under the supervision of the final rules of business competitiveness and ethics enshrined in Rationalia's OS. A free market system in which you are encouraged to participate not only as consumer and employee but also as business owner and entrepreneur.

All entities that are entrusted with delivering to you the essential functions will be regularly audited by so specialized third-party auditors along with the internal auditors of the Microports

Corporation. Moreover and crucially, the overall management performance of the Microports Corporation will be audited by a so specialized third-party auditor, and the results of this comprehensive auditing process will be made freely available to you.

As an individual, you can rest assured that you will receive personal justice. Any allegation, whether it be by a fellow citizen of Rationalia or the Microports Corporation, that you have contravened the rules & regulations laid down in the Citizen Handbook against an individual in particular or society in general, will be adjudged by a so specialized third-party auditor to ensure impartiality.

Rationalia's societal management OS and Citizen Handbook not only derive their legitimacy from your inalienable and final rights. Together they embody the culmination of the best-practice of self-governance, they are the hard won harvest from the often painful trial & error of laws and systems over the long bloody millennia of human history. Which means that, and we at the Microports Corporation firmly believe this, there is not much about our OS and Handbook that will need amendment, deletion or addition. However on that rare occurrence, where such amendment, deletion or addition does become necessary, under the orders of Rationalia's OS, direct democracy will unhesitatingly be called upon to serve its first role in your self-governance. Where there is a clamor from you, the citizenry, or the necessity is pressing and an element of the Citizen Handbook demands amendment or deletion or an element demands to be added (and of course any citizen of Rationalia can petition for or against such a proposal) through Microports' regular referenda app, you, the citizenry of Rationalia, will be polled. Up will pop a question, which until you respond to your citizenship account will be frozen and which you will not be able to respond to until the attached background reading is completed.

Given that Rationalia's societal management OS and Citizen Handbook are substantially final, it is direct democracy's second role in your self-governance of Rationalia that is its most vital.

Governance is the making of decisions, these decisions can be placed on a continuum of directionality. At one end of the continuum are those great majority of day-to-day, simple decisions that have no directional bearing on the future of you the citizenry. These choices exist to, and are only capable of, furthering the chosen direction; the only challenge that these choices present is to pick the one that most efficiently furthers the chosen direction. At the other end of the continuum are those small minority of complex decisions which establish or steer the future direction of you the citizenry. These ambiguous questions require the counsel of morals, consideration of the impact on various stakeholder's final rights and the study of the influence of and the effect on social, economic and technological variables. These directional decisions can justly, only be made by you the citizen, it is one amongst your final rights; and in Rationalia via direct democracy all directional decisions *will* be made by you. To implement this, all decision making situations that arise in Rationalia are rated on a twenty point scale, ranging from ones and twos of what color the road signs will be and when the garbage will be collected, to the directional zone where, to highlight just a few, it will be up to you to select, continue or discontinue public service and utility providers, to decide on subscription structuring and rates, and where your consent will be sought for infrastructure investment decisions. And so, every so often, up will pop a question, an important one, a directional one, sometimes even a future defining one, which until you respond to your citizenship account will be frozen and which you will not be able to respond to until the attached background reading is completed; and we are sure you will agree with us that this is, just as it should be.

But perhaps the ultimate check & balance, the ultimate assurance that we at Microports can give you about the progressiveness and superiority of the Direct Democratic Republic of Rationalia comes not from us, but indeed from a force responsible for delivering to you many of the wonderful goods & services, benefits and conveniences that you have grown accustomed to; a force we wholeheartedly foster within Rationalia; a force, a motivator which indeed we must sincerely credit for making us the market leader we are today; the force, the motivator of free market competition. We have no doubt that very soon you will be browsing through many more prospectuses much like this one, for Rationalia is only the first of its kind. Which means that if you, even in the slightest way whatsoever, feel that your rights, your best-interests are being denied, infringed, impinged upon, that your will is not being done, then you are free to unsubscribe from our citizenship services, delete your citizenship account with us and exercise your inalienable final right to choose from amongst the—by then—host of options offered by our worthy competitors.

And so secure in these safeguards, firm in your final rights, rightfully, finally handing you the reins of power via direct democracy, we at Microports humbly welcome you to your Direct Democratic Republic of Rationalia.

16

THIS PLACE, same-old familiar now seemed dreamy peculiar. And as any new place would, designs and dimensions, tints and textures, the potpourri of aromas, the beat of vital functions all at once coming through on a blinding sunshiny flux, suddenly overawed his senses. Like clouds on a breeze, it was OmniRealm that seemed to move, that seemed to surreally pass by, as if he were standing still. But he was walking. Walking with purpose to confront Bernays, twisters full of big question marks, loose ends and thought scraps swirling.

His chest beginning to bump-bump, Zen knock-knocked on Bernays's door and waited, stroking his right trouser pocket.

Though muffled, he was sure he heard "Come in"

"Zen!" Bernays smiled, as Zen single-mindedly strode toward his desk.

As if rehearsed, without a word Zen squared himself to the desk and Bernays, robotically reached into his pocket, palmed the book out trying his best to obscure the title, placed it firmly on the desk and removed his moist palm, revealing it.

"Director-General, tell me how the realms have come to be, from this" Zen formally demanded, thumping the book. And then, quickly remembering what nervousness had almost made him forget, he added "I have read it"

Placing his elbows on the desk and his upturned thumbs under his eyebrow ridges, so that the points of his other four fingers on each hand all touched, Bernays silently contemplated for a while.

Through the gap between Bernays's palms, Zen noticed Bernays's beady black bulbs occasionally stealing a covert scan of him.

And then after some more time had passed, right before Zen, who was rapidly running out of patience, re-demanded an explanation.

"MARKETING" proclaimed Bernays, his hands retracting, thumping as best they could the desk, leaving only those beady black bulbs to burn the word on to Zen's mind.

"MARKETING" Bernays reiterated.

In one simple way Zen wasn't surprised, the only other two people who had used variations of that word were Bernays's kindred spirits. But it was obvious, for Bernays it meant more.

"We don't label it that anymore of course," clarified Bernays, "but yes, MARKETING" he reiterated, his saggy mouth and scraggy lips slowly sumptuously savoring, sexually almost each syllable of the word 'MAR…KET…ING'.

Unexpectedly, Bernays reorganized into his contemplative configuration. This time though his burning beady black bulbs not occasionally stealing but unblinkingly locked in on Zen's eyes.

Fearing that Bernays might leave it dangling there, at 'MARKETING', a seed for self-learning but nothing more, as he always did; Zen nudged closer to the desk and clenched its edge, poised to demand for more.

"You see… by the early decades of the twenty-first century," Bernays abruptly dropped his hands and started, "governments were failing". After a pause, "Politics was failing" he went on, underlining with his index finger the word 'Politica' in the book's title, "Taxes, recessions, bureaucracy, inefficiency, scandals, terrorism—the entire *doesn't* works" he listed with a pleased snicker.

Zen sat back and hoped Bernays would unravel his explanation slowly, meticulously.

"Needless to say," Bernays continued now patting the book, "people had lost faith in their governments. Politics wasn't failing, it had already failed. But, but…"

Zen leaned closer, sensing that an important little clincher of understanding was about to be unveiled.

"…but, it wasn't as if this was an age of across-the-board decline" Bernays continued, shaking his head with conviction, "Oh no, no, no, while countries were dying, brands were beloved, entrepreneurs were esteemed, corporations were consecrated. This was no dark age Zen… but for governments and politics. Both were very much at the end of their product lifecycle, in the decline phase. Only a small minority of laggards, luddites clung to them"

The apparition of Muthu flashed and flickered before Zen's mind's eye.

153

"Rats jump from the sinking ship" proffered Bernays, a quizzical look of 'why not' contorting his nose and mouth, "Well, at least consumers should jump from sinking products"

Zen made a note of Bernays's interesting variation on a word he knew all too well.

"It is their inalienable right to do so" declared Bernays.

As Bernays spoke those two words that he had only ever heard together in Ports' book, a pivotal quandary lanced him—Was Bernays purposely letting on that he knew Ports?

"You don't know anything about Marketing do you?" asked Bernays empathetically, "Well of course you don't, how could you?". "Let me show you, yes, let me show you" he decided with a spritely upsurge of enthusiasm. "Arrange for the pod to take us to the pre-world, the last logged pre-world location will do. And you can bring this along with you" instructed Bernays, sliding the book toward Zen, his beady black bulbs intently rising to meet Zen's own eyes.

"Here we are" exclaimed Bernays, ushering Zen by the hand to the low hovering pod's cabin window, "Come on, open it wider, wider"

Down below, Zen recognized a settlement roughshod, ad-hoc much like his own. No rhythm, no rhyme, no reason discernible to the place. The only buildings not squalidly, precariously thatched together with cardboard, mud bricks and rusty sheets—mosques, churches and temples.

"You see those days," Bernays commenced in earnest, "we were self-centered and insensitive. Perhaps we had no other choice… in any case, we would make whatever it was that we could make and expect it to satisfy everybody. But people are different, don't you think Zen?"

"Yes" replied Zen obligatorily.

"Yes, they are different, diverse" resounded Bernays with verve, "And often these differences, this diversity is contradictory, conflictual. Look, look at the pre-world Zen, I'm sure you know better than me, you know firsthand the injustice, the misery, the uselessness of trying to satisfying everyone's wants with a one-size-fits-no-one product"

Bernays fidgeting his Embed lowered the pod, so that the clumps of dots soon grew to be identifiable as faces and bodies.

"And that's what Marketing is" elucidated Bernays, a thermal of self-righteousness rising his head, "Marketing is all about appreciating, understanding and satisfying individual wants"

The motley clumps of pre-worlders had dropped everything and were reverentially looking up to the pod.

"To each he can own" pronounced Bernays, fidgeting his Embed to release a fleet of parachutes toward the hungry horde below. "To each he can own" he re-avowed.

"And do you know how Marketing satisfies your individual wants Zen?" asked Bernays, the answer already antsy at the tip of his tongue, "SEGMENTING–TARGETING–POSTIONING". SEGMENTING then TARGETING then POSTIONING… that's marketing"

Again Bernays animatedly fidgeted with his Embed. Zen felt the pod ascend, the faces and bodies of the hungry horde becoming a clump of dots once more.

"SEGMENTING then TARGETING then POSTIONING" Bernays repeated the mantra.

Soon the pod was hovering over a NumLing amphitheater. At a point in its descent toward the theatre, Bernays excitedly shouted, "Look, look!" and halted the pod.

"Look at the segments, look at the segments within the segments" he marveled.

This NumLing theatre was either several times larger than the one that he and Maya attended or it seemed that way from this vantage point.

"Look, look" egged Bernays.

Then, instantaneously, it struck Zen what Bernays was going on about. The amphitheater looked like a large pizza pie except, and he was sure this was Bernays's point, each clearly demarcated wedge was obviously a distinct flavor. One large wedge was denim blue from shirt to tattered trousers, another saffron robed and the one next to it bearded and white skull-capped. But the most conspicuous contrast was between the black tented wedge and the tawdry topless one that let all hangout right next to it.

"SEGMENTATION" presented Bernays, a ring of voilà in his voice, "The marketer's, and marketing's first task is to divide the horribly heterogeneous market into harmoniously homogenous segments. But of course, it's never as simple as that. Oh no, no... you see Marketing should never be passive, content with just divvying up the market according to various obvious variables". "You see Zen, Marketing has a higher purpose" he sermonized turning toward Zen, "Marketing mustn't merely identify the wants that consumers know they have and are ready to say they have—oh no, much more—Marketing must unearth the under-lurking wants that consumers most definitely have, but haven't realized yet. The wants that, one might say, consumers 'intrinsically clamor' for" Bernays added with a smirk, patting the book that was back in Zen's pocket.

There it was again, another hint, but now Zen's attention was more concerned with what Bernays was preaching.

"You know that topless segment that disgusted you so when you caught first glance of it" whispered Bernays, getting closer to Zen and guiding his focus, "Right there, right there. Well, it is we who placed them there! They are not hopefuls at all! Oh no, just a bunch of ragtag random hippies that we pay to sit together through every NumLing cast topless (and soon naked). And do you know why?"

"Segmentation?" speculated Zen.

"To unearth these pre-world consumers' under-lurking wants Zen!" thundered Bernays, "To cajole and coax them out, for their own good. How else will consumers know that they must seek to satisfy their defining desires, if we don't make them felt?"

His beady black bulbs powering down, Bernays took a meditative pause.

"And then we marketers must introspect" he broke out thunderously, his wrinkly gray eye-lashed shutters popping open, "We must look within ourselves, we must ask and honestly answer the question 'Which segment's wants can we best satisfy?'. It is a matter of utmost moral significance to us marketers, Zen. Oh yes, if our hat fits, then and only then must we make them wear it. It goes against our Kotleratic oath to of course attempt to satisfy all segments with one product; but equally so to try and satisfy those segments which we are not best capable of satisfying"

"So that's…" Zen began.

"That's TARGETING!" Bernays bellowed, "That is Targeting, my dear Zen"

Bernays's left hand rose, swaying the loose fleshy sail hanging from his short-sleeved upper-arm, his thumb and middle finger clicked each other, his forefinger pointed up with purpose, he had an idea, "Let's go" he marshaled.

"So we have our wants" Bernays impassioned, raising and closing the fingers of his left hand, as the pod descended (to where Zen didn't know), "And we've designed our product from the very bottom up, its price, its packaging, where and how we sell it, every last devil of its details"

Bernays paused, his left hand still fingers closed and raised, and reeled Zen in with his beady black bulbs.

"And then," he continued, bringing his raised right hand, its fingers similarly closed, toward his left and then moving both hands toward his head until his bunched ten fingers impacted the loose flesh that draped his forehead, "and then… I shall show you"

The pod landed, Bernays led the way to the hatch, his legs spurred by the passion gurgling and bubbling in his mind. Holding the rail, more falling down each stair than stepping down, he escorted Zen to the ground.

"There" pointed Bernays.

But Zen was already scrutinizing it. A behemoth black burqa, like the one that tented the wedge next to the topless sliver, levitated over them obscuring almost the entire horizon. Through its boxy slit, no averted eyes peered out, but in the sternest black font only the running words— 'IF YOU BELIEVE THERE IS NO GOD BUT ALLAH, THERE IS NO REALM BUT BISMILLAH'. With a tiny (in relation) muted gray tick engraved just under the boxy slit.

"Just look, just look" Bernays exhorted, pointing to some specific element of the behemoth black burqa, "Just look at the modest brand impression, the puritanical monotone-ness. No bells & whistles here, no bells & whistles needed. They've bought the sky over this area so even in the brightest sunshine, there's a gloomy austerity that hangs over the place—don't you think?"

"Yes" Zen agreed, after his eyes zoomed out to register the drab overcast light that struggled through the barely translucent behemoth black burqa.

"Why even the font is frigid" marveled Bernays, "Like I said, right down to the very 'last devil of detail'. And I can prove just how effective this conspicuous lack of song & dance is! Oh yes, oh yes"

"Tell me Zen, at first and unbiased glance, what kind of realm you think Bismillah is?" posed Bernays with a presumptuous smile, cocksure of Zen's answer.

"Well, obviously it's an islamic realm" Zen started.

"Well obviously" Bernays interrupted, "But what specifically does it instantly feel like? Other than islam, what pops into your heart?"

"Ultra-Conservative" Zen immediately hastened back, "It's ultra-conservative"

"Preee-cisely" Bernays affirmed emphatically, "And you could not have thought it, felt it, to be anything else"

"Uh…" Zen began, thinking that Bernays had asked him a question.

"This is why… this is why, this… is an example of excellently executed… POSITIONING" Bernays climaxed, "Positioning Zen, is all about ensuring, informing… educating actually, it's all about educating the consumers of our target market that our product specifically, especially satisfies their individual wants. It's about clearing the air, stating who we are; making sure that we are not felt to be some jack-of-all-trades, that instead we are known unequivocally to be the master of one"

Bernays took a contemplative pause where he stood looking up with humbled awe at the behemoth black burqa.

"Marketing, and marketers have a higher… no, in fact the HIGH-EST calling, Zen" he then resumed his sermon, still looking up, his neck sails fully unfurled, "And I'll tell you why Zen. What is the purpose of anyone's life? To satisfy their individual wants, whatever they maybe— wouldn't you agree? Not to be told what these wants should be, not to settle for those goods & services that only satisfy some convenient group average, not to have the wants of others clash with and deprive you of your own; but to have your wants satisfied; uncompromisingly, undilutedly satisfied. To do so, your wants will have to be identified and unearthed, goods & services will have to be designed faithfully focusing on your wants and you will have to be educated as to how precisely these products satisfy your wants—wouldn't you agree?"

Again Bernays paused, not to contemplate, not so much to give Zen time to answer but to give young Zen's mind enough time to assemble his argument's building blocks.

"And so you see Zen," he resumed, chin rising notches more, neck sails unfurling full-mast, and Zen was sure his beady black bulbs burning with intensity, "this is why Marketing is the highest calling—it is Marketing that satisfies your needs, it is Marketing that fulfills the purpose of your life"

Bernays hadn't said anything on the way back quite obviously to let things sink in. When Zen tried to poke and prod him forward, every attempt along the lines of 'Director what is the…' was stubbed along the lines of 'ah, ah, ah… Segmenting, Targeting, Positioning, that's all you should muse and meditate on'. And even though the temptation teased him, he had resisted playing the rabble rousing card up his sleeve. Bernays *was* going to tell all, Zen had assured himself, but he was going to do it, in typical fashion, at his own deliberate pace and meter.

"Oh, incidentally," Bernays suddenly broke out, initiating dialog for the first time on the way back, "where did you get that book?"

Zen's heart rate spiked as he quickly assessed the truth to verify whether it had any potential to derail his strategy. It didn't.

"Um, from this old man in the pre-world, who lived near my settlement" Zen answered, "He lived in a place which had hundreds… thousands of books actually"

"Oh" responded Bernays, his eyebrows jumping up with amusement. Pouting his cracked lips out, his eyes growing distant, his head ever so slightly bobbling, "A last laggard in a library, I suppose" he remarked wistfully.

159

The next day, his menial and mostly nominal tasks as Bernays's aide completed in a mindless blur, and the previous night having mused and meditated on Segmenting-Targeting-Positioning, Zen, the talismanic tome tucked away in his pocket, at last got the call up from the old know-bag.

Bernays presided from his large leather throne, elbows on desk, in one of his contemplative configurations; the diagonal streaks of the mid-afternoon sun spotlighting him. He gestured Zen to sit opposite him, and poured some liquid from a bottle into a glass but his beady black bulbs didn't make contact for a few seconds yet.

"If you could sail to the stars on your bicycle, wouldn't that be marvelous Zen?" asked Bernays, his beady black bulbs turning to Zen, "Just your bicycle, just your bicycle, nothing more!"

From mechanical Segmenting-Targeting-Positioning to the fantastical, to this! Zen was discombobulated but he knew the answer was imminent, that Bernays was asking only a rhetorical question.

"And if I knew precisely how to make your bicycle so sail to the stars, is it not my duty to teach you?" roved Bernays rhetorically, "Well this Zen... this is the other half, the better half of Marketing!"

Into another glass, Bernays poured some more of the liquid and offered it to Zen.

"You see Zen," Bernays set off once Zen had taken a sip, "as they say— 'There are wants and then, there are *wants*'. Maybe right at this very moment you want to raise with both your hands a frisbee-sized juicy cheeseburger to your licking lips. Tantalize your taste buds, titillate your tongue with a succulent sandwich of two sesame encrusted, delicately toasted golden buns that cosset a whopping patty of freshly ground, flame-grilled beef, delectably doused with mouthwateringly messy mustard and pickles, crispy crunchy lettuce, the lava of molten melting cheese sumptuously topping it all off. You see this, this is an example of a simple, straightforward, sensorial want; a tangible want. But of course all your wants are not like this. What about esteem and prestige? What about freedom? What about dominance? What about sophistication, advancement, achievement? What about self-expression? What about meaning? What about contentment? What about love?"

Bernays's exhaustive enumeration exhausting him, the wise windbag waited a while for his second-wind.

"You see…" he restarted, not quite having regained it, "these wants—complicated, deep seated, intangible—these are the wants I was telling you about before. These are the wants that are most often under-lurking, these are an individual's defining desires"

Again Bernays recessed, this time in equal measure to gather his breath and his thoughts.

"But you see…" he resumed in a quieter tone, changing mode from rhetorical to explanatory, "products, actz & ens, through their form & function can only ever satisfy your simple, straightforward, tangible wants. So how do we marketers fulfil our higher calling, how do we marketers fully fulfil the purpose of your life, Zen?"

Bernays's beady black bulbs zeroed in on Zen so intently, so convincingly that he almost attempted to answer the question.

"Ha-ha-ha," Bernays reignited heartily, unfurling his arms and their flaps wondrously, "this is where the beautiful bountiful ingenuity of marketing and marketers comes into play. You see a product, an act or en is merely a bare axis…"

Bernays stopped mid-sentence. This time not for effect or second-wind but because, Zen inferred from his beady black bulbs, he had second-thoughts.

"Close your eyes Zen" he backtracked, "Now cleanse everything from your mind, and imagine the night sky without the sun and stars or anything else, just the pure blackness of night"

Zen now more discombobulated than ever, stared back wide-eyed. Seconds later, only then did it strike him that Bernays wanted him to actually shut his eyes, which he duly did.

"Now picture," Bernays went on conjuring, his beady black bulbs too, shut by the visualization, "just one bare axis, a bare rod floating amidst this pure blackness of night. This bare axis is the form & function of a product, of an act or en. How boring, how mundane, how one-dimensional right? Right, but this bare axis has one fantastic, one fantastical potential. You see, things can orbit around it. Keeping this in mind, now picture Zen that a philanthropic, humane, cosmic hand, like the hand of god, places in orbit around this axis esteem, prestige, freedom, dominance, sophistication, advancement, achievement, self-expression, contentment, love. In other words that this philanthropic, humane, cosmic hand places in orbit around this bare axis, your complicated, deep seated, intangible wants, your under-lurking defining desires. Now all you have to do is drive, ride, wear, apply, eat, drink, play with this axis; all you have to do is to grab out to buy this axis, to own this axis. For when you do—esteem, prestige, freedom, dominance, sophistication, advancement, achievement, self-expression, meaning, contentment, love—will orbit you; but much, much more, they will be yours... they will be you!"

The feel of two fleshy slaps of clammy cold shuddered Zen's eyes open. For a startled sec, it was as though eyes open all he could see was the same pure blackness of night that he had visualized eyes closed—it was Bernays's beady black bulbs burning just inches away. He had leant over the desk and had Zen's cheeks in his palms, a soapy antiseptic smell soused with some sharp overpoweringly musky notes made Zen feel as though he couldn't take another breath.

"This... this is what I meant by 'sailing to the stars on your bicycle' " Bernays drove home unblinkingly.

Then the warmth rapidly returned to Zen's cheeks as Bernays, and his antiseptic musky miasma, retreated into his leather throne to gather his thoughts once again.

"Now you see Zen," Bernays switched back to explanatory mode, "some axes simply don't lend themselves to having certain defining desires orbit them. Some axes, you could say, are a real grind! Salt and prestige, for instance, go together like chalk and cheese. And so, just like planets orbit the sun, and it is this sun that powers the planets and in turn the planet's satellites; it is brands—brand-suns—that radiate their light of defining desires upon products, which in turn these products simply reflect onwards"

Again Bernays leaned over the desk, his antiseptic musky miasma suffocating Zen, and clasped Zen's cheeks with the slap of his cold clammy hands.

"This is what I really meant by 'sailing to the stars on your bicycle' " he drilled, "Salt *can* reflect, re-radiate prestige, water *can* sparkle with refinement, a sweatband *can* pulsate you with the exhilaration of competition, lumps of coal *can* crystallize into love. The mundane *can* be transcendent. This... this my dear Zen, is the power, the omnipotence of BRANDING"

Abruptly, Bernays's hands yanked away, and began pouring from the bottle into Zen's glass. But instead of handing Zen his glass, Bernays brought it to his own nose and dramatically parodied a sommelier's whiff and tasting of wine before handing it to Zen, saying, "Drink it, drink it all"

"You are drinking... Fun; You are drinking... Youthfulness; You are drinking... Happiness" Bernays chanted, "You are drinking... Fun; You are drinking... Youthfulness; You are drinking... Happiness. You are having Fun; You are Young; You are Happy. You are drinking... Fun; You are drinking... Youthfulness; You are drinking... Happiness"

"OR," Bernays came to instant a reverberating stop, "are you merely drinking fizzy blackened sugar-water?"

Across the black ocean of grandiose promises, where light-brown fizzy tides foamed, through the refraction of moistened glass, Zen could see on the curvaceous bottle, those two *C*'s in cursive white and red. Bernays's lesson could not have been better branded.

17

NOTHING WAS forthcoming from Bernays after that. For days, weeks now, barely even broaching the subject was stonewalled by the refrain 'MARKETING' and the refrain 'BRANDING'. But Zen was sure that implied in this stonewalling was a 'That's enough for now', that most certainly there was more to come. Or was he? Was it time to play his hand? Or should he bide his time? That Bernays knew Ports had made Ports' Post Politica real—realer—to him, he could no longer dismiss it as some fairytale only old Muthu chose to live in. But there was one outcome he hadn't considered before. Playing his hand would mean confessing to Bernays that he had entered Bernays's hut and that he had been to that strange place which he was sure Bernays didn't want to show him, at least just not yet. And if Bernays blacklisted him for this, he would never be able to go back there and worst of all he could never extract anything more from the old know-bag. But then again if he did get blacklisted, back in the pre-world there was always good old Muthu, who surely would be delighted to tell him all about how from Post Politica came the realms. But no, no, he couldn't risk it; at least before he played his hand, he had to go back one more, one last time.

He had rehearsed it a million times in his head. 'Just like before', 'Just like before' he intoned to himself as he selected Bernays's home coordinates. Fingers figuratively crossed, Zen concentrated on every twitch and tick of the rising then falling old drool bag, hoping that the landing of the pod wouldn't somehow prick it bursting back to life. Slipping Bernays's Embed out, Zen as before, tiptoed to the hatch and then frisked down its steps.

This time, he must explore more of this strange place before reentering Bernays's hut, he resolved, and so Zen purposely headed any which way in the opposite direction. As he roamed in the long mauve and indigo infused shadows of the motley megalithic huts, a snag of ambivalence jabbed him. He so wanted to meet someone else from this outlandish outlier but if they made him and informed Bernays, him and his best-laid plan might soon be heading down the blacklist chute. Mid-quandary, the left turn of the street brought into view the entrance to a park, not named, and bare by realm standards, thought Zen, as he walked toward it. As he neared, he noticed a barely life-size statue of an old (but not nearly as old as Bernays) man with longish side-parted hair. Bernays had kept the most spectacular actz or 'products' as he called them, all to himself, Zen thought jocularly, slowing his pace just a bit as he went by the unspectacular statue to read the inscription, "I am against...". Clenching his thighs and calves, digging in his toes as if he were coming to a halt from a full-on sprint, Zen froze his forward momentum. Squaring his body to the just milliseconds ago unspectacular statue, he read again the inscription:

'I am against religion because it teaches us to be satisfied with not understanding the world'

A 'WHAT??' of overwhelming curiosity upended Zen's thought stream. Reading it again, he verified if he had missed or mixed up some negatives, a 'not' here or there that would have inverted the meaning of what he had first read in passing. But no. It read precisely the same after several careful reads as it read on first glance. Right below the inscription, Zen noticed that a rectangular area much shorter in length than the inscription had been effaced. He sat down on a bench next to the statue, from where he could still read the inscription and almost touch its stony face. The powdery mauves and indigos of dawn were stretching, yawning, awaking into the brighter, clearer caramels and yellows of the early morn. From the corners of his downturned eyes, energetic little characters began to emerge, all of them running at a predetermined purposeful pace. Somewhere at the very end of the priority list of his thoughts, he registered this as novel and strange—running surely not to get anywhere, and not it seemed running, solely to maintain minWellness and avoid eviction. But this was the last thing on his mind. This was no realm nor OmniRealm, this was even more so not the pre-world, he knew that; but all the same, he could never have imagined that this place was openly godless. Sure Muthu and Ports and he was certain Bernays were godless, but up until now he had assumed—especially of Bernays given his position as the Director-General of OmniRealm—that they had to keep it their 'dirty little secret'. But to describe to himself this place, which on reading the inscription was falling into place, Zen could use no better word than that word that Muthu had taught him. This was an atheist realm. He had never heard of it before, but then again citisumers were hardly concerned with anything beyond the contents of their stomachs and their own realm. And pre-worlders, well pre-worlders only ever selectively googled after information about realms that offered their favorite religious flavor. Or perhaps, this was an all-new realm or an even an experimental one. Either way this was an atheist realm. It made sense—Segmenting! Even before he had read the inscription, this place had sort of sent him this subliminal suggestion that Muthu and Ports (if he were alive)—the only other two people that were like Bernays— would belong here. Obviously so, because this realm was segmented based on their defining desire of godless atheism. Following logically on from this, looking up to the horizon, Zen searched. But there was no brand-sun. Perhaps, it was still experimental, he thought again as he rose to his feet to restart his roaming.

And as he roamed, he observed that the citisumers of this godless atheist realm were quite different from the citisumers of your average religious realm. Indeed, the citisumers of this realm were quite like its huts. Wearing different clothes—of denim, spandex, silk, corduroy, cotton—in different designs, ensembles and colors, sporting different styles and 'dos, each character in this place seemed to have borrowed from all the realms and for effect even from the pre-world, to weave for themselves their very own mélange. It was as if they had nothing in common but that—godless atheism.

Confident that he wouldn't be noticed, being as different from them as they were from each other, Zen roamed on. Until, a few more zigzags through random roads later, he was amazed by the sight of little tractors for only one (or four at the most it appeared) zipping across the large grayish-black divider between walkways. This was what the odd white and yellow painted lines were for, he thought to himself, as within them the whooshing variously colored and shaped pellets swiped by. Unlike the rusty brown pre-world tractors that crammed forty or fifty into their open trailers, these pretty pellets, Zen deduced from their carrying capacity and the infrequency with which he saw them (once every few minutes or so), were ridden purely for pleasure.

Yes, Muthu would fit right in here, and so very well might he, Zen fleetingly fancied. Placing his hand solemnly on the impression the book made through his trouser pocket, Zen slowed his gait and lifted his gaze to marvel at the self-belief of this godless place. Never apologetic, indeed proud of its iconoclasm, about its progressiveness positive, eccentrically enterprising; for a hallucinatory half-moment, this is what Ports' Rationalia must have been like he daydreamed, he saw. And so, with a sense of wonder but none of time, Zen wandered on, in many a way within the book much more than the place.

To a floral circle he came, that united at right angles four of those white and yellow marked large grayish-black dividers. On the green field across from it, a hut stood all alone. Zen shaded his eyes with a palm-made visor. Amidst the hail of sharp, dazzling golden arrows from the exuberant early morning sun, Zen's retinas registered something atop the red brick hut. Against the blazing blue that painfully pulsed his retinas—no it couldn't be, he thought—but nevertheless, he had to see. Darting diagonally from his side of the divider, arcing around the circle, he was at the foot of the hut. Looking up from this vantage was no less piercingly painful but now he couldn't deny that his retinas were right. From the highest spire of the red brick hut, with none of the frills or fanfare of the ones he had seen before in the pre-world or the realms, grew out a slender metal pole and horizontally intersecting it about three-quarters the way up, another shorter pole. It was a crucifix. This was a church. His mind as mesmerized as his eyes, Zen entered. Suddenly darkness. Not really darkness but an indoor gloom that in contrast to the iridescence outside came over his eyes as darkness. His pupils recalibrated, and as they did, he saw; no hive of activity nor holograms, just row behind row of brown wooden benches. He sat down and looked up at the angular wooden crucifix that unassumingly oversaw the austere church, his unease at being unable to pin this place down slowly, surely agitating an anger within him. Amidst the anger that was beginning to bubble and pop an incoherent thought—'Maybe this is an ultra-conservative christian realm like Bismillah, and that's why the austerity'. How ridiculous, Zen dismissed boiling over, thumping the wooden back of the bench with the side of his closed palm. How could this be an ultra-conservative christian realm when he had just seen an openly displayed quote denouncing religion? Bernays was up to something, Bernays was not telling him something, or everything, or anything at all; he had to know, but how?

Various permutations as to 'How?' along with time, came and went until quite a while later he was snapped out by the sight of a smallish character entering the church from one of its side entrances. Pretending to pray, Zen observed the character, an oldish woman, as she sat and gazed contemplatively at the austere altar and the unassuming crucifix, but didn't kneel or clasp her hands and fingers together in prayer. Intermittently, he observed, she would close her eyes, but even then, as closely as he looked, her mouth wouldn't (or he couldn't see it) quiver in prayer. Some while of breezy, easy, almost irreligious introspection later, the oldish woman, without so much as a capping-it-all-off glance of goodbye at the unassuming crucifix, started to saunter off toward the entrance she had come in through. And a few 'I should—No—I shouldn't' moments of hesitation later, Zen started after her. Outside the sun-flower up above, now high, was in full burning bloom, but the woman was nowhere to be seen. Pointlessly, Zen searched to the right and then to the left of the entrance knowing full well it was in vain, before heading back into the church and sitting, this time on the very first row of benches.

Slowly, into the quicksand of his thoughts, deeper and deeper, he sank. Deeper and deeper, he drowned. Where am I? What is this place? Not the pre-world certainly, nor OmniRealm, but neither a typical religiously flavored realm; an atheist realm maybe? But what of this church? An ultra-conservative christian realm? But no, where was the fervor? And there was that quote. And where in any case, was the brand-sun?

"Delusion is the solution", a swollen fist inside Zen's left chest, clenched and unclenched, clenched and unclenched, clenched and unclenched itself, racing, repeatedly, rapidly. He tautly gulped down his Adam's apple that had tried to squeeze through his strangled throat into his drying mouth.

"Delusion *is* the solution". Zen had no choice but to turn around and face-to-face the musky miasma.

"Delusion has always been the solution. You see... if you think about it, religion is the ultimate consumer product. Oh yes, yes, yes, first it segments, and like any good marketer would... like every marketer should, not merely on those wants consumers know they have and are ready to say they have. Oh no, no, no... prophets and priests, saviors and seers, cajole and coax, scare out some of their consumers' most defining desires—for meaning... for immortality... for, for a sense of morality; you know... for comfort and consolation, for forgiveness... for hope.

And then, oh and then, these mystic marketers target these most defining desires by designing their god... or their gods... or their karmas and nirvanas—of course down to the very last 'devil' of their details—to satisfy these most defining desires. Oh yes... god, gods, karma & nirvana—omnipresent, omniscient, omnipotent; nothing preceding them, nothing proceeding them, they'll do the trick... they're ponies that'll do many a trick. Oh they'll give you meaning, a grand narrative in fact.

And immortality? Not a problem. The escape from it? That's just as easy too;

And a sense of morality? Why that's industry standard;

Comfort and consolation? A 24-hour cosmic hotline is on standby to listen just to you;

And forgiveness? Well, you'll have to pray a little extra, but most certainly sir, that too"

This lyrical recitation did not appear to have waned the musky miasma, it did though at first relieve, then absorb and then quite a bit entertain Zen, and so it waxed on.

"Ha-ha... and then our mystic marketers, build to their heavens palaces so purposely exorbitant that when consumers gaze up from the foot of the long shadow cast by this *packaging* they are awestruck. They are daunted by what then most definitely has to be the omnipresence, omniscience, omnipotence of our mystic marketer's god, gods, karmas and nirvanas. And from these heaven-scraping palaces, our mystic marketers send forth missionaries and zealots to proselytize, to convert (in their jargon)... or in ours—brand ambassadors and brand loyalists to inform, to educate target consumers that their god, gods, karmas and nirvanas... their religion... their product... specifically, especially satisfies these consumers' individual wants. Is this not positioning?"

A beam of light squared by the left-hand side window above the altar, particles of dust sauntering within it, spotlighted Bernays's face. From his beady black bulbs and the light murky blue rims that increasingly encroached on them, grew out a blood-red reticulation of capillaries so dense that there remained almost no whites of his eyes.

"Ha-ha-ha... all of this is the marketing method no doubt, but it's not what makes religions the ultimate consumer products that they are" Bernays erupted, his arms, palms and fingers unfurling and rising. Then ironically, as if in prayer, Bernays froze.

Zen knew both the answer to Bernays's last poser and what the old know-bag was about to do; but this time the suspicion itched him that the cunning old know-bag was doing it mostly to get him out of this place.

Bernays thrust his hand over the back of the bench, palm faced upwards. Zen, his fingers brushing against the book, prised it out. Slightly averting his eyes from the shiny black beads, their murky light-blue rims and the blood-red reticulation that had set their sights on him, he placed Bernays's Embed on his palm.

It was a long journey from that conundrum of a place. Zen spent it glued to the glass of the cabin window, but as soon as they zoomed out from its wide but low huts, he could gather nothing more revealing about the place than that those large grayish-black dividers didn't divide, but in fact, crisscrossed and connected the place together.

Bernays descended the pod and brought it to a hovering standstill, it was the pre-world again. But everything was different. Yet, as Zen looked closer, the visual litter organized itself into a flashback that made him gasp a quick short shuddering breath and think of his mother. The roughshod, the ad-hoc, the no rhythm, no rhyme, no reason sheltering, the cardboard, the rusty sheets and every personal this & that, were soaked and strewn everywhere. The dried mud and leaf coatings of the scrawny dead, their agonized last gasps solidified, now clawed and pecked by at scavengers, now broken through, were oozing stringy guts and yellowy puss like cream-filled easter eggs.

"Look there… there… there" Bernays pointed severally.

Trudging through the mud and sludge, pre-worlders of all ages were at it with zeal. And emerging from the mud and sludge, were saplings of minarets and spires, dagobas and domes. Zen remembered how, not long but a lifetime ago, he and his mother were them. He remembered how they would, with blood and sweat, through tears, spend day and night rebuilding their church every time the flash floods hit. He remembered how the emptiness inside their stomachs would nauseatingly be filled to the brim with vomit from the stench of bloated bodies left behind by the receding brown waters. He remembered the hymns they would sing aloud as they toiled, tinged and tangled five times a day by the determined prayers of muslims who, like them, were rebuilding their mosque.

"Now you see why religions are the ultimate consumer good…" Bernays boomingly broke in from behind, "BRANDING"

Zen, though looking out at the washed apart world below, at his life before, was intent on listening to and learning everything Bernays was about to impart.

"Religions, you see my dear Zen, are really…" Bernays began explaining, "(or not really!)" he digressively chuckled, "Religions are really brands. The first brands you could say. And do you know why… and do you know how?"

171

Zen looking down at the pre-world below, replied with receptive silence.

"Oh... but you do" Bernays assured, "You see branding is when a philanthropic, humane hand places in orbit around a bare axis complicated intangible wants. And you know the thing about complicated intangible wants? Ha-ha-ha... there are just that, they are complicated and they are intangible. Their complicatedness, my dear Zen, means of course that the average mind can't easily understand them; break them down, sum them up, figure out what they are and what they're not, how they work and when and why they don't or won't. And their intangibility, my dear Zen, means that your senses are of little help to you in this processing task. Of a rotten apple, the registering by your faithful senses, your greatly accurate sensors, of a mushy feel or a squirmy worm will tell you all you need to know; but when it comes to complex concepts not so"

Bernays closed in behind Zen a little more, "This means... oh, this means my dear Zen, many things. It means that somebody must break down these complex concepts for the average mind, teach them how precisely they work. But do you know what it means most of all?"

Zen could now feel the moist warmth of Bernays's breath on the back of his left ear, "Oh and its wonderful Zen, really... unreally... wonderful". "It means that the goals that these concepts seek after, can be realized in here..." Bernays exulted, knocking on Zen's skull as if on a door to seek entry, "without actually being achieved out here" he continued, throwing his arm-sails widely apart to gesticulate his point.

A spin of confusion swiveled Zen around to face Bernays.

"You see..." Bernays started to re-explain, recognizing that Zen hadn't fully understood, "all minds, including the average mind, have certain complicated and intangible wants, defining desires. But of course the average mind can't understand the true mechanics, the true workings of these wants in the real world outside it. Take for instance... uh... individuality, Zen. It is too complicated a processing task for the average mind to figure out exactly what's to be done, what's not to be done, what's to be done in moderation and how precisely all this is to be done, in order to win themselves individuality in the face of others. So we sell them a shirt!"

"What?" shot Zen, his face crumpling, his eyes squinting, his confusion spinning.

"Yes, we sell them a shirt" Bernays insisted, "A shirt, which from cradle to grave, over and over again, we have promised, wins you individuality. But does it? Well, how can it? Everybody else in your segment is wearing it!"

Bernays held Zen squarely by the shoulders, "Oh... but that doesn't matter. It doesn't matter because you don't know, you are incapable of knowing how individuality works" he condescended, feebly trying to shake Zen, "But if we marketers have done our duty, risen to our higher calling, you will be so well educated that—HEY PRESTO—this threadbare thatch of threads will blow a neuron wind, a brain storm will gather, a mind mist will hover and all the grand, high-flown trappings of individuality will be yours"

"But not really" Zen interjected.

"Not really, not really..." Bernays momentarily agreed, still holding and again now feebly shaking Zen by the shoulders, "but ooooh so really Zen. Realer indeed, mightier, more magnificent than any can that can be won out here, my dear Zen"

Bernays paused, still holding him by the shoulders, though it felt to Zen as if he was being strangled by the jugular, "And do you know what Zen?" Bernays asked not letting go, "All the better... all the more effective, all the more efficient, if these neuron winds, these brain storms, these mind mists can be evoked not by the threadbare thatch of threads... oh no, no... but by none other than that lustrous life-giver, that..."

"A bran..." Zen tried.

"Yes Zen, oh yes, a brand-sun Zen... a beatific Brand-Sun" Bernays flourished.

The noose of loose fleshed hands wouldn't let go and it felt as though they were tightening around his jugular. As a half-measure to wriggle free, Zen tried to at least avert his eyes but the beady black bulbs followed them. Then, having securely clasped his shoulders, the hands turned Zen back around to the cabin window. Amidst the mud and sludge, the pious pre-worlders were trudging on.

"And so you see my dear Zen," Bernays began in a tone that suggested he was wrapping up, "religions are brands. Oh yes, the very first brands... the very best brands. Brands where the 'supposedly' philanthropic, humane hand—of god, gods or karma & nirvana (though the mystic marketers had a big hand to play in this as well!)—places in orbit around an axis (hardly ever a bare one though!) the satisfaction of the complicated and intangible defining desire for meaning... for immortality... for a sense of morality... for consolation... for forgiveness... for hope"

With this Bernays fell silent and his noose of loose fleshed hands fell away, leaving Zen to stand in the new light shone by his impartation. Zen's lower lip started moving sideways, roughening against his upper lip, this tick only interrupted every few times by his incisors biting a soon bloodying fold of his lower lip. Self-concept deflating at foolishness realized, regret, pity, frustration churning, teeth gritted in anger. What a waste his struggle was, all his and his mother's sacrifices, that ascension, all those likes, Muthu maligned, Maya muslimed; damn LifeTree, damn Jesus!—he cursed, he raged. And all those wretched pre-worlders toiling in ignorance, lies for meaning, dances for morality, jumping smoke hoops for forgiveness, drugged by consolation, chasing their mangy tails for hope. He had been made a fool of all those years, everything had been taken from him, he could never get them back. Damn... Damn... DAMN, his fists clenched, fantasizing about someone to punch.

The noise of pre-world clang and clatter and then the murmuring of chatter steadily increased in volume as Bernays fidgeted with his Embed.

"Listen... listen Zen" he shushed.

Zen, teeth still gritted, fists still clenched didn't want to listen, but he heard.

"Gather 'round everybody" a voice called out above the chatter, clang and clatter, "Gather 'round, gather 'round" it herded.

Despite his seething, Zen couldn't help but notice that below, the mud baked pre-worlders were dropping everything and forming themselves into the semblance of a semicircle.

"Oh yes Zen, marketing has learned a lot from religion" Bernays began to voiceover.

"Let us hold hands in prayer" the voice exhorted, and the semicircle stretched out like a string of cutout figures.

"Branding oh yes, but not just what branding can do and how to do this, oh no… much more"

"Let us thank God almighty for the mercy he has shown us, let us thank God for his love that never fails" the voice reverentially rang out.

"Religion has taught marketing, branding's most wonderful, it's apt to say—its most supernatural power" Bernays adjudged.

"God thank you, thank you for sparing us from this devil sent flash flood" the voice subserviently thanked.

"Look Zen, these people… these people have lost everything" Bernays sympathized, transparently to make his point.

"God thank you, thank you for giving us the strength to rebuild your church" the voice gratefully went on.

"God has broken all the promises that orbit him and his religion" Bernays disparagingly declared.

"God thank you, thank you for having taken those who we have lost to a better place, to your embrace; thank you for having granted them eternal life in your glorious kingdom" the voice sincerely thanked.

"But these promises Zen, not only do they not have to be achieved, the veritable opposite of them can come to pass out here" Bernays marveled.

"God thank you, thank you for all your blessings" the voice re-thanked.

"And yet, if people want them enough, all that needs be done is for the axis around which they revolve to be invoked for that neuron wind to blow, that brain storm to gather, for that mind mist to hover"

"God, we know that you only challenge the strongest of us, the…" the voice trustfully appreciated.

"For after a while Zen, if the yearning is fervent enough and for one's defining desires by definition it is—a neuron wind, a brain storm, a mind mist—that is all that satisfaction is, and nothing more. And to ensure this is so, along with this fervor, indeed *from* this fervor comes always a self-medicating dose of post-purchase rationalization"

"…and God we thank you for this opportunity to prove our faith in you, and God we thank you for your mercy, and God we thank you for your blessings, and God we thank you for your undying and eternal love for us…" the voice effusively came to a grateful climax.

And Bernays summed up, "Religion, my dear Zen, has always known and has taught marketing, that it is not god… oh no, no, no… but indeed—Branding—that works in mysterious ways"

Following the voice, the chorus rang out, "AMEN"

18

CHILDREN RACING dogs and goats, scavenging up the rubbish mountain's side, if only they could make it to the top they would see. They would see their lot: brown and dry, rusty and low; cut with ditches that snaked off with that gray sludge, filmed with plastic bag pink and blue, which oozed, excreted from the washing, bathing, pissing and shitting across its banks. But more so, they would see over the barricading border and over the hologram haze that levitated above it. They would see the neatness and niceness, the greenness of the lush broccoli topped spokes that radiated from a central grove where polished metal ballerinas poised in the most elegant of poses flowered to the tropical sun. But most of all they would see, that neither here nor there were they free.

"Unique, unique, unique indeed, Zen" Bernays broke in, making Zen zoom out till his eyes could only discern a split-screen between the broccoli carpet of lush green and a rusty brown sheet, "The only place on earth, where we allow the pre-world to creep so close to the realms"

The uneasy feeling that Bernays, the cunning gray eminence, was ever so slyly shifting the sand beneath his thoughts away from that place, crossed Zen.

"Director, what was that place?" Zen jumped-the-gun, "And I know it wasn't an atheist realm but I saw an inscription…"

" 'I am against religion because it teaches…'?" Bernays verified.

"Yes" Zen confirmed, "and of course we… uh, we met in a church"

"Ha-ha… an atheist realm" Bernays exclaimed, his furry white and brown eyebrows springing up in fascination and then his eyes away, up and to the right as though wistfully imagining it. "You thought it was an atheist realm" Bernays giggled mostly to himself, "So one could say Zen, that for you…" he giggled again, "the atheistic inscription on that stone tablet was a revelation" he giggled on.

"Well…" Zen tried to explain.

"No, no," Bernays interrupted, "there is no such thing as an atheist realm, but how apt… how apt indeed that you ask this now" he added, looking out the cabin window and smiling.

"But then, what…" Zen started, gaping his eyes, splaying his arms, upturning his palms in puzzlement at Bernays.

"You remember, Zen…" Bernays cut in loudly over Zen who determinedly tried to get a few more words in, "YOU REMEMBER… I told you, that while brands were beloved, entrepreneurs were esteemed, corporations were consecrated—countries were dying?"

"Yes" Zen gave in, Bernays's dictatorial decibel surge having had the intended effect.

"And, now you know," Bernays resumed back at his customary volume, "the force that made brands beloved, entrepreneurs esteemed, that consecrated corporations"

"Marketing?" Zen still cowered, played along.

"Yes, none other" Bernays replied, his tone imbued with reverence and pomp, his chin rising, "And marketing thought, my dear Zen, if it is the illuminating insights, the distinguished discipline, the worthy work of marketing that has come to be the most influential hand that guides society (we marketers being the faithful fingers of this guiding hand), then… then it is nothing less than marketing's moral duty to segment, to target, to position and of course to brand… countries"

His eyes closing as he inhaled a deep breath, Bernays gathered himself, then refocussing on Zen, slap-clasping him by the cheeks with his cold clammy hands, "We didn't just re-brand, re-market countries as some dismiss, oh no, no, no… we branded anew, we marketed anew, we discarded the old, we conceived—REALMS" Bernays erupted volcanically spewing spit and passion all over Zen's face.

Ports' rallying cry—'Imagine there's new countries'—zinged Zen's mind.

Then, starting with a series of small regular coughs, a full-on spasm of whoops overwhelmed Bernays; in between them his breath grew shorter, faster, more desperate. Concerned, Zen approached.

"I'm fine, I'm fine" Bernays assured, retiring to his leather throne, "But… (cough, whoop, cough)… it's best I go home now"

…That we the people, now well capable and sufficiently informed, now ready, now deserving, are, for the first time in history, finally granted true self-governance. Imagine there's new countries.

Throughout the night, Zen had read these words of Ports over and over again. It had to be that, it had to be that, it couldn't be anything else, he concluded each time. Yet each time he couldn't help but re-read and re-think before coming full circle, dismissing what he re-thought and concluding again that, what he thought had to be—was.

The next day, Bernays's vitality and vigor it seemed was well back, and there was something in the way he intently fidgeted his Embed that hinted to Zen that they were going back there.

Standing shoulder to droopy shoulder, together looking out through the cabin window, Bernays put what he meant to be an affectionate, avuncular, though what felt like a paternalistic arm, around Zen, "Delusion has always been the solution. But the only problem was… the only problem was, my dear Zen, that there were too many delusions competing to be the solution"

Zen, though uncomfortable in the feeble yet straightjacketing grip of the musky miasma, fought the urge to squirm free, trying instead to concentrate on what it was saying.

"You see Zen," Bernays began, "when marketing answered its higher calling, when marketing assumed the righteous responsibility of Segmenting, Targeting, Positioning and Branding countries… realms I mean. We marketers had to ask ourselves an all-important question"

Then Bernays paused momentarily, lowered his arm from Zen's shoulder, "Indeed marketers had to ask and answer a 'future defining' question" he emphasized, tapping the book cozily cosseted in Zen's pocket, "And what do you think that question was Zen?"

"On what to…" Zen tried to venture.

"Yes Zen, exactly" Bernays boomed back in, "Based on what do you we segment these new realms? And what better to segment on, Zen, than on that venerated, deified service provider which throughout the ages has oh so 'faith'-fully catered to the defining desires of the masses"

This time determined not to be denied Zen quickly rattled off, "But wasn't religion also dying and godless atheism growing?"

Stopped in his thought tracks, Bernays turned to Zen. On making eye contact his beady black bulbs made a quick reassessment and then rerouted.

"Well yes, but more so—No" Bernays started to reconcile, "In certain countries of the old developed world—Yes. But amongst the masses of the third world, by far the vast majority, religion was most definitely still alive and killing!"

'Developed world', 'Third world', the labelling was unfamiliar, but Zen assumed the differences were along the lines of those between the realms and the pre-world.

"And, oh Zen,'', Bernays's brown and white eyebrows and his index finger jumped up, expressing that a pivotal point had popped into his head, "what those who declared the impending death of religion by simply relying on a headcount of those who didn't believe, those who doubted and those whose doubts were growing, didn't count on was the 'Faith Potential' in all of us"

"Faith potential??" Zen shot back quizzically.

"Oh yes Zen, you see each and everyone one of us, some more than others though, are hardwired with the potential to believe in the irrational" Bernays declared, and then his index finger jumped up again, "In fact it is rationality that is rare. And even when it is there, it doesn't preside over all thoughts and things; and it hardly stays for long and never... never over the mass majority of men, my dear Zen... does it preside forever"

After this flourish falling silent, Bernays tilted his head contemplatively, his thoughts a million miles waylaid. And Zen, his hook being the cause, took an impish pleasure in this.

"It is true my dear Zen," Bernays then blossomed back out of the cocoon of contemplation that seemed to be claiming him, "that as peace has been to war, in human history, rationality has only ever been an aberration to irrationality"

Bernays turned to Zen and in now customary fashion, feebly got ahold of him by the shoulders, "It comes and goes, waltzes in and out, and any stability, any prosperity built on it, is soon swashed and backwashed away by the timeless tides and unwavering waves of irrationality". Trying in vain to shake him, Bernays expounded on, "No Zen, the linearists... uh, those who had 'faith' that history always moves forward—linear*hists*—as I like to call them, they were wrong. Prosperity and stability and the stability of prosperity can only ever be built on the bedrock of irrationality and unreason; they can only ever be built on faith, my dear Zen"

Then, still having Zen by the shoulders Bernays paused, an expression of 'Where was I?' complicating his saggy face, his thoughts rewinding almost visibly across his eyes like a videogram would.

"Yes, and so," he got back on track, temporarily letting Zen loose, "delusion has always been the solution, but there were too many delusions competing to be the solution. But not if... oh, but not if, marketing figured, we segment, target, position and brand based faithfully on your particular delusion's dress-up; based on your religion"

Bernays again took Zen by the shoulders, "Religion may have always known, my dear Zen, that delusion is the solution, but it was marketing that discovered that the devil is definitely in the details, that... Delusion*s* are the Solution*s*"

Letting go of one shoulder, Bernays dropped his left hand to near the right side of his waist, and began incanting. Each incantation heralded by a dismissive swiping motion of his left arm-sail diagonally from bottom to top, each time almost backhanding Zen across the face.

Dismissive swipe, near slap—"Never again will I suffer what I believe being blasphemed, being challenged, even being questioned"

Dismissive swipe, near slap—"Never again will I suffer being persecuted for what I believe in, will I suffer being shunned, will I suffer being ridiculed"

Dismissive swipe, slap—"Never again will I suffer even so much as having to acknowledge different beliefs from my own, will I suffer even so much as having to perceive different beliefs from my own, will I suffer even so much as a dust particle of doubt entering my mind to smear my spotless faith"

Holding his flapping left arm-sail raised after this last incantation, his chin and eyes rising imperiously in the direction and to the elevation of his outstretched arm-sail, Bernays climaxed, "Henceforth and for eternity, 'What I Believe in is Always Right'; my realm *is* me, my realm *is* I"

Zen felt the feeble grip on his left shoulder tighten as much as it could before pulling him closer. It turned him, the only moments ago million miles waylaid gaze now, suddenly, squarely setting its sights upon his eyes, "This my dear Zen... this... this is what we call Belief Marketing". "And you, me, we... Now!... we are all living in market segments" Bernays ceremoniously consummated, sweeping his other hand in a gesture as if to unveil the world below—split-screen between rusty brown and lush green.

19

ZEN WONDERING, Bernays in wonderment, stood looking out the cabin window for a while longer.

There was really no point; pieces were missing, pieces were messed up, some pieces meant one thing but others which looked identical meant something entirely else. Till Bernays decided to tell-all and put all together for him, the jigsaw wouldn't come together; there really was no point. But, his mind couldn't help itself. Not an atheist realm but then what? Bernays knew Ports but how? From Post Politica to the realms but why? Well, at least he had a working theory about that.

"No one trick pony" Bernays observed, starting off at no more than a whisper, "No one trick pony... not a one trick pony at all" he concluded at near conversational volume.

"Religion?" Zen asked, his brow furrowing both at the oddness of Bernays's behavior and out of curiosity about what he was muttering.

"No one trick pony, but a... oh yes, yes—religion, Zen" Bernays replied mid mutter, "It's not just about meaning, immortality, hope and all that other soap, you see. Oh no, no, no... much more"

Bernays re-squared himself to the cabin window. "Over there," he started, thrusting his right hand rightwards to indicate the brown rusty right of the split-screen world below, "sure religion blows neuron winds of meaning, immortality, hope and bubbles of all that other soap, but we also employ its versatile verses for quite another purpose. Well, actually, employ perhaps is not the right word, it's more of a case of us... uh, facilitating, helping along, one of religion's natural and inevitable byproducts—divisiveness. Oh yes, in the pre-world we simultaneously market the proverb—'What I believe in is always right'—while funding proselytization and sponsoring crusades"

Bernays's words sharply poked the scab over that old wound of indignation that had winced Zen back when he found out the truth about the crusades.

"Ah, but you Zen, you were a crusade assistant, so you know this first hand, don't you" Bernays remembered, "Yes, in the pre-world we offer religion a helping hand to hammer home the doctrine of our day— 'Divide and Rule Yourself' "

"And, and over here" Bernays went on, thrusting his left hand leftwards to indicate the lush green left of the split-screen world below, "Ha-ha, over here, same-same—neuron winds blow meaning, immortality, hope and bubbles of all that other soap—but different. Oh yes, over here, in our realms, Zen, along with morality neatly compartmentalized and the rare big philosophical question answered away; over here, the versatile verses of religion we most certainly do employ, Zen. To impart—yes—but most, most importantly, my dear Zen, to provide… to procure, divine sanction for good consumerism"

This too, just as much as the proselytization and sponsored crusades, Zen knew.

"Ha-ha, so you see my dear Zen," Bernays bloomed, thrusting both his arms out to either side, to lush green and rusty brown, "religion… religion is no one trick pony… oh no, no, no…" he started laughing, "but a, but a… many trick phony!"

Zombies staggered around admiring themselves. More than walking they stopped, and then tilted, angled, adjusted their heads and their bodies this way and that, then looked, then admired, then staggered forward again; always only for a few steps more, until they stopped and then started all over again. And just in case, all over the place, between the brand-fruit trees, around the vending buddies, on many of the walls, lining the walkways—were more mirrors.

Zen looked up from the mesmerizing maze of mirrors and the turbaned and head-scarfed zombies that they encased. In about the only plane that didn't gawk back at him, in the sky, a sheathed golden dagger presided, inscribed with the name 'Guru Globe II', the upper part of the lettering featuring a distinctive straight-line overstrike. Regularly the golden dagger revolved, revealing a square consisting of four smaller squares colored red, green, blue and yellow, with 'Realmsoft' in a blocky basic font typewritten underneath it.

Zen focused back down on Bernays, who was uncomfortably fidgeting with his turban, amidst the sea of zombies staggering by.

"A new invention," Bernays remarked, still fidgeting with his turban, "a complement to MeScape that I really wanted you to see Zen"

"MirrorMe" Bernays revealed, after he sat down on a nearby outdoor chair belonging to a café, "Still in the testing stages, but it's supposed to look and feel like you're in a mobile hall of mirrors. The funny warps have to be bought separately"

Zen noticed a head-scarfed woman, in baggy cream and gold silk pants (like the men and everyone else here wore) staggering closely by; her short tight tank top revealing a bare midriff that weirdly had tattooed around its naval, as if orbiting it, four or five objects. One of which Zen instantly recognized as being the dagger presiding over the sky, another a comb, he was sure. But what wouldn't let Zen's eyes go, was neither her realm uniform nor her orbit of tattoos, it was that she was an uneven patchwork of saggy old and supple young. Hanging jowls and high brows gave way to resigning shoulders and perky breasts, and then to a potbelly that tautly tummy tucked itself in tying together wrinkly tarpaulins for skin. Though facially she didn't look anything like her, she reminded him of Tresemmé. 'A lifetime ago, a lifetime ago'—he reminisced, as he kept staring at her. Not that stumblingly—tilting, angling, adjusting her hodgepodge of head and body in self-admiration—she could notice being stared at.

A while later a series of small regular coughs started from Bernays. Zen hardly noticed, still reminiscing, now retrospecting, reflecting, on how far he'd come, on how much he'd changed, on how naïve he'd been to have believed in the realms and in religion. Then, as had become more and more frequent, a full spasm of whoops overwhelmed Bernays, in between them his breath growing shorter, faster, more desperate. And this finally roused Zen from his reflecting.

"I'm fine, I'm fine" Bernays assured as always, this time though it seemed his bout of coughs actually were subsiding.

Giving it a few more moments to be sure, Zen sunk back to where he left off. As the silk trousered zombies, turbaned or head-scarfed, all in tight tank tops long or short, tattoos on their shoulders or midriffs, self-admiringly staggered on by.

How different things might have been if, instead of getting a participation as a crusade assistant, he got some other participation, Zen retraced pensively. He would've never discovered the real purpose of the crusades. Which meant he wouldn't even have been at a crusade meeting let alone have had that outburst that brought him to the attention of the MyRealm crusade director. Which meant he would've never have met the wheezing old know-bag now sipping some brew in front of him, and he would've never known, what he knew now—from which, there was no going back. An unlikely sequence of happenings, his mind unequivocally reasoned, he was better off for; though his heart didn't always feel the same way.

"You don't know why I brought you here, do you Zen?" Bernays asked, circulating his index finger around the rim of his white ceramic mug, a wry smile and a shine of self-satisfaction glazing his beady black bulbs.

It had to have something to do with this latest friend-device—MirrorMe. It had to, Zen figured, his concentration intensifying, his eyes stopped at the familiar round green crest featured on Bernays's white ceramic mug (this being Guru Globe II, Siren the mermaid wearing a headscarf).

"Look around you Zen" Bernays clued.

And Zen did. First to the background screensaver of self-admiring zombies staggering around and then closer inside the café itself. Where, out of necessity, the turbaned and head-scarfed zombies had momentarily swiped away MirrorMe to place their orders. Orders to which, after they had drunk them, the turbaned and head-scarfed zombies would make—to their mugs and cups, to green head-scarfed Siren the mermaid—a both-palmed praying gesture of thanks. But still, Zen couldn't flesh out beyond his intuition that it had everything to do with MirrorMe. So he zoned in on the zombie at the next closest table. To her left, to her right and from behind her, MirrorMe was her self-reflecting. The rectangular plane in front of her was divided equally between a translucent window of MirrorMe and a translucent window of SoulMate Mobile. But again, there was nothing out of the ordinary that jumped out from her four-sided compact. Not knowing what to look for, and not really expecting to find it, Zen zoomed even closer through the translucence of her mirror sides and her fine filamentous headscarf to her light ash blonde hair, even catching a glimpse of her pale blue eyes when they ever so often tilted, angled, adjusted for self-admiration. But nothing.

"You don't see it, do you Zen?" Bernays concluded.

"Uh…" Zen stalled, desperately not wanting to give up to the old ghost.

"Well, you *have* seen it Zen, you *do* see it Zen" Bernays assured, leaning over and clasping the ends of the small table they were sitting at, and in the process almost knocking over Siren's mug, "It's just that… it's just that… ha-ha, after a while even the elephant becomes a part of the room"

Bernays, on the crest of an idea it seemed, bounded up, propped for support by the table. His cold clammy hands then clasped Zen by the forearm and pulled him away from the café into the midst, into the zigzagging paths, of the staggering zombies.

"Look, look" Bernays exhorted, wildly throwing his arm-sails out. Then, sure in the knowledge that none would notice, let alone care, Bernays started pointing fingers at individual zombies as they staggeringly zigzagged by.

Again Zen zoomed in. But all he noticed was that following their usual tilting, angling and adjusting, many of the zombies, especially the women, would prominently pout their lips and their lower faces (as Tresemmé often would, he re-pictured). And when they pouted their lips so, they looked like ducks, he thought. But these were all trifles, none of them were bringing him any closer to solving Bernays's puzzle, dismissed Zen, trying to return to the bigger picture.

Bernays, to rub in his puzzling point, was now turban-and-all buffoonishly waving at the zombies that zigzagged close in front of him. To no avail of course, dismissed Zen, and then just as he thought this, because he thought this—an electrocuting eureka ding-donged his mind. All this time he had been focusing on a mere friend-device, on

MirrorMe, and Bernays had hinted that 'you *have* seen it', that 'the elephant becomes a part of the room'. This had nothing to do with Guru Globe II in particular, it had everything to do with citisumers in general.

But before Zen could proudly posit his solution to Bernays, he was dragged by a cold clammy claw on his forearm, sidestepping, skirting through the sea of zigzagging zombies and mini-zombies, then via a travelator to a large open-air stadium. And by the time Bernays had made his way up to the seats, the old windbag thoroughly winded was now coughing and whooping again.

"What do you see Zen?" Bernays asked through coughs and whoops, pointing to the heated contest unfolding on the field below.

Two teams of sweaty strapping young men, a ball...; Zen gleaned nothing extraordinary except perhaps the extra suit of technological armor each player donned.

"Nothing?" Bernays verified, "Now turn your Embed on"

With a flick of his fingers at his forearm, Zen duly did so. And a few seconds later, from his Embed a translucent screen that spanned his entire field of view appeared in front of him. Then each player, though still very much toing & froing in the competitive kinetics of the game—blurred. They blurred so much that none of their identifying features could be distinguished, and all that remained were shadow-puppets (each one somewhat recognizable only from their distinctive style of play) and the logo of the team they represented hovering above their heads. And running across the bottom of Zen's field of view, the invitation: 'Dear Citisumer Zen, welcome to MyGame bestowed upon you by Realmsoft. Choose the team and the player that is YOU'.

"You have to choose a team and a player since you haven't tried MyGame before. Have you chosen yet?" Bernays asked impatiently.

Zen quite randomly chose a player. Then all at once, everywhere around him the toing & froing of other players, their competitive kinetics now at eye level. Then the ball coming toward him—his. And then the sky and the Guru Globe II dagger, as if he was on his back, he *was* on his back—felled. And he knew by whom, he was away with the ball, away from him. He couldn't do anything about it, he tried, he twitched then wagged his hands and legs, but he needn't have, something was already being done for him, by him. And then back on his feet, the toing and the froing, the competitive kinetics now back at eye level, again the ball, from a teammate, coming toward him—his. It expertly handled by him, it expertly handled for him, he turned, he was turned—past one, by another, he swiftly slalomed forth, marauding into enemy territory, and then he heard the crowd roar as it had been doing right throughout the game, but this time "Zen, Zen, Zen…", then "LOooo…SER, LOooo…SER, LOooo…SER…" they heckled.

"OFF, OFF, OFF" Zen commanded, disoriented, unable to locate his forearm.

"Off the-edge-of-your-seat right onto the field" Bernays remarked, assisting Zen to turn MyGame off.

Zen, eyes blinking rapidly, bewilderedly, gradually readjusted back to his physical vantage point on the stadium's top tier.

"We won't be needing this for much longer" Bernays remarked, indicating panoramically with his right arm, "Oh no, never again will you be a spectator. From here on, it'll be YOU playing for YOUR team, from wherever YOU are… and at a pro skill level that is certainly not YOURS"

Zen's eyes, following Bernays's words as he explained, scanned the rows upon rows of empty soon-to-be obsolete seats that cascaded down from the upper rim of the cavernous stadium.

"The crowd that chanted your name and 'Loser, Loser' were…" Bernays started to state the obvious.

"…were holographic" Zen filled in the blanks.

"Yes. You were on the road-team you see" he observed in passing and went on, "We need spectators of course. It wouldn't be realistic for the VicSub… the, the vicarious subscriber, otherwise. And more basically of course, the actual pro athletes out there, would hardly be motivated playing to an empty stadium—would they now? It's just that consumers won't be the spectators"

Dramatically, and totally out of sync with the matter-of-fact explanatory brief that preceded it, Bernays turned and got ahold of Zen by the shoulders, his beady black bulbs not blinking for a few seconds.

"You must select with your heart Zen" he then solemnly advised, "For when you select a young player as he enters the league, Zen, his abilities and inabilities, his injuries and recoveries, his trades and teams, his ups and downs, his whole career becomes yours, it becomes your career… he becomes you… and there is no changing away from that. He becomes you… and then… oh and then… it becomes all about YOU" Bernays concluded in a laden, overly mysterious tone.

At that clinching moment, Zen was sure he had solved Bernays's puzzle.

But Bernays wasn't done. Before Zen could proudly posit his solution, that cold clammy claw got Zen by the forearm again and dragged him out of the stadium.

Many walkways, elevators and travelators later, huffing—then coughing, whooping—and puffing, Bernays led Zen to an enormous, wide open field. A field ablaze with several separate fires. And from these fires billowed smoke, yet not the distinctive smell of burning, which led Zen to surmise, as he and Bernays approached them, that these were holographic fires.

"In Sikhism they cremate, you see…" Bernays clarified, as they neared a funeral pyre.

By now Zen didn't need Bernays to tell him this. What really fascinated him was what was at the center of the flickering funeral fire— a life-size videogram that summed up the life of the deceased.

"…but crypts or gravestones, MyAfterLife is pretty much the same across the realms"

Zen read the levitating inscription underneath, as the holographic montage entered Davidpreet's teen years. First it was Davidpreet and his friends back when sports were still real-player, Zen noted sardonically. Then it was Davidpreet and his friend-devices, as he blessed himself with his first this & that, act & en. Then it was Davidpreet on his first date. And then with his first-date, it was Davidpreet… it was Davidpreet's first-time… on SoulMate. Zen's head flung away, right into the searchlight of Bernays's beady black bulb beamed gaze.

"Believe in god… but don't forget to upload your life" Bernays wisecracked, and began to giggle.

After his giggles had turned to coughs and whoops, "It wasn't available in…" Bernays started, before pausing to read the levitating inscription, "uh, Davidpreet's time, but now there's an option where along with a montage like this one, your entire life, every second of it, can replay forever". "God, gods and karma may promise you immortality up there, my dear Zen," Bernays then declaimed, pointing to the sky and winking at Zen, "but down in humble old here, it is we marketers that deliver you *e*mortality!"

If his solution to Bernays's puzzle was right, the old know-bag was on the verge of veering off and away on his favorite tangent, Zen fretted. "It's the defining difference between citisumers and pre-worlders that you've brought me here to show isn't it?" Zen blurted, trying to cut Bernays's thoughts off at the pass, "That's the elephant that has become part of the room"

The loose scrunch of liver-spotted flesh that was Bernays's face unfurled itself out to beam a broad proud smile. Bernays lowering his head ever so slightly, courteously gestured 'right this way' toward a bench at the closest edge of the field

'After you' Bernays gestured for Zen to sit down first on the bench. Above which levitated a signboard featuring the name 'MyAfterLife Meadow' with the slogan *Diamonds should be Forever'* underneath it, and a large square consisting of four smaller squares colored—red, green, blue and yellow—to its side.

After he had sat down, "You see Zen," Bernays began in a profound timbre, "by the early decades of the twenty-first century, pathological narcissism had risen to epidemic proportions. Oh yes, somehow we had moved from self-respect to self-worth to… self-esteem to self-love and then to self-infatuation, all in the span of a few decades"

Zen had never heard the word before, not even from Muthu or Ports, but Bernays had explained it well.

"Self-love was threatening to—stop—making the world go round" Bernays evoked his point with wordplay, "And the old systems, Zen, simply couldn't handle the new narcissistic normal"

Every word from Bernays resounding, resonant, Zen set his eyes on the self-admiring zombies zigzagging across the walkways surrounding the meadow.

"And how could they Zen? How could systems... designed for a long gone age, where man looked out and asked himself—'Where do you I fit in?', 'What must I do?—and dreamt—'What... what *can* I do out there?'—possibly continue to function in an age where man was obsessed more with the finer points of his fanny than with the conduct of his affairs... than with the conquest of his future?"

For the first time it seemed to Zen that Bernays, Bernays—the archangel of the Age of the Realms—was bemoaning, bemoaning the passing of a backward bygone age.

"The big picture, Zen, was destroyed... crumbled into seven billion petty little profile pictures" Bernays decried, his cracked gray lips then pursing, the center of his face made of loose shriveled flesh shriveling even more with lament.

His face still scrunched in this shrivel, Bernays sat, shaking his head slightly almost unnoticeably, for a few moments.

"Why I remember... let alone systems, hmpf, barely a conversation could function" Bernays reminisced, his eyes with his thoughts floating away far, far back in time, "It came to a point where even the most pressing social concern wouldn't concern the average narcissus next-door, because he considered himself apart from the whole. Why... why I remember we had a national election where voter turnout was under ten percent! And I think that same year, Facebook crashed for a week because people were uploading too many pictures and videos of themselves and this caused mass panic because the narcissuses thought that their pictures and videos were lost for good!"

'Elections', 'Voters'—more undeniable corroboration that the lifetimes of Bernays and Ports intersected, catalogued Zen.

"Why... two weeks before the Sao Paulo asteroid hit, fewer than twenty percent, I think I remember it was, of online users had heard about it, let alone knew what it was! And, and when asked to guess, most thought it was an eponymous cocktail or a dance hit about to go viral from Sao Paulo!". "This wasn't the narcissism of the revolutionary, the achiever, the social climber, the winner, Zen" Bernays explained, his thoughts trudging back, leaving his eyes still far back when, "The narcissistic mirror has many facets, you see. The narcissism of the revolutionary, the achiever, the social climber, the winner, this is a narcissism that relies, that must be supplied from without. Narcissistic supply is only secured when things: external, objective, important are conquered—no matter how self-centeredly—out here. Out here in the peer-reviewed world, out here in the consensus world"

An emanation of warm pride from about Zen's chest glowed forth—he was right! The puzzle had been solved. Bernays was echoing his thoughts (and nearly to the word too) about the difference between citisumers and pre-worlders—he was right!

"But what was rising was not this. What was rising was a… was a… inward admiring, conceited… not a self-seeking but a… a self-satisfied narcissism. Self-satisfied with every triviality, with every nook and fanny, with every dimple and pimple; a… a PETTY NARCISSISM"

This pronouncement was barely done vibrating his vocal cords when Bernays realized what he had done. A series of small dry regular coughs started jittering the loose liver-spotted flesh around his neck and jowls.

"But of course… but of course…" he sputtered, his words fighting through short desperate breaths and not yet subsided wailing whoops, "it was the systems that were outdated"

Allowing himself a little more time to re-gather his gusto, "Mass narcissism was the next stage in human social evolution and it *is* the ultimate stage in human social evolution, my dear Zen" Bernays about-faced, his expression animating, his cool and his fire returning, "Oh yes, yes, yes, and guess who realized it, Zen?"

"Marketing" Zen obliged.

"Yes, none other" Bernays affirmed, raising both his arms and ceremoniously snapping his fingers almost to signal his comeback, "And do you know why it is the ultimate stage in human evolution, Zen?"

"No" Zen answered, genuinely curious.

Turning to Zen, and so that he was backgrounded by a screensaver of staggeringly self-admiring zombies, Bernays got him by the shoulders.

"Well you see my dear Zen, any zeitgeist, any a... a norm of society, and from the individual perspective any disposition, any mindset, that seeks after real conquest out here..." he started to explain, letting go of Zen's shoulders momentarily to dramatically gesture 'out here', "by definition makes waves, creates ripples, causes change—doesn't it? Now this change can potentially be good, it can be innovation and invention, it can potentially be progressive in all those primitive and intermediate stages of man's social evolution that precede the ultimate and therefore rightfully final stage of social evolution. But when we reach this ultimate and therefore rightfully final stage, social change can only be disruptive and regressive—it can only be bad—don't you think?"

Zen, straightjacketed by Bernays's logic and spellbound by his charisma infused lucidity, didn't realize that Bernays would have preferred a 'Yes' before he went on.

"And this is where, marketing recognized that narcissism becomes invaluable" Bernays revealed, his grip trying to tighten on Zen's shoulders, "Oh yes, yes, yes... you see petty... uh, better we call it peaceable narcissism, is inert... innocuous... harmless, they are my dear Zen—storms in tea cups. Storms... storms in *me* cups. That make no waves, create no ripples, cause no change out here; unlike the other kind... the, the violent narcissism that was necessary to bring us here"

Bernays paused and it seemed took stock for a few seconds, still not letting Zen go.

"But... but you see Zen," Bernays sputtered, still organizing his thoughts, "it's not that marketing instrumentally chose pet... uh, peaceable narcissism to be the prevailing zeitgeist, the mass mentality of the new age. Oh no, no, no... that would be us marketers breaching our duty, our higher calling, which is of course to fulfill the true will of the people. You see marketing merely recognized that peaceable narcissism was rising precisely *because* the final stage of man's social evolution was ready to storm the gates. That, that peaceable narcissism is the batteries to the final social device that is the realms. And that, if these batteries were not included, then it would have been the duty of marketing and marketers to supply them. But of course, of course the realms came with batteries very much included, Zen"

Bernays then leaned back, letting go of Zen's shoulders, a sly smile of self-satisfaction curling the corner of his cracked gray lips. Zen for his part wanted to say something, at least ask something in the few seconds of intermission before Bernays burst back with the rest of his exposition but he couldn't. He couldn't, because he was still getting his head around the notion that this 'narcissism', as Bernays called it, wasn't at all a disease of the realms that portended its decline but instead its indispensable power source, its very heartbeat.

"And, and..." Bernays hastened, his brown and white furry eyebrows jumping up leaving his beady black bulbs against a vast liver-spotted expanse, "branding fitted like a designer glove! Oh yes, oh yes. You see, as you well know my dear Zen, the promises of brands, ha-ha, they are all made to the individual. YOU drive, ride, wear, apply, eat, drink, play with the axis, Zen, and esteem, prestige, freedom, dominance, sophistication, advancement, achievement, self-expression, meaning, contentment, love—will orbit YOU. They will be YOURS, they will be YOU. But there's more Zen"

'There always is' Zen snickered in his thoughts.

"And oh it's perfect my dear Zen" Bernays promised, again getting ahold of Zen by the shoulders. "The satisfaction of these defining desires are neuron winds, brain storms, mind mists, head holograms with very little to do with what really goes on out here—right?" Bernays asked and waited for Zen to acknowledge that he was following him thus far.

"Right" Zen nodded.

"And so, it follows that branding works best for those minds who, for whatever reason—their not capable, they don't care—know the least about what's going on out here—right?" again Bernays waited for Zen's go-ahead.

This time it took a little longer to process, but Zen eventually nodded.

"Right and pet...uh, peaceable narcissists, by definition almost, know the very least about what's going on out here!" Bernays climatically arrived at the solution, shaking Zen by his shoulders. "Hand in designer glove, hand in designer glove… narcissism fits branding—hand in designer glove" Bernays then merrily resounded, "Oh yes, yes, yes… so today we have beverage brands promising YOU youthfulness, rock brands promising YOU eternal love, clothing brands promising YOU self-expression, apparel brands promising YOU dominance, Embed brands promising YOU achievement—the procession is endless, but together… together my dear Zen, they deliver through YOU, the narcissus, mass self-contentment"

Again Bernays fell away and sat back, his eyes a black brew of passion and concentration; boiling, bubbling.

His head now well wrapped around 'narcissism', Zen couldn't help but think maybe Ports was wrong. Maybe the young people who Ports so believed in, were apathetic alright, but not because of their loss of faith in politics but because of their peaceable narcissism. And as Bernays argued, peaceable narcissists were never going to be revolutionaries. They were never going to be the revolutionaries that Ports hoped they would be; they were never going to bring about his Post Politica.

"Oh the realms my dear Zen, are most definitely the final stage of man's social evolution" Bernays rebounded.

Zen safely bet himself that Bernays was about to ask him why and answer his own question.

"And do you know why, Zen?" Bernays asked.

A half-smile hoisted one cheek and side of Zen's mouth.

"You see all the hegemonies… the, the social control systems of the past, have made either one or both of two mistakes" Bernays setoff, before adding parenthetically "Perhaps because they had to" and then continuing, "But in any case, most of them… most of them my dear Zen sought to establish control by brute physical force and the ever looming threat of this. Under their jackboot… ha-ha their jackbrute, it was OBEY or DIE"

Then Bernays was stopped, as if by the realization that Zen wouldn't be able to relate to what he had just explained. He got Zen by the shoulders, his beady black bulbs widening ominously against that vast liver-spotted expanse, "OBEY or DIE" his voice bellowed with an omniscience, with an omnipotence underscoring it, "OBEY or DIE"

After trying to shake him for several seconds longer, Bernays relented, and resumed in his explanatory tone, "But you see Zen, of course this couldn't last. Because even if the subjugation by brute physical force was supplemented by the most invasive and pervasive brainwashing, there is no brainwashing invasive and pervasive enough to completely, to radically eradicate man's natural resentment toward physical subjugation. So inevitably, especially when the economic fortunes of the jackbrute regime waned, the masses would at great cost of life & limb overthrow it"

Images from those words etched in his memory, Ports' opening words '… economic crises, the wars, the famines, the terrorist insurgencies, and the environmental destruction…', now evocatively flashed-back across Zen's mind.

"By the mid twentieth century, Zen, realizing the unsustainability of such jackbrute hegemonies, another kind of hegemony was rising" Bernays continued, sitting back against the bench. The right side of his mouth kinked up with a tiny smile as if he were reminiscing this (though Zen knew this to be impossible), "Yes… yes, instead of physical coercion, the best way it was thought to maintain social order was to provide the very opposite—mass comfort. First, the advance of technology facilitated mass creature comfort and then… and then it facilitated mass psychological comfort" Bernays explained, his gaze wafting somewhere out in the distance.

How possibly could this be unsustainable? Automatically wondered Zen.

"But you see my dear Zen, the hegemony of mass comfort made the second mistake that the intermediate hegemonies in human history were all prone to" Bernays declared, his enthusiasm as signaled by his eyebrows and his index finger perking up, "Oh yes, yes, yes… the mistake was that it was 'mass' comfort. And of course it should have been, it should always be, but it should never seem to be", Bernays, so enthused, confused Zen.

Zen's eyes squinted, his eyebrows squashed in.

Bernays chuckled, "Perhaps I confused you a little" he understated, "You see my dear Zen, man... man comes into this world with a drive to seek individuality. To be recognized as I, myself; to be recognized *for* I, myself. To be not a blade of grass that is alive only to submit a pixel of green to the lawn, but to be a precious flower of unique scent and hue that springs forth from it, that has its very own place under the sun"

Bernays then paused and tried to glean if he was making headway against the confusion. Zen's eyes and eyebrows slowly expanded back to their normal positions, he understood this last part, as well as (he was fairly certain) how it fit into Bernays's overarching point.

"Things and entertainments, devices and distractions, coddling and cuddling—comfort... by all means—Yes" Bernays avowed, "But insofar as... for so long as it was *mass* comfort, its hegemony could not last, it was not final. The hegemony of mass comfort, Zen, like all other intermediate hegemonies, was always susceptible, indeed inherently susceptible because it didn't... it couldn't honor the defining desire for individuality"

Bernays was now contradicting himself, Zen was sure—well, almost. He had just proclaimed that the realms and brands deliver *mass* self-contentment and now, just minutes later, here he was trying to convince him that any 'hegemony' that possessed it was inevitably doomed. Pursing his lips, Zen tried to suppress the smug smile emerging on his face, his cheeks rose a little nonetheless.

"Must be hard for you to fathom, I imagine" Bernays went on, before a thought or memory seemed to pause him, "Why, there was a thing called TV back then—did that old laggard in that library ever tell you about it?"

"Teevee?" puzzled Zen, "No"

Quite disconnectedly from the flow of the conversation, Bernays shut his eyes, clicked his fingers and quietly cursed to himself in a manner as if he had forgotten something.

"Yes, yes, no... a T-V" Bernays bumbled back, "All sorts of entertainment programs were mass broadcast to millions, hundreds of millions, sometimes billions of viewers at a time"

Again Zen's eyes squinted, his eyebrows squashed in.

"What I mean is," Bernays started to clarify, "any given entertainment program was mass broadcast to hundreds of millions at a time. Everybody would watch the same program or at most, could choose between a few!"

Bernays waited for Zen's bemusement. It wasn't forthcoming.

"Hard to fathom isn't it?" he tried again to draw it out, "This was typical of the age of mass comfort and that's why it couldn't last"

Again Bernays paused to gauge Zen's comprehension. Zen's thoughts discussed and deduced behind the scenes of an expressionless face and intent eyes.

"You see my dear Zen" Bernays resumed, "At some level everybody knew, or if they didn't already, could be made aware, that they were that insignificant blade of glass merely submitting a pixel of green to the lawn. That they were a nameless, faceless make-up-the-number, that their individuality was been dishonored, denied; that it was being smudged into sameness. And they did realize Zen, and down fell the hegemony of mass comfort, countries and all"

Not just yet, not just yet, let the old know-bag dig his own grave a little deeper, a little deeper, thought Zen, waiting for his moment.

Again Bernays gauged Zen's comprehension, "But of course, you see Zen, it is economically inefficient… impossible to individualize goods & services… actz & ens". Bernays then put his arm-sail around Zen's shoulder, enveloping him with his musky miasma and smiling in stained enamel yellow and root canal black, the most contented, blissful smile, "And that is why we have branding" he whispered and paused.

"And this is where peaceable narcissism becomes invaluable once more" he exploded, arm-sails flailing. Turning back to Zen and getting him by the shoulders, "Oh yes, yes, yes… you see that shirt we've sold to you, we've sold to all of you—economic efficiency" Bernays flared, his beady black bulbs lasers upon Zen's eyes, "Shirts all the same, but which nevertheless through the power of branding stir up brain storms of individuality"

From his shoulders, Bernays brought Zen even closer toward him, "And here is the best part" he whispered, "Before the advent of peaceable narcissism, there was a danger that you could verify these brain storms that we would stir. You know, actually look around outside you and question how the same shirt (or whatever other axis) we've sold to all & sundry can possibly... can possibly win you individuality. But with the advent of peaceable narcissism these brain storms of individuality, my dear Zen, they rage, oh yes... but they are, they are self-contained... in billions of me-cups"

Bernays finally let go. Zen and his heart sank back into the bench. The old know-bag hadn't contradicted himself, and that coup de grâce where at long last he would show the old know-bag up—that wasn't coming. In resignation, he asked anyway.

"But you said the realms deliver mass self-contentment"

"Ooooh, they do my dear Zen" Bernays crooned, "They do in reality, but for the narcissus, his brain storm brewing in his me-cup, ha—for him the 'mass', the other me-cups... well, they barely even exist!"

Then holding the armrest of the bench Bernays stood and unfurled his arm-sails to indicate his surroundings. Backgrounded by the screensaver of staggeringly self-admiring zombies, foregrounded by the flickering funeral fires of MyAfterLife, beneath Guru Globe's golden dagger and four-squared brand-sun, "We have mastered the science (the art some would say) of the mass production of individuality, my dear Zen; and with it, oh and with it, we have ushered in the ultimate hegemony, the final stage of man's social evolution" he exulted, closing in on Zen.

Extending his arm-sails toward Zen, Bernays clasped him by the side of the shoulders and attempted to raise Zen up. Zen somewhat resisted at first, but then complied.

Bernays's murky blue rimmed beady black bulbs were now only a few nose lengths away. And they grew bigger, they came closer, their hypnotic beams all the while growing more intense, until they were so close upon him that Zen could now smell the humid acetone breath of the old musky miasma, "Of 'I', 'I' will never tire, for how can 'I'? " Bernays rhapsodized, shaking Zen by the shoulders.

"Of 'I', 'I' will never tire, and nor will 'I' of things and entertainments, devices and distractions, coddling and cuddling; of comfort.

Of 'I', 'I' will never tire—no never; and secure, secure in My, 'I' religion, riding high on My, 'I' many-trick-pony, 'I' have arrived, oh 'I' have arrived—at the end of history"

Zen stood transfixed, his eyes for the first time not wanting to escape the two hypnotic beams emanating from Bernays's blood-red and murky blue besieged beady black bulbs.

"And in all the ages of the past, before 'I' was conceived, those others—the masses, had, they say—blind faith. But today... today, here in the realms, here at the very end of history: 'I'... 'I' have BRAND FAITH"

20

IN SUSPENDED animation. Now a nebula of thought and knowledge, not a part of, so from above, mind's-eyeing the pre-world and the realms, Post Politica and OmniRealm, that conundrum of a place down below—Zen returned. A vortex of abstraction. What to do next? In the short term and the long, of no concern, he returned to his nominal role as the Director-General's personal aide—not the same Zen. And when he did consider what to do next, everything that came to mind came from this vortex of abstraction. All he wanted to do was meet Muthu again and tell Muthu everything that Bernays had told him, confront Bernays about Ports, corner him about that conundrum of a place. The time was right, he assured himself, he was on his way to meet Bernays at his hut, at his home, at that conundrum of a place, which meant Bernays surely wanted him to know, he wanted him to ask.

The exotic asymmetry of the place hadn't at all lost its novelty for Zen, and so, unhurriedly, Zen ambled to the door of Bernays's hut. Where for a few moments he stood, savoring the anticipation, envisioning the facts and the artifacts that were about to be revealed to him. Then the long carpeted corridor, its dull gold light flickering from its chandeliers suspended from its high painted ceiling, its aisle of paintings and sculptures and ancient friend-devices. Zen darted in and searched out those artifacts which time hadn't permitted him to peruse on his clandestine first time. On the same side of the aisle, several glass boxes after Vic Crafts, a small glass box lassoed Zen's attention. Mounted within it was a rectangular round-edged friend-device that appeared to be switched on, and which revolved deliberately to display (on its back cover) that bitten cherry logo that appeared on Vic Crafts' beige box, though this time it was emblazoned in brilliant silver. Zen, nose nearly on glass, watched a few more revolutions of this, before moving on to another small glass box. In it was a double flapped friend-device that he recalled from his previous visit, this time though it was switched on. On the top flap, opened at about a right angle to the bottom flap (which contained a tray of buttons much less pronounced than those on Vic Crafts' beige box) a small two-dimensional picture and a variety of different writing, in various fonts and in various shaped boxes appeared. Zen leaned in, first reading on the grayish bar at about the top of the picture a strange code of characters that ended with /s.php?k=10080&id=4, before focusing in on the picture which featured a grinning young redheaded man perhaps only a few years younger than himself.

"Technological advancement unlike social advancement can, and must, proceed ad infinitum" a voice from behind startled Zen. As he rose, before he turned around, on the glass box he saw the unmistakable almost ghostly reflection of the old know-bag.

"But of course that doesn't always happen" Bernays remarked, visibly delighted to see Zen. "Come, come, come" he invited; Zen hoped to the room where he found Bernays's copy of Post Politica.

But not so. The room Bernays escorted Zen to was sparser, neater and far smaller than the one which he had found the book in, though just as old and old fashioned. As Bernays sat down on his imposing crosshatched and dimpled leather chair, perhaps aggravated by the dustiness of the room, his lungs launched the loose windbag of liver-spotted wrinkles, cheeks and chest ballooning then deflating, into one of his bouts of coughs and whoops.

After the coughs and whoops subsided, clearing his throat, "Interested in technology are you Zen?" he asked, "Or is it more in history?"

Zen answered but it was obvious Bernays wasn't listening. His beady black bulbs and his thoughts distancing out through the wooden framed window to the right of his chair, a look of regret, of lament, seemed to droop even more the already loose hanging features of his face.

"There are of course a few more riddles the realms have to resolve… a few required wrinkles that have been ironed out, Zen" Bernays stated out of the sky blue that his gaze and thoughts seemed lost in.

Suddenly, impetuously, Zen felt he couldn't wait any longer, uncontrollably his chest revved into drumming thud-thuds that reverberated all the way to the roof of his rapidly drying mouth.

"Take your Embed for instance," Bernays started to cleave off on a tangent.

"YOU KNEW HENRY PORTS" Zen thundered, both his hands frantically, bunglingly reaching about both his pockets to find the book, "I s-s-saw, I saw this same book made out to you by Henry Ports... in this, in this same hut" he stammered loudly, thumping the book on the table and then standing up.

Ever so gradually, the rays of a serene smile began dawning on Bernays's loose shrivel of a face, and abided there. His beady black bulbs projecting this serenity beheld Zen, in complete silence. And as they did, they becalmed Zen, making him sit down again.

"Oh yes, Zen" Bernays whispered, still serenely smiling, "I knew Henry Ports very well"

The drumming thud-thuds decelerated away into regular indistinct heartbeats. And another sensation—the joyous anticipation of the explorer who senses that he is on the cusp of a lifelong pursued discovery—began to diffuse from Zen's chest throughout his being.

Bernays reached down to the bottom drawer of the desk and took out a rectangular shaped thing, which at first Zen thought to be a large thin booklet. Flapping open its sectioned cover to fleetingly reveal a dark sheet of glass, he faced it toward him, appeared to check it and flapped it shut again. Then, "Come Zen, I have something to show you" he invited, gesturing to the door.

Into that aisle flickering with an aura of dull gold they went, Bernays, rectangular thingy in hand. Past glass boxes full of little friend-devices, and various striped, starred and spangled rectangular cloth banners, through a turn Zen had missed the time before, they walked. Until, they reached a statue carved out of beige stone, which, though elevated on a square base, was about life-size. It raised one hand, as if orating a point toward Zen and Bernays, but most distinct about it was that its head had been deliberately chopped off, as obvious from the clear-cut flat plane at the top of its neck. Zen's eyes zipped to the inscription on the stone base:

'In the future there will be no war, if for no better reason than it will be bad for business'

— Henry Ports

Neural fireworks of elation shot and sparkled across the pathways of his brain. Bernays wasn't deceiving him, he was standing in front of Henry Ports himself! Finally, finally, he was on the cusp, on the mountain top, and history's haze Bernays was about to blow away.

"Zen... meet Henry Ports" Bernays introduced, gesturing accordingly.

Allowing the awe inspired young man to revel a little longer in his sense of wonder,

"Come, come" Bernays prompted, "There is much I have to show you"

In the pod, on their way, Zen's mind so expectant that all was about to be told, wasn't nagged by all those usual questions, lanced by all those usual loose ends nor disquieted by that usual lurking suspicion of Bernays. Indeed, Zen for the first time relented, allowing himself to feel a grandfatherly affection for the old know-bag who had taught him so much, and soon—everything.

A trip that was zipped along by all the goings-on and all that was going-to-be, soon ended with Bernays fidgeting his with Embed, followed by that indicative series of broken jittery thuds.

But as the hatch opened, and he and Bernays (still with rectangular thingy in hand) descended down the stairs, Zen was surprised to see, presiding over the horizon, a square consisting of four smaller squares colored red, green, blue and yellow—it was Realmsoft's brand-sun. Above 'Realmsoft', from the spaces between the four smaller squares that together formed sort of a plus sign, a shimmering pearl white crucifix extended out, and above it appeared the name 'Adam's Peak'.

Zen thought about it, but not wanting to even consider the possibility, didn't ask Bernays where they were.

As always, a team of assistants awaited to whisk them to wherever it was Bernays had decided he was taking Zen. All throughout the way, though Zen kept telling himself not to, he couldn't help but look up at that brand-sun, and wonder. And every time he did, although he fought them away, those questions nagged, those loose ends lanced and those suspicions disquieted him.

"Zen... Zen we are here" Bernays's voice loudened, trying to awake him from his meditative fixation with the brand-sun up above.

Swarmed by a congregation of assistants, Bernays and Zen got off the Sky Cabriolet and were escorted through a tower, a participation tower it looked like, to one of its uppermost floors. As they ascended, perversely to Zen's great relief, a collective expression of foreboding gloomed the faces of the congregation of assistants. Dismissing his earlier disquiet as unfounded, putting it down to habitual suspicion, Zen's relief turned, it returned to elated anticipation. It was that Bernays was about to tell-all, it was that the old know-bag was about to reveal all the deep dark secrets of the realms, Post Politica and Henry Ports, that explained the ever darkening foreboding on the assistants' faces. But this would mean the assistants knew all as well, but only Bernays knew all, Zen's mind instinctively back-talked. But it had to be, it had to be, he wishfully concluded.

On reaching their destination floor, Bernays led the slow procession. "You are about to see one of our most dangerous experiments" Bernays announced to Zen, making sure the entire congregation would hear. They arrived at a viewing balcony, overlooking a large auditorium. On seeing what was going on below, Bernays's concentration visibly intensified. And a few seconds later clasping his thumb and forefinger together he began slowly, repetitively scrunching the loose wad of flesh that was his chin. The expressions on the assistants' faces had rapidly deteriorated from foreboding to revulsion, many were turning their heads away, unable to bear looking at the scene below.

It was odd, and at first glance it did instantly strike that something was amiss, but it certainly wasn't repulsive, Zen thought to himself, peering down with Bernays and only a brave few of the congregation. But then again, he empathized, his was not the perspective of the typical citisumer.

At the center of the auditorium which seemed quite old, as if it belonged in that place along with Bernays's hut, Realmsoft's four-squared brand-sun levitated. Its squared rays—colored red, green, blue and yellow—shining on and presiding over small circular assemblies of characters in which each participant character was conspicuously different from the next. Sarees next to burqas, cat-suits next to togas, baggy next to spandex, rainbow streaked next to pristine white, stood forcedly, stood awkwardly holding hands.

Just to be sure, Zen randomly zoomed into a few of the characters to verify from the insignia on their clothing that they were all Realmsoft citisumers—as far as he could tell, they were.

"Alright, you lot can go" Bernays permitted, allowing the thankful assistants to scurry away.

"You see, Zen," Bernays started, leaning over the balcony, "technological advancement unlike social advancement can, and must, proceed ad infinitum… you know, forever. But we've found that technological advancement has… well, let's say it has stagnated"

Still leaning over the balcony, Bernays loosened one arm-sail free and started tapping on Zen's forearm, "Take your Embed for instance" he cited, his gaze still peering down at the clashing assemblies floundering below.

Pushing himself off with his other arm-sail Bernays sprung himself around to face Zen, pierced him in the eyes with his beady black bulbs and then started to search for something in amongst the nearby seats.

"Ah, here it is" Bernays exclaimed, presenting the rectangular thingy to Zen, "Go on open it"

Zen remembering how Bernays had done it, though more delicately, flapped open its sectioned cover. Several columns of squircles, quite like those that made up SoulMate (of all things!—thought Zen) appeared on the sheet of glass.

Bernays commandeered Zen's right hand, momentarily destabilizing his hold on the glass sheet, and then taking Zen's index finger made him tap one of the squircles launching it into life, albeit in only two dimensions.

"The only thing that your Embed has on this, is that it's holographic" Bernays declared, his beady black bulbs trying eagerly but failing to make contact with Zen's downward fixated eyes.

"And Henry Ports used one just like this!" Bernays punch-lined, knowing that this would bring Zen's eyes and attention darting back to him. It did.

"Do know what imagination is, Zen?" Bernays asked, a sliver of that sly smile (which dawned when he used Ports to get Zen's attention) still lingering on his face.

"Yes" Zen replied, adding 'obviously' with the fitting facial expression.

"And do you know what the seeds of imagination, of creativity are?" Bernays asked, inviting him to sit down.

"Um…" Zen stalled, sitting down.

"The seeds of imagination, of creativity my dear Zen," Bernays romped on, "ha, they are wild grass seeds, foxtails, diaspores"

Zen's thought train screeched. He didn't completely comprehend what Bernays was saying, but he was sure that it was on an entirely different track than his own frantic search for an answer.

"Oh yes, yes, yes… the seeds of imagination, of creativity, are those pesky, prickly wild grass seeds which you don't want clinging to your trousers, to your skin, but do so all the same"

Launched by this metaphor, Bernays metaphorically leapt to his feet. Rectangular old Embed in one hand, taking Zen by the other, he headed out of the balcony, past the now dispersed assistants, gesturing to the ones that volunteered to follow him that there was no need to. Until, at the nearest glass epidermis of the tower, he stopped.

Letting go of his hand, Bernays got Zen by the eyes. The brand-sun of Adam's Peak—its shimmering pearl white crucifix extending out through those four smaller red, green, blue and yellow squares—reflected lucidly from his beady black bulbs.

"Look, down there" Bernays pointed, moving his index finger across the glass to indicate the line of citisumers sauntering through a walkway below, "What do you see?"

Zen knew that the answer had to be far more nuanced than 'citisumers', so he stalled with a few "ums", his thought train once more beginning to choo-choo.

"They are all the same!" Bernays preempted indecorously.

'Argh' Zen's mind winced, he had considered saying this but had dismissed it as being too obvious.

"Thanks… thanks to Segmenting… they are all the same" quickly put in Bernays, seeking to dispel any doubt that he was blaspheming his creed.

To Zen's eyes, the citisumers sauntering below now merged into one long blue line of marching ants.

"You see Zen," Bernays recommenced, his index finger pacing along the line of blue marching ants, "DIFFERENCES: different ways and different things and most of all different people, are to one's mind wild grass. Wild grass... wild grass with different, divergent, diverse diaspores that whether you want them to or not, at first painfully prick and then... stick to your mind. And which—given the right conditions—will cross-pollinate your own seeds of thought, and then..."

Bernays turned to Zen, "EUREKAAAAA" he bellowed, his bombast making him drop the old Embed thud on to the floor, "EUREKA..." he repeated, and then his eye caught sight of the fallen old Embed, "the apple will fall, ha-ha-ha-ha" he burst out in a spit spewing full blown belly-laugh. "Your imagination, my dear Zen," Bernays resumed after the laughs that turned into coughs subsided, "would have created something new, novel, never before known"

Bernays paused to regather his strength but more so his seriousness. Zen's eyes, like Bernays's index finger before them, returned to pacing slowly from left to right along the blue line of marching ants.

"But of course, like violent narcissism," Bernays harked back, a solemnness in his voice, "imagination, in this the final stage of man's social evolution, is a dangerous force"

Again Bernays paused. Zen's eyes still paced.

"Oh yes, yes, yes" Bernays bounced back, his voice regaining its usual effervescence, "And that my dear Zen, is why instead of allowing wild weeds to cross-pollinate each other, we have fields and fields, realms and realms, with all and different varieties of grass across them, but flourishing... flourishing within each my dear Zen... is only one stable and happy monoculture"

With this Bernays shuffled closer to Zen—whose eyes, whilst his ears were absorbing Bernays's every word and weed, were still pacing—and whispered into his ear, " 'United We Fall, Divided We Stand' "

For a few moments, the musky miasma let this sink in. Arrested by its presence so close upon him, and by a sudden critical inference, Zen's eyes stopped pacing and his brow furrowed.

"So then the pre-world should be 'flourishing' with imagination?" asked Zen sarcastically intonating 'flourishing' and then, turning to Bernays, "After all, the grass is *wilder* on the other side"

With a pleased smile, Bernays chuckled nasally by expelling short puffs of air from his nose, his beady black bulbs beamed with pride saying 'well done'.

"But Zen," he smiled, something obviously up his sleeve, "intelligence and imagination go together, like horsepower and carriage"

Zen first cussed himself, he had been a little too eager to prove himself to the old know-bag. And then he made light of it, in Bernays's tongue— 'He had jumped the *pun*'. He knew exactly what Bernays's cogent comeback would be.

"Now, this is not to say," Bernays, raising his index finger, began clarifying, "that the smart are all creative... no, no. It's just that illuminating light bulb moments aren't going to flick on in dimwit minds. Certainly... certainly, there is not much creativity to be found under the NumLing threshold required for ascension"

Bernays turned back to the glass epidermis, "Oh yes, now you shouldn't get me wrong Zen, things are just how they should be. Oh yes, yes, yes... with these here realms, we have separated the wheat—the intelligence— from... from the riffraff, from the dimwits dulling down below. And with these here realms, with these... with these petri dishes, each containing a monoculture, we have exactly what this the final and ultimate stage of man's social evolution requires: intelligence without imagination, cleverness without creativity, powerful engines capable of driving... horses capable of pulling their carriages... only, only in the straightest of straight lines"

After a pause, where he repetitively scrunched his chin, "But of course, an iota of imagination is still required to spur along the potentially ad infinitum advancement of technology" he qualified. Bernays then creakily squatted down to pick the fallen old Embed up, took Zen by the hand and hurried away from the glass epidermis.

Soon they were back at the viewing balcony overlooking the auditorium, short of breath but breathless to make his point, "And to ignite this iota of imagination, that is the aim of this experiment" Bernays heaved and sat down.

Zen kept standing, observing once again the conspicuously different assemblies consisting of sarees next to burqas, cat-suits next to togas, baggy next to spandex, rainbow streaked next to pristine white; his mind gradually assembling Bernays's latest lesson into coherence.

Zen's process of piecing together was only broken when he heard the old windbag, apparently having regained his second-wind, repetitively mutter something. He couldn't quite make out the first keyword, but each recitation ended, he was sure, with, "…must be wild", "…must be wild"

"When we do ignite this iota of imagination, we must take great care that it is a small and controlled explosion, Zen" Bernays suddenly, boomingly deviated, perhaps noticing that Zen overheard his mutterings.

Gesturing, then waiting for Zen to sit next him, "Oh yes, we must be careful, we are treading on egghead shells. But nevertheless, it is imperative that we vigilantly manage imagination Zen; that we master the art… the science of Imagi-nagement—as I call it. Perhaps you Zen, perhaps you can come up with a better term for it"

"But if we can't… that means that the realms aren't final, that they aren't ultimate—right?" Zen posed, looking out distantly, contemplatively over the balcony.

That radiance of pride, from Bernays's eyes and his smile, re-dawned; the warmth of its fond rays reaching out, caressing Zen's eyes as they turned to him seeking the answer.

"Oh but Zen… my dear, dear Zen… the realms *are* the final and ultimate stage" Bernays reiterated, his eyes and smile still radiating warmth, "Eliciting that iota of imagination ensuring no explosion of thought pollution, is no easy enterprise. But just like we look back on the sex stickler as one of our conquests, for this conundrum too, we will figure out a balancing act (or en)!"

"Sex stickler?" Zen bemusedly barked back, lip-syncing 'What' while waiting for Bernays to answer.

And then, just as Bernays started to answer, it occurred to Zen, "Yes, the sex stickler—the… sex… stickler" Bernays iterated, his beady little bulbs animatedly intimating that Zen already knew the answer.

"You mean SoulMate?" Zen ventured.

"That Zen, was our solution to the conundrum, not the conundrum itself" Bernays clarified and sprung up his furry white and brown eyebrows to say 'See if you can figure it out'.

Zen's gaze turned down a notch, his upper lip started to traverse right to left, left to right over his lower lip, as he tried to deduce backwards from SoulMate the specs of the sex stickler. But he was shaken from his deepening deducing by a low grumbling from the auditorium. Against their will it seemed, the motley assemblies were being escorted out of the auditorium. Zen turned to Bernays for an explanation.

"They're off to the long isolation stage" Bernays informed, his beady black bulbs floating up and away, obviously picturing this stage, "and then they are separated—the incubation stage—before they are reassembled; and hopefully this is where—as a group, and only as a group—they can come up with a creative solution to the problem they have been assigned"

For a while longer Bernays's beady black bulbs remained distant, still seemingly envisioning the stages, the implications and ramifications of the experiment. Then Bernays began to creak up, "Let's see them out" he enlisted, tucking the old Embed between his right arm-sail and his hip.

As they entered an elevated passageway, Zen slowed down and then detoured toward its glass paneling. Underneath bustled a hall, a hall segregated into small square cubicles. Each confined a citisumer and across the cubicles all the varieties that were previously clumped together—from sarongs to niqabs, from pantaloons to loincloth robes— were represented.

After engrossedly observing for a while the citisumers, as they appeared to talk to themselves whilst animatedly gesturing together images emanating from their Embeds, "What's going on down there?" Zen asked, eyes still glued.

"That's our quarantine chamber" Bernays answered, "Decontamination is the final stage of the Imagi-nagement process. Subjects are isolated and asked to relate in great detail how horrible their harrowing, and potentially infecting, exposure to foreign thought bodies has been. Then their own harrowing accounts are replayed to them along with expert advice on how to stave off thought infections. It's like iTime to get over weTime"

As Bernays concluded his explanation, Zen noticed that in some of the cubicles another set of characters were sitting down in large chairs especially reserved for them. And as his nose squashed in against the glass, he noticed that this set of characters, in fact were made up of replicas of around only eight or so distinct characters, one of whom—Dr. Stal McKnow—he was cringingly all too familiar with.

"Do you know what you should do…" Zen began to volunteer and paused to mentally tick-off that the replica sets of the eight or so characters, most of them middle-aged, spectacled, erudite looking, each exclusively paired up with a distinct strain of citisumer, "you should implement this only for non-NumLing related soon-to-be evictees. This way you get to use the best intelligence and if there is more than just a small imagination explosion, a thought infection, well… it's not like you will have to throw away a good citisumer, they were heading back to the pre-world anyway, where their imagination explosion will be diluted by the dulling dimwits down there. Ha… this way you literally get the best of both worlds"

This time Zen's thoughts off on the implications and ramifications of his idea, he didn't notice the translucent reflection on the glass pancling of Bernays, beaming broadly in stained enamel yellow and root canal black, proudly back at him.

A loose fleshed arm-sail came over his shoulder, with a featherweight mast it felt like of hollow bone, "Right you are… right you are, Zen"

Like convicts shackled by invisible chains, up the hatches of the awaiting pods, trudged the tangle of sarees and lungis, purdahs and pantsuits. Standing side by side, Zen and Bernays soon saw off the pods as they began to whirr away. As Zen's eyes breezily followed one of the pods away and across the twinkling azure, billowed here and there with white marshmallow puffs of cumulonimbus—suddenly—a needled syringe, full of angst, shot into his thought stream. Bernays, the sly sorcerer, had swerved shy of the subject of Ports and Post Politica, the cunning conjuror had changed the subject to the subjects of his experiment, Zen resoundingly realized.

"But what has all this got to do with Henry Ports and Post Politica" Zen broke out; not waiting for Bernays to answer, "Why have you brought me here?" he demanded.

Bernays inhaled a deep breath that arose his chin, before turning to Zen. And when, after a long pause, he did turn, he punctuated a something-up-my-sleeve smile with a quick wink.

Having delayed if not having allayed Zen, Bernays fidgeted with his Embed and soon a trio of assistants turned up. They escorted Zen and Bernays through to the final outermost station of the Sky Cabriolet network and promptly got back in the same carriage which was due to head back.

Along the way to wherever it was he was taking Zen, not a stray syllable slipped out from Bernays; just, when Zen would ask where they were going, that something-up-my-sleeve smile. At last and it appeared mostly because the old windbag was winded, Bernays, sweat stains sprawling out from his armpits, came to a rest at the head of a walkway so long that curving slightly inwards it stretched blurring into the horizon. To the right of them, beyond the vast expanse of rolling green botanical garden, a coconut plantation paralleled the path of the walkway until it too softened into a patchwork of slanting, slender brown bark topped with windmill blades of waving green strips.

Struggling to whoop in deep breaths from the surrounding heavy blanket of humidity, Bernays sat down on the walkway, his back against its low metal barricade and gestured for Zen to do the same. Rivulets of sweat water-falling from his chin, from the point of his nose, tasting tangy on the tip of his tongue, Zen sat down next to Bernays.

Not more than a few seconds later, beneath Adam's Peak's brand-sun, a rectangular matrix of large squircles appeared, at first all of them paled out in a sepia tone. Embossing forth from this sepia matrix background, a pattern of squircles began carnally oscillating and colored into life to spell 'SoulMate'; heralded by a femininely modulated electronic voice which jingled out throughout the land—'Don't Just Make Love… Make Self-Love'.

"The solution" Bernays remarked looking up at SoulMate, as the live carnal oscillations commenced, and asked "Have you figured out the sex stickler?"

SoulMate was the solution, Zen started to work backwards. It likeized sex. But getting more loves than hates or even as much as possible of both wasn't its primary draw for citisumers. It was that SoulMate was just another outlet for (to use the label that Bernays had taught him) their narcissism. Right, all of this was for certain, but 'sex stickler' and 'solution' implies that...—right there Zen got it! The pieces were with him all along, he realized! Well he had been gathering them ever since he jousted with El-El-Elantra, all the way back when he ascended.

"I figured it out!" Zen burst out, wanting to but stopping himself from clenching and vibrating his fists in celebration.

Bernays turned to Zen, raised one of his brown and white furry eyebrows in curiosity and, "Go on" he invited.

"Sex is the only thing in the realms which have a 'no prostitution' spec that is enjoyable that can't involve likes," Zen started to race away, "and because it can't involve likes this means that when people are having sex they are being like... um, economically inefficient—what they are doing doesn't make likes or use likes..."

"Sex is an uneconomic activity" Bernays summarized.

"Yes" Zen quickly agreed and raced on, "And because it's an uneconomic activity it should be reduced until it's only done for reproduction but it's enjoyable so that's never going to happen on its own, so..."

"So..." Bernays prompted, with a slight circular motion of his wrist.

"So... the natural enjoyment from sex has to be slowly chipped away at..." Zen declared and then paused to double-check the instrumentality of his decree, "Yes, the natural enjoyment from sex has to be slowly chipped away at and replaced with an enjoyment that, even if it doesn't directly involve likes, is tied to economic activity... to the economy. Yes... at first we must get our foot in the bedroom door by teaching citisumers that sex can be more than just physical pleasure, that it can get them 'this' and win them 'that'. And it doesn't matter what 'this' and 'that' are, as long they can in some way, some how be tied to the economy. This education must be so good and the 'this' & 'that' must be so hooking, that eventually natural enjoyment is the least sought after benefit from sex, sex then becomes merely a means... a means through which to reach an economically tied end. Hmpf... starting from just a foot in the bedroom door, soon they will be tied-up and in bed with us!"

Bernays chuckled, and playing the good conversational counterpart inquired, "And when we are in bed with them, what are the happy endings that we replace the physical pleasure of sex with?

"Well... one is attention, possibly along with belongingness and esteem, and the other..." answered Zen and made eye contact to acknowledge Bernays's contribution to what he was going to say, "well, the other is narcissism"

Looking back out at the matrix of carnally oscillating squircles, their counters (placed next to the thumbs-up and thumbs-down icons) totting up, Zen explained, "Getting loves & hates for sex is all about getting attention and hopefully belongingness and esteem but to get loves & hates you need to go through SoulMate which is obviously tied to the economy which means *you* are tied to the economy. And, and it's the same for the other end as well, to feed your narcissism you must record this important part of your life but again to do this you need SoulMate, your Embed, and all those cameras, lights and mirrors, which means even if you are only pursuing this end your sex life is tied to the economy"

Turning back to Bernays, who long since was awaiting him with that grandfatherly radiance of pride from his eyes and his smile, ready almost to hug him, "And that is the sex stickler and why SoulMate is the solution" Zen climactically consummated, and reclined back against the railing, contented.

But just as he did, as if there were a sharp nail sticking out from the railing, a loose end pricked him, "But why do so many realms have a 'no prostitution' spec in the first place?" Zen queried sitting upright again.

"Other than when the urge overcomes those that do patronize the second oldest profession, for them at all other times, and always for an overwhelming majority of the rest, prostitution and prostitutes squirms a visceral disgust" Bernays explained, "And because it is an instinctive, almost reflexive flesh crawl that is squirmed, there is little point working in religious sanction for it. That's what the realms that do... that did, have a pro-stitution spec soon found out"

Pouting his lips and nodding his head slightly up and down, 'Makes sense' Zen concluded to himself.

The sun on its slow immerse into the tree-lined, skyscraper topped horizon, was now just below the four-squared brand-sun. It shone through this red, green, blue and yellow film, through SoulMate's matrix of carnally oscillating squircles, a kaleidoscopic aurora that tinged the marshmallow puffs of cumulonimbus and all the world below.

For a while they laid back and basked in this aurora sharing a profound silence, their surroundings retreating, shrinking away until they were alone with their thoughts, until they were giants amidst the faint landscapes of their dreams.

Almost as if sleep talking through his daydream, "Yes, I knew Henry Ports very well" Bernays softly reminisced.

But Zen, gossamers of thought still breezing airy-fairy about his own daydream, didn't hear.

"Yes, I knew Henry Ports" Bernays pronounced louder, awakening Zen as if by a splash of cold water. A thump thump of anticipation starting out from the left of his chest, Zen turned to come eye to eye with old know-bag.

But Bernays's beady black bulbs were out in the distance, way back when, "Henry Ports was the founder of the Microports Corporation, a billionaire" they relived, "A great man... a great man, a philanthropist. When politics and governments were failing, when the decline of countries was rife, he felt... he felt the time was ripe for history to move forward (and it was), for a new system of governance to overthrow the old..."

"Self-governance" Zen interjected.

"No, that's what we have today" Bernays retorted with a snicker, before going on, "So he approached a state that had all but failed... surprise, surprise—a small third world state" Bernays chortled to himself, his beady black bulbs obviously reminiscing this as clear as yesterday, "And he offered to buy a huge swathe of its territory, and of course the failed state's crooked government pounced at the opportunity—it was the only way the sorry state could stay afloat". Bernays then paused, his thoughts seemingly digressing.

"And..." Zen impatiently prompted.

"And well..." Bernays resumed, and tapped on the impression that the book made on Zen's pocket, before proceeding without much fanfare, "he launched Rationalia"

Zen didn't realize himself doing this, but along the railing he shuffled closer to Bernays.

"A good start, anything to get away from those countries that were finished" Bernays remarked, disgust souring his face as he mouthed 'countries'.

Bernays wanting, for effect, to leap to his feet, instead had to support himself by the railing and stagger to them, "And there... right there by founding Rationalia, Henry Ports (without knowing it) had planted the seed from the which, in only a few years, the first realm would spring up" Bernays erupted, dramatizing his explanation by holding his hands, fists clenched, touching each other near his waist, before sprouting them up just above his head and flowering them out, fingers, thumbs and all.

Still on his feet, hands still flowered out, something seemed to pop into his head that made the old windbag burst and huff & puff out with laughter, amidst which he jested, "You could say that Ports' Rationalia was the *serendipitous* seed... that we marketers did need... to conceive... the realms"

Zen didn't entirely get it and he curtly indicated as much with a blank stare.

"You see my dear Zen," Bernays toned down, after his coughs and whoops had reluctantly subsided, "you see Henry Ports and his Rationalia showed us that for too long countries had been our oppressive overlord holding over us the sword of legitimacy. A legitimacy drawn from some long irrelevant and probably apocryphal antiquity and secured by promises of eternality. But Ports and his Rationalia showed us that a country is nothing so grand, that a country does its best when it is designed, used and assessed as nothing more than a consumer product. And..."

Bernays stood tall auguring a crescendo, "and, if a country is a consumer product my dear Zen, then... then we marketers thought it nothing less than our righteous duty to segment, target, position and of course brand countries" he sanctimoniously sermonized.

"What happened to Ports and Rationalia?" Zen interrupted.

This interruption as if a small splinter through his skin, made Bernays slightly grimace before heedlessly continuing, "And so just as the Microports Corporation had done, we marketers at the helms of the great corporations... uh, trepships, approached failing and failed states, making them offers that their empty coffers couldn't refuse"

"So what happened to Ports and Rationalia?" Zen persisted, searching for Bernays's beady black bulbs to corner them.

"And soon..." Bernays carried on unbowed, "soon there was an exodus from oppressive, obsolete countries into... ha, the promised lands, that were... that are the realms"

"WHAT—happened to..." Zen started to sternly demand.

"The only votes that really matter are consumer votes" Bernays inexplicably remarked, his eyes dismissively almost, averted from Zen.

Unanticipatedly Bernays's beady black bulbs turned on Zen, "And boardroom votes" he remarked, again totally inexplicably, and accompanied by a scoffing nasal exhalation and self-satisfied snippet of a smile, "Henry Ports was voted off the board of Microports!"

"Voted off the board?" Zen bewilderedly repeated, his features crumpling up at the center of his face.

"Yes, kicked out" Bernays cleared up, "Kicked out of the company that he himself founded"

'Ah'—Zen getting it—his head sank back.

"And in disgust and disapproval, Henry Ports disappeared never to be seen or heard from again; probably died in desolation" Bernays concluded shrugging his droopy shoulders, his eyes floating off to way back when.

"If there was still such a thing called history, we would laud Henry Ports as the prophet who took us to the mountaintop from which we marketers envisioned the promised lands" regretted Bernays pouting his downturned mouth.

Nowadays there's only SoulMate history, Zen derisively thought to himself.

"But 'A science which hesitates to forget its founders is lost' " Bernays countered aloud, initially to reassure himself but then boomingly to mount a comeback for Zen's benefit, having had lured himself into a lament, "Oh yes, yes, yes... a science which hesitates to forget its founders is most definitely lost. And history, well it was essential that we made history... so to say—extinct. For history my dear Zen, is full of not dead but dormant diaspores that at any time can come alive and cross-pollinate our citisumers' own seeds of thought, endangering our ecosystem of happy monocultures"

With this Bernays tremblingly sat back down next to Zen.

By now, as though inundated in a cup of plain tea, the kaleidoscopic aurora was infused with a deep dusky red that to Zen's eyes refracted SoulMate's squircles into a liquid blur. And the only image in his mind was of Henry Ports, the way he imagined him, on that one fine day, upon the fresh start of vast virgin green vistas, in his eyes the glint of a golden age, inaugurating the Direct Democratic Republic of Rationalia.

Reborn on Ports' transcendent day, and for an eternal moment alive only in it, the loudening whirr couldn't penetrate Zen's consciousness. Until, when it landed, Bernays got up and repeated, "Let's go Zen"

By the cabin window, Zen stood telekinetically in Rationalia, as Adam's Peak gradually zoomed out into a Lego land of foliage neatly interlocking with skyscraper. And just as, what he then saw surprised Zen back to the more pressing present, that customary loose fleshed arm-sail came over his shoulder.

"Fitting for many a reason that it's called Adam's Peak... fitting indeed" the musky miasma commented, looking down along with Zen at the split-screen between lush green and rusty brown below.

Zen's mind automatically rewinding and gathering every sound bite that Bernays had uttered about the place, told him via his gut, that Bernays had kept bringing him here because there was something significantly different about this place.

"Oh yes, yes, yes... fitting indeed. For this is where from the Garden of Eden the biblical Adam was evicted to" the musky miasma commenced propitiously, its arm-sail tightening around Zen until it snugly embraced him, "And this… this my dear Zen, is where the Adam of the realms— Henry William Ports founded the Direct… Democratic… Republic… of Rationalia"

Zen's rapidly moistening palm thumped thwack against the cabin window.

"Yes, down there in what formerly was known as Sri-Lanka"

21

HENRY PORTS the billionaire, Post Politica: Self-governance for all from Sri-Lanka's skies, came chopping, dreaming, cogitating. Came puffing direct idealism to blow clean away the state of dirt. To build on the paradise otherwise lost, with clay clamor bricks of final rights secured by sturdy polls of regular votes—democratic peaks for last Adams and Eves. Humid brewing and opportunistic leaves falling; a monsoon of marketers gathering. The old middlemen long gone, their successors after the storm sprouting flimsy flimflam film sets, foresting over, forgetting the ancient ruins of Rationalia. Fleeing.

Eddies of dust settled, silhouetting into a character frail and weak. Who came upon a kindred spirit hunched over his yellowing sheaves, asleep. It creaked to a seat, and let the old ghost twitch a little more in its sleep. Not having the heart, what could have been, oh, what could have been, it let him sleep. A disturbance of dust, a gasp of broken drool, rocking back to life, now eye to eye—his bête noir hadn't changed a bit. Eyes to beady eyes, they shared unspoken, stared long and poignant 'What could have been but was'. I'm sorry, I'm sorry. A small syringe through the neck—thud—his final rites a dusty funeral plume, the old ghost hunched, now forever, over his yellowing sheaves.

Zen awoke niggled, hurried by the feeling that he had overslept, he couldn't spare a moment, it could already be too late—who knew what the old know-bag would reveal with his last few breaths. With scant concern for getting properly dressed or indeed anything else but this, Zen single-mindedly headed for Bernays's hut.

From behind the ornate thick cloth curtains and the miscellany of antiques and artifacts, a muted gold translucence of morning backlit Bernays's deathbed. "Ah Zen" a bedridden Bernays mumbled, his whoops and coughs last gasping for breath. "Go, go" he feebly, tremblingly, wagged his wrist, shooing the medical assistant out of the room.

Zen sat by the side of Bernays in what had become over the last few days his anointed place.

Drawing in deep whistling whoops through his respirator, his entire small shrivel of a body despairingly rising and falling, only Bernays's beady black bulbs were perfectly still and they unflinchingly, unblinkingly set their sights upon Zen.

It seemed all too soon, nonetheless with a perverse anticipation Zen cleared his concentration to consume what could be the old know-bag's last words.

But those beady black bulbs burning as brightly they ever burnt, wanted it appeared nothing more than to behold Zen in an indelible silence. And as much as Zen's own eyes uncomfortably evaded them, here then there, they did not relent. It was as if it was Bernays's eyes that were really making a last gasp, a last gasp for affection; beseeching Zen with an innocence that was either never there before or which Zen had shut out, to feel something, anything at all for him. And when Zen out of awkwardness, had to stop evading them, an insuppressible pang of sympathy for old Bernays convulsed the regular rhythm of his heartbeat and choked up his throat. Old Bernays, who took him under his wing, who taught him all he knew, was breathing his last, his heart winced, a gray sadness of memories inundating it. Zen reached for and felt the loose cold flesh of Bernays's tube-intruded hand, he gripped it tight. The muted gold translucence now well upon his face, Bernays's eyes, like two polished black pearls shone this adoringly back at his protégé; one final smile of supreme contentment curled the corners of his cracked ashen lips.

The accelerating beeps rapidly led to the sounding of alarms, Bernays lay frozen in his last moment in Zen's arms. The medical assistants were now trying to ply Zen away from Bernays, or Bernays away from Zen, as he clung to him. Finally, Bernays was laid to rest on his deathbed in an instant rigor mortis, the corners of his cracked ashen lips curled into one final smile of supreme contentment; set against the dense blood-red reticulation and murky blue of his wide open eyes, his beady black bulbs adoringly beholding his protégé for all eternity.

Zen, on his way back, was confronted by his feelings for him, for old Bernays. He couldn't believe it, it wasn't true, Zen refused to accept at first, when he thought about what had just happened, when he thought of Bernays's death. And then Zen reminisced, he reminisced all the way back to the first time he met Bernays, huh '…products must have flaws'. About their journeying across the realms and how endearingly ridiculous Bernays would look whenever he had to get into the characteristic costumes of the realm they were visiting. About how he'd always get around to answering his questions but never as they were asked. And, Zen chuckled to himself, how most of the time he would ask and answer his own. He could hear again the old know-bag's voice, a cornucopia flowering with puns and ripe with exotic words, dramatically intonating up and down, exploding, to make his point. Looking back, Bernays was right, quirks do make people more lovable, Zen thought. Carrying his Embed in his pocket, having the—huh— devil-may-carefreeness to look like he did whilst being no less than the Director-General of OmniRealm (but then again, this wasn't solely a quirk, it was more a consequence of what he knew, Zen qualified). And it was what he knew, what he'd taught him—'oh yes, yes, yes'— everything about marketing and the realms, about religion, narcissism and history, it was what Bernays taught him that made the old know-bag, along with Henry Ports, the two most important citi… no, people in his life, Zen eulogized, taking his customary seat in the pod next to Bernays's leather throne.

His heartstrings plucked by gratitude, "Richard Bernays… Richard Bernays" Zen sentimentally summed up, beholding the late know-bag's leather throne.

As Zen sat there, focused on Bernays's leather proxy, fondly flipping over again the album of memories that he and Bernays shared, an infiltrator of unease snuck up on him. Now that Bernays was gone— Where, What… was he going back to? Was he going to be evicted and blacklisted by whoever it was that was going to succeed Bernays? He probably was. Zen fell back in his chair, his eyes turned down and to the left, he started biting his lips.

Out from the pod, the leaden weight of uncertainty heavy upon his shoulders, Zen walked slowly, haltingly to the OmniRealm admin tower, toward his fate.

Surely the verdict, which he couldn't bear to listen to, would be delivered in Bernays's office, Zen thought, as he climbed a few steps looking down at his feet. Maybe it was self-consciousness brought on by the thud-thudding anxiety over his impending fate now just a few floors away, but he sensed assistants dropping whatever they were doing to stare at him. He knocked, his knuckles barely hitting the leminiscate adorned door, he knocked again and waited a moment to knock again.

"There's no one in there" a female voice from behind startled him, "Director-General Bernays has died… don't you know?"

Zen paralyzed by his anxiety, stood staring at the door till the voice passed.

But, "Are you… are you Zen?" the voice nearing him, asked interrogatingly.

He had to turn. An old woman, not nearly as old as Bernays, but nevertheless old, in an unrealm way, completely unlike Tresemmé, stood in front of him expecting an answer.

"Yes" he replied meekly.

"Nice to meet you, I'm Rohini Freud" the old woman warmly introduced herself, extending her bejeweled hand toward him.

His anxiety somewhat abated by her friendliness, Zen scanning upwards from her bright red baggy pants, long ornately embroidered top and satiny green neck scarf, remembered seeing her around the OmniRealm admin tower.

"Well, Director-General Bernays has left instructions to allow you to use his private pod until the new Director-General assumes office" she smilingly informed him on realizing that Zen was a little too rattled to shake her hand.

Zen's brain-jerk response to this was, "And then what?"

"What… what do you mean?" the old woman sought to clarify, her head slightly side-to-siding.

"I mean like… like what am I going to do after I hand over the pod and the new Director-General assumes office… like you know in the long term?" Zen cleared up.

Her head rocked back gesturing 'oh', "Well… um, Director-General Bernays didn't… he didn't really specify" she answered, her pupils dilating with empathy for the young man.

Looking into each other's eyes, they separately contemplated Zen's fate.

"Well…" the old woman started and then paused to consider Zen's options, "I remember Director Bernays telling me that you have been blacklisted from MyRealm I and of course all LifeTree realms, but… but even though this counts against your ascension worthiness, you could always re-ascend to another realm provider's realm, couldn't you?"

The thought sickened Zen. Ascension was now to him akin to an unendurable demotion.

"Or…" the old woman wondered, "or, I suppose if, IF, a participation pops up here at OmniRealm AND you meet the higher NumLing threshold we require, I suppose you can stay on here. But even if you wanted to, those are all big IFs"

Dimwits dulling down below, the reek of backwardness, hunger the only staple, chaos the norm; all this maybe so, but was the pre-world all that bad, at least for him?—Zen reassessed. After all, he would be going back to his mother and to Muthu; and who knew what more intriguing ideas lay in store for him amongst Muthu's vast archive of books?

"Well Zen, you've got a bit of time to think about it" the old woman concluded to Zen, whose mind was indeed in another world.

"Yes… yes I do" he agreed, still envisioning going back home.

"Oh, and one more thing" the old woman remembered as she turned to walk away, "If you are visiting a realm in the pod, you must be accompanied by an OmniRealm participant"

When she had left him, and was nearly out of earshot, "And who is the new director-general?" Zen asked loudly.

She stopped, turned and doubled back a few paces, "Why… it's me, Zen" she answered with a gracious smile and as though ready to curtsy.

Zen lay on his bed, trying to convince himself that he knew all too well what he was going to see, so there was really no point in looking. But who was he kidding, he knew himself even better—there was a certain inevitability about what he was going to do.

22

THE POD landed, Zen braced himself. Then not really summoning the courage but ripping the plaster off the wound—putting action first, letting everything else fall where it may—in one motion he stood up and headed for the exit hatch.

Tunnel vision, the surroundings blurring, fast-forwarding by, into the midst of the crowd Zen squeezed and shielding his eyes from the late afternoon glare he looked around in all directions. There it was. Wanting to get it over with, single-mindedly swiftly slaloming through the crowd he entered the tower, was soon granted access and now was rising to his destination floor. TING—a sharp twinge, a taut pluck in his chest, as the elevator door opened; but for no reason. Hurrying to the floor's observation deck, he frantically almost looked around at the arrangements of white clothed sameness plugging away below. Then he zoomed into each face. Not her, not her, not her, his eyes manically scanned past, until—gulp. Throbbing hot blood carrying painful shards, nostalgia and mixed feelings, pumping from his chest coursing through his arteries and veins, thud-thud-thud-thud—there she was.

For more than an hour he sat, his eyes watching her, but looking in at himself. The OmniRealm assistant that he dragged along with him (who had to accompany him at all times) not understanding at all why. Then finally what he had been waiting for, the day's participation was at an end. The assistant tailing him, he headed out of the observation deck telling himself that now all he had to do was confirm what he already knew; and trying his damnedest to deny that dangling in her eyes was the tiniest twinkle of hope.

Out of the Sky Cabriolet station into the square he, they, followed her, nudging, pushing, not averse to shoving. All he had to do he told himself was to get in front of her, hold her squarely by the shoulders look into her eyes and that would be that. But that tiny twinkle that he thought he saw, that had turned his simple in-and-out plan head-over-heels, made him want much, much more.

Running so fast that he overshot her by several meters, he stopped and turned. Entranced by something or another going on in her Embed she sauntered along not noticing him, he stood perfectly still for her, his only movement that of his heart thud-thud-thud-thudding. Amidst a head tilted, lips duck-pouted, self-admiringly look, she bumped straight into him. His eyes already fixated where he knew, after she gathered herself, her eyes would look, he waited thud-thudding for a millisecond more.

But her eyes promptly back to her holographic mirror haze, she said "Sorry" without so much as looking at him and off on her way she continued.

Scurrying in front of her, he held her tightly by the shoulders; from above the skyline of burnished metal & glass minarets, the rays of the LifeTree emblazoned green crescent moon directly in his eyes, "Maya" Zen beheld her.

Not nearly as astonished as Zen expected her to be, indeed blankly staring back at him, all she quite absurdly said was, "Your Embed is in your arm" before trying to struggle her shoulders free of his grip.

And when she did, "It's Saudah... Sa-u-dah" she pronounced sternly.

Zen gripped her again by the shoulders. Now an alarm of fear going off, her whole body shrunk into itself.

"Maya, Maya" Zen insisted, he beseeched, hoping that she was in there somewhere.

Her covered head slightly turning away from him, her body continued to cower, shrivel in fear. Bending with her, he stooped to look her in the eyes. And amidst all this, holding her this close, his eyes couldn't help but register how much her face had been changed; but in her eyes he saw nothing, he saw nothing but fear.

Zen's hands fell away and he stood straighter, still in the hope that she would realize that he wasn't about to hurt her, still in the hope that she would look him in the eyes, talk to him. But free of his grip, her covered head still turned away from him and stiffened in fear, she started to diagonally shuffle off and when a few steps removed, she began to scamper away to safety.

Stupefied, Zen stood, currents of white cloth swirling around him, as the frightened, voluptuous, white spandex hourglass that was Maya, gradually dissolved away into one of them.

"Oh yeah, they allow that now" remarked the assistant as they headed for the Sky Cabriolet, interrupting the chant that Zen's mind kept playing on loop 'This is what I expected… This is what I expected… This is what I expected'.

"What?" Zen asked, not really interested but needing something to escape this cyclical rehashing of hurt.

"There" pointed the assistant skyward.

As his eyes registered the familiar matrix of squircles, "Oh Soul…" Zen began but then halted; his eyes bugging out in amazement.

"It's called Nikahbook here" corrected the assistant.

Now along with his eyes, his mouth hanging open, Zen gawked up at the unfamiliar spectacle oscillating within the all-too familiar matrix of squircles. In every position, just like everywhere else, posing self-admiringly, just like everywhere else, carnal oscillations. Walking backwards from the Sky Cabriolet tracks, Zen adjusted himself into a better vantage point against the slanting rays of the evening sun. Yes, they were neither white shadows nor puppets, they were real men and women, real New Caliphate citisumers, but from head to toe, from head to toe they were fully clothed. The bearded men in long flowing white robes all of them topped off with a white skullcap and the women, the women clothed like Maya in white spandex from hair, head to toe, leaving—where the positions allowed—only their faces for themselves and all to see.

"But they don't allow it everywhere" qualified the OmniRealm assistant, who had stepped back along with Zen, "It's only in the Nikahbook that they show in this neighborhood of the realm… they call it the Marriagehood"

GASP—the knife of heartbreak stabbed Zen in the chest, he couldn't breathe, it felt like his stabbed heart wouldn't beat, all he could do was murmur, bleed—"Maya"

A DULL heartache, like the aftermath of a violent cramp, had anguished his chest muscles for days, maybe a week, or more, he didn't know. Holed up in his apartment, supposedly to give himself time to think about what to do next, all he actually did was relive over and over again his time with Bernays and the old man's demise; serrated shrapnel from New Caliphate (he couldn't bear telling himself her name) unpredictably re-lacerating old and new wounds from time to time. And each time he got reinjured he'd tell himself, not to think about that, that it was solely Bernays's demise that made him hurt this way, but each time he took respite in the thoughts of Ports and Bernays, just when he thought he had convalesced, flashes, voices, shrapnel from that day would make him—arghhhh—writhe in hurt.

'Think about something, think about something else', in a forced moment of clarity it struck Zen as odd that Rohini Freud hadn't yet asked for her pod back. For that matter, she hadn't pressed him to make a decision nor in fact had she made any contact with him at all. Indeed, what should he do? Zen asked himself finally, relieved he was crawling out of the slippery sided gray abyss of hurt. And as he crawled, a pinpoint of sunlight—he must meet Muthu again, tell him about Bernays and all that he revealed to him; and thank him, yes thank him for gifting him the book that was the first domino of this all. To think that the last time he saw Muthu, Maya was still Maya and ready to ascend to MyRealm I with him—arghhhh—the shrapnel writhed Zen again. 'Must meet Muthu again… must meet Muthu again' Zen desperately fought back, 'If Maya had ascended with me to MyRealm, I would never have known what I know now, and I'm better for it… I'm better for it', he went on the attack.

Pressing a pillow over his face, its OmniRealm leminiscate the last thing that blurred before black, Zen told himself to sleep on it. But he just couldn't. Tossing and turning, writhing and thinking, one thing was for sure, to OmniRealm well maybe, but there was no way he was re-ascending to a realm. And more and more he was leaning; back home wasn't so bad he kept telling himself, his mother, Muthu and all his books of course, but also Ramwi would most definitely take him back. In any case, Zen figured, whether he was going to stay there or not, he should definitely put what were most likely his last few days with the pod to good use and visit his mother and Muthu. And having made up his mind thus, sinking into the cool comfy cushiness of his mattress, Zen fell soundly asleep.

On the journey there, a mini smile painting itself on Zen's face, across his mind played a halcyon montage of memories and expectations. Thud... bump... thud... bump... thud... bump... clunk-clunk-clunk-clunk-clunk-clunk, the pod landed. His mini smile breaking into a full pearly grin, his bag strapped across his chest, joyous anticipation red-carpeted his last few steps out of the pod.

He opened the hatch—on an overwhelming gust of greasy smog, a raucous din, pierced from the background by blaring tractor horns. Zen looked down at the pre-worlders all seemingly in tattered brown rags who had gathered in awe to pay homage to the OmniRealm pod. Taken aback, he nevertheless smiled again and descended.

As he set foot on the stony ground, tufts of weeds sprouting from here and there—hands. Hands, hands from all directions thrust out at him, their heads tilted in self-pity, begging, demanding, the largesse they had grown accustomed to. Shoving each other aside, some got ahold of him, some bowed their heads and prayed to him.

"I'm from OmniRealm, I'm from OmniRealm" Zen shouted trying to part the barricade of beggars but it didn't seem to matter.

As they closed in on him, growing claustrophobic in their rancid vinegary odor, palms open thrusting his hands to either side, Zen shoved back and repelled himself free. Rusty carcasses of tractors the only outcrops from the parched brown landscape, tumbleweeds of rubbish blown about by dusty winds and unlike the realms from the horizon to the sun, bare, bare sky, the only towers belching black columns of smog; a stranger looked out across a somehow eerily familiar land.

The tractor jerking him up and down, side to side, so much so that his jowls flapped, Zen rumbled to his settlement. And so immersed in applying Bernays's explanation of the pre-world—huh, 'the dimwits dulling down below'—to what he saw around him, he scarcely gave a thought to how he was going to explain himself to his mother. As the bobbing tractor wobblingly rounded a large temple complex, being built (it looked like) by missionaries from a hindu realm, Zen pictured, he heard old Bernays enunciate in his hyperbolic style 'Oh yes, yes, yes… in the pre-world we offer religion a helping hand to hammer home the doctrine of our day—'Divide and Rule Yourself'.

"Right here, right here" Zen shouted above the rattling of the tractor, making it jarringly grind to a halt.

Paying his likes, he jumped off, his cheeks rising and stretching out into a broad smiley face. He knocked forcefully on the corrugated-metal makeshift door of his hut which hadn't changed a bit. A few knocks later it started to creek, impatiently he swung it wide open and, barely giving his mother a millisecond to freeze in her flabbergast, he bear-hugged her emaciated skeleton, the thick oily smell of her hair nostalgically comforting him.

"Oh my God Zen, oh my God" she sniffled still in his tight embrace, "You're back"

"Yes Ma" he whispered, feeling a tear of hers trickle down his face.

Letting go of the hug, holding her by the shoulders, he looked into her haggard scraggly face, his eyes welling up with a deep brown stirring of sympathy and love.

"You're back, you're back on a crusade aren't you, Zen" she delighted.

His happy bubble burst by this, Zen didn't have the heart to dump the difficult truth on his poor mother, at least not just yet, "Uh… yes, yes" he went along.

"Well, let's get you something to eat, you must be hungry" she mothered him in.

A restlessness fidgeted Zen as he forced down the last few clumps of porridge.

"Where are you going? Don't you want to have some more?" his mother asked, when Zen sprung up from the rickety table, his last clumpy mouthful barely having made it as far as his gullet.

"Um… to see Muthu" he replied chewing and gulping, fighting down what was already in his stomach.

He could still remember the way, past the precariously slanted rusty pylons that he always ran past, to the reek of the sludgy canal on which all sorts of things floated by and then over it, over it and through the heap of rubbly buildings that scavengers were always picking apart, and then just a little bit more to Muthu. Yes, Zen could still remember but having envisioned doing what he was doing now so many times over the last few days and weeks, along the way there he couldn't believe what was happening, what he was doing. It felt like with every beat of his heart, his perspective kept rapidly vacillating between his own eyes and him watching himself from afar on his way back to Muthu, it felt quite unreal.

A huge rusty brown metal shutter, that closed off the entrance to the graffiti defiled crossing of the canal, arrested Zen's perspective. Rust flaked through the painted letters, and at first Zen attributed their illegibility to this. But as he stepped closer, placed his palm against the brown flaking roughness and scanned them closely, he was sure that this was a completely different type of lettering which he was totally unfamiliar with. Scanning downwards just beneath the first set of letters, Zen saw the tops of a second set of letters which he instantly recognized. With his bare palms he scrubbed aside the dried stains of mud that covered the rest of the lettering until he could discern 'Crossing Closed'. But he wasn't about to let anything stop him, with all his might he tried to pry the two rusty halves apart, again, again, stopping to regather his strength, again and again, but the halves didn't budge an inch, not even with the help of a metal rod wedged in between them. Giving up, he stepped back, and surveyed for a plan B but with no other crossing in sight the sludgy lines of rubbish wiggled out in both directions until they disappeared into the bare horizon. Argh, he should have never given the pod back so soon, he kicked himself. In desperation, he even looked down at the sludge below to ascertain its depth.

"Hey, hey" he shouted running toward a tattered brown outline scavenging in the distance, "Hey, hey"

As Zen sprinted toward the brown outline that focused into a man, in fear he began scampering away.

"Wait, wait" Zen shouted, "I'm from OmniRealm, I'm from OmniRealm"

Hearing this, the pre-world scavenger stopped, turned and thrust out his grimy hand and tilted his head, a mendicant expression sorrowing his face.

"When was this crossing closed?" Zen demanded breathlessly.

In silence the thrust out grimy hand wagged, its eyes meeting Zen's and making something quite clear.

Zen quickly transferred some likes.

"It was about two or three weeks ago"

"Who closed it?" Zen interrogated.

The grimy hand wagged again. Zen paid up.

Impatiently twitching as the transaction happened, the moment it was completed, without answering, the scavenger scampered off. Zen didn't bother running after him.

He turned and resurveyed to his right the sludgy line, tracing his eyes along it all the way out to the horizon and then he did the same to the left. Once more he set his sights on the huge rusty brown shutter, walked up to it and tried and tried again to pry it open with his makeshift crowbar, but to no avail. Somewhere behind the swirling dust and smog filled pre-world sky, the sun, its circularity smudged into a roundish orange blotch, was fast setting. It was far too late to set off along the canal, his mother must already be worried, but tomorrow, bright and early tomorrow, this is exactly what he would do. He would walk, he wouldn't stop until he found another crossing to the other side, to Muthu.

The ominous rumbling of the low angry sky cracking bolts of electric purple roots through the thick smog and heavy air, had sent it seemed the entire pre-world running for cover back to their huts, so alone Zen walked back to his settlement. And as he walked, he contemplated the darkened desolate pre-world wasteland, the voice of Bernays echoing, whispering through the winds of his thoughts. Passed each broken milestone, Zen's opened mind went back, way back to before Ports' Post Politica and Bernays, and reassumed as a sort of thought experiment all that he had believed as a pre-worlder.

He felt faceless, just another piece of the riffraff, unwashed, with a shudder Zen felt claustrophobic in his previous ignorance. His mind cringed in embarrassment at how he must have first appeared to Muthu. Oh how grateful he was that Muthu tried to take him under his wing anyway, that he gave him the book that led him to Bernays, the book that changed everything. Zen felt for the rectangular impression of the book in his right trouser pocket, the first few pellets of slanting rain the only thing stopping him from opening it to reread out of thankfulness Muthu's thoughtful inscription to him.

The next morning, Zen was up early with an eagerness that uncomfortably nagged him, for it was reminiscent of those NumLing mornings. Dismissing this with the excitement of his imminent reunion with Muthu, he started to stuff a few supplies for the trip there into his bag.

"Zen... Zen" his mother called, "There's someone here to meet you"

But it wasn't just someone, behind Francis, there were four other familiar faces.

"We heard that you were back on crusade from MyRealm I, everybody's talking about it around the settlement. God bless you and God bless LifeTree, Zen" announced Francis, whom Zen had known for as long as he could remember, the four familiar faces nodding whilst smiling buffoonish awestruck smiles at Zen.

A slow pitter-patter against the tinny roof of the hut, quickly accelerated to a powerful blowing whoosh.

"The faithful of the settlement want to hold a thanksgiving mass in your honor, Zen" his mother informed, almost having to shout to be heard above the incessant whoosh.

Zen completely cornered, took a quick short gasp and held his breath. And when he let it out, though still frozen in wide-eyed surprise, an almost imperceptible sheepish little smile ever so slightly tugged at the corners of his mouth. His eyeballs turned to his mother, she was beaming back at him with pride.

Before he could get another word in it seemed (not that he had the heart to say no) his mother had got appropriately dressed and huddling together under her oft-repaired now polythene sheathed umbrella, they were hurrying through the muddy paths of their settlement to the church. On nearing the church, as the rain eased off, scores of catholic pre-worlders introduced themselves and making the sign of the cross on their chests they walked solemnly behind Zen and his mother chanting various homilies to god, Jesus Christ and LifeTree. Whilst in the background, on the very edge of the settlement, a tattered brown rim of non-catholic pre-worlders looked on, reminding themselves ever so often to disguise their awe with menacing growls and waving fists.

Just about as their cavalcade caught first glimpse of the church (which Zen noticed had been radically reconstructed), his mother, holding him by the wrist, gushed, "Oh Zen, I'm so glad you're back, it's a Godsend, it's a Godsend from the realms I tell you". "It hasn't rained here for months and the river had almost half dried up, and then you come... and look" she pointed to her heavens.

How could he tell her? What could he say to this? Zen masked his grimace with a fake uneasy smile and hastened toward the church.

As if being dragged to the gallows Zen entered the church, looking fixedly down at his feet, his gaze averted from the faithful who had flocked to venerate him. They sat and soon Francis began the service— singing, uttering one inanity after another which Zen soon tuned out from, until it was nothing more than a muffled background babble to his thoughts.

Into the face of each dulling dimwit he peered; huh, when pre-worlders' heads weren't tilted in pity they were tilted in piety, he quipped to himself. If only they were taught what Ports and Bernays had taught him, Zen contemplated. If only pre-worlders and citisumers, if everybody were taught what he know knew. But Ports had failed, but perhaps he had failed and the marketers prevailed, only because he assumed that everybody was ready, that everybody knew. Where in fact they needed to be taught, taught not only what Ports knew about final rights, democracy and technology, but equally as importantly what Bernays knew about religion, what he knew about narcissism but most of all what he knew about marketing. But this would mean, it would mean that this was not the…

"Zen, Zen" his mother whispered, poking him, she was already kneeling.

Looking down at her and the rest of the kneeling congregation around him, he tried to force himself to, but the thought of it squirmed him like the thought of putting a live worm in his mouth. His eyes darted to the doorway, he considered it, but as they zoomed back to the kneeling congregation, Francis, whose head had been turned down in prayer, was giving him what he interpreted to be a glare, which like a palm pushing down on the top of his head made Zen kneel, not in prayer but with the determination that somehow he must get out of here.

The second his mother had finished her prayers, Zen had wanted to leave but she made him wait until every last one of the eager faithful had personally paid him their respects.

"God bless. Joy is LifeTree" the very last one intoned.

Outside, all hopes of embarking on his long journey to Muthu today were being washed away by a deluge that only spared the newly raised church.

As they waited for the rain to abate, "Where's the cross I gave you?" his mother queried, taking the inside of his left forearm in her hands and curiously darting her eyes back and forth between it and his scarred forehead.

The deluge had lasted for three whole days. Its muddy light-brown waters, inundating the settlement and in places infiltrating his hut, unbearably confining Zen to the drone of his mother's regular prayers (which, quite torturously, he had to participate in lest he compromised his cover). Mercifully though, after the ear itch of her piteous pleas and her increasingly probing questions about the crusade he was supposed

239

to be on, let up for the day—when his mother went to sleep—to the background of the never-ending whoosh against their tinny roof, the night, it belonged to Zen's thoughts. And this night, as every night, he envisioned his reunion with Muthu—of how he'd present to him the arguments of Bernays, of how no doubt hot and impassioned Muthu would retort. Looking around his ramshackle hut, every bit of furniture, every appliance, every device, originally meant for some other purpose or long since broken, Zen thought back to the cleanliness, the conveniences, the comforts that all worked together like clockwork in the realms. In a way (though of course he wouldn't have it any other way), it was not unreasonable to adjudge that Bernays had done him a disfavor by revealing to him the truth. For now, even if he were allowed back, he could never make himself go back there. And from this thought, for the first time the question of what he would do after his reunion with Muthu perturbed Zen. He couldn't, for it would devastate his mother, and he shouldn't for it would endanger both of them, betray his loss of faith to anyone. And sure, when soon his mother figured out that there was no crusade, that he was evicted from MyRealm I, she would be terribly disappointed. But all of this was not what really perturbed Zen. Muthu and his books were fine from afar, from within the bereavement and upheaval that the loss of Bernays had caused him, but now he was here and the thought of living the rest of his life with the brain-deadened dumbwits of the pre-world made him feel like the stinking floodwaters just below his raised bed of boxes were rising, that the rusty corrugated-sheet walls were closing in on him; it made him feel like he couldn't breathe. His thoughts and feelings in disarray, neither here nor there, nowhere to go, back and forth, he tossed and turned, until, hours later, it took fatigue to finally put Zen to sleep.

The next morning, altogether against the flow of the vexatious thoughts and feelings that tormented him the night before, Zen, bleary little hexagons of light twinkling from the end of his eyelashes, opened his eyes feeling a deep sense of satisfaction. For in his sleep an 'Aha!' moment had come to him that revealed exactly what that conundrum of a place where Bernays lived had to be all about.

On the bright yellow pinpricks of sunlight from the tiny holes in the corrugated-metal walls of his hut and the warm oven-like radiation from its tinny roof, more cause for delight came at Zen. The rains had ceased, the sun was out, and soon he would be reunited with Muthu, Zen thrilled, jumping out of bed for joy.

He hurriedly packed all the things that he needed for the long trek along the canal and approached his mother well-prepared with an expedient explanation as to where he was going.

"Where are you heading off to, the floods haven't even gone back yet?" his mother preempted.

"The MyRealm I crusade starts off at the old canal today" Zen informed monotonously, just as he had rehearsed in his head.

"Ohhh!" she perked up, casting off it seemed a burdensome weight of worry from her shoulders, "Then I must start praying for a successful crusade and your safe return, Zen"

As she hugged him, "God bless…" she invoked.

Zen dismissively guessed the rest.

"Joy is LifeTree… Joy is LifeTree" she gently breathed into his ear.

The floodwaters hadn't completely receded yet. Large still lakes of muddy light-brown water remained embanked by dark brown marshland. A naughtiness of scrawny little pre-world children splashed around in one of them, nearly soiling Zen as he passed by, only for a mother-head to pop out from an adjacent hut to scold them back inside. This shouldn't bother him, nothing should bother him, Zen tried to convince himself, soon Muthu and he would be debating Ports and Bernays. But as much as this was his beckoning light at the end of the tunnel, Zen couldn't escape the nagging reality that it was also the end of tunnel. He had come full circle, from the pre-world to the realms and here, now back to the pre-world, nearly back to Muthu—but what then? Certainly not there, not the realms, and to his dismay he had found on coming back, not here, not the pre-world—so nowhere; there was nowhere for him, he told himself as he walked, his head hanging in resignation. But just a few paces later, chin up, chin up, soon he would be reunited with Muthu, soon he would be reunited with Muthu, Zen pepped himself up and quickened his steps.

From the towering height of the sun in the sky, he could say that he had been walking for hours, those same thoughts gyrating his feelings from resignation to anticipation and then drooping back again to resignation. A mile or so up a gradual plane, and perhaps it was just a mirage of hope, but in the distance, opposite a settlement that looked from afar quite like his own—another crossing. Zen stopped and shaded his eyes with a palm-made visor. Emanating from the skies and the ground it felt like, the percussions of a cymbal reverberated through his entire body and being. Striding, jogging, running, slipping in a shiny rink of still undried mud, soon he was sprinting toward it. This crossing wasn't closed! His feet thudding against, scarily bending its sheet metal floor, he made it to the other side.

By the time he traversed back along the canal, passed the closed crossing and found his way inland to the rubbly edge of the teetering grid of buildings amongst which Muthu took refuge in, the first gloom of evening was beginning to beset its rubbishy, building debris intruded paths. And bloodthirsty squadrons of mosquitos were descending on the scavengers—hooved, tailed and footed—that scrounged around them. His ankles twisting and then snapping back as he walked over booby-traps of gnarled metal pipes and broken-off bits of wall and bricks, Zen remembered his way to Muthu. Suddenly in a rare opening between the rubbish and debris, something he saw intrigued Zen with its familiarity. He stopped and perused for a while the elongated patch of rough grayish-black ground and its purposely broken line of white painted rectangles, which though stained looked just like those he had seen snaking all throughout that place where Bernays had lived.

With each recalled crumbling milestone along the last bit of the way, his chest like a thick leather sheath tautened from his collarbone to his ribcage, his heart increasing its tempo, beating from inside against it, first like a drumstick, but now, as he got closer and closer, more and more like a mallet. Thud… thump… thud…thump, a left at the crooked four arrowed post that made a lot more sense now, thud-thump-thud-thump-thud-thump Zen neared the half-imploded building. Over the heap of rubble left by the caved in doorway, the smell of dead rats thickening, he entered. From the pit of his stomach, cluster bombs shooting in all directions sharp tiny needle pricks, the mallet taut against his chest, reverberating through his parched gulping throat, throbbing his whole head with boiling hot blood—THUD-THUMP-THUD-THUMP-THUD-THUMP—Zen took the last few steps toward Muthu's cave of books and mortar.

At his desk, an old man sat looking out wistfully into the distance of his thoughts and reminisces. Pulling a sheaf of paper and a pen from a drawer, he looked at both, smiled to himself, and entitled the first page.

The smell unbearable, like two rancid heavy humid fists punched through his nose and through to the back of his mouth, gagging, instantly nauseating him. But it was what he saw that weakened his thighs, almost making him collapse. Shattering him and the time and things around it into an inerasable cracked glass tableau of grief that would haunt him for evermore; in the here and now it left him denying his eyes, refusing to believe what he saw. The next few moments a disbelieving blur, somehow he found himself, his nose numb to the nauseating smell and his hands numb to the fat slimy yellow maggots wriggling up them, hugging the half-eaten carcass that had stiffened—seated, head down against a book.

Placing his pen down on the paper, the old man clumsily evoked from his shirt pocket a vast holographic panorama that spanned his entire field of view. Within it so many squircles had to be accommodated making the live holograms within each so tiny that they all looked exactly alike. The old man summoned a batch closer to him, as they approached they grew bigger and with parental pride he doted his eyes on the uniformed ants within each squircle happily going about their lives of work and play and pray. He took in a deep, long breath of accomplishment and fidgeting with his shirt pocket played his favorite song.

The two swelling pools of tears upon the desk embraced each other and began dripping onto his trousers. Sniffling, wiping them off from the source with the back of his left index finger, he once more put his hand around the half-eaten carcass but as he did, a pang in his cheeks giving him an early warning, a surging second tsunami of tears burst out with a wail. For a few whole minutes he cried, until an exhaustion that felt as though all the nutrition in his body had been cried away in those tears, began to dry them up. Again, he sniffled back his runny nose and wiped his swollen eyes. And as the glassy translucence of tears cleared, he saw—its edges only slightly larger than the yellowing edges of the book—the whiter outline of a sheet of paper nestled within the book. While carefully wresting its tombstone loose from the stubborn carcass, he caught a glimpse of all he needed of the book's title, but it felt smoother and looked glossier. He placed it on the desk, its end splattering the blob of tears. Next to it, paying homage, he placed his own copy and observed a moment of silence, his eyes concentrating on the glossy jacket of the book. And before he took out the sheet of paper which he hoped against hope was a letter written to him, he turned the book over. Then absolute darkness, absolute emptiness, there was nothing in the entire universe, just him suspended in the black nothingness and the smiling image of the man on the back cover of the book pulsing toward his disbelieving eyes—then pulsing back, pulsing toward his stupefied eyes then pulsing back. He gulped down the mucus left in his throat by the tears and with memory flashes of face-shots pulsing at him from the black nothingness, he swiveled his neck to the half-eaten carcass and then dartingly back again to the back cover of the book, over and over again. It couldn't be—he still tried to cling on. But no, but no, but no—face-shots flashing, swiveling once more to the half-eaten carcass and then to the back cover—but no, his grief glazed eyes weren't refracting delusions through their tears—Muthu was Ports.

Imagine there's no countries
It isn't hard to do
Nothing to kill or die for
And all religions too
Imagine all the people living life in peace

Opening his eyes having had closed them to relish the beauty of the verse, the old man began writing.

An Interesting Case Study in using the Two-Sided Appeal

Those whom we seek, on account of the very attributes we seek in them—their intelligence, their imagination, their unblunted critical faculties—will be most responsive to the use on our part of a carefully curated two-sided appeal…

…Of course in this particular case, I was the beneficiary of what one might justifiably call for more than one reason—a stroke of serendipity. The boy came to me, due at least in part to yet another serendipitous encounter, already almost won over by the other side (the Portside if you will!). But of course—never be so hasty as to judge a book by its cover…

…And this is where unfortunately certain unsavory tactics had to be used. But on the whole I assessed them to be justifiable, given that this young man in the meritocratic world that we marketers have created, has the potential to very soon rise to be our Director-General…

The old man's favorite song playing on loop, continued.

Imagine all possessions
I wonder if you can
No need for want or hunger
All shopping goods for man
Imagine all the people enjoying all their worlds

Beginning to fitfully breathe again, loose ends, flashbacks, regrets, all clamoring like pinballs, zinging here, there and everywhere through his thoughts, ricocheting against the inside of his skull, he stared unblinkingly at the picture. Where leaning against a larger than life-size sculpturing of the italic lettered brand-sun of the Microports Corporation, Henry Ports—Muthu—smiled pleasantly back at him whilst sitting—dead—being devoured away by maggots, right next to him; exactly where he had always been.

Finally, Zen slid his hand along the desk and pinched the folded sheet of paper, still not having the emotional strength to slip it out. Just as much as Muthu's body was by death, his own head, overwhelmed facial expression of raised eyebrows and wide-wide stretched eyes, and his torso and legs, were stiffened by a tumult of emotions. Moving only his left hand and the fingers on it, he managed to unfold the sheet of paper, and tweezing it with his index and middle finger, he held it out to the last, rapidly graying, smoky red embers of evening. It was for him.

My Dear Zen,

If you are reading this letter you know by now who I am. Forgive me for not being forthright with you from the outset but I always wanted my ideas to stand tall in front of you on their own two feet, on their own merit. From what I came to know of your insatiably curious intellect, I trust that you have read Post Politica. To which, from the time you left, I have dedicated all my thinking. And my contemplations have led me to the inescapable conclusion that I was wrong, and radically so; that I was naïve to the nature of the masses.

You see Zen, it is too simplistic a definition that regards the masses as simply the vast number of men out there. It is far more illuminating to define the masses as the great and consistent majority of men in any age, society or population who regardless of their intelligence and capability, care not about the sources, nature and workings of their contentment, but only that it is there and theirs. Just as they (and in this case you and me) scarcely worry about and seek the hows & whys of the working of our bodily organs when these organs are functioning in good health, leaving such questions and concerns and the attendant research to the tiny minority of medical specialists. The cells and organs of the societal body—politics, economics, culture and technology—as long as together these deliver their lifeblood, their contentment, these are to the masses—taken for granted, utterly boring, rightly autonomic functions, just as much as the breathing of their lungs and the beating of their hearts.

But of course Zen, you and I are different. We are in this regard among the tiny minority of sociological specialists whose responsibility it will always be to concern ourselves, to study, research and inform ourselves about these cells and organs of the societal body. So that we can, working quietly, unobtrusively in the background, ensure their healthful functioning, their unfailing delivery of contentment to the masses. And when executing this vital function we must hold at the forefront of our thoughts and strategies this intrinsic, eternal truth about the masses. To hold otherwise, I see now, is nothing more than to fall prey to elitist projection. And this is where Rationalia failed, this is where I failed. Failed—perhaps so that you can succeed Zen.

Henry Ports

Beholding these words of Muthu, of Ports, flowing inky black against a pristine sheet of white, the very last things visible before the conquest by pitch blackness was complete—an intersecting cross-firing of neurons, a recently heard sound bite, the idea ghosts now an eureka insight—epiphanically his decision came to Zen.

Fighting down a series of small regular coughs, yet remaining fixated on what was now the only hologram levitating in front of him, the old man waited momentously, watching his protégé. On seeing his right hand move toward his left forearm, before he heard the ping he knew was imminent, a full-on spasm of whoops overwhelmed the old man and in between them his breath grew shorter, faster, more desperate. Yet through his violent coughing that swung and shook his loose liver-spotted jowls, a supremely contented smile in stained enamel yellow and root canal black dawned on his face. Hearing the clinching ping and then an alarm from a friend-device next to him; whooping, coughing, now convulsing but his master plan not permitting him to again prolong his agony, his beady black bulbs set against the dense blood-red reticulation and murky blue of his wide open eyes—suddenly froze—but not before he scribbled down his last line:

'…For whatever the hegemony may be, the oligarchy must always be wild.'

You, you may say
I'm a citisumer, and I am the only one
I hope some day you'll join me
And the world will live for one